lover of small-town life, ~~~~
two spoiled dogs in the Colorado mountains.

Tyler Anne Snell genuinely loves all genres of the written word. However, she's realized that she loves books filled with sexual tension and mysteries a little more than the rest. Her stories have a good dose of both. Tyler lives in Alabama with her same-named husband and their mini "lions." When she isn't reading or writing, she's playing video games and working on her blog, *Almost There*. To follow her shenanigans, visit www.tylerannesnell.com.

Visit millsandboon.co.uk
for more information

MISSING IN BLUE MESA

CINDI MYERS

LOVING BABY

TYLER ANNE SNELL

MILLS & BOON

First Published in Great Britain 2018
by Mills & Boon, an imprint of HarperCollins*Publishers*
1 London Bridge Street, London, SE1 9GF

Missing in Blue Mesa © 2018 Cynthia Myers
Loving Baby © 2018 Tyler Anne Snell

ISBN: 978-0-263-26558-3

39-0218

MIX
Paper from
responsible sources
FSC™ C007454

This book is produced from independently certified FSC™ paper to ensure responsible forest management.

For more information visit: www.harpercollins.co.uk/green

Printed and bound in Spain
by CPI, Barcelona

Chapter One

She didn't have much time. No more than twenty minutes—probably less. No telling what would happen if he caught her in here. Everyone said he wasn't like his brother, but how could they be sure? The two were twins—identical twins. If one of them was a murderer, who was to say the other one wasn't capable of that, too?

Michelle jammed the piece of wire into the keyhole on the door to the motor home again and felt the catch give. She could thank Mom for that particular skill. How many times had she locked little Michelle out of their trailer while she was entertaining her boyfriend, or when she was sick of the kid? Then she'd get drunk and forget to let her back in.

Or that was what she said.

Better to thank Joey Staskavitch for teaching her how to pick the lock to get back in on her own. She wondered whatever happened to Joey. He was probably in jail, or dead. That was where most of the boys from her neighborhood had ended up.

Starfall—her real name was Michelle Munson, though nobody here knew that—pushed open the door to Daniel Metwater's motor home and stepped into the darkened living room. The noise from the festivities in the center of the encampment faded, though orange light from the bonfire cast grasping shadows across the walls and furniture. "Prophet" Daniel Metwater was dancing around the bonfire, leading his followers in mesmerizing chanting. They loved it. They could listen for hours to their Prophet's words about how they were special and better. Most of them had never been special to or better than anyone, but he made them believe it.

Michelle tiptoed across the room, headed for the back of the motor home, and Metwater's bedroom. That was where he would keep anything private. Anything he didn't want his adoring followers to know about.

The bedroom door, at least, wasn't locked. No one but his closest disciples were allowed in here—and the women he bedded, who considered it a privilege to sleep with the Prophet. Michelle wasn't one of those women. He had tried to seduce her when she first joined his little cult, but she'd put him off with a chilling stare. The gorgeous Daniel Metwater, like his twin, David, wasn't used to being turned down, but he must have seen something in her that made him wary, because after that he left her alone.

Alert for any sounds outside the room, she eased open the top dresser drawer and riffled through the contents. She worked quickly, passing over the clothing and toiletries. The bedside table held only books and sex toys. She wrinkled her nose. Not going to go there. She shut the drawer and hurried to the closet. Dropping to her knees, she felt along the floor and the back wall. That was where she would stick a safe, but all she encountered was two pairs of shoes and a pile of dirty clothes.

After glancing over her shoulder to make sure she was still alone, she flicked on the penlight she had tucked into the pocket of her jeans and swept the beam along the floor and up the walls. Nothing interesting there. Frowning, she rose. Where was the locket? Her tent mate, Asteria, Metwater's "secretary" and the person closest to him, had described it in such detail. "Gold, with a pear-shaped diamond in the center that is at least two carats," Asteria had said. She would know. Before hooking up with Metwater, she had been Andi Matheson, wealthy socialite and only daughter of a high-profile senator. She had seen her share of two-carat diamonds, though she claimed to now prefer the simple, nonmaterialistic life of following the Prophet through the wilderness. Right. Only people who had spent all their life around money could make a spiritual discipline out of giving it up.

"It looked old," Andi had said about the locket. "He said it was a family heirloom. He plans to give it to the baby after she's born." She had cradled her eight-months-pregnant belly and smiled. "To think that he loves her so much already that he'd want to give her something so valuable."

Michelle had to bite the inside of her cheek to keep from pointing out that Daniel Metwater didn't love anyone but himself. The locket was an heirloom, all right— but not from his family. Michelle's foster sister, Cass, had inherited the necklace from her grandmother. She had been wearing it the night she was murdered by David Metwater.

Michelle left the closet and returned to the front room. She should have asked Asteria about a desk. Metwater probably had one, and maybe he kept the locket there. Maybe he had other things that had belonged to his brother, too—papers or a diary or anything Michelle might be able to use to prove that David had killed Cass.

The police said Cass had died of an accidental heroin overdose, but that wasn't true. She didn't do drugs. The night before she died, she had confided to Michelle that she had learned some things about her new boyfriend, David, that upset her. "I'm going to confront him," she said. "I need to know the truth."

The truth was, David Metwater had murdered Cass so that whatever she had learned about him wouldn't get out.

Michelle spotted the desk between the living and dining areas—a built-in shelf with a couple of drawers. A laptop sat open on the shelf, and her fingers itched to take it. She'd probably find all kinds of interesting information on that…

She shook her head. Too risky. She had come here for the locket, and time was running out. The drums outside had quieted, which meant the evening "services" were winding down. She pulled open the desk's center drawer and swept the beam of the penlight over the contents—paper clips, pencils, pens, business cards, a tube of lip balm—no locket. She shut the drawer and was reaching for another when light flooded the room. She froze, heart hammering painfully, unable to breathe.

"What do you think you're doing?" Daniel Metwater demanded.

Michelle turned to face him, but before she could reply, he crossed the room in four strides and grabbed her by the shoulders. His normally handsome face was a mask of rage. He shook her so hard she bit her tongue, tasting blood. *I'm dead*, she thought, as she stared into his cold, hard eyes. *I'll never see my son again.*

Special Agent Ethan Reynolds, FBI, stared down at the collection of half a dozen battered metal license plates arranged on the conference table at the headquarters of the Ranger Brigade, the multi-agency task force he was attached to. Before joining the Rangers, who were responsible for dealing with crime on the vast stretches of federal land in southwestern Colorado, Ethan had never realized how many criminals operated in the relatively deserted interior of national parks, wilderness preserves and protected recreation areas.

"You've verified these are all from stolen cars?" he asked his fellow agent, Immigration and Customs Enforcement Officer Simon Woolridge.

"Every one," Simon said. "A wildlife biologist with the Forest Service found them in an abandoned badger den near the end of Redvale Road. The Forest Service laid down a traffic counter on that road a couple of weeks ago and noticed heavier-than-expected traffic, so they were on the lookout for anything unusual."

"That's right about when this latest rash of thefts started," Ethan said. "So the thieves take the stolen cars to that remote area and strip the plates—then what?"

"Replace them with new tags," Simon said. "Probably forged dealer tags. They could print those up on any laser printer. Then they wait until dark and drive them out again, to a chop shop or even straight to Mexico."

"Then we need to stake out the site and grab them when they show up again," Ethan said.

"Unless they've moved on to a different location," Simon said. "The heavy rains two days ago washed out the road pretty badly. It doesn't look as if anyone has been up there since that storm. My guess is they're still in the area, but they've relocated."

Ethan glanced toward the large map of the Rangers' territory that filled one wall of the conference room. "How do we find that location?"

"We've alerted the park Rangers and the Forest Service, and anyone else who's likely to be in the area to be on the lookout for cars with dealer tags and anything meeting the description of the stolen vehicles," Simon said. He stabbed a finger at a point on the map. "The biologist found the license plates here. Does the location make you think of anything?"

"It's very near Daniel Metwater's camp at the base of Mystic Mesa." Ethan nodded to the red flag someone had positioned on the map. Metwater, scion of a wealthy industrialist and self-styled Prophet, had finagled a long-term camping permit for himself and roughly twenty followers in the Curecanti National Recreation area.

"It's less than ten miles by road," Simon said. "You could travel between the two sites over a network of old logging roads without ever having to risk being seen on the highway."

"That doesn't mean Metwater or any of his people had anything to do with the car thefts," Ethan said.

"No, but it doesn't mean they didn't," Simon said. "I find it interesting how many recent crimes have a connection to that bunch."

"Metwater would point out that he's never been convicted of a crime," Ethan said. Not that he didn't agree with Simon. He had made a study of cults as part of his FBI training and he knew that groups like Metwater's attracted the disaffected and disenfranchised. Some people in the group would have less respect for laws and authority. A certain smaller percentage would be criminally dangerous.

"My mother thinks I never swear," Simon said. "That doesn't mean it's true."

"Do you plan on questioning Metwater?" Ethan asked.

"I thought we should drive over to his camp tonight and see if anyone is missing—someone who might be out boosting cars in the dark."

"I like the way you think," Ethan said. He hadn't been to the camp in a few weeks. The Rangers were under orders not to harass Metwater and his followers, though each side had different definitions of what constituted harassment. Metwater felt the presence of any member of the Ranger Brigade anywhere near his camp infringed on his rights to live as he pleased. The Rangers contended Metwater and his followers were potential witnesses to any of the many crimes that oc-

curred on public lands, by virtue of being the only people living in the area.

They took Simon's FJ Cruiser, heading out of the
national park and into the adjacent Curecanti National
Recreation Area, toward the distinctive mesa where
Metwater had made his camp. Forty minutes later
Simon parked the cruiser between a rusting pickup and
a doorless Jeep in the lot outside Metwater's camp. He
switched off the headlights, and inky blackness closed
around them. The moon hadn't yet risen, and though
what looked like a million stars sparkled overhead, they
didn't give much light. The two men waited a moment
for their eyes to adjust to the darkness. Ethan breathed
in deeply the scents of sagebrush and wood smoke.
"Ready?" Simon asked.

"Ready."

They made their way up a narrow path toward the
camp. Something skittered into the underbrush to
Ethan's left and he flinched, hand on the butt of the
Glock on his hip, then forced himself to relax when he
realized it was only an animal—maybe a fox or a rac-
coon. Voices drifted to them as they neared the camp.
They emerged into a clearing surrounded by more than
a dozen trailers, tents and cobbled-together shacks. The
remains of a bonfire glowed in a stone-lined pit in the
center of the area, and the shadows of adults and children flitted about the dwellings, voices rising at the officers' approach.

Metwater lived in the large, modern motor home at
one end of the camp. A pregnant young woman with
long blond hair emerged from the white tent next to the

motor home, a flashlight in one hand. Ethan recognized Andi Matheson, a former socialite and senator's daughter, who had taken the name Asteria when she moved in with Metwater.

"Miss Matheson."

She jerked her head up when Simon addressed her, and froze. "Is something wrong, Officers?" she asked.

"Just a routine patrol." Simon stopped in front of her, his lanky frame towering over her.

"At this time of night?" she asked, her expression angry.

"People think they can get away with things with the darkness to hide them," Simon said. "We like to catch them by surprise."

"You won't find anyone trying to get away with anything here." She tried to move around him, but he took a step to the side, blocking her.

"So everyone is tucked tight in their beds?" Simon asked. "No one missing?"

"I don't keep track of everyone." She darted around him and walked past Ethan. The two men turned and followed her to the motor home. She stopped at the bottom of the steps and looked at them. "You can't see the Prophet without an appointment," she said.

"We know Mr. Metwater is always happy to cooperate with an investigation," Simon said. Did Asteria note the sarcasm in his voice?

"What investigation?" she asked.

"Have you seen any strange cars around camp?" Ethan asked. "Newer models? Anybody in the group get a new ride recently?"

"No. What is this about?"

"Maybe Metwater will know." Ethan had started to move past her when the door burst open and a woman stumbled out. She caught her foot on the top step and fell—right into Ethan's arms.

He staggered under the impact, but managed to stay upright and hold on to the woman. She stared up at him, eyes wide and full of terror, dark, curly hair a tangle around her sharp-featured face. Blood trickled from one corner of her mouth.

"Hey, it's okay." Ethan spoke softly. "What happened?"

The terror in her eyes didn't abate. "Help me," she whispered, before slipping into unconsciousness.

Chapter Two

Michelle fought past the fog that surrounded her, struggling back into consciousness. She had to flee or something terrible would happen. She opened her eyes and stared into the face of a man she didn't know. A new wave of fear revved her heart and she tried to pull away from him.

"Shh. It's okay." His voice was soft, his hands gentle, even as he continued to hold her arm. "Look at me," he said. "My name is Ethan. Ethan Reynolds. I'm not going to hurt you."

She stared into moss-green eyes so full of compassion and tenderness, tears burned at the back of her throat. She never cried. Crying was a sign of weakness and she couldn't afford to be weak. Especially not now.

She pushed herself into a sitting position on the cot where she had been lying, though he kept one hand on her arm, steadying her. They were in the tent she shared with Asteria. Someone had lit the big oil lamp that hung from a post in the center of the room, a wavering circle of yellow light shining down on them. She had only a vague memory of rushing out of the motor home and falling… A fresh shudder of terror rocked her at the recollection.

"You must have hurt your head when you fell," Asteria said. She sat on the cot beside Michelle and pressed a wet washrag to the side of her face.

Michelle winced as pain radiated across her cheek and jaw. "I don't remember," she lied.

Out of the corner of her eye, she watched the man, Ethan. He had released his hold on her and moved to sit at the end of the cot. He had short, dark hair and good shoulders that filled out his khaki uniform shirt in a way she would have admired if she had been less distracted. As it was, he studied her with an intensity that sent a tremor through her. His eyes reflected compassion, but danger, too. "You didn't fall," he said. "Someone hit you. Was it Daniel Metwater?"

She closed her eyes, but she couldn't shut out the memory of Daniel Metwater's handsome face twisted in rage, his fists slamming into her over and over, pummeling her toward the door. He had demanded to know why she was in his trailer and she had foolishly blurted the truth. "I want the locket," she said. "Cass's locket. I know you have it."

After that she had been sure he would beat her to death. What if he came after her again? The thought made her stomach flip.

"The Prophet would never hurt anyone," Asteria protested. She stood, the damp cloth she had been holding to Michelle's face landing on the rug beside the cot with a soft *plop*. "He doesn't believe in violence."

"Tell anyone about this and you're dead." Metwater's

parting words came back to Michelle. "You'll go out for a walk one day and no one will ever see you again. Mention that locket again and your son will die. You'll never see him again."

Part of her had been as naive as Asteria, believing Metwater would never hit her. She had been so wrong. "Hunter!" Suddenly frantic, she looked around for the child. "Where is Hunter?"

"He's right here." Michelle hadn't realized that a fourth person was in the room, another in the circle of women who had been drawn to Metwater. Sarah stepped forward, the smiling little boy in her arms. He held out his chubby arms to Michelle and she gathered him close, burying her nose against his neck and inhaling that sweet baby smell.

"What's your name?" Ethan asked. "Your real name?"

They were supposed to only use their Family names with the cops. It was one of Metwater's rules. "You have a new identity now," he had preached. "The police don't need to know anything about your past." She was done with obeying his rules.

"It's Michelle," she said. "Michelle Munson."

Ethan stood and began pacing. He stopped in front of her, taller than she had thought before, radiating masculine power and suppressed anger—anger not at her but on her behalf. "Did Daniel Metwater hit you?" he asked again.

She closed her eyes and rested her cheek against Hunter's face. He was the only good thing that had ever happened to her and she would do anything to protect him. "I fell," she said.

Ethan pressed his lips together, clearly not pleased

with her answer. "If he hit you, I can arrest him and charge him with assault."

And he would be back in camp before lunchtime tomorrow. Daniel Metwater had plenty of money to pay a top lawyer. He would come back, and he would make sure Michelle paid for her betrayal. She raised her eyes to meet Ethan's, her gaze steady, giving away nothing. "The Prophet doesn't believe in violence," she said.

"What were you doing at the Prophet's place, anyway?" Asteria asked. "You were supposed to be at the fire circle with the rest of us."

Did Ethan hear the fear behind the question? Asteria worried she was losing her position as the Prophet's favorite.

"I went to him for counseling," Michelle said, though she knew the answer wouldn't ease Asteria's fears. Daniel Metwater sometimes "counseled" young women in his bed. He had never pretended to be faithful to Asteria, or to anyone else, but the poor girl apparently couldn't stop hoping.

Ethan sat beside Michelle on the cot once more. Hunter turned his head to look at the man, the little boy's eyes wide with curiosity. "How old is he?" Ethan asked. He offered his finger and, grinning, Hunter took hold of it.

His question caught her off guard. Was he really interested in her son, or only trying to lull her into trusting him? "Nine months," she answered.

"Taking care of a child by yourself is a big responsibility," Ethan said.

"I can handle it." She pulled Hunter closer.

"Looks like you're doing a great job." He freed his finger from the little boy's grasp, and his eyes met hers once more. "If you get hurt you won't be able to look after him."

She ignored the shudder that went up her spine at his words. She didn't need this cop warning her about how to behave. She had been looking after herself for a long time. She jutted out her chin. "I'll be fine."

"Be careful, that's all." He took a business card from his shirt pocket and held it out to her. "If you ever need help, or just want to talk, call me. Anytime."

She took the card and closed her fingers around it. People said things like that all the time, but they almost never meant it. But maybe Ethan Reynolds did.

He touched the cut on her lip, the lightest brush of his fingers, sending a shimmer of heat through her. "If you tell me who did this, I promise I won't let him hurt you again," he murmured.

"It was just clumsiness," she said. Clumsy of her not to guess how Metwater would react to her taunts about the locket. "It won't happen again." She wouldn't make the mistake of being alone with the Prophet again. He had lashed out so fiercely he had taken her by surprise, but next time she would be smarter. She would find a way to get the proof she needed that his brother had killed Cass. When she did, she would do everything in her power to make sure he never hit a woman again.

ETHAN EMERGED FROM the tent to find Simon waiting for him. "I was about ready to come in there after you," Simon said. He glanced over Ethan's shoulder. "What happened? How is Asteria and the other one—Stardust or whatever she calls herself?"

"Starfall. Michelle. Her real name is Michelle. She's pretty bruised up, and obviously terrified, though she's trying not to show it. Asteria is fine. Concerned for her friend, of course."

"What happened to her?" Simon asked. "To Starfall?"

"She says she fell, but I think somebody beat her." He shifted his gaze to Metwater's motor home. No light shone from inside the dwelling.

"I didn't get anything out of any of the people who were still standing around here," Simon said. "They say they were at the bonfire and didn't see or hear anything."

"Let's see what Metwater has to say." Ethan started toward the motor home.

"I knocked, but no one answered," Simon said, falling in step beside Ethan. "I figured I'd wait for backup before I broke down the door."

"Maybe it won't come to that." Ethan pounded the door, a thunderous sound in the still darkness. "Open up!" he shouted. "Police!"

No answer.

Ethan glanced back at Simon, who had already drawn his weapon. "Metwater has a license for a handgun," Simon said. "I'd just as soon not give him a chance to use it."

Ethan nodded and drew his Glock. "On three," he said. "One. Two. Three." He hit the door hard, landing a fierce kick beside the lock, the metal crumpling under the blow. He hit it again with his shoulder and it burst inward. He immediately ducked around the jamb, waiting for an explosion of gunfire that didn't come.

Simon's eyes met his and he nodded. Ethan went in

first, gun at the ready, Simon at his back. Simon hit the light switch, illuminating a sofa, recliner, table and lamp. Nothing out of order and no obvious place for anyone to hide. Adrenaline making him hyperalert, Ethan pounded down the hallway to another door. He didn't bother knocking, but burst in, onto a scene of chaos.

A man cursed and a woman screamed—and kept on screaming. Ethan flicked the wall switch to the left of the door, and a single bedside lamp glowed, revealing a young woman standing in the corner, frantically trying to cover herself with a sheet she had dragged from the bed. Her mouth was open, and tears streamed down her face.

Daniel Metwater, naked and red-faced, sat up on the side of the bed. "Freeze!" Simon ordered, and fixed his weapon on him.

Metwater glared at them. "What is the meaning of this? The district attorney has ordered you people to leave me alone. I'll have your jobs, and then I'll sue you for everything you own. I—"

"Shut up," Ethan said. "And keep your hands where we can see them."

Metwater looked as if he might argue, but finally raised his hands to shoulder level. But he didn't stop talking. "You can't bust into a man's home in the middle of the night for no reason," he said.

"Shut up." Simon gave the order this time.

Ethan addressed the woman. "Are you all right, ma'am?" he asked.

She closed her mouth and swallowed, then nodded.

"What's your name?" Ethan asked.

"Sunshine."

"What's your full name?" he asked. "Your real name."

"Sunshine is my real name. Sunshine Hartford."

She looked barely eighteen, with strawberry-blond curls and freckles. "Ms. Hartford, how long have you been here with Mr. Metwater?" Ethan asked.

"N...not long." She pulled the sheet up higher over her breasts.

"How long?" Ethan asked. "Give me your best estimate."

"She's been here almost an hour," Metwater said.

"I told you to be quiet," Simon said.

"How long have you been here?" Ethan asked again.

"I guess like he said." She bit her bottom lip and glanced at Metwater. "About an hour?"

She was lying, but there wasn't much Ethan could do about it now. Confident Simon had Metwater under control, he holstered his Glock and took out a small notebook. "Give me your contact information and then you can get dressed and wait for us outside," he said.

He waited until the young woman had gathered her clothing and left the room, the sheet still wrapped around her. Then he turned to Metwater again. "Get up and put on some pants," he ordered.

With a sneering look, Metwater scooped a pair of loose-fitting white trousers from the floor and tugged them on. He tied the cord at the waist. "What are you doing here?" he asked.

"What happened between you and one of your followers—a woman called Starfall?" Ethan asked.

The expression in Metwater's icy brown eyes never

changed. "What about her? If she's gotten into some kind of trouble, that's her problem, not mine."

"Not very sympathetic for a man who claims to be the head of a family," Simon said.

"We witnessed her coming out of this motor home less than half an hour ago," Ethan said. "She was bruised and bleeding. She fainted."

"I don't know why she would be here." Metwater looked around, found a shirt and pulled it on, but didn't button it.

"I didn't ask if you knew why she was here," Ethan said. "What happened while she was here? How was she hurt?"

"I have no idea."

"Where were you when she was hurt?" Simon asked.

Metwater shrugged. "Since I don't know when she was hurt, or even if she was hurt, I can't answer that."

"Where were you thirty minutes ago?" Ethan asked.

"I already told you—I was here with Miss Hartford."

"So you admit you were here, in this motor home, at the time Starfall was hurt," Ethan said. "Yet you don't know how she was hurt?"

Metwater's smile held no warmth. "I was otherwise occupied. With Miss Hartford."

"Is Miss Hartford one of your followers?" Simon asked. "I don't remember seeing her around before."

"She's an aspiring disciple," Metwater said.

"We're going to question Ms. Hartford," Ethan said. "Are you sure she'll confirm your story?"

"She will."

Ethan fought the urge to knock the smug look off

Metwater's face. "Did you have an argument with Starfall?" he asked.

"No." His smile faded. "Does she say that we did?"

"She's too upset to question right now," Ethan said. He wanted to keep Metwater off guard as much as possible.

"She'll confirm we didn't argue," Metwater said. "Unless she lies. She sometimes has a problem with honesty. It's something we're working on."

"I'll find out the truth," Ethan said. "And I'll make sure the person who hurt Starfall is charged and prosecuted."

"Knock yourself out, Officer." Metwater stood. "But now it's time for you to leave. Expect to hear from my lawyers."

Ethan took a step toward Metwater. If this so-called Prophet thought Ethan was going to be intimidated by empty threats, he was in for a rude awakening.

"Come on." Simon's voice snapped Ethan out of his rage. "We're wasting our time here."

Ethan turned and led the way out of the motor home. "I wanted to deck him, too," Simon said when they were outside. "But it wouldn't be worth the hassle the suits would put you through later."

Ethan nodded and took a deep, calming breath. "We should talk to Ms. Hartford," he said.

"She's long gone." Simon looked around at the empty campground. The only light was from the few dying embers of the bonfire, and a thin glow of gold showing at the entrance to Asteria and Starfall's tent. "We'll track her down tomorrow."

"I want to check on Starfall one more time," Ethan said.

Asteria met them at the door of the tent. "She's sleeping," she said, in answer to Ethan's unvoiced question. "She was pretty shaken up, but I think she'll be okay. She's pretty tough."

"Did she tell you anything about what happened?" Ethan asked.

Asteria tucked her hair behind one ear. Deep shadows hollowed her eyes and she looked exhausted. "She wouldn't say anything. She got angry when I asked her about it."

"Has Daniel Metwater ever hit any of the women in camp before?" Ethan asked.

Asteria gaped at them, wide-eyed. "No! He would never do that! It isn't possible." She smoothed back her hair. "I should go to him now. He'll be very upset about your accusations, and he's expecting me. I was on my way to him when all this happened." She waved a hand toward the cot where Starfall slept.

She started to move past them, but Simon put out a hand to stop her. "What do you mean, Metwater is expecting you?" he asked.

Defiance shone behind the fatigue. "I was going to spend the night with him. I often do."

"If he was expecting you, what was Sunshine Hartford doing there?" Simon asked.

"Sunshine? Do you mean that girl who's been hanging around here?" Asteria furrowed her brow. "I thought I saw her at the fire circle tonight, but she wasn't with the Prophet."

"She was with him a few minutes ago," Ethan said.

"She was with him in his bed," Simon added.

Asteria stared at him. "What?"

"He told us he and Ms. Hartford had been together for the last hour," Simon said.

"That can't be right," she said.

"Why can't it be right?" Ethan asked.

"Because…" She bit her lower lip, then shook her head. "Just, because." She looked back toward the cot. Starfall lay on her side, the blanket pulled up past her ears. Only the tumble of her brown curls showed against the white of the pillow.

Simon touched Asteria's elbow, turning her attention back to him. "Why can't it be right?" he asked.

"He was supposed to be alone!" The words burst from her, and her eyes shone wetly. "Not with Starfall or Sunshine or anyone else. He asked me to come to him."

"Maybe he had something else in mind for tonight," Simon said.

She shook her head. "No. He isn't like that. You don't know him at all or you wouldn't say something like that."

"Maybe you don't know him that well, either," Simon said.

She stepped back into the tent. "Go away and leave us alone," she said. "You're not welcome here."

"We'll leave for now," Simon said. "But think about what's happened tonight. If Daniel Metwater would lie to you about being alone tonight, what else has he lied to you about?"

Ethan gave her a hard look. "And what are you going to do to stop the lying?"

Chapter Three

Michelle was still on Ethan's mind the next morning as he made his way down the quiet residential street on Montrose's south side. Staying emotionally distant from victims was a necessary part of the job—let yourself get too wound up about the things people did to each other and you'd never sleep at night. But Michelle got to him. She looked so wounded and fragile, yet he sensed real strength in her.

He turned onto his parents' street and nodded to a jogger on the sidewalk. The neighbor's sprinkler sent a shimmer of water over the perfectly trimmed yard, and the aroma of wet grass and pavement drifted in through his partially open window. He pulled into the driveway, wondering how long it would be before he stopped expecting to see his father waiting at the front door. Dad had been gone six months now, but every time Ethan came to the house he experienced that jolt of expectation followed by disappointment.

His mother came to the front door and held open the screen, waiting for him. She wore pale blue scrubs and white clogs, ready for her nursing shift at Montrose

Hospital. She looked so small to him—smaller than she had been when he was a boy, and smaller than when his dad had been alive. She smiled as he approached and stood on tiptoe to kiss his cheek. "This is a nice surprise," she said. "What brings you out so early?"

"I just stopped by to see how you're doing."

"I'm fine. I went shopping yesterday and they had some nice melon. Would you like some?"

"That's okay, Mom. I already had breakfast." He looked back at the neighbor's sprinkler. "I'll try to come over this afternoon and mow the lawn," he said.

"You don't have to do that," she said. "I can hire someone. Mrs. Douglas across the street has someone. I can ask her who she uses."

"You don't have to do that, Mom. I'll take care of it." His dad had kept the place immaculate when he was alive—grass cut every week, hedges trimmed, flowers mulched. Dad paid all the bills and took care of the cars and even drove Mom shopping once a week. Now she was having to do all those things herself. Ethan wondered if it was too much for her.

"First chance I get, I'll change the oil in your car," he said as he followed her into the house. "It's probably past time for that."

"I can take it to one of those quick oil change places," she said. "You have enough to do without worrying about me."

But Ethan did worry. One of the reasons he had jumped at the chance to join the Ranger Brigade was that the new position would allow him to live close to his mom—to look after her.

"Do you have time for coffee?" she asked as she led the way to the kitchen. "I was just going to pour myself a cup."

"Coffee would be nice." He sat at the kitchen table—his usual spot, to the left of the chair where his father had always sat. From this position, he had a good view of the backyard, and the patio he and his dad had put in during Ethan's senior year of high school—a patio currently occupied by a trio of tabby cats, busy devouring a dish of crumpets.

"Still feeding the neighborhood strays, I see," he said.

"They're not strays." His mother slid a blue mug of coffee in front of him, then took her seat in her usual place across from Ethan. "They're feral cats. They've never had a home, but grew up in the wild."

One cat finished and retreated to a fence post to groom itself in the sun. "You planning on adopting them?" Ethan asked. A pet might be good for her, keep her company.

"That's not how it works with ferals," she said. "You can't really tame them. They'll never give up their independence. The best I can do is feed them and provide a sheltered spot for them to get out of the weather." She indicated a pile of blankets in a corner of the covered patio.

"Sounds like a good way to end up with a whole zoo of wild cats," Ethan said.

"Oh, no. They've all been neutered. See how their ears are notched? That tells everyone they were fixed."

The cat on the post did indeed have a notch cut out

of its right ear. "Maybe you should think about adopting a domestic cat, then," he said. "Wouldn't you enjoy the company?"

"I enjoy feeding the ferals and having them around, without the commitment to a full-time cat," she said.

"Just be careful, Mom," he said. "Don't let one of them bite you or anything."

"You sound just like your father."

Though she was smiling, the remark pained him. The reaction must have shown on his face, because she quickly changed the subject. "How is your new job going?" she asked. "Are you working on anything interesting?"

"We're trying to track down some car thieves we think might be operating on public land." He sipped the coffee. "We were out at Daniel Metwater's camp last night, seeing if they knew anything."

"He's that good-looking preacher fellow, isn't he?" His mom shook a packet of sweetener into her coffee and stirred. "I've read things about him in the paper— all those young people camping out with him. Just like the hippies back when I was that age." She laughed. "One summer your father decided to grow his hair long and your grandmother was worried to death that he was going to become one of those flower children."

"Dad had long hair?" Ethan couldn't picture it. For most of his life, his dad hadn't had much hair at all.

"Oh, it was just one summer," she said. "Then he got a job in the oil fields and he had to cut it. I quite liked it, though. He had prettier hair than I did." She laughed again. "What are they like, the followers of that Prophet?"

"Mostly young," he said. "Some men, but a lot of women and children. Most of them are probably harmless, but he's attracted his share of people who are running from something—including the law."

"I can't think the children have much of a life, camping in the woods like that," she said.

"We try to monitor them, make sure there's no abuse or neglect." He frowned, remembering the bruises on Michelle's face.

"What is it, dear?" his mother asked. "You look upset."

"Last night when we were out there, we ran into a woman," he said. "Or rather, she ran into us. She'd been beaten—pretty badly. But she insisted she had fallen and wouldn't tell us who had hit her."

"Oh, no." His mom made a tsking noise. "We get women like that in the emergency room sometimes. They're too afraid to tell the truth, I think."

"This woman was afraid." He pushed his half-empty cup aside. "I'm going to go out there this morning and talk to her again. Maybe I can persuade her to file charges."

"I hope you can help her," his mom said. "No woman should be treated that way. Your father would have died before he raised his hand against me."

"Yeah, Dad was a great guy." He pushed his chair back. "I'd better get going. I'll be over later to take care of the lawn."

His mom walked with him to the door. "Thanks,

sweetie." She kissed his cheek again. "And don't worry about me. That's my job."

It was his job, too, now that his dad wasn't around. Trying to ignore the heaviness in his chest, he returned to his cruiser. He couldn't take away his mom's or his own grief, but he could do whatever he could to make her life easier. She wasn't like Michelle—alone with no one to defend her.

MICHELLE WOKE TO Hunter's crying—a reassuring sound, since she had been having a dream in which he was lost and she couldn't find him. She sat up on the side of her cot, groaning as pain radiated through her body, and the memory of last night returned, like a fresh blow. She put a hand to the tender, swollen flesh around her mouth, and carefully stood, then shuffled toward the crib.

The baby was soaking wet, so she changed him, then sat on the side of the cot once more to nurse him. She was weaning him, but right now she needed this closeness, giving him something only she could provide. Asteria was nowhere in sight—not surprising, since she spent most of her nights lately with Daniel Metwater. Michelle held her son closely and replayed the events of last night in her head.

She had been stupid to think Metwater wouldn't lash out at her. Stupid to believe he would hand over the locket in exchange for her promise of silence. Not that she intended to keep that promise, but she was good at conning people. She had been doing it most of her life.

But Metwater was a con, too. He knew how the game

was played. And now that he knew she was on to him, she would have to be careful. She would have to make sure Hunter stayed safe.

She brushed the hair from the baby's forehead and he smiled up at her. Her heart clenched. Until she had had Hunter, she had had nothing—no one.

She slipped a hand into her pocket and felt the business card the Ranger had given her. Ethan. A high-class-sounding name. Someone named Ethan probably wouldn't drop out of school or end up in jail for boosting cars or dealing drugs, the way the boys from her neighborhood did. Ethan went to college. He got a job upholding the law instead of breaking it.

Ethan didn't look twice at Michelle Munson from the wrong side of town. But Ethan Reynolds had looked at her. She had stared into his eyes and felt that he was seeing her—not the cool, smart-talking tough girl role she had assumed before her age reached double digits, but the real her—the woman who had been hurt, who was fearful of a future she couldn't control. Most of the time she forgot that woman even existed anymore, but somehow this cop had seen it.

The knowledge made her feel vulnerable—a sensation she didn't like. She was the only person she could rely on to look after herself and her son. That meant she couldn't let anyone make her feel helpless. Daniel Metwater controlled people by making them believe they weren't capable of making the right choices for their lives. They needed him to make those choices for them—to control their money and tell them when to eat and what to think. When she had first come here, she was amazed at how many people were willing to give up everything to someone who promised to make them feel good.

The flap of the tent pushed open and Asteria ducked inside. She carried a cup of coffee and handed it to Michelle. "I thought you might need this," she said.

"Yes. You're a saint." Michelle took the cup and drained a third of it in one long swallow. At least the Prophet hadn't made them give up coffee, the way he had talked them into giving up meat two days a week and cell phones and movies, and she had lost track of how much else. If she hadn't promised herself she would do whatever she had to in order to prove that Cass was murdered, she would have left this place a long time ago.

"How are you feeling?" Asteria sat on the cot beside her.

"A little sore." She watched Asteria out of the corner of her eye as she spoke. She had to be careful here. She couldn't afford to upset Metwater's biggest fan. "That was some fall."

"What were you doing at the Prophet's trailer?" Asteria asked. "And don't give me that lie about counseling."

"Why don't you believe I went to him for counseling?" Michelle asked.

"Because you're not the counseling type. You don't confide in people."

No, she didn't. And even if she did, she wouldn't reveal anything personal to a man like Metwater. She didn't want him to know so much as her shoe size, in case he could find a way to use it against her. "I went there to complain," she said. "The men in this camp are lazy bums who don't do their share of the work. He needs to put some of them on kitchen duty, instead of making us look after the children and prepare all the meals while they sit around and wait to be fed." She had no trouble getting into this rant, since it was one she had voiced before. The other women agreed with her, but none of them were willing to do anything about it.

Most of the tension went out of Asteria's shoulders. "You shouldn't bother him with something like that," she said. "Not late at night."

"It wasn't that late." She shifted Hunter to her other arm and took another drink of coffee. "Anyway, he wasn't there."

"If he wasn't there, why did you go inside?"

"The door was unlocked. I only stepped into the living room and called for him. I mean, it wasn't like I was going to go into his bedroom or anything." She held her breath, hoping Asteria would believe her.

"So you didn't see him at all?"

"No. I waited a few seconds, then turned and left. I must have caught my foot on the step on my way out." The cop, Ethan, hadn't believed that lame story for even a minute, but Asteria was buying it the way the former socialite would once have snagged a coveted designer gown in her size.

"Did you see anyone else?" Asteria asked. "Either in the motor home or on your way there?"

Someone else? That was an interesting development. "Who?" she asked.

"Did you see Sunshine?"

"Sunshine?" Starfall tried and failed to match a face to that name.

"The girl who's been hanging around lately."

Ah! The girl who had been shamelessly flirting with Metwater. Starfall saw where this was going now. "No, I didn't see her," she said. She hadn't seen anyone but Metwater and his fist.

"I knew those Rangers were lying," Asteria said. "They told me that when they questioned the Prophet about what had happened to you, he told them he was with Sunshine. They were just trying to upset me so that I would tell lies about the Prophet."

If you're sleeping with a guy, it's probably okay to call him by his first name, Michelle thought, but she kept quiet. Asteria—the former Andi Matheson—had bought Metwater's line about being a holy seer one hundred percent. She was his favorite follower—and also his wealthiest—and she couldn't even see the connection between his favoritism and her money. "What kind of lies did they want you to tell?" she asked.

"That he hit you. Which is ridiculous, because you know how much he hates violence."

Right. "I've heard him say several times that he hates violence," she agreed. Though he had had no trouble trying to beat her brains in last night. She still wasn't sure how she had managed to break free and run for the door. If the two Rangers hadn't been standing right outside, would he have pursued her and maybe even killed her?

She set down her coffee mug, suddenly sick to her stomach. "I need to take a shower," she said. Some of the men had built a shower shack at the other end of camp. Water came from a plastic barrel that sat on top of the shack. The sun heated the water, and the plastic showerhead had an on-off switch that allowed the person showering to control the flow. It wasn't the Ritz, but it wasn't bad.

"Do you want me to watch Hunter while you do that?" Asteria asked.

"That's okay. I'll take him in with me." Hunter liked to sit on the floor and play in the puddles that collected around her feet. Until she was sure she was safe, she wasn't going to let the baby out of her sight.

She finished the coffee, then collected a towel, soap and shampoo, and picked up Hunter. "Let's go take a shower, buddy," she said, bouncing him on her hip. He giggled, dimples forming on either side of his mouth. Smiling in return, she headed toward the shower shack.

She had just turned onto the path to the shower when Daniel Metwater stepped out in front of her. She stumbled to a halt, heart racing, searching for a way out. But the woods grew close to the path on either side and Metwater blocked the way forward. She could turn and run, but he might be able to catch her.

She stood, frozen, as he approached and put a hand on her shoulder. "I heard you had a bad fall," he said, gaze focused on her bruises. "Are you all right?"

The absurdity of his words, and the false concern in his voice, shocked her out of her fear. She stumbled back, wrenching away from him. "No, I am not all right." She checked to make sure no one was close enough to overhear them. "And I didn't fall. You and I both know it."

"As long as no one else knows." He wrapped his hand around Hunter's arm. Now if she tried to pull away, the baby would be hurt. "I meant what I told you," he said. "If you want Hunter to stay safe, you won't say a word about this—or about that locket—to anyone."

She wanted to spit in his face—to tell him that she was going to expose his brother as a murderer and him as a fraud. But she couldn't do that. She had to protect her son, and find a way to keep them both safe until she could get the proof she needed. "I know how to keep my mouth shut," she said. "I haven't told anyone about what I know, and I've been here for months."

"Make sure you don't."

She left, wanting to run but forcing herself to walk. She could feel his gaze boring into her back all the way to the shower shack, and when she reached the shack and glanced back, he was still watching, the hatred in his expression making her tremble all the way to her toes.

SUNSHINE HARTFORD VIBRATED like a terrified rabbit. Her left leg bounced and her upper lip twitched as she stared, wide-eyed, at the trio of officers gathered around her at Ranger Brigade Headquarters. Ethan and Agent Carmen Redhorse had picked her up at her apartment in Montrose and brought her in for questioning, thinking if they could rattle her a little she would be more likely to confess the truth.

But Ethan hadn't intended to frighten her so badly

she couldn't speak. "You don't have anything to worry about, Miss Hartford," he tried to reassure her. "You haven't done anything wrong. We only want your help in drawing a clear picture of what happened last night at Daniel Metwater's motor home."

"A woman was injured." Carmen leaned toward the young woman, her voice soft but firm. "You can help us find who hurt her."

"I… I was with the Prophet," she stammered. "You saw me there."

"How long had you been with him?" Ethan asked.

"He told you. We had been there an hour."

"Yes, that's what he told us, but that can't be right, can it?" Ethan tried to keep his tone conversational, nonaccusatory. "Was the bonfire even over that long?"

She squirmed like a kid who had to go to the bathroom. "I didn't have a watch with me."

"Did you hear or see anyone else in the motor home while you were there?" Ethan asked. "Maybe someone in another room?"

She shook her head. "No. When you're with the Prophet, it's as if no one else is around."

Out of view of Sunshine, Carmen rolled her eyes. "Did he say anything to you about anyone else?" Ethan asked. "Did he mention anyone by name?"

"He said if I saw Asteria, I had to pretend I hadn't been with him," she said.

"And you were okay with that?" Carmen asked. "Lying to another woman?"

"It wouldn't be lying, exactly," Sunshine said. "And

I would be obeying the Prophet. You can't be a good disciple if you aren't obedient."

A classic manipulator's line, Ethan thought.

"Did you know that lying to the police is against the law?" Ethan asked.

"The Prophet answers to the highest law. I'm sure he wouldn't ask me to do anything harmful."

"So you admit you're lying," Ethan said.

Her expression clouded. "I haven't seen or spoken to Asteria," she said. "So I haven't had to lie about anything."

"What about how much time you spent with Metwater?" Carmen asked. "Are you lying about that?"

She wrinkled her nose, and her voice took on a strident edge. "I told you—I don't wear a watch. I wasn't keeping track of the time. He said it was an hour, so it must be an hour."

"All right," Ethan said. "Take me through the sequence of events last night. When did you arrive at camp?"

"The fire circle is always at dusk, so I got to the camp a little before—about eight thirty."

"What next?"

"I walked into camp. The bonfire was going and a lot of Family members were already there. I found some women I knew and stood with them. We waited about fifteen minutes and then the Prophet came out." A smile transformed her from sulky teen to beautiful woman. "He was wearing a loincloth and had painted his face. He was beautiful."

"And he does what at these fire circles?" Every cult

had its rituals. The researcher in Ethan was curious about Metwater's rituals.

"First, he gave us a message about how we should live. He talked about sharing—about how the rest of the world lives in an economy based on hoarding, but in the Family, everyone shares, and that makes everyone better off, instead of only a few people."

Carmen made a snorting noise. Sunshine gave her a sharp look. "Go on," Carmen said. "I didn't mean to interrupt."

"After the message, the drummers started up, and the Prophet led us in a chant. Then he began to dance. It was mesmerizing."

"What do the rest of you do while he dances?" Ethan asked.

"We chant. And sometimes the Prophet asks other people to dance with him." Her cheeks glowed pink. "Last night he asked me to dance with him. I was so excited I couldn't even feel my feet touch the ground."

"How long did you dance?" Ethan asked.

"Not long. We went around the fire and when we reached my place in the circle, the Prophet kissed my cheek. Everyone was watching and I felt so special." Her eyes shone with the memory. Metwater certainly had her under his spell.

"What happened next?" Ethan prompted.

"The chanting and dancing went on for a little while longer. Then the drums quieted and the Prophet gave us his blessing. Then everyone left the fire circle and went to bed."

"Where did you go?" Carmen asked. "Did you go with the Prophet?"

"Not right away. I stood around talking with some of the other women—Sarah and Moonglow—and a guy named Alex."

"What did you talk about?" Ethan asked.

"Nothing in particular. I wanted to know more about what it was like to live in the Family. I want to join, but the Prophet says they aren't taking any new members right now. Apparently, they had trouble with some cops pretending to be interested in joining and using that to spy on the group. Can you believe that?"

Ethan's eyes met Carmen's and he suppressed a smile. She had lived with Metwater and his followers for a couple of weeks last month, by pretending to be a prospective member. Her undercover work hadn't revealed any evidence of criminal activity in the group, but it had led to contact with a Fish and Game officer tracking smugglers. Carmen had helped with the case and now she and the Fish and Game cop were engaged.

"So you didn't go to Metwater's motor home with him right away?" he asked Sunshine.

"No. I stood around and talked for a while. I was thinking I should probably go back to my car when the Prophet walked over and asked me to come back to his motor home with him." She blushed again. "Just like that, he singled me out. It was amazing."

"Did you see anyone or talk to anyone on your way to the motor home?" Ethan asked.

"No. He took my hand and practically dragged me back there with him."

"What happened when you got inside the motor home?" Ethan asked. "What did you see?"

"Nothing, really. He had all the lights turned off. He took me to his bedroom and told me to undress. He started undressing, too. We got under the covers and started making out. And then you interrupted."

"That doesn't sound like it would take an hour to me," Ethan said.

"I don't see why the time matters so much," Sunshine said. "The important thing is that we were together and I didn't see anybody else—certainly not a hurt woman. I mean, I'm sorry she was hurt, but the Prophet wouldn't do anything like that. He loves women."

"He certainly loves to use them," Carmen said.

Sunshine stood and brushed off her skirt. "Can I go now?" she asked.

"Yes, you can go," Ethan said. "I'll take you back home." He dug in his pocket for his car keys but stopped when the front door of Ranger Headquarters burst open.

Starfall staggered inside, her face pale as death except for the bruising along her jaw and around her mouth. She stared at Ethan with haunted eyes, and when she spoke, her voice was a ragged gasp. "Hunter…my baby…he's gone! You have to help me get him back!"

Chapter Four

Panic clawed at Michelle's throat and clouded her vision. Every breath burned and her pulse pounded in her head. *My baby's gone. My baby's gone. My baby's gone!*

A steadying hand gripped her arm and a man's firm but gentle voice cut through the clamor of her thoughts. "Take a deep breath. I'm going to help you. Sit down over here and tell me everything that happened."

Ethan Reynolds led her to a chair and someone brought her a cup of water. She drank it and struggled to control her breathing. "My little boy, Hunter, is missing," she said. "Daniel Metwater took him, I know he did. He threatened to hurt him and now he's done it." She choked back a sob.

Ethan sat in a chair across from her, his knees almost touching hers, his hand firm on her shoulder. "Michelle, look at me," he said.

She looked into brown eyes so full of concern and compassion that a fresh flood of tears filled her eyes. "I know it's hard, but you have to be strong," he said. "The more information you can tell us, the more we'll have to use to find your baby. And we will do every-thing in our power to find him."

He was right. She had to be strong. And she was strong. She wouldn't have made it this long if she wasn't. She took a deep breath and began. "I was in the shower," she said. "We have this shower shack, with a plastic barrel of water on the roof. The sun warms the water and there's a showerhead with a switch you can turn on and off. I took Hunter into the stall with me. He likes to play in the water and I wanted to keep an eye on him." She had only turned away for a second…

"What happened then?" Ethan prompted, once more pulling her back from that awful abyss of panic.

"I had just turned on the water and was wetting my hair when someone dumped a bucket of paint over the side of the stall. The top is mostly open and I know there was some paint sitting around—the plan was to paint the shack, but no one had gotten around to it yet." She was rambling, filling in too many details, but she couldn't stop herself.

"Who dumped the paint—do you know?" A wom-an's voice this time. Michelle turned her head and rec-ognized Carmen Redhorse—the cop who had lived with them for a while. She and Michelle hadn't exactly got-ten along—Michelle had tried to scam the cop Carmen was now engaged to.

"I don't know who threw the paint," she said. "I couldn't see anything. That was the problem. I had paint all over me—in my hair and in my eyes. I screamed and I was trying to wash it all out. I was worried about it drying that way, in my hair and my eyelashes. I turned the water on full blast and grabbed the shampoo. I couldn't see or hear anything. By the time I got it all rinsed out, Hunter was gone. Someone must have reached in and grabbed him while I was blinded. Either Metwater or someone he ordered to take Hunter."

"Why do you think it was Metwater?" Ethan asked.

"Because he said he would hurt Hunter if I didn't keep quiet about what happened last night, and about what I knew about his brother."

"So he is the one who hurt you last night?" Ethan asked.

"Yes. But I couldn't tell you about it. I couldn't tell anyone. I kept quiet, the way he said." But it hadn't made any difference, apparently.

"What was that about his brother?" Ethan asked.

She sighed. How could she make this cop understand, when the story was so convoluted? But she had to try. "My sister, my foster sister, Cass, dated Daniel Metwater's twin brother, David. She thought she was in love with him, but she was worried. She had found out something about him—something bad. She wouldn't tell me what it was, but she told me she was going to confront him. She thought this bad thing couldn't possibly be true, that he would prove it wasn't true and they could go on. Instead, she died that night of an apparent heroin overdose. But Cass didn't use drugs. I know she didn't. He killed her so she wouldn't reveal the bad thing she had found out about him. I'm sure of it."

"That's terrible," Carmen said. "But what does it have to do with Daniel Metwater?"

"Cass had a locket—gold, with a big diamond. She inherited it from her grandmother. She was wearing it the night she disappeared, but when police found her body, the locket was missing. A few days ago Asteria told me Daniel had showed her a gold locket and promised to give it to her baby. It sounded like Cass's locket. If I could get hold of that, it would help me prove that there was a connection between Cass and the Metwaters. It might be enough to get the police to dig deeper into her death. More than anything, I want to clear her name and prove David Metwater was a murderer. It's why I joined up with the Family in the first place."

"So you went to Metwater's motor home last night to get the locket," Ethan said.

"Yes. Only he came back earlier than I expected and he caught me looking for it. He was furious. He started hitting me and telling me he was going to hurt Hunter, too. I thought he was going to beat me to death. Somehow I broke free and ran out of the trailer—that's when you found me."

"Why didn't you tell me any of this last night?" Ethan asked. She heard the frustration in his voice—she couldn't blame him.

"I was afraid of him," she said. "The way he beat on me, I'm sure he was ready to kill me. And I had to protect Hunter."

"Did Daniel Metwater specifically threaten to take Hunter?" Carmen asked.

"He said he would hurt him. He said it last night, and again this morning. He stopped me on the way to the showers and he said if I wanted Hunter to stay safe, I needed to keep my mouth shut. I told him I would, but I guess he didn't believe me."

"What did you do when you discovered Hunter was missing?" Ethan asked.

"I pulled on my clothes and ran out of the shower, calling for him. I thought maybe he wandered off. I stopped everyone I met and asked if they had seen him, but no one had. Then I went to Metwater's motor home and pounded on the door. I screamed that I wanted my baby. He said he didn't know anything about my baby and I needed to stop being so hysterical." She could have killed Metwater in that moment. She had tried to push past him, to search for Hunter, but he had two of his bodyguards hold her back. "I accused him of taking Hunter and he told everyone I had lost my mind. After that no one would help me, so I came here." She slumped forward, head in her hands. "I didn't know what else to do."

"We'll help you." Ethan took one hand and gently pulled it away from her face. "We'll put out an Amber Alert for Hunter. Everyone will be looking for him. We'll search the camp and we'll question Metwater. We'll find your son."

She nodded. If they acted quickly, maybe Metwater wouldn't have had time to take Hunter away somewhere.

"All those articles you had collected about David and Daniel Metwater," Carmen said. "The ones I found in your trunk—they were because of your sister?"

Michelle stared at the other woman for a moment, before she remembered that Carmen had, indeed, searched her trunk—and she had discovered the item Michelle had been using to blackmail the Fish and Game officer

Carmen was now engaged to. "I didn't know you had seen the articles," she said.

"I didn't read them all," Carmen said. "But I looked through them enough to see they were all about Daniel and David Metwater. I thought maybe you were trying to blackmail him, too."

"I wish," Michelle said. "I saved every article I could find, hoping it would give me some clue as to what really happened to Cass that night. The local police wouldn't believe she had been murdered, so they weren't doing anything about it. It was up to me."

"So you decided to join Daniel Metwater's family," Ethan said.

"Yes. I called myself Starfall because I didn't want to risk Metwater recognizing the name. Cass and I weren't related by blood—her family took me in as their foster child when I was a teenager, but Cass might have mentioned me, so I thought it was safer to assume a fake name. A lot of the people who join his family do that. Asteria did it. She used to be some wealthy socialite."

"Do you mind if I call you Michelle?" Ethan asked. "At least when Metwater isn't around?"

She nodded. "I'd like that. Since he took my baby, I don't want to have anything to do with him." She sat up straighter. "And I don't care if he knows who I really am now. I'm not going to let him get away with this."

"Neither are we." Ethan's expression was grim. "I promise you—neither are we."

HALF AN HOUR later Ethan glanced over at the woman who sat in the passenger seat of his FJ Cruiser. Starfall—Michelle—was still pale, the bruises around her mouth from where Metwater had hit her last night a painful-looking purple. "You hanging in there?" he asked.

She nodded and turned toward him. "What do you think he's done with Hunter?"

"I don't know." It wasn't the answer she wanted, but it was all he had to give her. "Would Hunter have gone with him willingly, do you think?"

"Probably. He's a friendly boy, and he's never had any reason to be afraid of anyone or anything. I made sure of that."

"What about his father?"

She stiffened. "What about him?"

"Is it possible he would take the boy? That happens sometimes with custody disputes."

"No." She shook her head, curls bouncing. "He's been out of the picture for months now. He was a mistake."

"Still, he might decide he wants his son." Ethan couldn't imagine having a child who wasn't a part of his life. "What's his name? We can check his whereabouts."

"It's Greg Warbush. The last I heard he was in Seattle. But you're wasting your time looking for him. He wouldn't take Hunter. Greg was never even interested in him. He even said he wasn't sure Hunter was his." She shrugged. "Maybe he was right."

Ethan tried not to let his feelings show on his face, but his expression must have betrayed something, because she said, "I was in a bad place after Cass died. She was the only family I really had—the only person I was close to. I went off the deep end, drinking and sleeping around. I snapped out of it when I found out I was pregnant. I didn't want my kid growing up the way I had—unwanted. I straightened up and tried to make it work with Greg, but I guess when you start out that way, the relationship is doomed."

The way she said that word—*unwanted*—as if it was just another fact in her life—sent a chill through him. Ethan's parents had always been there for him. He couldn't imagine living a life where the only person you cared about—the only person you thought cared about you—was a foster sibling.

"Is there anyone else who might want to harm you or your son?" he asked. "Someone with a grudge against you? Someone who is angry with you, for whatever reason?"

She sighed and tilted her head back to stare up at the ceiling. "I'm sure you've talked to Officer Redhorse. If you have, you know I'm not the most popular person in camp. I'm not the kind of person who gets close to other people, and I've done things to make enemies."

"What kind of things?"

"I find out people's secrets and use that to get them to do what I want." Her eyes flashed, defiant.

"You mean blackmail?"

"Nobody in camp has any money. And most people don't have big secrets, either. But if I need a guy to fix my car and he says no, I'll snoop around until I catch him doing something like siphoning gas out of the Prophet's ride and I'll threaten to tell unless he make the repairs I need. I'm not saying I'm proud of it, but I do what I have to do to survive."

Part of him could admire her resourcefulness, even

if he didn't approve of her methods. "By your silence, I can tell you don't approve," she said. "But don't worry. I promise I won't try to scam you."

"I think I'm smart enough to spot a scam," he said.

"Did I mention that I'm very, very good?"

Her teasing tone gave him hope—she was holding it together under horrendous circumstances. That told him more about her strength than any show of force. "Thanks for warning me," he said.

ONLY A COUPLE of vehicles sat in the parking area outside Metwater's camp. Ethan parked his vehicle, and two other Ranger units slid in beside him. Task force members Carmen Redhorse, Simon Woolridge, Marco Cruz and Michael Dance fell in behind Ethan as Michelle led the way up the trail through the woods. She was practically running as she neared the compound. They emerged into the clearing and the first thing that struck him was the silence. No children played, no one lounged in front of the camps, no groups stood around talking. "Where is everyone?" Michelle asked, looking around.

"We'll spread out and check things out," Marco said.

"I'll see if Metwater is home," Ethan said. He headed for the motor home and rapped on the door. It opened quickly. Asteria scowled at him. "If you're looking for the Prophet, he's not here," she said. "He's with the others, searching for Hunter." She frowned at Michelle. "Why did you bring the cops here? Why aren't you searching for your boy?"

Michelle shoved past Asteria, into the motor home. "Was Hunter here?" she asked. "Did you see him?"

Asteria looked confused. "What do you mean? Of course he wasn't here."

"Daniel Metwater threatened to hurt him," Michelle said. "He was near the shower shack before I went in. He must have seen his chance and snatched my baby to frighten me."

Asteria took a step back until she was pressed against the wall. "You need to leave," she said. "The Prophet told us you were crazy and I didn't want to believe him, but I see it's true."

Ethan put his hand on Michelle's shoulder—she practically vibrated with anger, and he was sure if he hadn't been there to hold her back she would have launched herself at Asteria. "Where is Metwater now?" he asked.

Asteria didn't take her eyes off Michelle as she answered, "He and the others are searching the woods just outside camp past the shower shack. We thought Hunter might have wandered into there—he's barely crawling, so he couldn't have gone far."

"Let's go." Ethan led Michelle toward the door. "Maybe they've found something."

That bit of hope got her moving. But when they were outside, she glanced over her shoulder, back toward the motor home. "She would lie for him," she said. "But I can't believe she would do anything to harm Hunter. She loved him."

"Maybe she really doesn't know anything." He put a hand at her back. "Show me this shower shack."

She led him across the clearing, past a cluster of tents, to another narrow path that cut through thick underbrush. Halfway along, she stopped. "Metwater threatened me here," she said, halting a few dozen yards down the path, where trees closed in on either side. "He must have cut through the underbrush and been waiting for me."

"Did he follow you after he talked to you?" Ethan asked.

"He started walking back toward camp, but he could have turned around when he was out of sight."

They continued to a wooden hut, open at the top except for a platform, on which sat a blue plastic barrel. The door to the hut was open A bearded young man was inside, painting the walls a light blue-gray. "What are you doing?" Michelle demanded.

He stopped in mid-brushstroke. "The Prophet told me to paint in here," he said.

"Why aren't you out searching with everyone else?" she asked.

"He told me it was more important to paint."

"Were there any paint marks on the walls before you started?" Ethan asked. The young man must have been working for a while—all four walls were mostly coated with paint.

The man scratched his head. "I don't know. I didn't pay any attention. Anyway, I'm almost finished."

Ethan nudged Michelle. "Let's find Metwater," he said. He could hear voices now, perhaps a sign the searchers were nearby.

"That's the same color paint that was dumped on me," she said. "Metwater must have ordered it painted to hide the evidence."

"Maybe." The voices grew louder and they emerged into a second clearing, this one empty of dwellings, but full of people. Ethan spotted Metwater right away—with his long, dark hair and all-white clothing, he stood out amidst his ragtag group of followers. "Metwater, I want to talk to you," he called.

Metwater raised his head and fixed his gaze first on Michelle. Ethan couldn't read his expression. When his gaze shifted to Ethan, Metwater looked calm—too calm. "I understand a child went missing from camp," Ethan said as he and Michelle approached the self-appointed Prophet.

"His mother reported him missing," Metwater said. "We haven't found any sign of foul play—and no sign of the child."

"He's missing because you took him," Michelle said.

Metwater turned away from her to address Ethan. "Officer, could I have a word with you? In private?"

"You'll be all right here for a moment, won't you?" Ethan asked Michelle.

She gave a stiff nod, then looked away.

He walked a short distance away with Metwater. "This is far enough," Ethan said, turning so that he could keep an eye on Michelle. She looked very vulnerable and alone standing there, arms folded and shoulders hunched, hair falling forward to hide her face.

"I'm guessing she came to you with a wild story about my having kidnapped her child," Metwater said.

Ethan said nothing.

Metwater sighed. "I don't blame Starfall," he said. "She's had a very hard time of it since her partner left. She's not well liked in camp, though I've done my best to make her feel a part of the Family. Some people simply aren't emotionally equipped for bonding."

"What are you getting at?" Ethan gave him a hard look. "You don't think her son is missing?"

"Hunter isn't here," Metwater said. "But I don't think any of our members are responsible for his disappearance. I'm certainly not."

"What do you think happened?" Ethan asked.

"I think Starfall hid the child away to draw attention to herself and to make trouble for me."

Michelle's distress over her son hadn't been faked; Ethan was sure of it. No one was that cold. "What makes you say that?" he asked.

"I told you, she has been under a lot of strain. All these wild fantasies about me harming her or the child." He spread his arms wide. "I live in a camp full of women and children and I've never laid a hand on any of them. Why would I? What would I gain from harming any one of them?"

If Ethan could discover the answer to that question, he would be one step closer to the truth. "She says you have a locket that belonged to her late foster sister," he said.

Metwater's expression hardened. "She's a liar, Officer. Spend enough time with her and you'll learn that."

"We'll talk more later," Ethan said, and moved back to Michelle's side. The raw hope in her eyes at his approach sent a physical ache through him. He would have given a lot to be able to share good news with her at that moment. "I'm sorry," he said. "He says he doesn't know anything."

"He hasn't had time to take Hunter very far away,"

she said. "He must be somewhere nearby. Maybe someone is hiding him in one of the trailers. We should look now, while everyone is gone." She moved past him, headed back down the path toward camp. But she had taken only a few steps when a clamor rose behind them.

Together they turned to see a tall, bare-chested man with red hair running toward Metwater, something in his hand. He showed Metwater the item and they exchanged a few words. Then Metwater turned and motioned Ethan and Michelle over.

"What have you found?" Ethan asked.

"It's a child's sock." Metwater turned to the redhead. "Show him, Eugene."

Eugene opened his hand to reveal a small white sock—white except for a reddish brown stain dampening the heel.

"That looks like Hunter's sock," Michelle said. "The one he was wearing." She reached for it, but Ethan stopped her. "Where did you find that?" he asked Eugene.

"Not far. I can show you."

"What's that on the heel?" Michelle asked. She leaned forward for a closer look.

"I believe it's blood," Metwater said. "Very fresh, and quite a lot of it."

Ethan wanted to throttle him for taking such pleasure in shocking Michelle. But he didn't have time for that now. "We don't know what it is right now," he said. "Or where it came from. It might not even belong to Hunter."

But his words were too late to provide any comfort. Michelle blanched dead white, and with a keening wail she slumped to the ground.

Chapter Five

Michelle was making a habit of waking up in Ethan's arms. Under other circumstances, it wouldn't be a bad way to return to consciousness. But before she had time to enjoy the pleasant sensation of being cradled in his strength, the memory of that bloody sock flooded back, and she had to bite the inside of her cheek to keep from wailing.

"Take it easy," he said, supporting her into a sitting position. She was on the ground, Ethan beside her and people standing all around her. She recognized people from the camp, as well as some of the officers who had come into camp with them.

"I'm fine," she said. She had to be. She had to keep it together for Hunter. Gripping Ethan's arm, she pushed herself to her feet. "I want to see where they found that sock."

She thought Ethan might argue with her, but instead, he turned to Eugene. "Show us where you found it," he said.

"Uh, sure. Over here." Eugene led the way and half the camp fell in alongside them, including Metwater.

"You people all have to stay back!" one of the

officers—the good-looking Hispanic guy named Marco—said. He and the other two men—Simon and Michael—herded the crowd back. Ethan, Michelle and Metwater kept following Eugene, who stopped in a brushy area maybe one hundred yards from the edge of camp. The ground all around them was trampled and dusty.

"It was hanging on a branch here," Eugene said. "Or anyways, really near here. I didn't mark the exact place."

Ethan knelt and examined the ground. "No sign of blood anywhere around here," he said. He stood and took out an evidence bag, dropped the sock in and labeled it.

Michelle longed to hold that sock, to cradle it in her hand, to put her nose to it and see if her son's scent still lingered. But she couldn't do that. That little sock was evidence now. But evidence of what? She refused to let herself dwell on the possible answers to that question.

Marco and Carmen joined them. "We need to get these people out of here and get a crime scene team in here," Carmen said.

"And we need to conduct our own search for the missing boy," Ethan said. "Starting with the camp."

"I can't allow you to search our homes without a warrant," Metwater said.

"We're talking about a missing baby," Ethan said. "If you don't want to cooperate, I promise you we can get a warrant."

"What are you hiding, Metwater?" Marco asked.

"You're wasting your time," Metwater said. "While

you're conducting a useless and intrusive search of the camp, the real kidnapper will be getting away."

"So you're willing to admit now that Michelle's son is missing?" Ethan asked.

"Is that what she told you her name was? Are you sure that's not another lie?"

Michelle didn't know if she had ever hated another man as much as she hated Daniel Metwater at this moment. The power of her rage frightened her. "You're one to talk of lies," she said. "Your whole life is a lie. All these people think you're some great spiritual teacher, but I know the truth."

Something flashed in Metwater's eyes—something very like fear. But the expression was quickly masked. "You will leave this camp at once," he said. "You are no longer welcome here."

"I won't leave without my son."

Ethan put a hand on her shoulder. "Let's go back to your tent," he said. "You can wait there while we search."

"I want to help search," she said.

"The best thing is for you to wait," he said. "I know it's hard, but I promise we'll let you know as soon as we find anything."

She waited until they were at her tent before she spoke again. "My name really is Michelle," she said. "I have my birth certificate. And my driver's license. I can show you."

"You don't have to show me," he said. "I believe you."

She had to look away then, afraid he would see in her eyes how much his words meant to her. She cleared her throat. "What are you going to do while I wait?"

"One of our team members has a dog who's trained in search and rescue," he said. "We'll get him out here and hope they can pick up a trail."

She looked around the tent, at the empty crib, the box of diapers, the baby blanket draped across the end of her cot. "I feel so helpless," she said.

"Do you want me to call someone to stay with you?" he asked.

"No. I'd rather be alone. I'm used to it."

He put his hand on her shoulder again, and she gave in to the urge to rest her cheek against it, for just a moment. Then she remembered who this was—a cop she scarcely knew—and she straightened and stepped away. "I'll be all right," she said. "Go—and find my baby."

When he was gone, she sank onto the cot and picked up the baby blanket. *Hunter, don't be scared, baby. Mommy is going to find you.*

"IF THERE WAS a scent here, I know she'd find it, but the scene is too compromised." Customs and Border Patrol Agent Randall Knightbridge stroked the neck of his Belgian Malinois, Lotte, who sat by his side, panting heavily. The dog and Randall had spent the last hour carefully searching the area from Michelle's tent to the shower shack to the place where the sock had been found. Lotte had alerted a few times, but every time the trail petered out after only a few yards.

"Thanks for trying." Ethan gave the dog a pat and surveyed the stretch of trampled ground extending fifty yards or more past the general boundaries of Daniel

Metwater's camp. "No sign of blood, either, so I guess that's a good thing."

"Lotte definitely would have picked up any human blood," Randall said. "People walking over that wouldn't hide the scent from her nose."

Carmen, Michael and Marco joined them. "We searched the last of the tents and trailers," Michael said. "No sign of the missing kid."

"We found a few illegal drugs and some questionable IDs, but no sign of an out-of-place toddler," Carmen said. "For what it's worth, most people seem pretty upset about Hunter's disappearance."

"Nobody is offering up any clues to what happened, though," Marco said. "No one else was around the shower this morning."

"No one will admit to hearing Metwater threaten Starfall or her baby," Michael said.

"Her name is Michelle," Ethan said. "She only used Starfall so Metwater wouldn't realize she's related to a woman his brother was dating, who died under mysterious circumstances."

"If Metwater took the child, he got him out of here in a hurry," Marco said. "How much time do you estimate passed between when Starfall—I mean Michelle—discovered him missing and we got here?"

"About two hours," Ethan said. "Plenty of time to give the kid to someone else to hide."

"Or to kill him and bury the body," Michael said, his expression grim.

"We need to get the blood on that sock tested," Ethan said.

"I'll take it to the lab this evening," Carmen said. "Meanwhile, what are we going to do about Michelle?"

"I don't think it's safe for her to stay here," Ethan said. "Metwater already beat her up once."

"He kicked her out, didn't he?" Michael asked. "Does she have any family or friends in town she can stay with?"

"I don't think so," Ethan said.

"We can try to find a place for her at the women's shelter," Carmen said. "Though they're usually pretty full."

"The other half of my duplex is vacant," Ethan said. "Maybe she could stay there."

"If she could put up with having you for a neighbor," Michael said.

Carmen looked thoughtful. "It might not be a bad idea. She'd be safe, but close by if we needed her."

And she wouldn't have to be alone, Ethan thought. The emptiness in her voice when she had told him she was used to being by herself pulled at something deep inside him. She might be hard and a little prickly, but he figured she had her reasons. He might not be able to bring her son back to her tonight, but he could show her he was on her side.

The other Rangers headed to their vehicles, and he made his way to Michelle's tent. "Hello?" he called at the door.

"Come in."

He lifted the flap and stepped inside. For a primitive dwelling, the women had made it as comfortable as possible, with rugs on the floor and colorful blankets draped over the cots and camp chairs. A suitcase lay open on Michelle's cot, and she was folding clothes into it. At his approach, she turned to him, the longing in her eyes so raw it made his throat tighten, hurting for her. "I don't have any news for you yet," he said. "But we didn't find any signs of violence." Which didn't mean there hadn't been any, but he wanted to offer her what comfort he could.

She looked down at the suitcase and picked up a tiny shirt. "I was just packing a few things—my clothes, but Hunter's, too. I'll have to come back later for the crib and other stuff. He'll need them when you find him."

When you find him. He hoped he could live up to that trust. "You can't stay here," he said.

"No. I have a little money saved. I'll get a cheap motel room in town." She closed the suitcase and zipped it shut. Her hair fell forward, revealing the pale skin at the back of her neck. He had to fight the urge to bend down and inhale the scent of her there, to run his fingers over the soft flesh. She was such an enticing combination of satin and steel—so strong and yet so vulnerable. "Could I come to Ranger Headquarters during the day—just to be close if anything does happen?" she asked. "I don't think I could bear sitting in a motel room all day, not knowing what was going on."

"Of course," he said. "But you don't need the motel room. I have a safe place for you to stay."

Her eyebrows pulled closer together and her lips thinned. "Where?"

"I live in a duplex near the national park. The other half is empty right now. The property is owned by the federal government. You can stay there. You'll be safe and close—and Metwater will never think to look for you there."

Her expression relaxed. "I'd like that. Thank you."

He picked up her suitcase. "Let's go. We'll send for the rest of your stuff later."

"All this gentlemanly behavior is going to go to my head," she said. "I'm not used to it."

They left the tent and started across the fire ring. They had only taken a few steps when Metwater stepped out of his motor home. "Starfall!"

Ethan was probably the only one to notice her flinch at the sound of Metwater's voice. The hard expression on her face gave nothing away as she turned toward him. "I don't have anything else to say to you," she said.

"But I have something to say to you." His long strides quickly closed the gap between them. He held out his hand. "Give me the keys to the car."

She lifted her chin and looked him in the eye. "What car?"

"The one you've been driving. It belongs to me."

"It does not! I never signed your stupid agreement to hand over all my worldly goods."

"No. I'll have to speak to Asteria about that oversight."

"She didn't have anything to do with it," Michelle said. "I simply never turned them in."

"It doesn't matter." He smiled, a look that might have charmed under other circumstances. "Greg signed the papers—the car was in his name."

"No." She shook her head, curls dancing. "That car is mine. Greg gave it to me when he left. It's the only thing he ever did give me, the bum."

"It wasn't his to give," Metwater said. "He had already relinquished the title to me. I can show you the paperwork, if you don't believe me."

"You're going to take her car?" Ethan asked. "Why?"

Metwater shifted his gaze to Ethan, the sneer still firmly in place. "Because it isn't her car. The Family is a cooperative group. When a new member joins, she signs over all her possessions for the use of the group. We believe in negating the self for the good of the whole."

"You said the car belonged to you, not the group," Ethan said.

"I am the guardian of my family's possessions."

"It's just another scam," Michelle said. "Everyone else may not see through it, but I do."

Metwater looked at her again. "You should be careful what you say," he said. "Especially in front of a police officer." He turned to Ethan. "If you look into her background, Officer, I think you'll find she's far from innocent."

"He doesn't know what he's talking about," Michelle said. She opened her purse and pulled out the car keys. "Take it. It's not worth anything, anyway." She hurled the keys into the dirt at his feet and turned away. "Let's get out of here."

"Don't pretend you don't know what I'm talking about," Metwater called after her. "Or have you already forgotten Madeline Perry?"

Michelle faltered and swayed. Before Ethan had time to react, Metwater delivered his parting shot. "This isn't the first child you were responsible for who disappeared, is it?"

Chapter Six

When Michelle started moving again, she ran. Ethan glared at Metwater, then hurried after her. He found her waiting by the passenger door of his cruiser. He unlocked it and she climbed in. "Let's get out of here," she said.

He stowed her suitcase in the back, then slid into the driver's seat. He waited for her to explain Metwater's accusation—to tell him who Madeline Perry was. But she only stared out the side window, fists clenched, back stiff. If he tried to question her now, it would only come across like an interrogation. He would have to wait until she was ready.

By the time he parked the cruiser at the curb in front of the duplex, her refusal to speak made the air seem heavier and harder to breathe. He retrieved her suitcase from the back and led the way up the walk. She followed a few steps behind him.

He unlocked the door and opened it. "It's furnished, so you should have everything you need," he said. "We keep the kitchen and bathroom stocked with the basics, in case any visiting officials need to use it."

She took the suitcase from his fingers and moved past him, inside. His resolve broke and he blurted, "Do you want to tell me what Metwater was talking about?"

She turned to face him, her eyes empty, her expression bleak. "You're a cop," she said as she started to close the door. "You figure it out."

He stood on the stoop, staring at the closed door for several seconds, debating whether to beat on the wood and demand to settle this now, or wait until morning when he hoped she would have cooled off.

He settled for walking next door to his half of the house and going straight to his computer. A search with the keywords *Michelle Munson* and *Madeline Perry* turned up more than one hundred hits. He hunched forward to read the first one, a decade-old article from the *Chicago Tribune*.

"A confidential source in the district attorney's office has identified the chief suspect in six-year-old Madeline Perry's disappearance as her sixteen-year-old babysitter. Though the source declined to divulge the name of the suspect, against whom charges are expected to be brought shortly, the original report of Madeline's disappearance was made by sixteen-year-old Michelle Munson, who is identified in the original police report as the child's babysitter. Miss Munson is the foster child of Phillip and Georgia Little, next-door neighbors to the Perrys. Others in the neighborhood describe Miss Munson as 'a very troubled young woman.'"

ETHAN READ MORE newspaper articles, which described the disappearance of six-year-old Madeline from her parents' backyard on a Tuesday afternoon in June. The babysitter, Michelle Munson, reported that she had gone inside to prepare a snack for Madeline, who was swinging on her play set, and when she returned ten minutes later, the child was gone. She searched the area for half an hour before calling the police.

Story after story painted Michelle as a child who had been abandoned by her mother at around age ten, who had lived in a series of foster homes since that time, and had reportedly spent time in a juvenile detention center after being caught shoplifting. She had reportedly been very jealous of Madeline's home and possessions, often commenting on how nice the child's clothes were and how she wished she could live in a house like hers with parents like hers. The implication in most of the articles was that Michelle had killed Madeline and hidden the body in an attempt to take her place in the Perry household.

A fuzzy black-and-white photograph that accompanied one article showed a slight girl with a mass of dark curls, dressed in an ill-fitting jumpsuit, being escorted into court by two uniformed guards.

Ethan read faster, searching for an article that reported on the trial and its results. He found nothing about the trial, but a front-page story from November of that year reported what the paper termed "a startling development." Madeline Perry had been found alive and well in Mexico City, living with her mother, who had divorced her father two years' prior and lost custody of the girl in a heated court battle. Madeline and her mother both confirmed that Michelle Munson had nothing to do with Madeline's disappearance. Instead, her mother had been watching the house for days, waiting for her chance to grab her daughter and run.

Ethan sat back in his chair, drained. For almost six months sixteen-year-old Michelle had lived in hell, accused of the most horrible crime—killing a child—with no family, no friends, no one on her side. In the end, she was exonerated, but by then she had lost everything. He could find nothing about what had happened to her after Madeline was found. Certainly none of the papers printed apologies, and as far as he could determine, no one stepped forward to help the girl.

Anger, raw and searing, filled him. How could someone have let this happen? No wonder Michelle had built such a tough shell around herself—she had had to in order to survive.

And why was Metwater bringing it up now? Did he really think this story was going to make Ethan less sympathetic toward Michelle? Was the fact that she had been falsely accused before supposed to lead the Rangers to believe she was guilty now?

He thought of her now, separated from him only by a wall, but perhaps more alone than she had ever been. Her child was missing and she had no one to lean on. No one to comfort her.

Except him. He wouldn't let her go through this alone—not when she had suffered so much already.

He went next door and knocked. When she didn't answer, he knocked again.

"Go away," she called through the door.

"No."

He waited, scarcely daring to breathe. He had raised his hand to knock again when the door opened. She was pale, her eyes swollen and red-rimmed. "What do you want?" she asked.

"I know about Madeline Perry," he said. "I read the news articles online. I'm so sorry you had to go through that."

"I don't need your pity." She started to close the door again, but he shot his hand out, stopping her.

"I'm not pitying you," he said. "I'm angry that you had to go through that."

She studied his face as if weighing the sincerity of his words. "If you're angry, I guess that makes two of us," she said.

"Does that mean you'll let me in?" he asked.

She took hold of the front of his shirt and pulled his face down to hers, her lips pressed to his in an urgent kiss that sent heat crackling through him. Before he even had time to respond, she drew away again. "Yes," she said, and tugged him inside.

MICHELLE'S LIFE HAD become a nightmare from which she couldn't wake. She was being carried along in a flood, out of control. That a man who was a cop—a profession that had never been kind to her—would be the one steady thing she could hold on to didn't make sense to her. But nothing made sense these days.

A hard life had taught her that the only way to cope when the worst you could imagine had happened was to focus on right now—you got through this moment, and then the next, and then the next. Anticipating the future was too frightening, and dwelling on the past too sad.

Right now, in this moment, she was with the one person who believed in her. She wanted to hang on to the moment, to prolong it as long as possible. As soon as the door shut behind him, she pulled Ethan to her once more and kissed him again. She arched her back and pressed her body to his, reveling in the hard plane of his chest and the firm hold of his hands as he angled his mouth against hers and returned the kiss.

Ethan's tongue swept across her lips, a sensual invitation to deepen the contact. She opened to him, wanting to be closer, to learn his secrets and perhaps to share a few of her own. She caressed his back, the muscles shifting at her touch, then brought her hands around to his chest, to fumble at the buttons of his shirt.

He captured her hand in his and broke the kiss. "What are you doing?" he asked, his voice husky, his eyes glazed with passion.

"I'm taking off your clothes," she said, undoing another button. "Feel free to help."

"I don't think that's a good idea," he said.

"No? You kissed me as if you thought it was a very good idea."

"You're a crime victim. I'm supposed to be looking out for you, not taking advantage of you."

She turned her attention from the buttons to his face. "That is so touchingly noble and ethical, Officer Do-Right," she said. "But do I look like a woman who's being taken advantage of?"

He ran his tongue over his bottom lip. Did he have

any idea how sexy he looked, all noble and indecisive? She placed one finger on that same bottom lip. "Answer the question, Officer."

"You look like a strong, sexy woman who knows what she wants," he said.

"Good answer. And what I want right now is you."

He didn't waste any more time talking, but gathered her into his arms and kissed her until she was breathless. No more Mr. Indecision, he led her toward the bedroom, which held a chair, dresser and most important for their purposes—a made-up queen-size bed. Eyes locked to hers, he removed his utility belt and draped it over the back of the chair, then finished undoing the buttons on his shirt and removed it to reveal a muscular chest lightly dusted with brown hair. Her breath caught at the sight, and her knees felt wobbly.

He took her in his arms again. "You're sure this is what you want?" he asked.

"I need this," she said. "I need to not think about things, to just be with someone who isn't judging me or expecting anything from me."

"I'm not judging or expecting." He stroked her hair back from her face. "I just want to be with you."

She grabbed the hem of her shirt and tugged it over her head, then pushed down her skirt, leaving her standing before him in her panties and bra. She wasn't worried about what he might see—she had earned every stretch mark and blemish honestly, and she knew enough about sex by now to understand that the physical was only a small part of what made an encounter good.

In any case, the smile on his face, and the way he caressed her hips and kissed the valley of her cleavage, let her know he liked what he saw. She pulled him toward the bed and they fell together on it, already entwined, learning the shape and feel of each other. All his earlier hesitancy was gone—he matched her move for move, teasing her and thrilling her, replacing her pain and sadness, at least momentarily, with an awareness of her body and the pleasure it could both give and receive.

He patted her hip and kissed the tip of her nose. "I have to take care of one thing," he said. "Be right back."

He rose and went into the bathroom. She propped herself up on one elbow and enjoyed the view of him, naked, walking away from her. This was one cop who definitely kept in shape.

He returned quickly, a foil packet in one hand. She collapsed back on the pillows, surprised into laughter. "When you told me the place was furnished, I didn't think you meant *everything*."

He unwrapped the condom and rolled it on. "Officers on temporary assignment or special guests sometimes stay here, so we try to keep it stocked with whatever we think they might need."

"Guess you take that motto to *protect* and serve seriously," she teased.

"Oh, yeah." He knelt over her, parting her legs with one knee. "Though sometimes it's more of a pleasure than a duty."

She slid her hands up his arms to thread her fingers through the hair at the back of his head. "I'm ready to be served, Officer."

He slid into her and began to move, and she lost the

power of speech. Forget her plan to keep him waiting and call the shots—his skilled mouth and hands and sex had her surrendering to him, losing herself to sensation and passion. He leaned down and kissed her closed eyelids, and whispered in her ear. "You don't have to do anything," he said. "Just let go."

His voice, deep and hypnotic, and the words he spoke, so full of tenderness and caring, acted as a soothing balm to her frayed nerves and frantic mind. She did as he said and let go, floating on waves of sensation, climbing higher toward a breathless release that made her cry out with joy.

His own cries soon joined hers as his climax shuddered through them both. She clung to him as he slid out of her and settled beside her, his head on her breast. She stroked his hair, her eyes still closed, clinging to that brief moment of bliss.

"That was…intense," he said after a long moment.

"Mmm-hmm." She snuggled closer, and he wrapped his arms around her. She wanted to ride this wave of pleasure right into sleep—to shut worry and fear out for a little while longer.

But her brain wasn't going to allow it. As the afterglow faded, the reality of what was happening to her rushed back with the impact of a sucker punch. She rolled over to face Ethan. "How did Metwater find out about Madeline?" she asked.

"Probably the same way I did—I searched online for your name and hers."

"He wasn't supposed to know my real name."

"Maybe Asteria searched your things and found out for him."

She lay back down, her head nestled in the hollow of his shoulder. "Maybe." The idea hurt more than she cared to admit. She had thought Asteria was her friend.

"That must have been horrible for you, when Madeline disappeared," he said.

She had never talked about that time with anyone—mostly because there had never been anyone to talk to—no one who cared enough to ask. "At first I was terrified something terrible had happened to her," she said. "She was a really sweet little girl, and the two of us had gotten close. But it didn't take long to realize that everyone was blaming me. After all, I was the kid with no family. I'd already been in trouble with the law."

"What about your foster parents?" he asked. "Didn't they defend you?"

"When people first started saying I had hurt Madeline, the Littles couldn't distance themselves from me fast enough. They called my caseworker and insisted I be removed from their home. I was a bad influence on their other children. So I ended up back in a group home. At least, until they sent me to jail." She shuddered at the memory.

He caressed her shoulder. "I can't believe no one thought to look at the mother. So many child abductions are carried out by the noncustodial parent."

"They thought they had found their guilty party in me, so they didn't need to look any closer. They wanted the quick and easy solution, to make a splash in the papers."

"But you were exonerated. I don't understand why Metwater even brought it up."

"Because he hates me. And he wants you to doubt me. Sometimes that little seed of doubt it all it takes." She braced herself, waiting for his answer. Maybe Metwater's plan had worked. Maybe Ethan—despite the intimacy they had just shared—*did* have doubts about her innocence or her sanity or her trustworthiness. He wouldn't be the first.

"I don't doubt you," he said. "And I don't trust anything Metwater says. Why does he hate you?"

"Some people would say I'm an easy person to hate." At least if people didn't like you, they usually left you alone. Maybe that wasn't the healthiest way to get through life, but it had worked for her so far.

"Don't say that," he said. "It's not true."

She raised herself up to look down on him. "How do you know? You hardly know me."

"I know you're a survivor. You're a good mother. You're smart."

He thought she was smart? The idea sent a flutter through her heart and she lay down again, not wanting him to read her agitation in her expression. "Maybe he hates me because he knows I'm right about his brother," she said. "David did murder Cass."

"Or maybe it's more than that," Ethan said. "Maybe he thinks you know what his brother was involved in."

"I've wondered about that. Whatever it was, maybe Daniel was involved, too. Maybe it had something to do with the Russian mob. They ended up killing David, so maybe Daniel is afraid they'll come after him, too, if word gets out. That would be enough to make him hate me."

"I'd love to know what David was doing that worried your sister," Ethan said.

"Me, too. I was hoping if I stuck around Metwater's *family* long enough I could find out."

"We'll find out," Ethan said. "But later. Right now we need to find Hunter."

The mention of her son was like an arrow to her heart, the pain she had been fighting off for the last hour returning tenfold. She struggled to take a deep breath. She had been strong for so long, but was she really strong enough to get through this? Not alone.

"Will you stay here with me tonight?" she asked, hoping she didn't sound desperate. If he said no, she wouldn't beg, no matter how much she wanted to.

He gathered her close and kissed her forehead. "Just try and make me leave."

ETHAN WOKE TO gray light in an unfamiliar room, unease heavy in his chest. Then he identified the sound that had woken him—muffled sobbing from the woman beside him.

Michelle lay on her side, her back to him, curled into herself, the blanket pulled over her head. The choking, wrenching sobs made his chest hurt, and his first instinct was to pretend he didn't hear and find a way to slip out of bed and escape into the bathroom.

But that was the coward's way out, and he wasn't a coward. So instead, he reached out and pulled her to him, and kissed the top of her head and held her tightly. "I'm right here," he said. "I won't leave."

"I never cry," she sobbed, bunching the sheet in her fists. "I hate crying, but I can't help myself. Hunter—" A fresh wave of tears washed away whatever else she might have said.

"I can't even imagine how hard it is," he said.

"It's like someone has cut out part of my heart. I would rather they had hurt me than to have taken him." She buried her face against him and sobbed until her tears wet his shoulder and his arms ached from holding her trembling body. Lovemaking had breached the barrier between them, but this was a deeper kind of intimacy.

At last the sobbing subsided. She sat up, wiping at her eyes. "Thank you," she said. "I doubt your job description includes dealing with weeping women."

"You might be surprised." But was that really how she thought of him—as a cop first? Even after the closeness they had shared last night, she still didn't trust him. She didn't trust his badge.

"I'm going to take a shower," she said.

"I'll make coffee."

He dressed and moved to the kitchen, where he found the makings for coffee, but not much else. They'd have to stop by the store sometime today and get some food. He was waiting for the coffee to finish dripping through the brewer when his cell phone chimed. He fished the phone out of his pocket and saw he had a text from Carmen. A glance at the clock showed a little past seven. She was up early.

He was reading the text when Michelle came in, dressed in fresh jeans and a T-shirt, her hair still wet from the shower. "What's wrong?" she asked. "You look upset."

"I just got a text from Carmen. They got the results back from the lab on the sock Eugene found."

She clutched the counter and sucked in a deep breath. "What are the results?"

"I don't know." He pocketed the phone. "The commander wants us both at headquarters at eight o'clock."

Chapter Seven

Michelle barely managed to choke down the cup of coffee Ethan handed her. The fact that the Rangers wanted her at their headquarters, to deliver the test results in person, had to be a bad sign, right? She didn't ask Ethan—she didn't want him to confirm her suspicions. Neither of them said anything until they were almost to Black Canyon of the Gunnison National Park, where the Ranger Brigade had their headquarters, and then he reached over and took her hand, surprising her.

"Whatever the test results, don't give up hope," he said.

She cleared her throat. "Having a baby is all about hope," she said. "I never had any before I had Hunter."

He squeezed her hand. "We're going to find him."

"I know you'll try." That was more than anyone else had done for her in years. More, really, than she had done for herself. She had told herself she was hiding out with Daniel Metwater's group in order to prove Cass didn't overdose on drugs, but really, living with a reclusive group that didn't require her to have a job or interact with the rest of society had been a kind of cop-out. Things would have to be different once they found Hunter. She'd have to find a place to live and a job and start to give him the kind of stable, normal life she had always longed for.

She thought she had calmed down a little by the time they arrived at Ranger Brigade Headquarters, but her heart started racing again when she and Ethan were greeted by no fewer than six of the Rangers, including the commander. "I'm Commander Graham Ellison," he introduced himself. He had a firm handshake, a stern expression and closely cropped graying hair that made her think of army drill sergeants in the movies.

"What's going on, Commander?" Ethan asked.

"That's what we're trying to find out," Ellison said. He motioned to a rolling chair someone had pulled to the center of the room. "Ms. Munson, sit down, please."

She didn't like the way he ordered her to sit—albeit politely—instead of asking if she would like to sit, but she really didn't have a choice. She doubted her shaking legs would support her much longer. "Just tell me what the results were of the blood test on Hunter's sock," she said as she lowered herself into the chair. "Is it his blood?"

"It isn't." Carmen rolled a chair over to sit beside Michelle. "It wasn't even human blood. The lab said it's from an animal—most likely rabbit."

"Rabbit?" Had she heard right? Relief flooded her at the knowledge that it wasn't Hunter's blood staining the sock, but rabbit? "I don't understand."

"Someone is trying to play games with us," Commander Ellison said. He moved to stand in front of her, fixing her with the stern gaze she associated with principals and prison guards. "Is it you?"

"No!" She sought Ethan's face in the crowd of officers gathered around her. "What are you accusing me of?"

"Daniel Metwater seems to think you've set up some kind of hoax to draw attention to yourself," the commander said. "If you have, I promise there will be serious consequences."

"This isn't a hoax." Ethan stepped forward. "Her son is missing and she didn't have anything to do with it."

"Metwater is trying to make me look bad in order to divert suspicion from himself," she said.

Ellison scowled as if weighing the merits of her claims. She fought not to shrink under his gaze. Ethan believed her, but maybe he was the only one.

Ethan rested his hand on her shoulder, steadying her. "Michelle isn't guilty of anything but making an enemy of Daniel Metwater," he said. "But there is something you need to know." He looked at her. "It's bound to come out sooner rather than later, especially if Metwater is talking about it."

Yes, Metwater would make sure everyone knew about Madeline Perry. Michelle sighed, then lifted her head and looked the commander in the eye. "When I was sixteen, a child I was babysitting disappeared," she said. "I was arrested and charged with her murder, after a bloody handkerchief with her blood on it was found in my coat pocket." She told them the whole story—that the handkerchief was from a nosebleed Madeline had had that morning, about the DA and police chief who wanted to make a name for themselves by closing the case quickly—and about the foster child with no family to speak for her, whom no one would believe because she already had a record for shoplifting an expensive blouse and a necklace from a clothing store she couldn't afford to shop at.

"I was in a juvenile facility, awaiting trial, when a family friend spotted Madeline with her mother in Mexico," she said. "They released me without an apology. I had no one to go to, until Cass's family heard the story somehow. They took me in, and Cass became the sister I never had. She's the only reason I ended up with Metwater's group. Now that he knows I know the truth about Cass's death, he wants to get rid of me, and he'll do whatever he can to make that happen."

She braced herself for what she was sure would come next—the suspicious looks and halfhearted expressions of sympathy. Instead, Carmen leaned over and took her hand. The other woman—a cop, Michelle reminded herself—had tears in her eyes. "What a nightmare to have to live through," she said.

"Thank you for telling us about this," the commander said. "I'm sure it wasn't easy. But it could help us. Whoever is responsible for your son's disappearance may be using this incident from your past to throw suspicion on you or frighten you into silence."

"Daniel Metwater has motive and opportunity," Ethan said.

"The search of his motor home didn't turn up any evidence," Marco said. "And no one we talked to reported ever seeing him with the boy. In fact, no one saw the boy this morning."

"There aren't that many people in the camp," Carmen said. "If Metwater chose his time right—when people were occupied with chores—it might be possible to avoid seeing anyone."

"Or his followers might be reluctant to snitch on their Prophet," Michael said.

"I think we need to lean on Andi Matheson," Ethan said. "She's closest to Metwater. They practically live together."

"Andi is eight months pregnant," Simon said. "We won't win any friends if it looks like we're bullying her."

"We won't bully her," Michael said. "We'll simply encourage her to tell the truth about Metwater. We'll offer her our protection."

"She won't tell you anything," Simon said, his expression sour. "She thinks Metwater hung the moon and stars."

"She may look loyal on the outside, but I think she's getting a little disillusioned with the Prophet," Michelle said.

The others looked at her as if they had momentarily forgotten she was there. "Asteria doesn't just worship Metwater," she said. "She's in love with him. But he doesn't feel the same way about her. He doesn't make any secret of sleeping with other women."

"We could use that to persuade her to cooperate with us," Marco said.

"You don't have to trick her," Michelle said. "Just remind her that you're trying to find Hunter. She loves him and she's probably worried about him. She won't want to think Metwater had anything to do with his disappearance, but if she knows anything, her love for Hunter will win out over her infatuation with Metwater, I think."

"I'll go with you to interview her," Simon said.

"I want to go, too." Michelle stood. "I need to get my trunk and some of Hunter's things I left behind." She could see Simon was about to object, so she added, "She'll be more likely to cooperate with you if she sees that I trust you."

In the end, Ethan and Simon traveled in one car, while Michelle ended up riding with Carmen. Michelle was more comfortable around the other woman than she had been previously, but she still didn't completely trust her.

"Jake says hello," Carmen said as they headed toward the turnoff for Metwater's compound. "He has his Fish and Wildlife agents on the lookout for Hunter."

Jake Lohmiller, Carmen's fiancé, was the Fish and Wildlife agent Michelle had tried to scam—and yes, had flirted with—when he first came to the area. Knowing he and Carmen had discussed her made Michelle want to squirm in her seat. "I'm surprised he would want to help me," she said.

"He likes strong women. He always said it's one reason he ended up with me."

"Yeah, well, you didn't try to extort money out of him."

Carmen laughed. "It served him right. I still give him a hard time about losing his badge. What kind of cop does that?"

Michelle wondered if she had slipped into an alternate dimension—one in which the cops were nice, people believed her and she didn't feel the need to always try to game every situation.

If only Hunter were here with her, she might even grow to like this version of reality.

She followed the officers down the trail into camp from the parking lot. Suddenly, the place she had called home for the past few months felt threatening. The people gathered outside the tents and trailers stared openly, but she knew just as many others watched from behind cover. Some of them would be angry, feeling she had betrayed the Family by bringing the police into their lives. Many would wonder what had happened to Hunter—and if she had anything to do with his disappearance.

Ethan moved up beside her. "Simon and Carmen and I are going to interview Asteria," he said. "Will you be okay out here by yourself?"

"Of course." She had been looking after herself for more than a decade. She certainly didn't need a bodyguard. "I'll wait for you in my tent. I can finish packing up everything."

"Sounds like a plan." He patted her shoulder and, along with the other Rangers, moved toward Metwater's motor home.

Michelle headed for the white tent nearest the motor home. Greg had bought it from some hunters in Montrose. After he moved out, she had invited Asteria to live with her, since the senator's daughter didn't have a place of her own. Metwater probably claimed the tent belonged to him now. She didn't care. It wasn't as if she was ever going to live in it again. Once she and Hunter were together again, she would take her savings and make a fresh start. Maybe she'd go back to school, or start a business. She was smart and resourceful, and she didn't need anyone else to decide what she should do.

Ethan and the others had assumed Asteria was in Metwater's motor home, but she didn't spend all her time there. Maybe she was in the tent. If so, Michelle would have a chance to talk to her first. She could make her own plea for Asteria's help in finding Hunter. With a child of her own soon to be born, Asteria would be especially sympathetic to Michelle's pain. She would want to do whatever she could to help her.

Michelle quickened her pace. By the time the trio of officers was climbing the steps to Metwater's motor home, she was pushing back the flap of the white tent.

Yet again, a sense of unreality shook her. The rugs that had softened the floor and the scarves that had added color to the tent walls had vanished. The cots where she and Asteria had slept were gone, as were the chairs, tables and lamps, Hunter's crib and the baskets and bins where the women stored extra supplies.

"My trunk!" Michelle rushed into the tent, to the place at the foot of her cot where her trunk—containing all her pictures, the newspaper clippings about Cass and David Metwater she had saved and Hunter's birth certificate—had been. She turned in a slow circle, hoping to spot this precious depository for her few keepsakes, but the tent was empty, as if it had never been occupied.

She raced from the tent and up the steps to the motor home, where she beat on the door, rage blinding her to the stares of those around her. The door opened and Ethan took both her hands in his. "What is it?" he asked. "What's wrong?"

"Everything's gone," she said.

"What do you mean?" He led her into the motor home, where Metwater and Asteria stood with Carmen and Simon.

"The tent is empty. All my things—all Hunter's things. My trunk! It's all gone." She turned to Metwater. "What did you do with it all?"

"You left," Metwater said. "Asteria decided to move in with me. I redistributed the items in the tent, and disposed of whatever was no longer needed."

"That trunk was mine!" She tried to launch herself at him, but Ethan and Simon held her back.

"You're wrong," Metwater said. "Everything you had is mine now. Everything."

Chapter Eight

The stricken look in Michelle's eyes tore at Ethan. He moved between her and Metwater. "Are you talking about her son—Hunter?"

"No." He made a dismissive gesture. "I don't have Hunter. I already told you, she's a liar. You shouldn't believe anything she says."

"Maybe in this case, you're the liar," Ethan said. "It's something I intend to find out." Ignoring Metwater's glare, he turned to Asteria. "Ma'am, would you come outside with us for a moment? We need to ask you some questions."

"I can answer your questions here," she said.

"No." Carmen took her arm. "We want to talk in private."

Ethan braced himself for an argument. Asteria, like Metwater, had made no secret of her loathing for the Rangers. Judging by her stormy expression, her opinion hadn't changed.

"Go with them," Metwater said. "The sooner they find out you don't know anything, the sooner they'll leave us alone."

Lips pursed in a stubborn pout, Asteria let Carmen lead her toward the door. Ethan took Michelle's arm and tugged her after them. Outside, he released her. "We need to talk to Asteria alone," he said. "You can wait with my cruiser if you like."

"I need to find my trunk," she said.

"We're going to try to get Asteria to tell us what Metwater did with it," he said.

She didn't look happy with the answer, but she turned abruptly and walked away. He watched her leave and was struck by how slight and vulnerable she looked. Her fierce attitude often made her seem larger.

He turned and followed Carmen and Asteria into the tent. Carmen had found a folding chair for the pregnant woman to sit on. Asteria perched on the edge of the chair, eyeing the Rangers warily. Ethan remembered seeing pictures of socialite Andi Matheson in the newspaper and online. The sometimes model had dated sports figures and rock stars and had made more than one "most beautiful people" list. Now she looked listless and uncomfortable, her hair dull and skin sallow. "How are you doing?" Ethan asked. "Are you feeling all right?"

"Why do people always ask me that? I'm fine."

"You look tired," Carmen said. "Have you seen a doctor during your pregnancy?"

"That's none of your business."

So much for trying to persuade her they were on her side. "What can you tell us about Hunter and Michelle?" Ethan asked.

"I can't tell you anything," she said.

"Do you say that because you truly don't know anything, or because you're afraid of Daniel Metwater?" Carmen asked.

Something he couldn't read flickered in her eyes. "I'm not afraid of the Prophet," she said.

"You're closer to him than anyone else in this camp," Ethan said. "Maybe you can help us understand him better."

She said nothing, but he thought she didn't look as hostile. "You saw Michelle the morning Hunter disappeared, right?" he asked. "How did she look?"

"What do you mean? She looked fine."

"She says Daniel Metwater beat her when he caught her in his motor home the night before."

"The Prophet doesn't beat people." She said this in the same tone of voice she might have declared that he didn't eat pig's feet or wear polyester—as if doing so was beneath him.

"Someone hurt her, though. She was still hurting that morning."

"She had some bruises," Asteria admitted.

"How did she behave with Hunter?"

Asteria shrugged. "Normal."

"What was she doing with him?" Carmen asked.

"She was taking care of him. Cuddling him."

"So she wasn't angry with him, or distant?"

She frowned. "No. Starfall is a good mother."

"When she left your tent to go to the showers, did she take Hunter with her?" Ethan asked.

"Yes."

"Did you see her or Hunter after that?"

"I saw her when she ran back to camp looking for him."

"Where was Daniel Metwater while she was in the shower?" Ethan asked. "Did you see him?"

"I don't know."

He tried to hold her gaze and failed. She stared down at her lap, picking at a patch on her long skirt. "When was the first time you saw Daniel Metwater after Michelle headed to the shower?" Ethan asked.

"I saw him coming out of his motor home on the way to breakfast." She lifted her head, her expression defiant. "He goes to breakfast about that time every morning. There's nothing sinister about that."

"I never said there was. Did you see him anywhere else? Anywhere near the showers?"

"No. I went back into the tent and lay down." She smoothed her skirt over her belly. "I was tired."

Maybe she was telling the truth. Or maybe she was trying to protect Metwater. "You didn't see Metwater with Hunter?"

She shook her head, lips pressed tightly together as if holding back words. Time to change tactics. "Why did he take Michelle's trunk?" Ethan asked.

Asteria blinked, her blue eyes troubled. "She left and didn't take it with her."

"But she intended to come back for it," he said. "Everything in it was valuable to her—family pictures and important papers. Hunter's birth certificate was in that trunk."

Asteria shifted in the chair. "He thought it was abandoned."

"Can you help us get her things back?" Ethan asked.

She looked away. "I can't."

"Where do you keep things like pictures and personal items?" Carmen asked.

Asteria looked around the now-empty tent. "I have a lockbox. Why?"

"What if Metwater took them away from you?" Carmen asked.

"Imagine how that would feel," Ethan said.

Asteria shook her head. "He didn't take Starfall's trunk—she left it."

"What did he do with it?" Ethan asked. "Did he open it?"

"No. It was locked."

"Then you did see it." He moved in closer, leaning over her. "What happened when he couldn't open the trunk?"

"I don't know!"

"You do know something. Why are you covering up for him? It's not as if he's faithful to you."

He couldn't mistake the hurt in her eyes at that remark, but he pressed on. "If Daniel Metwater would take a woman's most precious possessions, how do you know he didn't take her child, too?" he asked.

"He didn't. He wouldn't."

"Help us find Hunter, Andi. He needs his mother."

Tears streamed down her pale cheeks. "I don't know anything about Hunter," she whispered.

"What about the trunk?" Carmen asked.

She bowed her head. "He had a couple of guys haul it off. He told them to destroy it."

"Who?" Ethan asked.

"Eugene and Derek. I don't know what they did with it. I really don't!"

"Where can we find Eugene and Derek?" Ethan asked.

She shook her head, mute.

Ethan turned away. The job was supposed to make him tough enough to ignore a woman's tears, but he wasn't there yet. "You can go now," he said. "Thank you for your help."

She jumped up and hurried away. Carmen moved past Ethan. "I'll start looking for Eugene and Derek, but my guess is we're not going to find that trunk."

"Maybe we'll get lucky," he said.

But luck wasn't on their side. No one in camp had seen Eugene or Derek that morning. Ethan suspected at least some of them were lying, but pressing the issue wasn't getting them anywhere. "I'll break the news to Michelle," he said. "We've got a chopper coming in this afternoon to do an aerial search for Hunter."

"I hope the little guy is all right," Carmen said. "Even though I don't care for Daniel Metwater, I never saw him as the type to hurt a kid."

"I think he's a sociopath who's capable of anything," Ethan said.

He found Michelle slumped against his cruiser, arms folded over her chest, head down. She straightened at his approach. "Well?"

"Asteria says Metwater couldn't open your trunk, so he gave it to two guys named Eugene and Derek and told them to get rid of it. Do you know them?"

"Eugene is the guy who found that bloody sock," she said. "Derek is just a bully. The two of them are loyal to Metwater because he lets them throw their weight around. That's the only kind of men who stay with him for long—that, and a few hangers-on who are hoping for a chance with all the women he attracts."

"Why did Hunter's father leave?" He couldn't imagine walking out on the mother of his child, or leaving his son without a father. He held the passenger door of the cruiser open for her. "I know you said he wasn't interested in being a father, but did something specific happen to make him quit the Family?"

"He thought I was obsessed with the Prophet." She slid into the passenger seat and reached for the seat belt. "I couldn't tell him the real reason I wanted to be here—about Cass and David Metwater and everything. He was too much of a talker. I knew if I told him he wouldn't be able to keep the information to himself." She shrugged. "He hated living out here, and he was too immature to be a father. I couldn't depend on him."

"You and Hunter deserve someone you can depend on."

"It's okay. I'm used to looking after myself."

He turned toward her, the anger he had been suppressing too long, surfacing. "I get that you're capable of looking after yourself, but you shouldn't have to. You should have people in your life you can depend on to be there for you."

"Yeah, well, I should be able to eat ice cream three times a day without gaining weight, too. The world isn't perfect. I'd think a cop would know that."

"I know it." He started the cruiser and shifted into Reverse. "But I don't have to like it."

He backed out of the parking lot and headed down the rutted forest service road, following the rooster tail of dust raised by Carmen's vehicle. Michelle remained silent, though he could feel her gaze on him. "What I don't like is how men like David and Daniel Metwater get away with anything," she said. "And no one listens to the people they hurt, like me."

"I'm listening," Ethan said.

"Yeah, you are. But I thought you'd be able to do more. Why don't you arrest him?"

"It doesn't do any good to arrest someone if you don't have the proof you need to keep him in jail," Ethan said. "We don't have anything that links Metwater to your son's disappearance."

"He stole my trunk. Isn't that enough to lock him up, at least for a little while?"

"He's saying you abandoned the trunk, and that it was his property anyway because of the agreement everyone signs when they join the Family."

"I didn't sign the agreement." She gripped the dashboard as they bounced over a washboarded section of road. "And I didn't abandon the trunk."

"We'll keep looking for it, but you might want to start trying to get copies of the important papers that were in it—birth certificates, that sort of thing."

"You don't think I'll ever see the things that were in there again."

"I'm saying it's possible they're gone for good."

She fell silent again. He scanned the landscape of

sagebrush and juniper, wishing he could find the right words to give her something positive to hang on to. Her son had been missing over twenty-four hours now. Every hour that passed lessened the chances they would find Hunter alive. The idea made him angry all over again.

"Is that smoke over there?" Michelle said. She pointed out the front windshield. He leaned forward and squinted at the thin gray column rising up from the ground. A simple campfire wouldn't make that much smoke, unless it had gotten out of control. Wildfire was a constant concern here in the high desert. One errant cigarette butt or abandoned campfire could lead to the destruction of thousands of acres of public land.

He shifted into Low and turned the cruiser off the road and began bumping his way toward the column of smoke. Michelle leaned forward in the seat, straining to see ahead of them.

Ethan braked the cruiser well back from the blaze. The fire had consumed an area about four feet square. Whoever had set it hadn't tried to be subtle. Ethan could smell the gasoline as he climbed out of the driver's seat. He pulled a fire extinguisher from the back of the vehicle, then started toward the blaze, Michelle on his heels.

He pulled the pin on the extinguisher and sent a cloud of suppressant over the smoldering ground at the perimeter of the main blaze. Michelle broke a green branch from a nearby piñon and began beating the ground with it, extinguishing sparks as she moved forward.

Ethan hit the center of the blaze with the full force of the extinguisher, engulfing the flames and coating everything in white. When he could no longer see flames, he took the branch from Michelle and used the end to tease apart the smoldering logs to reveal a blackened shape beneath.

Michelle gasped. "It's my trunk," she said.

She would have reached for it, but Ethan held her back. "It's too hot to touch," he said. And everything in it was likely ruined—the top had caved in and fire had all but consumed most of one end. "We'll get a crime scene team out here to investigate," he said. "They'll save whatever they can of the contents."

"He wants to destroy me." She stared at the smoldering trunk, eyes unfocused, the words so soft Ethan wasn't even sure she realized she had said them.

He touched her arm, lightly, the way he would approach a sleepwalker. She glanced at him, no recognition in her gaze. "He wants to destroy me, the way his brother destroyed Cass," she said. "But I won't let him. I won't." Then she turned and walked back to the cruiser, leaving Ethan standing on the blackened ground.

Chapter Nine

Ethan drove Michelle back to Ranger Headquarters, and then he and a crime scene team returned to the smoldering remains of the trunk. The team photographed the area, took measurements and hauled the trunk away for processing. "You've done all you can for today," Commander Ellison said when Ethan reported back to headquarters. "Take Michelle back to the duplex and both of you try to get some rest. The helicopter we asked for got diverted to the Front Range, but we've rescheduled the air search for tomorrow."

"Will do." Ethan walked over to where Michelle sat slumped at a desk, a cold cup of coffee at her elbow. "Ready to get out of here?" he asked.

She nodded. She didn't say anything until they turned onto the highway from the park road. "Nights are the worst," she said. "I'm exhausted, but every time I close my eyes I think about Hunter, alone somewhere in the dark." She bit her lip, and he could feel the force of her willing herself not to cry.

"I think we're all really good at torturing ourselves with thoughts like that," he said. "For weeks after my dad died I couldn't sleep for wondering if I could have done something to save him. He had a heart attack while he was painting the back fence. I told myself I should have painted the fence for him, or persuaded him to hire someone to do the job." He shook his head. "Useless to think all that, but I couldn't stop myself."

Michelle angled toward him. "When did he die?"

"Six months ago." He tightened his grip on the steering wheel. "It's one of the reasons I took the job with the Ranger Brigade. My mom lives in Montrose and I wanted to be close to her."

"That's really nice," she said. "And I'm sorry about your dad. But if his heart was bad, even if you had painted that fence, wouldn't the problem have shown up some other time?"

Ethan nodded. "Of course it would have. And the truth is, my dad liked painting things. He died doing something he enjoyed, and I guess we can't ask for better than that."

"I'll bet he was a really nice guy," she said. "Because you're a nice guy. I never knew my father. I'm not sure my mom even knew who he was. The one thing I really beat myself up about is being too much like my mom that way—I should have been more careful, and waited to give Hunter a real dad."

"Lots of kids these days don't have two parents and they do okay," Ethan said.

"Yeah, but I can't help thinking a boy needs a good man in his life."

Ethan's dad had been a good man—the best. He glanced at Michelle. "Would you mind if we ran by to see my mom for a few minutes?" he asked. "I like to check on her a few times a week. My dad was the kind of guy who did everything for her, and I think she's having a tough time now that he's gone."

"Sure," she said. "I'd love to meet her."

The first thing Ethan noted when he pulled into the driveway at his mother's house was that the yard had been mowed and trimmed. Nancy Reynolds came out onto the front stoop as Ethan and Michelle stepped out of the car. "Mom, this is Michelle Munson." He made the introduction as his mom walked out to meet them. "Michelle, this is my mom, Nancy."

"You're that poor mother whose little boy is missing, aren't you?" His mom took Michelle's hand in both of hers, her face creased with concern. "I saw the reports on the news. I've been praying they find him."

"Thank you," Michelle said. "Your son has been a big help to me."

Nancy nodded. "He is a big help to me, too."

"Mom, who did the yard?" Ethan asked.

"Althea Douglas gave me the name of the people she uses and they came out this afternoon." She surveyed the yard. "I think they did a pretty good job. They'll come every week now."

"Mom, I told you I would take care of it."

"You have plenty to do without worrying about my yard." She pulled Michelle toward the house. "Come on. I've got a surprise to show you."

Ethan followed the two women. His mom pressed the button to open the garage door and it slowly rose to reveal a shiny blue sedan with dealer tags. "It's the first brand-new car I've ever owned," she said, excitement making her voice sound high and girlish. She turned to Michelle. "Ethan's father always bought used cars. Which is very practical, I'm sure. But I always wanted something new." She leaned over and patted the fender of the car, an Accord.

Ethan fought a storm of emotions, from worry to anger. "Mom, why didn't you say something to me?" he asked. "I would have gone with you."

"I wanted to do this for myself," she said. "It was important to me to do it on my own."

"I hope they didn't take advantage of you," he said. His inexperienced mother would have been a target for an unscrupulous salesman.

"I didn't accept the first price he quoted," she said. "I made him come down, and I did my research online so I knew what was fair."

"It's beautiful," Michelle said. "And I love the color."

"Let me take you for a drive," his mom said. "She rides like a dream. Just let me get my purse." Before Ethan could protest, she ran back into the house.

"I can't believe she just went out and bought a new car," Ethan said, staring after her. "What was she thinking?"

"She always wanted a new car," Michelle said. "Why shouldn't she have it?"

Ethan didn't have an answer to this question. It wasn't the new car he minded, so much as his mother's impulsive—and as far as he was concerned, uncharacteristic—behavior. Maybe this was the first sign of early dementia. Today she was buying a new car—tomorrow she might donate her savings to a fake charity.

She emerged from the house, holding up the key fob. "I don't even need an old-fashioned key," she said. "Can you believe it?" She climbed into the driver's seat.

"You sit up front with your mom," Michelle said as she opened the back door.

Ethan slid into the front passenger seat. "Leather seats," Michelle said. She ran an appreciative hand over the upholstery. "Nice."

"Kenny—that was my husband, Ethan's father—didn't like leather seats. Impractical, he called them."

"But you didn't want practical," Michelle said. "You wanted good-looking. Luxurious, even."

"Exactly!" His mom beamed and backed the car out of the garage. "And right now I want to treat the two of you to dinner," she said.

"That's okay, Mom," Ethan said. "You don't have—"

"All three of us have to eat," his mom said. "So hush, and let me buy it for you." She raised her voice to be better heard in the back seat. "Ethan never wants me to spend money. I keep telling him that his father left me well provided for, but he doesn't believe it."

"You have to be careful, Mom," he said. "Dad took care of all the finances, so you haven't had a lot of experience with all that."

"Believe it or not, I still know how to add and subtract," she said. "And I know how to handle money. You don't have to worry about me winding up penniless on your doorstep."

"It's really sweet of you to offer to buy dinner," Michelle said. "But going to a restaurant where the press might see us isn't a good idea."

"Then I know the perfect place," his mom said. "Trust me, the press will never find you there."

Which was how the three of them ended up at Dixie's Drive-in. The old-fashioned drive-in on the outskirts of town boasted killer onion rings, real ice cream shakes and fresh-ground burgers on toasted buns. "We used to come here almost every Saturday night when Ethan was young," his mom said after they had placed their orders.

"This was always where Dad took me when he wanted to have a serious talk," Ethan said. "We'd order burgers and rings and after the food came Dad would make whatever announcement he wanted me to hear and we would eat. I think he liked that the food kept us from having to say too much more once he was done with his speech."

"What kind of announcements?" Michelle asked.

"This is where he told me about sex when I was eleven years old." Ethan chuckled, remembering. "He had a whole speech about the physical realities of sex and he recited it in a monotone, and very fast. His face was as red as the bottles of ketchup. I let him get through the whole thing before I told him my best friend, Mark Greeley, had already told me everything and that I had already French-kissed Carol Sue Beemer behind her father's barn when I went over to help harvest corn."

"Shame on you," his mom said. "Your poor father agonized over having 'the talk' with you for weeks. I finally told him he had to get it over with before he drove me crazy."

Ethan settled back in his seat. The car smelled so new—not like any vehicle the family had ever owned. "We talked about other things, too," he said. "About grades and sports, where I wanted to go to college, what I wanted to do for a living."

"He was always so proud of you," his mother said. "'My son, the FBI agent,' he would say."

"He always told me he hoped I found a woman like you," Ethan said.

His mom dabbed at her eyes. "For goodness' sake, I hope you find a woman better than me." She gave a watery smile. "Someone who knows how to balance her own checkbook and isn't terrified of spiders."

"Fearlessness is overrated," Michelle said. "Ethan likes taking care of people, so he needs a woman who needs to be looked after."

"We all need looking after sometimes, don't we?" his mom said. "I think sometimes the toughest people need that most of all."

MICHELLE ACHED FOR her son. She dreamed she was standing by that fire in the wilderness, walking through the ashes, opening the blackened trunk. Hunter, her beautiful boy, smiled up for her. But when she bent to lift him up, she discovered it was only a doll that looked like Hunter—plastic and staring and not her boy at all.

She woke crying, Ethan holding her tightly against him. She pressed her face into his chest, breathing in the clean cotton scent of the T-shirt he wore, and the more elemental fragrance of his skin, warm and male, comforting and exciting even in the midst of her grief.

She clung to him, yet hated that she did so. You couldn't hold on to people. If you tried, you only ended up hurt. If you counted on others for help, you'd only end up weaker than ever. Better to fight your own battles. Better to not need anyone else.

But when his arms tightened around her and he murmured soothing words in her ear, she could only hold on more. She had always been strong, but this time she wasn't strong enough to let go.

Last night, after dinner with his mom and the drive back to the duplex, fatigue had dragged at her. She didn't ask Ethan to stay with her, but when he did, she had been beyond relieved. She didn't think she would have slept at all if she had had to spend the night alone.

After a while she was able to pull herself together and ease out of his arms. "What time is it?" she asked.

"Almost seven," he said. "I have to be at work at eight. Do you want to grab a shower while I fix breakfast?"

She pushed her hair out of her eyes. "A shower would be good. But I don't feel like eating."

"I don't imagine you do, but it will probably be a long day." He stood and began pulling on clothes. "You need to eat something."

She shuffled into the shower, trying to decide how she felt about this—about him taking care of her—fixing breakfast and telling her to eat. She was a grown woman. She didn't need someone telling her what to do.

She still couldn't believe she had said that last night, about Ethan needing someone to look after. It was probably true, but was that really something you should say to a man's mother? All she had really meant to do was to subtly point out that she was not the woman for Ethan— just in case his mom started getting ideas.

Not that she didn't like Ethan—she was crazy about him. He was probably the best man she had ever met. But she had worked hard for many years to be someone who could always look after herself, and Ethan was never going to really appreciate that.

She couldn't imagine being like his mother—having to rely on other people for everything from mowing the lawn to handling her checkbook. Props to her for getting out there and learning new things, but it sounded as if she still had a ways to go. It had been a long time since Michelle had had a checking account, but she still knew how to take care of one. She knew how to change a tire and pick a lock and how to work her way through the paperwork maze of social services. She knew what she had to do to take care of herself and Hunter.

Hunter. Maybe they would find him today. Surely they would. Last night Ethan had explained they were bringing in a helicopter to search the area for any signs of the little boy. And volunteers from town were going to do a grid search of the wilderness around the camp. There was still the possibility that he had wandered off on his own and was lost somewhere in all that empty land. She shuddered at the thought. But children that young could survive amazing things, couldn't they? She had read stories like that—toddlers wandering lost for days, drinking ditch water and eating wild berries, eventually found safe and sound. That could happen for Hunter, too.

But her gut told her her son hadn't wandered off on his own. Someone had taken him—Daniel Metwater or someone Metwater controlled.

Ethan had coffee and scrambled eggs and toast waiting in the kitchen. "Should I go with the volunteers to search this morning?" she asked as he set a plate in front of her.

"You can, though it might be better if you stay at headquarters, in case we get any news." He took the seat across from her and began slathering strawberry jam on a piece of toast. "We've got another group of volunteers that will be putting up fliers all over the area. Someone might remember seeing Hunter."

"Why are people doing this?" she asked. "All these volunteers, I mean? They don't even know me."

"People care," he said. "Especially when a child is involved. They want to do what they can to help."

A knock on the door startled them. Ethan set down his toast and rose, frowning. He left the room and she heard the door open and muffled voices. A moment later Ethan returned. "It's a reporter from the *Montrose Daily Press*," he said. "He wants to speak to you."

Her stomach knotted. "I don't want to talk to anyone."

"You don't have to," Ethan said. "I'll send him away."

When he left the room again, she followed, trying to stay out of sight behind him. "She doesn't want to talk to you," Ethan said.

"Just a few words and a picture," the reporter said. "It will help the volunteers to see who they're helping."

The thought of all those people helping her when

she didn't even know them nagged at her. She stepped forward. "All right. But just a few words."

"Great." The reporter, a stocky young man with thinning blond hair, beckoned her forward. "Step out here where the light is better."

She moved onto the front steps of the duplex, and was startled to see half a dozen reporters congregating there. Camera flashes momentarily blinded her and for a moment she was sixteen again, standing in front of her foster parents' home, surrounded by an angry crowd who thought she had killed a little girl.

Only Ethan's hand pressed against her lower back kept her from fleeing back inside. She cleared her throat. "I want to thank everyone for their help," she said.

"Tell us about your son," the reporter prompted.

"Hunter…" Her voice broke and she struggled to control it. She didn't want to break down, though that was probably what some of them wanted. People liked drama. "Hunter is a good little boy," she said. "Always cheerful and loving. He's fearless, too. He loves meeting new people. If you find him—when you find him— you'll see."

"Do you think your son's disappearance has any connection to the disappearance of Madeline Perry, a child who was also under your care ten years ago?"

Her shock over the question must have shown on her face. The cameras flashed again, and she put up a hand to protect her eyes. Ethan moved up beside her, his hand still at her back. "Before you go making accusations, you'd better get your facts straight," he said, his voice full of anger. "Madeline Perry was kidnapped by her mother, who had lost a custody dispute with the child's father. Ms. Munson had nothing to do with the disappearance."

"That's not what my source said," the reporter said.

"Who is your source?" Ethan asked.

The reporter smirked. "You know I can't reveal that."

"Your source is wrong."

He ushered her inside and closed the door and locked it. She leaned against the wall, shaken. "Daniel Metwater fed the reporter that information," she said. "He's doing everything he can to get at me."

He led her back into the kitchen and sat her at the table, then refilled both their coffee cups. "Why is Metwater after you?" he asked.

"I don't know. Maybe because of his brother—because of what I know about David."

"Were they so close he would hurt you to keep you quiet?"

"They were twins. People say twins have a special bond."

"Or maybe he was involved somehow in David's crimes and he doesn't want that to come out." Since their first conversation along these lines he had tried to figure out some connection between the two brothers that would lead to his harassment of Michelle, but he had come up with nothing.

"I'm not going to let him beat me." She pushed away the half-eaten breakfast. "I'm tougher than he thinks."

"I'm not going to let him beat you," he said. "And if

he's responsible for what you and Hunter have suffered so far, I'll make sure he pays."

The fierceness of his words made her throat tighten. She couldn't believe all cops took their jobs so seriously—there was something very special about Ethan Reynolds.

Breakfast done, Ethan fended off the reporters who crowded around as they made their way to his cruiser. Michelle half expected to see a similar horde outside Ranger Headquarters, but either the press hadn't made their way here yet, or the Rangers had warned them off.

Inside, they found Carmen and Simon examining the contents of the burned trunk, which were spread on tables in the conference room. Everything reeked of smoke and most of the items were unrecognizable, reduced to twisted shards of black.

"They used diesel fuel as an accelerant," Simon said. "We found some tire tracks in the area, but nothing we can link to a specific vehicle."

Michelle stopped in front of what was left of her photo album. She started to reach for it, then stopped and looked at Ethan. "May I?"

"Sure."

She slid the blackened book toward her and gingerly lifted the cover. Relief flooded her when she saw the first page. "The edges are a little scorched, but I think most of the pictures are okay." She flipped through the pages, stopping on her high school graduation photo. She looked so impossibly young at first glance, though anyone who studied her eyes might see some of all she had been through by that age.

"Is that you?" Ethan asked.

She nodded. "I like the picture, so I kept it."

She turned the page to a group of snapshots of Hunter—as a newborn in the hospital, then slightly older, in the bath, smiling his wonderful smile. She blinked back tears and closed the book. "I can't accept that he just vanished," she said.

Ethan pulled another book from farther down the table. "Are these the articles you saved about David Metwater?" he asked.

She forced her attention to the scrapbook in front of him. "Yes. I started collecting them after Cass's death." The scrapbook hadn't fared as well as the photo album in the fire—many of the pages were scorched to the point where they were unreadable.

"We can probably find most of this stuff online." Simon joined them. "If we reassemble the collection, maybe we can pinpoint something in there Metwater is worried about."

"If you have a computer I could use, I could start looking," she said. That would give her something to do, and something to focus on while she waited on word from the searchers.

"You can use my laptop," Carmen said. "We'll set you up with a desk. Send anything interesting you find to the printer."

She hadn't used a computer in months. A couple of times since joining up with Metwater, she had looked up things on the desktop units at the local library— mostly checking for any updates on Cass's or David Metwater's deaths.

An internet search for the names Daniel Metwater and David Metwater pulled up a number of articles, some familiar, some new to her. A small article in an alternative Chicago paper caught her eye. Entitled "The Making of a Prophet," it detailed Daniel Metwater's transformation from industrialist to evangelist. "Metwater says the death of his twin affected him deeply and made him see the futility of his materialistic way of life. He longed for peace and found it in a retreat to the wilderness. Afterward, he felt called to teach others the lessons he had learned.

"However, our search revealed the Prophet did not divest himself of his worldly goods. In fact, his fortune has increased since he began leading his group of followers in the Colorado wilderness. One requirement of joining the group is that members contribute their possessions to the Family—of which Metwater is head. His latest coup is the recruitment of prominent socialite Andi Matheson. Daughter of the late Senator Pete Matheson, Andi has a personal fortune estimated at several million dollars. Much of that money is tied up in trusts that will revert to her—and presumably to Metwater—when she turns thirty later this year."

Michelle printed off this article. She wondered if Asteria would be so favored after she turned thirty and signed over all her millions to Daniel Metwater.

She scrolled through more articles, reading about the brothers' inheritance of their father's manufacturing millions, about David's murder and rumors of embezzlement from the family firm and ties to the Russian Mafia. Daniel Metwater presented himself as the squeaky-clean son, the good twin who had only tried to help his brother and now grieved his passing.

She found a couple of articles about Cass—only one mentioned that the hotel room she was found in after she died had been rented to David Metwater. After a few days her name disappeared from the news altogether, forgotten by all but those, like Michelle, who had loved her.

She was so absorbed in her research, she failed to notice anything going on around her. Only when Ethan stopped by her desk did she look up, blinking. "Something's come up," he said, and the grim expression on his face made her heart pound.

She half rose from the chair, then sank down again, too wobbly to stand. "What is it?" she asked. "Have they found Hunter? Is he—?"

"We haven't found him." He gripped her shoulder, his eyes locked to hers. "As far as we know, he's all right. But we've received a note."

"A note?" She looked around, confused.

Simon joined them and handed her a single sheet of paper, encased in a plastic envelope. "This came in the mail a few minutes ago. Postmarked in Montrose, addressed to you, in care of this office."

She blinked, bringing the block letters typed on the paper into focus:

WE HAVE YOUR KID. WE WANT ONE MILLION DOLLARS FOR HIS SAFE RETURN. TELL YOUR RICH FRIENDS TO PAY UP OR YOU'LL NEVER SEE HIM AGAIN.

Chapter Ten

Ethan took the note from Michelle. Her hand trembled and all the color had drained from her face. "Is this a ransom note?" she asked. "For a million dollars?" She shook her head. "Why would anyone think I have that kind of money?"

"Who are these rich friends the note mentions?" Simon asked.

"I don't have any rich friends," she said.

"What about Andi Matheson?" Simon asked. "Asteria. You and she shared a tent at Metwater's camp."

"Yes, but—I never thought of her as rich."

"She is," Simon said. "Though most of the money is in a trust, she still has access to some of it."

"Or Metwater does," Ethan said. "Don't his followers sign over their money to him?"

"Then maybe Metwater is the rich friend they're referring to."

"Who sent this?" Michelle asked.

"That's what we're trying to find out." Simon took the letter from Ethan. "Do you have any ideas?"

She shook her head. "No. It's crazy."

Simon tapped the evidence envelope against his palm. "Metwater seems pretty money-motivated to me," he said. "Maybe this is a ploy to get at some of Asteria's money outside of the funds that are tied up in her trust."

"I don't know why he would need to do that," Michelle said. "She would give him anything he wanted."

"Are you sure about that?" Ethan asked. "If she knows he's cheating on her, maybe withholding money would be a way for her to get back at him."

"Or maybe he thinks she could break the trust for something like this," Simon said. "I think we should bring him in for questioning."

"You're going to bring him here?" Michelle asked. "He won't like that."

"Good," Ethan said. "I want to make him as uncomfortable as possible."

"And while he's here, we'll send a team out to the camp again," Simon said. "Maybe without Metwater around, his followers will be more likely to answer our questions honestly."

"I guess getting this ransom note is a good thing, right?" she asked. "It means Hunter is still alive, and not wandering alone in the wilderness—or worse."

The yearning in her expression tore at Ethan. He wanted to lie to her, to tell her that yes, that was the case. But kidnappers were just as likely to ask for ransom for someone who was already dead. Or some people might try to make money by capitalizing on something they had only heard about on the news. He didn't want to raise Michelle's hopes, only to have them dashed later. "We don't know," he said. "I hope so, but we can't be sure."

She nodded. "The note didn't say anything about how I'm supposed to get in touch with the kidnappers, or how to get the money to them—if I could come up with such a crazy sum."

"They'll probably follow up with another note or a phone call," Simon said. "We'll be ready when that happens. We'll try to trace the call. A letter will be tougher, but we'll do what we can to try to track down the sender."

"What do I tell them when they get in touch?"

"We'll give you a script to follow," Ethan said. "And we'll be right there with you. You don't have to deal with this on your own."

She nodded, but he had the sense she didn't really believe him. Hunter was her child—this was her private pain. He couldn't ease her suffering or take that burden from her, though each day he knew her he wanted to do that more and more.

She was a tough, prickly person who seemed to go out of her way to keep others at a distance, but he had glimpsed the sweetness she carried deep inside her. He wanted to find a way to show her that it was safe to let that side of her show more—to let other people into her life.

To let him in.

ETHAN AND SIMON, with Marco Cruz and Michael Dance as backup, drove to Metwater's camp at the base of Mystic Mesa to bring him in for questioning. "You know he's going to put up a fight," Simon said as he pulled his cruiser into the parking area for the camp.

"I hope he does," Ethan said. "I'd like an excuse to give him a little taste of what he dealt to Michelle."

"I hear you." Simon checked his Glock, then slid it back into the holster at his hip. "I'm not so concerned about Metwater—I think he's mostly talk and a coward. Guys that target women and children usually are. But he keeps a bunch of young muscle around him. They're the ones we need to watch out for."

"We can handle them." Marco tapped the stun gun on his belt.

Ethan glanced up the path toward camp. "My guess is he knows we're here by now. He'll have had look-outs."

"Let's go," Simon said, and led the way up the path.

The compound looked deserted, all the trailers and tents shut tight, an eerie silence hanging over the clearing. A breeze stirred a child's beach ball in front of one trailer, and laundry flapped on a line hung between two trees, but the camp looked abandoned. "Do you think Metwater orders them to hide when the cops show up, or is it just their guilty consciences at work?" Simon asked, looking around.

"They're watching us," Ethan said. He walked up to the door of the motor home and knocked. No answer. Michael and Marco moved around to the back of the RV, just in case Metwater decided to duck out a window. Ethan knocked again. "Open up, Metwater," he called. "We need to talk to you."

The door opened, faster than Ethan had expected.

He had his gun drawn before Metwater stepped out. Metwater scowled. "Are you planning to shoot me?"

Ethan eased the gun back into the holster and struggled to control his breathing. "We need you to come with us to Ranger Brigade Headquarters," he said.

"No." Metwater folded his arms across his chest and scowled.

"You don't even know why we want you there," Simon said.

"It doesn't matter. I'm not going."

"We weren't making a suggestion." Simon took hold of Metwater's arm, but the Prophet shook him off.

A muscular young man stepped out of the motor home behind Metwater. He didn't say anything but stood next to the Prophet, muscles flexed.

"Don't even think of trying anything," Simon said. He unclipped the stun gun from his belt and reached for Metwater's arm again. "Don't make this harder than it has to be."

"Don't touch me!" Metwater jerked back and spat the words, his face flushed with rage. "You have no right." The muscle lunged for Simon and the Ranger fired the stun gun, the prongs catching the young man in the shoulder. He groaned and staggered back, then fell backward into the motor home.

Metwater stared at his bodyguard, who was writhing on the floor as Simon knelt beside him.

"We need you to come to headquarters and answer a few questions," Ethan said. "Cooperate and you could be back in time for dinner."

"And if I don't cooperate?"

"Then we'll charge you with impeding a police investigation and take you into custody," Ethan said.

"I don't have time to go with you now," Metwater said. "I'm preparing for an important presentation I'm giving in Omaha next week."

"You won't be going anywhere next week if you don't cooperate," Simon said. He had removed the stun gun leads from the young man and left him in the care of a young woman, who had emerged from the back of the motor home, possibly from the bedroom.

"Where's Asteria?" Ethan asked.

"She isn't here." Metwater glanced at the young woman. She looked up at him with a worshipful expression that made Ethan a little queasy.

"Where is she?" Simon asked, menace in his voice.

"I sent her away for a while. All this turmoil wasn't good for her."

"Where did you send her?" Simon moved closer, crowding Metwater up against the doorjamb.

"That's none of your business."

Simon's body tensed. Ethan was sure his fellow officer was going to deck Metwater—or hit him with the reloaded stun gun. He stepped between them. "People seem to have a way of disappearing from your camp lately," Ethan said. "First Hunter Munson, now Andi Matheson. You need to tell us where she is."

Metwater pressed his lips together and remained silent.

Simon turned to the young woman, who still knelt on the floor beside the young man, who was sitting up now, and glaring at the two officers. "Where is Asteria?" Simon asked.

"I... I don't know," the young woman said. "She and the Prophet left this morning. She took a suitcase with her. He returned a couple of hours ago."

"Did she go willingly?" Simon asked. "Was she upset or afraid?"

"She seemed okay to me," the young woman said. "It's hard to tell with her, though. She's not the warm and friendly type."

"What did they leave in?" Ethan asked. "Did someone drive them?"

"The Prophet drove." The young man spoke, with the nasal, clipped tones of the upper Midwest. "He used that old beater Starfall used to drive."

"We'll get a team in to search the car," Simon said, his gaze fixed on Metwater. "If we find anything suspicious, all the lawyers in Colorado won't be able to help you."

Ethan took hold of Metwater's arm. The man tried to resist, but Ethan held tight. Simon took hold of his other arm, pulled it behind him and snapped on the cuffs. "Am I under arrest?" Metwater asked.

"You're a person of interest," Ethan said. "We need you to answer some questions about the disappearance of Hunter Munson and Andi Matheson."

"Asteria hasn't disappeared. She's perfectly safe. And I already told you I don't know anything about Hunter."

"We've had a new development in the case," Ethan said. "We need your input."

"I don't have to talk to you. I want my lawyer."

"You can call him from headquarters." Ethan nudged him forward, toward the steps.

Marco and Michael rejoined them in front of the motor home. "Question anyone you can find in camp," Simon said. "See if any of them know where Andi Matheson went this morning."

"She's resting and doesn't want to be disturbed," Metwater said.

"Tell us where she is and you'll save yourself a lot of trouble," Ethan said.

"You're the ones who are going to be in trouble once I get hold of my lawyer," Metwater said.

Ethan tugged him toward the cars. "I'm more worried about Ms. Matheson than I am about your lawyers," he said.

Metwater clammed up then, and Ethan tucked him in the back of the cruiser. Neither he nor Simon spoke on the long ride back to Ranger Headquarters, though Ethan sensed his partner's agitation. They had left Michael and Marco to deal with the other residents of camp, and to wait for the crime scene team to search Michelle's car. He only hoped they would turn up something positive.

At Ranger Headquarters, they led Metwater into the conference room. "I want to call my lawyer," he said as Simon uncuffed him.

"Fine. Tell him you're a person of interest in the disappearances of Hunter Munson and of Andi Metwater," Ethan said. "And tell him we want to know why you sent a ransom note for a million dollars to Hunter's mother."

He had hoped to catch Metwater off guard with

the accusation, but the Prophet's response was not at all what he expected. Metwater dropped into a chair, his face pale. "A ransom note? What are you talking about?"

"Show him," Ethan said.

Simon retrieved the evidence envelope and held it up in front of Metwater. "Look familiar?"

Metwater scanned the note, his expression growing more agitated by the second. He jumped up from the chair. "Those idiots!" he shouted, and tried to push past Ethan.

Ethan didn't think; he reacted. He landed a punch that dropped Metwater to his knees, and the Prophet toppled to the floor, out cold.

Chapter Eleven

Michelle hated being stuck in this back office with a computer, unable to hear or see what was going on elsewhere in Ranger Headquarters. But Ethan had stressed that she couldn't be involved in questioning Daniel Metwater, and it would be better for everyone if he didn't even know she was here.

She guessed she could understand that—but that didn't mean she didn't want to keep tabs on what both Metwater and the Rangers were up to. Yes, Ethan and the other Rangers had been great with her so far, but they were still cops, and she didn't trust them to put her interests first. Only she could do that.

So when she heard the hum of conversation in the front room rise, she crept to the door of the office where they had put her and peeked out. Sure enough, Daniel Metwater stood in the middle of the room, surrounded by Rangers. The angry, arrogant expression on his face made her stomach churn. She wanted to launch herself at him and demand he tell her what he had done with her son—to kick and scratch and destroy him the way he was trying to destroy her.

Ethan took Metwater's arm and led him toward the conference room. Only then did she see that the Prophet's hands were handcuffed behind him, and giddy relief staggered her. She clung to the doorjamb while relief surged through her. If they had Metwater in cuffs, that must mean they had arrested him. Had they found some proof linking him to Hunter's disappearance? Would she be reunited with her son soon?

She forced herself to remain quiet and hidden as Ethan and Simon led Metwater into the conference room and shut the door. She had to give them time to question him—to make him tell them what he had done with Hunter.

Eyes closed, forehead pressed against the smooth wood of the door, she tried to picture the reunion with her son. He would smile his beautiful smile and reach out his chubby little arms for her. She would hold him and rock him and breathe deeply of his sweet scent, and reassure him that he was safe.

The door to the conference room opened and Simon emerged. He retrieved something from his desk, then went back in. A few seconds passed, and then a loud shout from the conference room made her jump. Sounds of a struggle, a loud smack, then a thump that shook the floor beneath her feet.

She came out of the office. Lance Carpenter ran past her. "What's going on?" she asked. He didn't answer but kept going, so she followed. She burst into the room in time to see Metwater facedown on the floor, Ethan kneeling in the middle of his back, cuffing him. "What happened?" she asked.

Ethan looked up at her. "You aren't supposed to be here," he said.

"But I am. So tell me what happened."

"We showed Metwater the ransom note and he went ballistic," Simon said.

Ethan rose and pulled Metwater to his feet. "Want to tell us what that was about?" he asked. "Who are the idiots you were referring to?"

"I want to talk to my lawyer."

"Fine." Ethan pushed Metwater toward the door. "Lance, call Montrose lockup and tell them we're bringing in a prisoner."

"You can't arrest me," Metwater protested. "I haven't done anything."

"We'll start with assault on a police officer and go from there," Ethan said. "Simon, take him for me. I'll catch up in a minute."

Simon took hold of Metwater, and Ethan crossed the room to Michelle. "You come with me," he said.

She folded her arms over her chest and took a step back. "What if I don't want to?"

His expression softened. "Please?"

"All right." She followed him back to the office where she had been waiting before.

He closed the door behind them and faced her. "Did you find anything else interesting online?" he asked.

"I printed out a few more articles, but none of them had any new information."

"We'll have a couple of people take a look at them— maybe we'll spot something."

"What happened with Metwater?" she asked. "I saw

you brought him in in handcuffs—did you arrest him? Did you find something to link him to Hunter? Did he tell you where Hunter is?"

He put a hand on her shoulder. "We don't know anything more about Hunter," he said. "I'm sorry."

She struggled not to let her disappointment show. "Then tell me what's going on."

"Andi Matheson—Asteria—has disappeared."

She definitely hadn't been expecting that. She gaped at him. "What?"

"She left camp this morning with Metwater—in your car. He returned a few hours later without her. He admits that much, but he won't say where she is—only that she went away to rest."

She swallowed hard. "I can't believe he would hurt Asteria. Not that he cares about anyone but himself, but she was worth a lot of money to him."

"Do you know if she had a will? It's possible she left everything to him, in which case she might be worth more to him dead than alive."

She shook her head. "I don't know. But I don't think so. She never said anything about it. Wouldn't she have to see a lawyer for something like that? She never mentioned it." She hugged herself, trying to ward off the chill that engulfed her. Asteria had been her one friend in the camp, and she was so close to having her baby.

"It's possible Metwater is telling the truth and is just being a jerk by not telling us where she's hiding," Ethan said. "Do you know where she might have gone? Did she mention a favorite place, or a friend or relative she might turn to?"

"No. She always said she had no one—that the Prophet and his followers were her only family now. She said she never wanted to go back to her old life."

"We've alerted area law enforcement to be on the lookout for her, and we'll contact area hotels in case he stashed her in one of them. And we'll lean on him to reveal her whereabouts, though his lawyers will try to prevent us talking to him."

"Simon said he went crazy when he saw the ransom note," she said. "What was that about?"

Ethan stepped back. "We don't know. He shouted 'those idiots' and lunged at me."

"It sounds like he knows whoever wrote the note."

"Yeah. It sounded like that to me, too." He grasped the doorknob. "I have to go now, and I'm not sure when I'll be back. If you want to get out of here, you can ask someone to take you back to the duplex."

"I want to stay here, in case some news comes in about Hunter," she said. "I just wish there was something more I could do."

"I know it's hard," he said. "But you need to hang on and let us take care of this. We're doing everything we can."

She nodded and he left. She sagged into the desk chair. She wanted to believe that he would *take care of this*, but wasn't that the polite thing that people said? In the end, Hunter was her child. She was the one who suffered most from his disappearance. And when this was all settled, one way or another, she was the one who would have to deal with the outcome. Ethan and the others would go on with their lives and she would have to find a way to go on with hers. Alone. That was the way things always ended up for her. She couldn't let herself believe that would change now, just because she'd met a cop who showed more compassion than most, and he was a man who touched parts of her no one else had ever been able to reach.

METWATER'S LAWYER WAS waiting for him when he arrived with Ethan and Simon at the Montrose County Jail. "What are the charges against my client?" the attorney, a stocky man with a full head of silver hair and a reputation as a legal bulldog, demanded as soon as the two Rangers marched Metwater into the building.

"Assaulting an officer, and interfering with the investigation of a crime, for starters," Ethan said. "He's also a suspect in the disappearances of Hunter Munson and Andi Matheson, aka Asteria."

"Defending oneself against police brutality is not assault," the lawyer shot back. "Refusing to answer questions without an attorney present is not interfering with an investigation, and you don't have as scrap of evidence to tie him to the disappearance of either of those people."

"Amazing," Simon said. "You know all this before you've even spoken with your client."

"I'm familiar with how you people operate." The lawyer glanced at Metwater, whose stony expression hadn't changed. "I want a conference room and the opportunity to speak with my client in private."

"You can do that," Ethan said, "after we process him." Even as he filled out paperwork, then led Metwater downstairs to be photographed and fingerprinted, Ethan held out little hope that Metwater would stay in jail for long. He had money and influence, and the best they could expect was to keep him a few hours before he posted bail.

He was surprised, therefore, when only a few moments after Metwater was led into an interview room to meet with his attorney, the Prophet sent word that he was ready to speak with Ethan and Simon.

"My client is prepared to make you an offer," the attorney announced when Ethan and Simon were seated across the table from Metwater and his counsel.

"How generous," Simon said. "What makes him think we're interested?"

"Mr. Metwater is prepared to tell you where Asteria is staying, in exchange for you dropping all charges against him. Charges, I might add, which will never hold up in court."

"If they won't hold up in court, why does he want to deal at all?" Ethan asked.

"He would like to avoid the hassle of a trial and return to his home. His followers need him."

"His followers need him like they need hemorrhoids," Simon muttered.

Ethan cleared his throat. "Your client needs to tell us what he knows about the disappearance of Hunter Munson."

"There's nothing to tell," the lawyer said. "He doesn't know anything."

"When we showed him the ransom note we received,

he said something about idiots—and then he exploded," Ethan said.

"You must have misunderstood him. He doesn't know anything."

Metwater sat with his arms folded, expressionless, a silent, brooding figure more statue than man. Ethan glanced at Simon. "We need to talk about this."

The lawyer gestured toward the door. "By all means."

In the hallway, Simon paced. "We've got him cold on the assault charges," he said. "We've got video of him trying to hit you."

"And what will that get him?" Ethan asked. "A slap on the wrist. Everything else we've got is weak. Meanwhile, Andi Matheson could be the key to this case."

"How do you figure that?" Simon asked.

"I don't think going away was her idea. I think Metwater sent her away so that we couldn't get to her. She knows something about Hunter's disappearance. She's eight months pregnant and Hunter is a missing baby—no matter how loyal she is to Metwater, that's got to be preying on her mind. She's going to tell us what she knows."

"Maybe if we talk to her, we can persuade her not to go back to Metwater's camp," Simon said. "She needs to see what a creep he is."

"Right, but we need to talk to her. And we can't do that if we don't know where she is. Given time, we might find her on our own, but depending on where Hunter is, we might not have the time."

Simon stopped pacing, shoulders slumped. "So we take Metwater's deal."

"We take the deal, and gamble that whatever Andi gives us will be enough to nail him with a bigger charge later," Ethan said. "We've still got the assault on Michelle we can hold over his head. I think I could persuade her to press charges now."

"Why wouldn't she press charges when it first happened?" Simon asked.

"She has a bad history with the police. They took her through the wringer when that little girl she was babysitting disappeared." It still angered him when he thought about her going through that, so young and so alone. "It didn't help that Metwater was making so much noise about her being responsible for her son's disappearance. She thought we would believe him."

"I don't believe anything he says." Simon glanced toward the closed door to the interview room. "How do we know he won't just tell us a lie this time? What if we let him go and find out Andi isn't where he says she is?"

"Then we pick him up again," Ethan said. "That will be part of the deal—he can't leave town until our investigation is over. We'll have someone watch the camp to make sure he stays put."

"The commander will love that idea—not."

"But he'll agree, because he knows how important this is."

Simon nodded. "Let's do it, then."

Metwater and his lawyer broke off their conversation when the two Rangers returned to the room. "Well?" the lawyer asked.

Ethan ignored him and addressed Metwater. "You tell us where Andi Matheson is and if she's there, we drop the assault charge and the charge of interfering with our investigation."

"She's at the Brown Palace in Denver," Metwater said. "I took her to the airport this morning, and arranged for a car to pick her up and deliver her to the hotel. She hated to leave me, but I persuaded her it would be best for her and her baby to get out of this tense situation for a while."

The lawyer stood. "I believe we're done here."

"You can go," Simon said to Metwater. "But we'll be keeping an eye on you. And we had better not find out you lied to us."

In the hallway once more, Ethan looked up the telephone number for the Brown Palace Hotel and Spa. "Pretty fancy retreat," Simon said. "You ever been there?"

Ethan shook his head.

"It's one of the oldest hotels in Denver—very Victorian and luxurious. Lots of presidents and famous people have stayed there. Metwater might have made a mistake, putting her there."

"How do you figure that?" Ethan asked.

"It will remind her of her old life as a rich socialite," Simon said. "A few nights of sleeping on expensive sheets and having spa treatments and she might not want to come back to the wilderness."

Ethan transmitted the number and listened to it ring. On the third ring a pleasant woman's voice answered, "The Brown Palace Hotel and Spa. How may I help you?"

"This is Special Agent Ethan Reynolds with the FBI. Do you have an Andi Matheson registered there?"

"One moment please, Agent Reynolds."

Ethan waited, and a moment later a man came on the line. "This is the general manager, Roger Able," he said. "How may I help you?"

"I'm looking for a woman named Andi Matheson. She hasn't done anything wrong. I'm merely trying to determine that she's safe."

"Our guest information is confidential. How do I know you're who you say you are?"

"I'll give you a number you can call to verify my credentials." He rattled off the number and Able promised to call it, then call him back. Ethan ended the call.

"We should have held Metwater in custody until we had this all settled," Simon said.

"We know where to find him," Ethan said. "And Michael is following him."

His cell phone rang and he answered it. "Agent Reynolds, I've checked our registration, and we don't have an Andi Matheson registered here," Able said. "We don't have anyone named Matheson."

"How about Asteria? Or Metwater?"

"One moment please."

Simon's scowl deepened. "We should have asked Metwater what name she was registered under."

Able came back on the line. "I'm sorry, but we don't have anyone by those names, either."

Ethan bit back a groan of frustration. "We're looking for a blonde young woman, very pregnant, who checked into the hotel this morning," he said.

"I don't know of anyone here who fits that description," Able said. "But I only came on this afternoon."

"Then I think the best thing is for you to send me a list of all your registered guests."

"I can't supply that information without a warrant."

It was the answer Ethan had expected, but he had to try. "I'll be in touch," he said, and ended the call.

"I'll go to the hotel in Denver," Simon said. "If she's there, I'll find her."

"That's probably the best way to make sure she's really safe," Ethan said.

"I'll clear it with the commander," Simon said, and pulled out his phone.

While Simon talked to Commander Ellison, Ethan called Michelle. "You must be exhausted," he said. "It's going to be a while before I'm free. Let me take you back to the duplex while I have a few moments free and you can try to get some rest."

"All right. Your side or mine?"

Was it a good sign that she was asking the question? "Wherever you feel more comfortable," he said. "You're welcome to stay in my side."

"All right." He wasn't sure how to interpret that— was she going to stay in his side of the duplex or hers? He guessed he'd find out when he got home—whenever that ended up being.

"Have you heard anything from the volunteers who are looking for Hunter?" she asked.

"I'm sorry, no."

"I watched a local news broadcast and they showed his picture. Maybe someone will see him and recognize him." She sounded so down—clinging to this frail hope with her last strength.

"I hope so." He wanted to be able to give her good news, but right now the only positive in this whole case was that they hadn't found Ethan's body. "Hang in there," he said. "I'll be home as soon as I can."

"I'll be okay." But the words held no conviction.

Simon approached as Ethan stowed his phone. "I've got the okay to go to Denver to find Andi," he said. "I'll drop you back at headquarters, then head over to my place to clean up and pack."

"All right." Ethan planned to spend some time going over the printouts Michelle had compiled about Metwater. Maybe he would see something there that would give him a clue to the man's thought processes, why he was targeting Michelle and what his next move might be.

Activity was winding down at headquarters when Ethan arrived. The commander and a few others had gone home, though they would be in early in the morning to start another round of searching for Hunter Munson. Michelle looked drained, dark half-moons beneath her eyes and skin so pale it was almost translucent. "Is there anything you need before I take you back to my place?" he asked. "Anything you want to eat or drink—ice cream?"

She tried to smile but didn't quite make it. "Thanks, but I don't need anything from a store."

No—all she needed was the one thing he couldn't give her—her son. "What are you going to be doing this evening?" she asked as they climbed into his cruiser.

"I'm going to do some more digging into Daniel and David Metwater's backgrounds," he said. "I'm hoping

I'll spot something that will tell me why you have him so worried. If I can figure out his motive, maybe I'll have a better handle on what he's done with Hunter."

"So you really do believe Metwater took Hunter," she said.

"I believe he probably had something to do with Hunter's disappearance, yes." He glanced at her. "That doesn't mean I'm not keeping my mind open to other possible suspects."

"I overheard people talking today," she said. "Rangers and volunteers and others—and some of them still think Hunter wandered away on his own."

"At this point we can't risk ruling out anything or anyone," he said. "We don't want to look in the wrong direction and miss the one clue that will lead us to finding him."

"I know, but—"

His phone rang, shrill and insistent. He glanced at the dash screen that showed an incoming call and sighed. "What is it?" she asked.

"My mom." He tapped the button to ignore the call.

"Why aren't you going to answer it?" Michelle asked.

"She probably just wants to talk, and I don't have time for that right now."

"I don't mind if you pull over and talk to her," Michelle said. "It's not as if I'm in a big hurry to get to the duplex and spend more time waiting."

"It's not that." He shook his head. "Sometimes I don't know what to say to her. When she talks about Dad, it makes me sad. When she asks me things like what color she should paint the living room, I have no idea.

I mean, what's wrong with the color it is now? And things she should ask me about—like that new car—she doesn't say a word."

"Wow—you really are wound up about that car, aren't you?"

He risked another glance at her. She was regarding him calmly, some of the fatigue gone from her eyes. "You think I'm making too big a deal of it, don't you?" he asked.

"I think you're a good son who misses his father and wants to take care of his mother," she said. "And like most men, you think your job is to fix things. Your mom doesn't need that."

"Then what does she need?"

"You could ask her. But you might try not offering an opinion or advice at all. Just listen. When she talks about your father, maybe share some of your own good memories of him. It might help you, too. Tell her whatever color she paints the living room is fine by you. And tell her you're proud of her for handling the car purchase by herself. It's a big deal, and she's proud of herself for doing it, so you should be, too."

The phone rang again. This time, he answered, Michelle's advice—which he wasn't sure he agreed with—spinning in his head. "Oh, Ethan, I'm so glad I was able to reach you." His mother sounded breathless—a little teary, even.

Ethan pulled the cruiser to the side of the road. "What's wrong, Mom?" he asked. "What's happened?"

"My car! Someone stole my new car!" Her voice rose to a wail on the last words.

Chapter Twelve

"Calm down, Mom. Take a deep breath and tell me exactly what happened." Ethan tried to sound calm, to handle his mother the way he would a distraught witness.

"I went to have my nails done—you know I have that done every other week," she said. "All the spaces in front of the salon were full, so I had to park at the end of the lot by the street. When I came out, the car was gone."

"Are you sure?" Ethan asked. "It's a new car, so you're not used to it. Maybe you parked in a different spot than you remembered."

"Ethan Reynolds, I know where I parked my own car."

He winced at her tone of voice—the same one she had used when she learned he had been caught cheating on a history test in eighth grade, and when he had gotten his first speeding ticket at age seventeen. "Did you call the police?" he asked.

"Yes. And they took a report over the phone, but the officer didn't sound like he took me seriously. So now

I'm calling you. You're FBI—you ought to be able to find my car."

"I'll do what I can, Mom. I promise." He wrote down the description of the car and the name of the officer who had the theft report, and promised to call her when he knew more, then hung up and pulled back onto the road.

"Your poor mother," Michelle said after a moment. "She must be beside herself."

"She was pretty upset." He tapped his fingers on the steering wheel. "The local cops won't appreciate a fed homing in on their case."

"They'll understand when you explain the car belonged to your mother," Michelle said. "Besides, can't you tell them it's Ranger business? You handle car thefts, don't you?"

The image of a collection of license plates spread out on the conference room table flashed into his head. "We do," he said. "Do you remember the night Simon and I came to Metwater's camp—the night he beat you?"

"I'm not going to forget that night—ever."

"We were there to question him about a car theft ring we think was operating near the camp. We thought maybe one or more of his followers might be involved. Did you ever hear anything about that—Family members getting money from stolen cars or car parts or anything like that?"

"Nothing like that, exactly. We have a guy, Roscoe, who was sort of our family mechanic. He worked on my car a few times and he kept a lot of other folks' rides running. But he also made money selling junked cars he finds out there. I guess people haul wrecks out there and dump them sometimes."

"Or maybe they aren't all wrecks," Ethan said. "Maybe some of them used to be new cars."

"I don't think so," Michelle said. "I mean, he didn't only sell junk cars. He sold old appliances and stock tanks and anything else he found abandoned. The stuff I saw him with was always old and beat up and rusty."

"Still, I think I'll have a talk with him," Ethan said.

"I hope you find your mom's car," she said.

"If an organized gang like this one stole it, it's already been cut into pieces or is on its way out of state," Ethan said. "Probably the best I can do is help her file the insurance claim and pick out a new one."

"Ask her if she wants help with the papers," Michelle said. "Let her pick out her own car."

"Right." He grimaced. He still had a lot to learn about handling women, including his mother.

ETHAN DROPPED MICHELLE off at the duplex, then headed to Ranger Headquarters. She prowled the rooms, unable to rest despite her exhaustion. She distracted herself by examining Ethan's belongings, trying to imagine the life he lived here. He wasn't overly neat, or a slob, the kind of man who valued utility over appearance. The kitchen contained the basics, but nothing extra—no mixer or juicer or anything extraneous. His bookshelf contained law enforcement texts, nature guides and some historical novels. The only picture on his wall was a painting of an elk bugling, against a backdrop of snowcapped peaks.

His furniture was identical to the items in the other half of the unit, which meant it had probably been here when he moved in. The one exception was a sturdy but worn leather recliner, positioned for watching the flat-screen television. She settled into this chair, and it was almost as if Ethan had wrapped his arms around her. The leather carried his scent. She imagined him sitting here, feet up, remote in hand, as he flipped through channels, looking for a game. He had probably spent many such evenings for the chair to conform to the shape of his body this way.

She hadn't bothered asking him if he had a girlfriend or if he dated. He struck her as something of a loner—lonely, even. Though she had spent much of her life on her own, she rarely thought of herself as lonely. Though now she was so grateful not to have to endure the pain of waiting and wondering about her son without Ethan to steady her.

She was almost asleep when her cell phone buzzed. She shifted to dig it out of her pocket and frowned at a number she didn't recognize, then sat bolt upright, heart racing. What if it was the kidnappers? She didn't have the script Ethan had promised. She had no way of tracing the call.

The ringtone continued, insistent. With shaking hands, she swiped to answer it. "Hello?"

"Hello, Starfall? It's me, Asteria."

"Asteria?" It took half a second for the name to register; then a second surge of adrenaline jolted her. "Where are you? Everyone's so worried about you."

"You don't need to worry about me," Asteria said.

"I'm fine. The Prophet sent me to a spa to rest. I didn't really want to go, but he convinced me it would be the best thing for the baby."

"Where did he send you?" Michelle asked.

"I'm in Denver. And I'm fine, really. Have you had any word about Hunter?"

"Nothing yet."

"Oh, no. I was hoping they would have found him by now."

"They haven't." The pain of this truth stabbed her all over again. "Asteria—Andi—do you know anything at all about what happened to him? I know you wouldn't have had any part in taking him, but maybe Metwater said something or did something—"

"He didn't. I even asked him directly if he knew anything about Hunter's disappearance."

"What did he say?" Not that she expected he would tell the truth, but his answer might be revealing.

"That's one reason I called," Asteria said. "I wanted you to know that the Prophet had a vision. He said in the vision he saw Hunter safe and happy. He's fine and you don't need to worry."

Michelle gripped the phone so tightly her fingers ached. "The only way he could know that was if he had something to do with Hunter's kidnapping," she said.

"No!" Asteria protested. "The Prophet has a true gift. His visions are real."

"His visions are a way of manipulating his followers," Michelle said. "Andi, wake up!" She deliberately used the woman's real name, to remind her of who she really was. "Don't let him manipulate you, too."

"I called because I thought you'd be happy to hear some good news," Andi said. "Instead, you tell me I'm stupid."

"I don't think you're stupid," Michelle said. "But you're being naive if you think everything Daniel Metwater tells you is true."

"He's the only one who has ever accepted the real me." She sounded teary now. "You're the kind of person who always sees the worst in people, instead of all the good they do."

Michelle couldn't deny the charge. For much of her life, that had been true. But lately, she'd felt something shifting inside her. "I see the good in you," she said. "And I care about you—and about your baby. Just promise me that if you have any doubts—or you're ever in trouble and need help—you'll go to the Ranger Brigade. They care, too, and they'll help you."

"I can't believe you, of all people, are recommending I rely on the police for anything," Andi said.

"I can't believe it, either," Michelle said. "But it's true. They've done everything they can to help me, and I know they would help you, too."

"I don't need their help. I don't need anyone's help. And I'd better go now. I'm sorry I called."

"I'm not sorry," Michelle said. "It was good to hear from you, and I'm glad to know you're all right. But please, think about something. If Daniel Metwater did have something to do with Hunter's disappearance—if he would take a child from his mother—what would he do with your baby?"

"I can't believe you'd say something so awful," Andi said, and ended the call.

No, Michelle thought. *You just don't want to believe your Prophet would do something so awful.*

ETHAN PORED OVER the computer printouts about the Metwater brothers until his head ached and his vision blurred, but he could find nothing to link Daniel to his brother's crimes or to anything else he might have needed to keep Michelle from revealing.

At last, he put the files aside and drove home. The light was on in the front room, and when he unlocked the door and stepped inside, he was surprised to find Michelle asleep in the recliner, an afghan his mother had knitted draped over her. At least someone was getting some rest. He was tempted to leave her there, but as he passed the chair, she stirred.

"What time is it?" she asked, blinking and wincing at the light.

"It's after midnight. I'm sorry I woke you."

"It's okay." She pushed aside the afghan and stretched. "Your chair is really comfortable," she said.

"It was my dad's." That and a hunting rifle were the only two things he had wanted of his father's. As far back as he could remember, the leather recliner had been his dad's throne, the place where he read the paper, watched the ball game and meted out both punishment and advice to his only child.

"It's yours now," she said, rubbing one hand up and down the arm of the chair. "It smells like you."

He didn't know what to say to that, and decided instead to answer the question she hadn't yet asked. "I didn't find anything in the files," he said.

"I didn't really think you would, but thanks for trying." She yawned and sat up straighter. "Before I forget, Asteria called. She said she's safe and staying at some spa in Denver."

"Metwater told us she was at the Brown Palace, but it's nice to have that confirmed. Is that why she called—to let you know where she was?"

Michelle shook her head. "She said something else that she thought I'd be happy to hear, but it only made me angrier."

He sat on the sofa adjacent to the recliner, only inches away from her. "What was that?"

"She asked Metwater if he knew anything about Hunter's disappearance. He told her he had had a vision. In the vision he saw Hunter, safe and happy. I tried to tell her that if Metwater knew that Hunter was safe, it meant he had something to do with him being taken from me—either that, or he's lying to make her stop worrying."

"But she doesn't see it that way," Ethan said.

"No. She thinks he's really a prophet and his visions are real. I told her she shouldn't trust him, but of course she didn't listen. She said I always thought the worst of people." She clasped her hands, her fingers laced. "The thing is, she's right. I have always looked for the worst in everyone."

"From what you've told me, you've had good reason not to trust people," Ethan said.

"Maybe. But I'm trying to change." Her eyes met his,

weary but focused. "I told her if she ever needed help, she should contact the Rangers. I told her she could trust you—that I trusted you."

He leaned over and took her hand and held it. "I'm glad I've earned your trust," he said. "I'll do everything in my power to keep it."

She leaned forward and kissed him, then closed her eyes and rested her head on his shoulder. "What happens now?" she asked.

"Now? We're both exhausted. I think we should go to bed."

"All right."

He stood and pulled her up beside him. Then, leaning on each other, they walked to his bedroom and helped each other undress. They climbed under the covers and she snuggled close. He thought she might have been asleep before he turned off the light. That, he realized, was proof of how comfortable she had become with him.

It took longer for him to go to sleep, his mind too full of everything that had happened—with Michelle and Hunter and his mother and Metwater. Tomorrow he would need to follow up on the theft of his mother's car, and maybe find time to go by Metwater's camp to question Roscoe. He might have another go at Metwater, also—ask him about the *vision* he had described to Asteria. It seemed he had scarcely drifted off before his phone rang. He groped for it on the bedside table and answered groggily.

"Ethan, it's Carmen. Did I wake you?"

"What time is it?" He squinted at the bedside clock.

"It's almost eight."

He swore under his breath and swung his feet to the floor. "I'll be in as soon as I can," he said. "I had a late night last night."

"I'm not calling to rag on you for being late," Carmen said. "I wanted to let you know we just had someone call in with a report of two young men and a baby staying at an old motel in Cimarron. The caller thought that was odd. It may be nothing, but we should check it out."

"I'm on it." He pulled a pad of paper and a pen from the bedside table. "Give me the address."

Carmen read off the address. "Simon is already on his way."

"I thought he went to Denver."

"He had car trouble last night and got such a late start he decided to wait until this morning. He wasn't likely to get anything out of the folks at the Brown Palace in the middle of the night."

"Tell him I'll meet him in Cimarron," Ethan said.

"You and half the force," Carmen said. "None of us want to be left out of this one."

He ended the call and turned to find Michelle sitting up in bed, staring at him. "What is it?" she asked.

"We got a report of two guys with a baby—it could be Hunter."

She threw back the covers and headed toward her clothes. "Wait," he said. "It also might be nothing. Don't get your hopes up."

"Hope is all I've got," she said. "I'm coming with you."

"You can't."

"Why not? I'm his mother."

"I promise you, if it is Hunter, as soon as it's safe to do so, you can see him," Ethan said. "But I can't let you walk into a potential hostage situation. Having you there might even make the kidnappers less likely to cooperate."

She continued dressing. "I'm going with you."

He walked around the bed and took her shoulders. "Michelle, look at me."

She glared at him. "He's my baby. He needs me. I need him."

"Yes, but I need you to stay safe while we make sure he's safe, too. Do you remember you said you trusted me?"

"Yes. Because I thought you were on my side."

"I am on your side. And I need to keep both you and Hunter safe." He gave her a gentle squeeze. "I promise, I will bring you to him, as soon as it's safe to do so. But I can't do my best for him if I'm worried about you, too."

"Then don't worry about me," she said. "The only person you need to worry about is Hunter."

He cupped her cheek in his palm. "I can't avoid worrying about you. That's how important you've become to me."

The hardness went out of her eyes. She wet her lips. "All right. I'll stay here. But save my boy. Bring him back to me."

"If this baby is Hunter, I'll get him back to you." He had taken an oath that he would give his life, if necessary, to protect and serve, but he had never meant the words more than he did now.

Chapter Thirteen

In the cruiser, Ethan called Carmen again. "Give me an update."

"Colorado State Patrol is already headed that way to sit on the place and make sure these guys don't leave until we've checked them out. The rest of us are mobilizing. Where is Michelle?"

"I left her at my place. She wasn't happy about it, but I tried to make her understand it wouldn't be safe for her or Hunter to have her there."

"Ouch. That's tough."

"You're telling me. I promised her as soon as it was safe to do so, I'd bring her to him."

"You did the right thing."

"Yeah. But I'm not sure she believed that." He slowed as he neared the small community of Cimarron, which boasted one gas station, a post office and a few campgrounds and motels mainly utilized by fishermen and people visiting Blue Mesa Reservoir or Black Canyon of the Gunnison National Park. "I'm almost at the motel," he said. "I'll do a drive-by and see what I can see."

The Magpie Inn consisted of a row of seven connected rooms, all facing the highway, a big picture window in each room giving a clear view of the road and the parking lot. The office sat to one side of the rooms. Anyone in the rooms or the office would spot a police vehicle as soon as it drove in, so Ethan sped past. If anyone at the motel saw him, he hoped they would think he was on his way somewhere else.

Just beyond the inn, a silver and blue Colorado State Patrol unit had parked on the side of the highway. Ethan swung his cruiser in to park behind it. A uniformed deputy stepped out of the patrol car to greet him. "Mike Gladwell," he said, shaking hands.

"Ethan Reynolds." Ethan nodded toward the motel. "Can you tell me anything about this place?"

"The owner is an older couple, the Johansons," Gladwell said. "The wife is the only one there right now. I talked to her on the phone when the call first came in. She says the two guys registered as brothers—Thad and Tom Smith. The baby is Thad's son, Timmy. They're in room six—next to the last on the end farthest from the office."

"I suppose that could be their real names," Ethan said.

"I ran the plates on the car," Gladwell said. "It's a rental—rented to Thad Smith. They rented a car seat along with the car."

"Who called this in, do you know?" Ethan asked.

"The motel owner, Mrs. Johanson, thinks it's the wife of a couple in the room next to the Smiths, on the end. The lady was asking the owner about these guys—

she said it didn't look to her as if they had a clue how to take care of a baby."

"Anything else we should know?" Ethan asked.

"Mrs. Johanson said they haven't acted like your typical vacationers. No sightseeing or hiking or fishing or anything. They've pretty much stayed in the cabin, out of sight."

"Where is the owner now?" Ethan asked.

"I talked her into locking up and going to her house up there." Gladwell pointed up the hill from the motel. "She'll stay there until I give her the all clear, and she promised to call her husband and let him know not to stop by here. He planned to spend the morning fishing."

Two other Ranger cruisers pulled in behind Ethan's vehicle and Carmen, Lance and Simon got out. After introductions, Lance asked. "What's the plan?"

"Someone needs to watch the back while Simon and I approach the front," Ethan said.

Simon nodded. "We'll park behind the office," he said. "Where they can't see us. Then we'll approach their door from the side, on foot."

"We'll take the back," Carmen said.

"I'll watch the parking lot exit," Gladwell said.

"All right," Lance said. "Let's do it."

They checked their weapons, then took their positions. Simon pulled his cruiser in behind the office and he and Ethan stayed close to the building, out of sight of anyone in the rooms. They moved quickly, weapons drawn. When they reached the room the Smiths were registered in, they positioned themselves on either side of the door and Ethan knocked.

No one answered, but the curtains over the window twitched. Ethan knocked again, harder. "Mr. Smith, we need to speak with you, please."

The door opened, and a man in his twenties with shaggy brown hair and the bronzed skin of someone who spent a lot of time out of doors peered out. He wore a faded blue T-shirt and tan cargo shorts and was barefoot. "What's going on?" he asked.

"Child welfare check," Ethan said. "Do you have an infant here with you?"

"Uh…"

Ethan figured he was about to lie, but at that moment a baby began to wail, somewhere in the room behind the young man. He glanced over his shoulder. "That's just my son, Timmy."

"May we see him, please?"

"Why?"

"A woman called in a concern about his welfare."

Thad—if that was really his name—swore under his breath.

"We need to make sure the child is all right," Simon said. "If you could just bring him to the door for a moment."

"Uh, sure." He stepped back and shut the door. The sounds of movement and low, muffled voices followed.

Ethan's eyes met Simon's across the door. "What do you think?" he asked.

"I think if he doesn't come out of there in thirty seconds, we go in," Simon said.

The gun blast tore through the door, sending wood splinters flying. Both officers flattened themselves on the ground. Ethan began scooting backward, away from the room, his eyes on the door. Though he held his weapon at the ready, he didn't dare fire blindly into the room, for fear of hitting Hunter.

"Let us go and the kid won't get hurt," Thad called. "Try anything and he's dead, I swear it!"

MICHELLE HAD TO muster every reserve of strength to keep from racing down the driveway after Ethan as his cruiser pulled away. While objectively, his words about keeping clear and staying safe, letting the Rangers do their job, all made sense, her mother's instinct to be with her child and protect him threatened to overwhelm any practical logic. Hunter needed her. He was probably frightened and confused right now, and she was the only one who could comfort him.

She forced herself to stand and go into the kitchen. She'd make coffee, and then maybe find something to watch on television. She would do her best to distract herself, all the while waiting for the call that would tell her her son was safe.

She was pouring coffee into her cup when a knock on the door startled her so much she almost dropped the carafe. She froze and the knock came again, louder this time. Was it another reporter, wanting to badger her with questions? Or someone from the Rangers with news about Hunter?

Heart pounding, she crept across the floor to the door and peered out the security peephole. She choked back a cry of alarm when she found herself staring into Daniel Metwater's intense dark eyes. He pounded the door again. "I know you're in there, Michelle." He sneered her name. "Open up so we can talk."

Her first instinct was to remain silent and refuse to answer, but even as she was pondering this, he backed up and gave the door a vicious kick. It shook in its frame. A second kick had it buckling inward near the doorknob. She looked around wildly for something— anything—with which to defend herself, and spotted the phone. If she called, could Ethan or one of the others get to her in time?

She had just reached the phone when the door burst open and Metwater rushed in, smashing his way toward the kitchen. Her coffee cup shattered as he grabbed hold of her arm and wrenched the phone away. He hurled it to the floor and stomped on it, bits of plastic flying as he crushed it. She stared at him, unable to speak. Gone was the mild-mannered, charismatic Prophet, replaced by a fierce, angry bully. He dragged her across the room and shoved her onto the sofa. "You're going to sit there and you're going to listen to me," he ordered.

Be tough, she told herself. *Don't let him see how scared you are.* She sat up straight and forced herself to look him in the eye. "Whatever you have to say, you'd better say it quick. Ethan will be home any minute. When he finds you here he'll have you back in jail so fast you won't know what hit you."

"Your boyfriend isn't going to bother us," Metwater said. "He and that other cop, Woolridge, were headed in the opposite direction last time I saw them."

"How did you find me?" she asked.

"I followed you from Ranger Headquarters last night."

"You're supposed to be in jail."

"They had to drop the charges," he said. "I knew they would. They didn't have a scrap of proof that I was guilty of anything but being someone they don't like. Everybody knows the Rangers like to harass me and my followers."

"Asteria called and told me what you said about Hunter—that you knew where he was. That's proof you had something to do with his disappearance."

"It doesn't prove anything. I'm a prophet, remember? I have visions and I know things." He moved toward her. "The way I know that you're not going to cause me any more trouble."

She jumped up and tried to run away, but he grabbed her arm and yanked her back onto the sofa. "You're not going anywhere," he said. He kneeled over her, pushing her back into the cushions.

She forced herself to keep looking at him, trying to read his intentions in his eyes, but all she saw in his expression was the mania of a fanatic, and a hatred that chilled her to the core. "I hate liars," he said, his hands on her arms tightening so that she bit back a cry of pain. "You've been lying to me ever since we met—pretending you wanted to follow me when all you really wanted was to bring me down."

"I don't care about you," she said. "I only wanted to know the truth about your brother, David."

He laughed, throwing his head back, his body shaking with mirth. "You want to know the truth? You wouldn't believe it if I told you."

"Your brother killed my sister," she said. "He gave her those drugs and let everyone think she had over-dosed."

"No, he didn't do that." He shook his head. "I don't expect you to believe me, but my brother didn't do any of the things people think he did. But he'll never have the chance to clear his name. Isn't that ironic? He and your sister—your foster sister—have that in common."

"Did you know Cass?" she asked. "Did you ever meet her?"

"Yes, I did. She was a lovely young woman. And a very stupid one. If she had kept her mouth shut, she might still be alive. But she had to say the wrong thing to the wrong person. Just like you." He squeezed harder, and she whimpered. She tried to fight him, but it was like pushing against a wall. Where was Ethan? If only he would come back with Hunter in time to save her.

Metwater straightened and pulled her up alongside him. "Come on," he said.

"Wh…where are we going?"

"Out." He dragged her toward the door.

"I'm not going anywhere with you." She tried to pull free, but he shook her and slapped her, hard, blurring her vision.

"Shut up!" He yanked open the door and pulled her outside. She blinked at the familiar car in the drive-way. Her car.

She opened her mouth to speak and tasted blood. Icy terror gripped her so that her vision blurred and it hurt to breathe. She couldn't go with him. If she did, she would never come back alive, she was sure. She dug in her heels and hung back.

"Stop it!" He yanked her forward with one hand while he pulled the keys from his pocket with the other.

She looked around wildly—for a weapon, for someone who could help her, for anything she could use to get away. But there was nothing. The other duplexes on this short dead-end street were all home to other members of the Ranger Brigade, who were all away, trying to rescue her son. No traffic passed on the road that connected to the street, and the neat, sparse yard offered nothing she could use as a weapon.

Metwater opened the passenger door and dragged her toward the car. She made herself go limp, her heels digging into the dirt, resisting him with all her strength. He grunted and took hold of her with both hands. "Let me go!" she shouted, and kicked at him, ignoring the pain that shot through her as he wrenched her shoulders. She managed to free one hand and clawed at his face, her nails raking across his skin.

Enraged, he let out a roar and grabbed hold of her hair, yanking her head so far back she thought he might break her neck. She spit at him and writhed in his arms. If she pulled him to the ground, maybe she could crawl away from him…

"No!" he shouted, and slammed her against the side of the car. Pain exploded in her head, and a flash of bright light blinded her, right before darkness engulfed her and that riptide she had been fighting earlier pulled her completely under.

Chapter Fourteen

Ethan crawled backward along the walkway in front of the row of hotel rooms until he reached the corner of the building and cover. He pulled himself to his feet and looked back in time to see Simon disappear around the opposite corner of the building. They were both safe, but what about the men and the baby in that room?

His telephone buzzed and he answered it. "We heard the shots," Carmen said, her voice just above a whisper. "What's going on up there?"

"They fired on us," he said. "They've got Hunter in there and they said they'll kill him if we try anything."

"Who are they?" she asked. "Why did they take Hunter?"

"No idea. Did we ever track down Michelle's ex?"

"No. We weren't able to find him."

"Maybe he's one of these guys." Ethan wiped the sweat from his forehead. "It doesn't matter. We have to figure out how to get Hunter out of there before things go south."

"We need to get a hostage negotiator out here," she said. "Maybe we can talk them into giving up the baby."

"I've had training as a hostage negotiator," Ethan said. "I'm going to call the commander and see what he wants to do."

"Okay. Simon is with us now. He seems okay."

"Good. We don't want anyone hurt if we can help it." He hung up and punched in Commander Graham Ellison's number. The commander answered on the first ring.

"What's going on out there?" Ellison asked. "A report came in on the scanner of shots fired."

"We've got two guys, registered as Thad and Tom Smith, with a baby we're pretty sure is Hunter Munson," Ethan said. "Simon and I went to the door of their room and asked to see the baby. I spoke to Thad, who pretended to cooperate, then opened fire and screamed if we tried anything, he'd kill the kid."

"You okay?" Ellison asked.

"I'm safe. So is Simon. He's behind the building with Carmen and Lance. We've got a CSP deputy posted at the road. Before we got here he persuaded the motel owner to move to her house nearby, so she's out of the line of fire."

"Don't do anything until I get there with reinforcements," Ellison said. "Keep quiet and let them sweat a little."

"Will do." He ended the call just as Simon slipped up beside him from behind the building. "You okay?" Ethan asked.

"Yeah." He nodded toward the kidnappers' room. "What's the plan?"

"The commander and the rest of the team are on their way. We're to sit tight until they get here."

"Is anyone staying in any of these other rooms?" Simon asked.

Ethan had been so focused on Hunter and the kidnappers, he hadn't even thought about other people who might be in harm's way. "I'll find out," he said. "Gladwell knows the owners. He can tell us how to get in touch with them."

Keeping out of view of the kidnappers, he slipped behind the office and made his way to the road. A second Colorado State Patrol car had parked behind Gladwell's. Both CSP deputies walked back to the rear of the second car to meet Ethan. "Everybody okay?" Gladwell asked.

"So far," Ethan said. "We're waiting for our commander and some more of the team to get here. Do you know if there are other guests staying here?"

"I asked Mrs. Johanson and she says she had three other rooms rented, but their occupants are all out sight-seeing or fishing or other stuff," Gladwell said. "I'll give you her number and you can double-check. I know she'd appreciate an update about what's going on. We'll keep any other guests away if they come back before this is resolved."

"Thanks."

"What's the game plan?" Gladwell asked.

"My commander is on his way," Ethan said. "We'll try talking first, see if we can get them to hand over the kid."

"We can get a sniper over from CSP if you need one," the second deputy said.

"Thanks," Ethan said. "We've got that covered, I think." Marco Cruz had that kind of experience. They'd position him where he had a clear view of the door and window of the room, though the Smith brothers had the curtains pulled over the latter. Still, if they stepped out the door, Marco might have to chance a shot. Ethan had been on a hostage situation once where, after more than twelve hours of negotiating for the release of two children, he persuaded the kidnapper to accept a delivery of pizza. As soon as he stepped onto his front porch to pick up the boxes, the sharpshooter nailed him. It wasn't the ideal outcome, but they had saved the two kids.

Ethan would do whatever it took to save Michelle's kid. Hunter deserved a chance to grow up. And Michelle deserved to see her son again.

Ethan rejoined Simon. "Gladwell says all the other guests are out. I'm going to call the owner, Mrs. Johanson, to double-check and to find out more about the layout of the rooms." He punched in the number Gladwell had given him.

"Johanson," a man answered, his voice gruff.

Ethan identified himself and brought the man up-to-date on what was going on with the Smiths. "I wanted to know more about the layout of the rooms," he said. "Is there a door connecting the room the Smiths are in to the rooms on the other side?"

"There is," Mr. Johanson said. "It should be locked and bolted from the other side, though."

"What about windows?" Ethan asked. "Anything large enough for a man to crawl out of?"

"There's a small window in the bathroom at the

back," Johanson said. "But it's only about eighteen inches wide. I don't think either of the Smiths could fit through it."

"Okay. Does the room have a phone?"

"All our rooms have phones and satellite TV. People expect that these days."

"I'll need the number for the phone in their room. We're going to try to negotiate with these guys."

"I feel terrible about that kid," Johanson said. "I guess we should have realized something wasn't right, but we don't watch much news and we're just not the type to expect the worst from people. Let me get you that number."

He came back on the line after a moment and rattled off the phone number, which Ethan wrote down in his notebook. "Is there anything we can do?" Mr. Johanson asked.

"Just stay in the house. We'll let you know when it's safe to come out."

"Here comes the cavalry," Simon said as Ethan pocketed his phone. Two Ranger Brigade FJ Cruisers swung in to block the entrance to the motel, and Commander Ellison and the rest of the Ranger Brigade climbed out. Simon and Ethan made their way over to meet them.

Ethan brought them up to date on the situation, opening his notebook to sketch the layout of the rooms. "We could put a team in the room next door and come in that way," Marco said.

"Risky unless we know exactly where the baby is," Commander Ellison said.

"I might be able to find that out when I talk to them," Ethan said.

"The back window is a little small to try going in that way," Ellison said.

"Carmen might be able to get in that way," Simon said.

"I wouldn't want to send her in alone," Ellison said. "But we'll keep it in mind."

"We come at them from both sides, it'll be easier to pin them down," Simon said.

Ethan shook his head. "Too much risk of the baby getting caught in the cross fire."

"Ethan, you get them on the phone," Ellison said. "Maybe we can talk them into surrendering. Meanwhile, Simon and Michael, you get into the room next door. We'll keep Carmen and Lance on the back of the building, and tell her to be ready to go in the window if necessary. Marco, you take up a position where you have a clear shot at the front of the room."

What is that roaring in my ears? And why is it so dark?

Michelle groaned, and the roaring faded, her vision gradually clearing. Her head throbbed, and her arms ached. What was she doing lying in the back of a car? She struggled to sit, the task made more difficult by the fact that her hands were tied behind her back.

"It's about time you woke up."

She stared at the three-quarter profile of Daniel Metwater's face as he piloted the car down a paved highway, past a landscape of sagebrush fields and rocky cliffs. "What are you doing?" she asked, the words emerging as a strangled croak. She coughed and tried again. "Where are you taking me?"

"I haven't decided, exactly," he said. "I've been driving around, waiting for you to wake up and considering my options."

"Why are you so angry with me?" she asked. "What did I ever do to you?"

"It's not what you have done, but what you potentially could do," he said. "The best way to handle a problem in your life is to address it before it becomes serious. You may recall a teaching I presented on that topic at the campfire circle one evening not too long ago."

He must have interpreted her frown as puzzlement. "Of course you don't remember," he said. "I always suspected you of not paying attention."

No one had paid attention to his nightly sermons—or what he called "teachings"—most of the time. Even the uber-faithful like Asteria would tune out after a while. Good looks and charisma could take a man a long way, but they weren't enough to cow two dozen healthy adults into hanging on to his every word night after night. But Michelle knew better than to anger Metwater by pointing this out. "What do you mean—what I could potentially do?" she asked.

He glanced up at her in the rearview mirror, then back at the road. "One of my gifts is reading people," he said. "I can almost always watch a new follower for a day or two and figure out what he or she is looking for from me, and I determine how to fill that need. It's what makes me a great leader."

A great manipulator, she thought.

"For instance, more than anything, Asteria wants a home and security. She wants to feel safe. I can give that to her and to her child."

"And in exchange, she gives you everything," Michelle blurted.

Metwater nodded. "The definition of a fair exchange is one in which each party receives what he or she wants, so I would say the exchange between Asteria and myself is infinitely fair. You, however, were much more difficult to read. I realized right away, of course, that this was because you were being deceptive."

He had realized no such thing. He had paid scarcely any attention to her in the first weeks after she and Greg came to the camp with Hunter. "If you thought I was such a liar, why did you let me stay?"

"Because I wanted to know what your game was. The best way to defeat an enemy is to know him."

"Was that one of your teachings, too?"

He laughed. "It was. Think of all the useful things you would have learned if you had been paying attention."

"So what do you think you know about me?" she asked.

"You're not malleable."

It wasn't the answer she had been expecting. "Why is that bad?" she asked.

"It isn't necessarily bad," he said. "I'm not malleable, either. But nonmalleable people don't mesh well in groups—unless they're the leader. I can't have someone in my group I can't control."

She somehow refrained from rolling her eyes. "Fine,"

she said. "So you kicked me out. End of story. Why kidnap me now?"

"You're too dangerous, especially now that you're in bed with the cops."

He had chosen that particular figure of speech on purpose, she was sure. "I don't care about you," she said. "I only care about David, and what he did to my sister."

"If you start digging around in David's past, it could come back to hurt me. I've come much too far to let that happen."

That made her curious, as he must have known it would. Which also meant he had no intention of letting her live long enough to dig further into his past. "Since we're baring our souls here," she said, "tell me the truth about what happened to Hunter. Where is he? What did you do to him?" Her voice broke on the last words, and she blinked hard, forcing back tears. She wouldn't break down in front of this arrogant jerk, no matter what.

"Some guys I knew in Chicago owed me a favor," he said. "They agreed to come down and babysit your little boy. You don't have to worry about him—he's all right."

Relief rocked her back in the seat, and she swayed, light-headed. Metwater wasn't the type to spare her feelings, so he must be telling the truth.

He slowed the car, then pulled onto the side of the road. She sat up straighter. The landscape hadn't changed—rolling stretches of sagebrush, rocky cliffs, achingly blue sky. "Why are we stopping?" she asked.

"I was thinking about my brother," he said. "About

when they found his body. Have you ever seen some-one who has drowned?"

She shook her head, then, realizing he couldn't see her, added, "No."

"Being in the water really messes up a body," he said. "By the time they found my brother, he was so disfig-ured no one could identify him. Dental records didn't help—we both have perfect teeth. They identified him based on a tattoo. I had to go in and look at it and bring pictures that showed him with the tattoo."

"Wh…why are you telling me this?"

"Because I wanted you to know that's what it's going to be like for you." He put the car in gear and turned back onto the highway. "Only a little farther now," he said. "I just have to find deep enough water."

WHEN EVERYONE WAS in their places around the motel, Ethan pulled out his phone. He texted Carmen.

Can you hear anything in there?

Some movement. The baby was crying a little bit ago, but he's quiet now.

I'm making my call now. Ethan replied.

Good luck.

He punched in the number Mr. Johanson had given him and waited. On the fifth ring, a man picked up. "Yeah?"

"This is Agent Ethan Reynolds with the Ranger Brigade. Is this Thad or Tom Smith?"

"What difference does it make to you? You all need to back off and leave us alone if you don't want this kid to get hurt."

"We don't want anyone to get hurt," Ethan said. Though he kept his gaze fixed on the door to the room where the kidnappers waited, out of the corner of his eye he saw Simon and Michael inching along the front of the building, toward the door of the end room. "I'm sure you didn't plan for things to turn out this way." He needed to establish a connection with Smith and keep him on the line and distracted as long as possible.

"This was supposed to be a simple job," Smith said. "Snatch the kid and hold him for a few days."

A job. Meaning the Smiths were employees? "Whose idea was it to take the baby?" Ethan asked.

"Not mine. I wish I'd never laid eyes on the kid."

"So the person we should really be going after isn't you—it's the person who hired you."

"I'm not saying anything."

"Why? Because you're afraid of the person who hired you?"

"Because I'm not stupid. I roll over on him and I'll end up at the bottom of a river somewhere."

The door to the end room closed behind the two Rangers. Ethan hadn't heard anything to alert him that the Smiths were aware of their new neighbors. "Was the ransom note his idea or yours?" Ethan asked.

"What difference does it make?"

"I'm just trying to figure out what you want. If I

know that, maybe we can come to an agreement that gets us both what we want."

"Hey, I didn't just fall off the turnip truck. No cop cares about what I want."

Ethan remembered Metwater's outrage when they'd shown him the ransom note. "Those idiots!" he had shouted. "How much did Daniel Metwater promise you for taking the boy?" he asked.

"Not nearly enough. Hey! I never said it was Metwater."

"You didn't have to. How much did he offer?"

Silence. "Come on," Ethan prodded. "Help me make my case against him and it will go better for you."

"Five thousand," Smith said. "We were just supposed to keep the kid for a few days while he taught some woman a lesson."

It wasn't enough that Metwater had beat up Michelle—he had to steal her baby, too. "But it took longer than you thought," Ethan prompted.

"Yeah. And the kid hardly shuts up. He cried all night last night. We hardly slept."

"That's rough." Ethan pretended to sympathize. "He sounds quiet now."

"He's asleep."

"You have a crib in there?" Ethan tried to picture where a baby bed might fit into the small room.

"We put some pillows in the bathtub and put him in there. He seems to like it, and we can shut the door if he starts wailing again."

Ethan's heart leaped at this news. He grabbed his

notepad and scrawled a message to the commander. "Text Carmen that the baby is in the bathtub, asleep."

Ellison glanced at the note and nodded. Ethan forced his attention back to the call. "You must be pretty bored in there," he said. "What do you do to pass the time?"

"Mostly we watch TV and sleep." Someone mumbled in the background and Smith chuckled. "My brother says to tell you he's cleaning his gun."

"If you come out now, and leave the baby behind for us, I'll make sure the DA knows you cooperated," Ethan said.

Smith made a snorting sound. "We're not moving until we get a solid deal—none of this *maybe* business."

"I'll see what I can do," Ethan said. "I'll need to make some calls and talk to a few people. In the meantime, can I get you anything—food, beer, diapers?"

"We're good."

Ethan ended the call and looked at Ellison. The commander gave him a thumbs-up. "Simon and Michael are in place," Ellison said. "They were able to open the door on their side while you were on the phone with Smith. We'll come in the front while they come in the side."

"We know they're armed," Ethan said. "They'll start shooting right away."

"We think we can overpower them before they know what hit them," Ellison said. "We're going to fire tear gas in before we go in. We'll have gas masks, but they won't."

"Neither will Hunter," Ethan said.

"Carmen is at the back window with Lance," Ellison said. "She thinks she can get in the window—

which is already open a few inches. He'll boost her up and she'll go in and grab the baby and hand him out to Lance while the Smiths are dealing with their surprise visitors. The gas won't have had time to reach the bathroom yet, especially with the door closed."

Ethan nodded. It sounded like a good plan, but he knew too well that things could always go wrong.

Chapter Fifteen

"What's my role?" Ethan asked.

"Get Smith back on the phone," Ellison said. "Pump him for more information about Metwater's involvement. Get him worked up if you can—agitated and distracted. Try to get him to look out the window at you—that will put him farther from the connecting door when we go in."

Ethan nodded. All he had to do was keep his cool, and let the team do its job. "Do you need a minute?" Ellison asked.

"No, I'm good." He held up the phone. "I'm ready when you are."

"Go when Randall and I are in the room with Simon and Michael."

He waited while the commander added a helmet and shield to his riot gear. Ellison and Randall Knightbridge, who was similarly outfitted, slipped out of sight behind the motel office, then reappeared at the corner of the building. Moving stealthily, they made their way to the door of the end room and disappeared inside.

Ethan called the Smiths. Someone answered right

away. The baby wailed in the background. "What?" Thad demanded.

"I need you to tell me more about Metwater," he said. "I need to be able to convince the DA that you can give us information we can't get anywhere else. I need him to see that you're too valuable to pass up the opportunity to get you on our side."

"Yeah, and if I tell you everything I know now, you won't need me at all," he said. "Tom, shut that kid up. I can't think!"

"He'll stop crying in a minute," Ethan said. "Try turning on the TV. They like to hear the voices."

"I'll try anything." After a moment the sound of a television came up. Miraculously, Hunter's crying stopped. "Hey, it worked!"

"Just leave him in the bathtub and he'll probably fall back asleep in a minute," Ethan said. In any case, the noise from the television would help cover up any sounds from the room next door. "I don't need much, I just need a little to make the DA happy. You mentioned Metwater's connections. What did you mean by that?"

"What do you think I mean?" Smith asked. "Chicago? Connections?"

"You mean the mob?" Ethan asked. "I thought his brother was the one who was tied up with the Mafia."

"That's what everybody thought, but they were all wrong."

"How do you know this?" Ethan asked.

"Uh-uh. I'm not going there. In fact, we're done talking."

"Don't hang up!" Ethan said. "Tell me about this

woman Metwater wanted to teach a lesson. What was his beef with her?"

"Man, I don't know," Smith said. "All he told us was that we had to keep the kid out of sight for a few days until she learned her lesson. He said he'd give us five thousand bucks to babysit and that's all I needed to know."

"But then he didn't pay you."

"He didn't come through with the money and he couldn't tell me when the job would be over."

"So you decided to make the best of things and sent the ransom note," Ethan said. "That way, at least you'd get something out of the deal."

"That's about it. We had to cover our expenses, you know? And this way, the kid ended up back with his mother. We're not heartless."

"I can see that. And the DA will take that into consedera—"

An explosion cut off his word. Shouting, and thuds. Ethan clutched the phone to his ear and stared at the front of the hotel, but the curtains to the Smiths' room remained closed, providing no clue about what was going on inside. Then two figures raced from behind the building. Carmen, followed by Lance, jogged along the far side of the parking lot to reach Ethan. She cradled a blanket-wrapped bundle to her chest and was grinning from ear to ear. "He's okay," she said, before Ethan could ask. "We've got EMTs on the way," Lance said. "They'll take him to the hospital for a checkup. His mom can meet us there."

His mom. Ethan ended the call to the Smiths and

punched in the number for his duplex. The phone rang and rang. "Michelle probably isn't answering because she thinks the call is for me," he said.

The door to the motel room burst open and a bearded young man with long brown hair stumbled out, his hands cuffed behind him, followed by Commander Ellison, and a second handcuffed man handled by Simon and Randall. They hustled the prisoners over to the cruisers and put them in the back seats.

Ellison pulled off his helmet and joined Ethan, Lance and Carmen, who was still holding Hunter. The baby was wailing, loudly, his face red from the effort. "I think he needs a bottle and a clean diaper," Carmen said as she jostled him in her arms. "I hope the EMTs come prepared."

"I tried to reach Michelle, but she's not answering the phone," Ethan said. "Maybe she's asleep."

Ellison clapped Ethan on the back. "Go give her the good news in person. Then you can bring her to the hospital to be reunited with her baby."

"What about Metwater?" Ethan asked.

"Marco and I are on our way to his camp now to arrest him," Ellison said. "His lawyers aren't going to get him off the hook on this one, I promise."

Ethan left, forcing himself to keep close to the speed limit. Sometimes in his job he got the opportunity to do something really good. This was one of those times. He couldn't wait to see Michelle's face when he told her they had found Hunter safe and sound. After so much in her life going wrong for her, this time things had gone right.

The setting sun painted the graying sky with streaks of pink and orange behind Ethan's duplex. Purple thunderclouds loomed in the distance, and the air was heavy with the promise of a storm. Ethan parked in the drive and strode up the walk, grinning in anticipation of sharing the good news about Hunter. But the damaged front door stopped him in his tracks. "Michelle!" he called.

When she didn't answer, he drew his weapon and approached cautiously. He nudged open the damaged door and stepped inside. Only dark, still air greeted him. Maybe Michelle was taking a nap, though he couldn't imagine she would sleep until she knew her son was safe.

He flipped on the light and started for the bedroom, but was only a few feet into the room when he stopped and stared at the overturned bar stool, shattered cup and scattered bits of plastic on the floor. Heart hammering, he knelt and put a fingertip to the coffee pooled among the shards of china. Cold. Then he spotted another dark puddle a foot from the coffee, and icy fear gripped him. He took the flashlight from his utility belt and played it across the stain, noting the syrupy burgundy-brown shimmer of blood.

"Michelle!" he shouted, and ran toward the bedroom. Empty. He checked the bathroom and the guest room, and looked into the tiny fenced backyard. Nothing. But he found her purse on the sofa, and her sweater on the peg by the door. Keys in one hand, cell phone in the other, he jogged back to the cruiser.

"Ellison." The commander's voice was crisp, warning the caller not to waste his time.

"Michelle's gone. The house is empty and there's sign of a struggle and blood on the floor."

"Stay there," Ellison ordered. "I'll send someone. Stay put until they get there."

"Yes, sir." Ethan slumped against the cruiser and stared toward the house. Where was he going to go, anyway? He had no idea where Michelle might be, or what had happened to her.

He stayed outside until a Ranger Brigade cruiser pulled over to the curb. Simon and Randall got out, along with Randall's police dog, Lotte. "The commander said something happened with Michelle," Randall said.

"I came home to tell her we'd found Hunter, and the house was empty," Ethan said. "There's an overturned chair, a broken coffee cup and a little bit of blood on the floor. Her purse is still there, and her sweater. I don't think she would have left without them if she had had the choice." He was surprised at how calm he sounded, how detached and businesslike, when inside his emotions were in turmoil.

"Let's take a look," Simon said, and led the way up the walk.

They took pictures and measurements, and searched the duplex for anything Ethan might have missed. Lotte sniffed Michelle's handbag and sweater and on the command "Find" trailed the scent to the end of the driveway. Simon found another spot of blood on the curb and took a sample for the lab.

"I'd say someone came in a car and she left with them," Simon said. "Either voluntarily or involuntarily."

"The blood tells me it was involuntary," Randall said.

"Who have we got watching Metwater?" Ethan asked.

Simon and Randall exchanged looks. "When the call came in about the hostage situation, the commander pulled me off that duty," Randall said. "Metwater didn't show any signs of going anywhere."

"Somebody should check if he's still in camp," Simon said.

"I'll do it," Ethan said.

"We'll run these samples to the lab and put out an APB for Michelle," Simon said. "And one for Metwater, too, in case he's done a runner."

"Hang in there," Randall said. "We'll find her."

Ethan nodded and climbed into his cruiser. He only hoped they found Michelle before it was too late. There hadn't been a lot of blood, but any at all was too much when it was someone you cared about.

Someone you loved. This was a heck of a time to realize he was in love with Michelle, but a crisis brought everything into clearer focus. Maybe there were more than a few reasons why the two of them shouldn't be together, but right now the only one that mattered was that it was tearing his heart out to think of her hurt or in need. He would do anything to save her—anything to be with her again. That was the kind of glue that kept people together in spite of their differences and difficulties, he thought. If only he had the chance to prove that theory to her.

He watched for signs of Michelle along the road as he drove toward Metwater's camp, scrutinizing every car and truck and camper that passed. When he turned off the paved road, he pushed the cruiser as fast as he dared, rattling over washboarded sections and bouncing over potholes with a force that threatened to shake parts of the vehicle—or parts of him—loose.

At last, he screeched to a halt at Metwater's compound and jogged up the trail to the camp. He bounded up the steps to Metwater's motor home and pounded hard on the door. "Open up, police!" he shouted.

"He's not there."

Ethan turned to see a shirtless young man with a shaved head and a torso full of colorful tattoos. "What did you say?" he asked.

"He's not there," the man said. "He left about an hour ago—maybe a little more."

"Where did he go?"

The man shrugged. "Don't know."

"Was he by himself?"

The man considered the question. "Yeah. I think he was."

That was probably the best answer Ethan was going to get. "How did he leave?" he asked. "Did someone drive him?" That was Metwater's usual habit—to have someone else drive him on his errands.

"Nah. He was driving that old car of Starfall's."

"What's your name?" Ethan asked.

"Roscoe."

He didn't offer a last name, but Ethan didn't need to know it. "You're the mechanic, right?" he asked. "The guy who salvages junk cars?"

Roscoe looked wary. "How do you know that?"

"Starfall mentioned that you'd worked on her car for her."

"Yeah. It's old, but it's in pretty good shape."

"You ever work on other cars—for people other than Family members?" Ethan asked.

"I could. Why? You got one that needs fixing?"

"I'm wondering if you ever crossed paths with guys who were bringing in cars from town," Ethan said. "Stripping them for parts, or maybe altering them before moving them on to other locations."

Roscoe took a step back. "You're talking about stolen cars." He shook his head. "Nuh-uh. I don't mess with that."

"But you might know someone who does? Someone else here in camp?" Ethan looked around—the few people who had been out and about when he arrived had vanished, though he suspected more than one pair of eyes watched him from the cover of tents and trailers.

"Nobody here in camp," Roscoe said. "The Prophet wouldn't allow it. He's always talking to us about being honest and respecting other people's property."

"Fine. Nobody here in camp. But somebody has been boosting cars in town and stripping them down out here on public land." He gave Roscoe a hard look. "If I find out you know who it is and you don't tell me, I'll have to assume it's because you're involved. A guy like you, with mechanical ability, would be a real asset to an operation like that. And if you already have a record…" The last point was a guess on Ethan's part, but an educated one, since some of Roscoe's artwork looked like jailhouse tats.

Roscoe paled. "All I know is a couple of guys named Smith asked me if I'd be interested in working for them."

Smith again. "Describe them."

"Young. Brown hair, kind of long. Brothers, I think, but the younger one takes the lead, does most of the talking."

"Any first names?" Ethan asked.

Roscoe shook his head. "I never heard any."

"How did you meet them?" Ethan asked.

"They came up to me at the salvage yard about a month ago. I had a load of scrap I'd hauled in to sell. Not cars, but a couple of old washing machines, some couch springs—you wouldn't believe the trash people dump out here."

"And this Smith guy just walked up to you?"

"Yeah. He said he'd heard I was good with cars and he needed someone like me to do some work for him."

"Did he say who recommended you?"

Roscoe frowned. "I didn't ask. I figure it was some-body I knew on the inside. I told him I didn't do that stuff anymore—that I was straight and going to stay that way."

"What did he say to that?" Ethan asked.

"He laughed." Roscoe scowled. "Made me mad. I told him where to go and got in my truck and left."

"So he never actually said he was stealing cars?" Ethan tried not to show his disappointment.

"He didn't have to. I know the types. Not too long after that, the guy who runs the salvage yard, Frankie, told me the cops were on the lookout for a car theft ring."

"You ever see the Smith brothers again?" Ethan asked. "They ever come by to visit the Prophet?"

"No way! I'm pretty sure that's why they laughed at me. When I told them I'd gone straight, I told them I was following the Prophet and he didn't hold with stealing. When people don't understand religion, the easiest way to put it down is to laugh at it."

Or maybe they had been laughing because they knew how wrong Roscoe was to believe the Prophet was so lily-white and honest. "Any idea where they're operating?" Ethan asked.

Roscoe shook his head. "I don't know and I don't want to know."

"They boosted my mother's car yesterday," Ethan said. "Brand-new Accord. She's pretty upset about it."

"Aw, dude, I'm sorry," Roscoe said. "I hope she had good insurance. These guys will have it stripped down or driven off to Mexico within twenty-four hours. I mean, I never saw their operation, but they struck me as pros. The name of the game in that business is speed—get the evidence off the street so you can't be linked with it and caught."

"Except you were caught," Ethan guessed.

Roscoe surprised him with a grin. "Yeah, but only because I got greedy. I boosted a sweet Corvette and thought I could give it a new paint job and hang on to it. Stupid. But for the best, too. Otherwise, I might never have seen the light, you know?"

Ethan nodded. "Thanks for telling me what you know about the Smiths."

"Sorry about your mom's car," he said. "If you see Starfall, tell her I said hi. And I hope they find her kid."

"We found Hunter," Ethan said. "But now Michelle—Starfall—is missing."

"No!" Roscoe shook his head. "Some people sure have bad luck."

"Luck didn't have anything to do with it," Ethan said. "We think she might be with Daniel Metwater." He was careful not to say he thought she had been abducted. He didn't want anyone to think their Prophet was being accused of anything and needed protecting.

"Maybe she's trying to talk him into taking her back," Roscoe said. "I bet he will, if she has the right attitude. He only kicked her out because she needed a little tough love. We all do, sometimes."

Ethan didn't bother correcting the young man. He handed Roscoe one of his cards. "Call me if you hear anything more about the car thieves—or if you see Starfall."

"She in some kind of trouble with the cops?" Roscoe asked, studying the business card.

"We just want to make sure she's okay," Ethan said.

He debated questioning others but decided not to waste any more time. He raced back to his cruiser. As soon as he was in cell coverage again, he called in to Ranger Brigade Headquarters. Simon answered the phone. "What have you got?" he asked.

"Metwater left camp more than an hour ago. He was driving Michelle's old car. The maroon Chevy."

"Yeah, I know it," Simon said. "We'll put out a bulletin to watch for it. Anything else?"

"I talked to a guy named Roscoe. He's the group's mechanic, makes extra money selling salvage metal. He said a couple of guys named Smith—brothers—approached him about working for them parting out stolen cars."

"Another side project for Metwater, or their own idea?" Simon asked.

"Roscoe thought Metwater didn't know anything about it, but he comes across as a true believer in the Prophet."

"I'll see what I can get out of the Smiths," Simon said. "See if they knew anything about Metwater's plans for Michelle. Where are you now?"

"About fifteen miles from headquarters. I'm going to patrol around here for a while, see what I can spot."

"Good idea," Simon said. "Keep an eye on the weather. We're supposed to have a storm coming in—could bring flash flooding."

Ethan looked out at the dark clouds massed in the dusky sky. Wind bent the trees along the side of the road. "I'll be careful," he said, and ended the call.

He headed toward the lake, away from Ranger Headquarters. Where was Metwater most likely to go? He had no idea. For all he had studied and observed the phony Prophet, he knew very little about how the man thought. He called the commander. "Simon updated me about the situation," Ellison said. "Have you learned anything new?"

"No, sir. Are you still with the Smith brothers?"

"I am."

"Ask them if they know of anyone else who was helping Metwater—anyone not in his *family*," Ethan said. "Ask them if he ever talked about what he would do to Michelle. I'm trying to figure out what he's up to."

"Will do. I'll let you know as soon as I find out anything."

"Yes, sir." He ended the call and gripped the steering wheel tighter. All he needed was a clue—some little lead that would send him in the right direction. Metwater could be halfway to Denver by now—or very nearby, down one of the countless side roads that wound through the wilderness area. Ethan was tempted to turn off onto one of those roads, but he needed to stay in cell phone range in order to wait for the commander's return call.

Michelle was a survivor. He needed to remember that. She had been through so much already—more than most people could endure. Yet she had kept going. She would do everything in her power to stay alive for her son.

His phone rang and he snatched it up. "Hello?"

"The Smiths aren't talking," Commander Ellison said. "They're waiting for their attorney to show up, but he's already advised them not to speak with us."

"I'm going to take a look in the country around the camp," Ethan said. "Metwater knows that area best, so he might stick to familiar ground." What he didn't say—what he knew the commander was also thinking—was that if Metwater planned to kill Michelle, he would know places to hide the body where it would never be found.

Ethan ended the call and turned the cruiser around, headed for the turnoff to Metwater's camp at the base of Mystic Mesa. As he passed a dirt turnoff that led down toward the lake, he thought he saw a burgundy-colored sedan shrouded in a cloud of dust.

He braked hard, mind racing. Had the car really been Michelle's old beater, or was his imagination playing tricks on him? He swung onto the narrow road and gunned the cruiser, fishtailing wildly as he struggled to keep up with the vehicle ahead. All he could see now was the occasional glow of brake lights and the dust rising like mist in the glow of his headlights.

He cut the lights, relying on the dim remnants of daylight to guide him. He didn't want whoever was in that car to realize he was following. Light flashed on water, and he braked as he realized they were almost to the lake. He pulled to the side of the road and parked, letting the other car drive on down to the shore. He took out his phone to call in his location and suppressed a groan at the message that he had no service.

Wind buffeted him as he stepped out of the cruiser, bringing with it the scent of rain and damp sage. Jagged lightning tore the sky on the far side of the lake, and the headlights from the first car showed whitecaps on the dark water.

Ethan crept toward the parked car, shrinking back into the shadows when the driver's door opened. Metwater climbed out, then opened the back door and pulled someone out. Michelle fell to her knees, her hands tied behind her back, and Metwater hauled her up roughly. Ethan couldn't see her that well in the growing darkness, but he recognized the tangle of brown curls around her face, and the defiant posture with which she faced her captor.

He debated going back to the cruiser for his rifle, but taking the time to retrieve it might mean the difference between life and death for Michelle. He didn't think Metwater had brought her here at this time of evening to go swimming. Ethan moved forward down the slope toward the pair by the water.

A rock shifted beneath him and he fell, skidding down the slope. He rolled, drawing his weapon as bullets thudded into the dirt where a fraction of a second before he had lain. Michelle screamed and Ethan peered from behind a log where he had sought cover in time to see Metwater grab her by the hair and pull her in front of him. Now Ethan couldn't fire on Metwater without endangering her.

Metwater dragged Michelle toward the water lapping at the shore. She tried to pull away, kicking at him, but he held her fast and she slipped in the mud. He shoved her hard into the lake, holding her under the surface. If Ethan didn't act quickly, Metwater was going to drown her. He tried to aim his pistol at Metwater's back, but the Prophet's movements made it impossible to focus on the target.

Michelle had stopped fighting and lay still under the water. Enraged, Ethan grabbed up a piece of driftwood and charged toward Metwater, swinging the stick like a club. He struck Metwater on the side of the head, driving him away from Michelle. Ethan lunged into the water, groping for her hand. He found it and dragged her up, hauling her to shore just as Metwater leaped on him.

Ethan struggled to his feet and drew his weapon. "No!" Metwater roared and struck his arm hard, jolting the pistol loose. It landed in the lake with a splash and

Metwater grabbed Ethan's shoulders, trying to force him down into the water. The two men grappled, slipping in the mud and gravel.

"Run!" Ethan screamed at Michelle. She was on the shore on all fours, coughing violently.

Metwater was on top of Ethan now, one hand around Ethan's throat, choking him, the other grappling for his gun at his hip. Ethan fought for breath, struggling to remain conscious, to keep fighting long enough for Michelle to get away. Metwater had his own pistol out now, the barrel pressed against Ethan's forehead. He closed his eyes, waiting for the end.

Then Metwater's grasp on him loosened, and the Prophet groaned and staggered to his feet. Ethan struggled to rise also as Metwater turned toward Michelle, who stood a short distance away, the stick of driftwood in her hand. Metwater lunged toward her, and Ethan leaped on his back, his arm around the Prophet's throat, choking him. "Run!" he shouted at Michelle again, and this time she listened, taking off into the brush alongside the lakeshore.

Ethan tightened his grip on Metwater, squeezing hard, until the other man stopped fighting. He loosened his hold, intending to put Metwater in cuffs, but before he could reach his utility belt, Metwater turned on him once more. Face contorted by rage, he shoved Ethan away from him.

Ethan staggered back, struggling to keep his footing. Metwater scooped up his pistol and aimed it at Ethan, who only had time to dive behind a currant bush before the bullet thudded into the dirt to his right. He scrambled backward, seeking better cover, but Metwater relentlessly pursued. With no weapon and little cover, Ethan's only chance was to outrun the Prophet, and pray that the bullets that rained after him didn't find their target.

He ran hard, feet sending up sprays of gravel, zigzagging among the brush and driftwood that crowded this part of the lakeshore. Metwater stopped firing, though Ethan thought he heard the Prophet pounding along the shore after him.

"Ethan, here!"

He looked to the side and spotted Michelle standing at the edge of the water, beckoning him. As he drew closer, he saw that she held on to the bow of a battered green kayak. "He can't get to us if we're out on the water," she said, shoving a paddle into his hand and preparing to climb into the boat.

"There's a storm coming up," Ethan said, looking up at the angry clouds barely visible against the blackening sky.

"There's nowhere else to go," she said, already in the boat. "Nowhere to hide, no way to get away from him. I promise you, he won't give up. At least this way we have a chance."

They would have a chance if they could get back to his cruiser, but to do that they would have to negotiate a steep bluff in the dark, with Metwater in pursuit. Still, Ethan didn't like their chances on the water. He was about to tell Michelle as much when a bullet clipped the rock to his right, sending chips of granite flying. He glanced back over his shoulder and saw Metwater closing in.

"Hurry!" Michelle pleaded.

He stepped into the boat and pushed off with the paddle. He could feel her paddling also, and together they pulled away from shore. In the gathering dusk, he could make out a point of land to their left, and headed around this, hoping to get out of sight of Metwater as quickly as possible. Once Ethan was sure they were safe, they could beach the kayak and make their way back up to the road and, eventually, to his cruiser and safety.

Metwater shouted from the shore, his words swallowed up by the rising wind and the slap of waves against the kayak's fiberglass hull. A dozen more strokes with the paddles and Ethan couldn't hear him at all—or see the shore, or much of anything else, but dark sky against dark water. The sensation was eerie and disorienting. He kept paddling, afraid if they stopped the wind would blow them back to Metwater, but he stared into the darkness, trying to make out some landmark to steer by.

"I don't hear him anymore," Michelle said.

"No. But like you said—he doesn't give up. He's still out there."

As if to prove him right, light glowed from shore— the headlights of the car, twin spots shooting across the water. But the kayak was beyond the reach of the light. "What are we going to do now?" she asked.

"We have to get farther down the shore," Ethan said. "If we get around this point of land, we should be able to come into shore again. He'll probably still be looking for us, but he won't know where we are."

"Then I guess we'd better get paddling."

Chapter Sixteen

They paddled, but the wind was picking up and though Ethan couldn't see anything in the darkness, it didn't feel to him as if they were making much progress. Lightning streaked across the sky, revealing the rocky shoreline several hundred yards away—the storm had blown them even farther than he had thought. Thunder crashed, and rain began to lash them, icy needles stinging bare skin.

"It doesn't feel like we're getting anywhere!" Michelle shouted above the roar of the storm.

"Keep paddling!" he shouted. 'We've got to get to shore." Waves slapped against the fiberglass hull, buffeting them, making the boat more and more difficult to control. Rain continued to pound down, cold water puddling around his feet in the open boat.

The boat turned sideways and waves threatened to swamp them. Water streaming into his eyes, Ethan fought to turn the boat into the gale. The boat rose, bow out of the water altogether, and then they were falling, tossed up and over, falling through the darkness into the icy, churning water.

Michelle fought her way to the surface, sputtering and thrashing as yet another cold wave engulfed her. "Ethan!" she shouted, water streaming down her face and into her eyes. She struggled to stay afloat, looking wildly around her.

"Over here!"

She spun around and saw Ethan waving to her from where he clung to the kayak, which was upright once more. She swam to him and joined him in clinging to the boat. Neither spoke for a long moment as the waves tossed them about. Chill seeped into her, and her teeth began to chatter. "We should get back in the boat," she said.

"It's too full of water."

She dipped her hand down into the boat and realized he was right—the body of the kayak was almost filled with water. She wanted to scream in frustration. After everything she had been through, she wasn't going to die of exposure here in the middle of a lake. "What are we going to do?" she asked as lightning flashed. For a fraction of a second, she caught sight of Ethan's face, pale but determined, across from her.

"Can you get on my side of the boat and kick?" he shouted above the storm. "I thought I saw land up ahead."

Carefully, she maneuvered around the boat, terrified that if she let go the waves would sweep her away. After agonizing minutes she positioned herself next to him. "Kick hard!" he shouted, and she put her head down and kicked.

They had been at it long enough for her legs to begin

aching. Her fingers were cramped from clinging to the kayak. She was about to tell Ethan it was hopeless when her foot struck something. Then her other foot touched bottom. Ethan was already standing and reaching for her. They clung to each other, staggering out of the water, pushing the waterlogged kayak in front of them.

When they were all the way out of the water, Michelle sank to her knees, struggling to breathe, trying to ignore the shivers that rocked her. Ethan tugged at her arm. "Come on," he said. "We have to find shelter and a way to keep warm."

She didn't see how they were going to find any of that in the darkness, but just then he switched on a flashlight. The beam sent a thin disk of light across the landscape, showing driftwood and scrub brush and the kind of debris that often washed up at lakes—fishing lures and water bottles and beer cans. "I guess this thing really is waterproof," Ethan said as he helped her to her feet. He played the beam over the area around them, then pointed inland. "Let's get into those trees. Maybe we can make some kind of shelter."

Make it out of what? she wanted to ask, but since the alternative was standing here in a downpour by herself, she followed him.

A few yards inland they found more trash—some boards and what looked like an old tarp. Ethan spread out the boards over the wet ground, then shook out the tarp and draped it over them. She told herself not to think what might be on that tarp. It was raining so hard the worst of the grime would have been washed off, right?

Ethan wrapped one arm around her and pulled her close. "When the rain lets up a little, I'll try to start a fire," he said.

"Let me guess," she said. "You were a Boy Scout."

"An Eagle Scout," he said.

"Of course." She rested her head on his shoulder and closed her eyes. "I don't care what you were—you saved me. Metwater was going to kill me. And then I thought he was going to kill you." Her voice broke on the last words. The thought that he could have died while trying to rescue her shook her.

"I wasn't going to let him kill you." He rubbed her shoulder. "Hunter is waiting to see you."

She was so numb it took a moment for his words to sink in. She stared at him, even though she could only see the dim outline of his face in the darkness. "Do you really have him? Is he all right?"

"He's fine. We took him to the hospital as a precaution, but he's fine."

"Where? What happened? Who?"

He chuckled. "Hold on and I'll tell you the whole story. It was just like you suspected—Metwater was behind it all." She listened, stunned, as he told about the Smith brothers and the little motel where they attempted to hold Hunter hostage. He described the rescue in the briefest terms, but even so it sounded incredibly brave and daring to her. "I can't believe you found him." She threw her arms around him and kissed his cheek. "I can't ever thank you enough."

"You don't have to thank me." He snuggled her close again. "I'm glad we were able to find him."

"And now here we are, stuck who knows where."

"In the morning we'll be able to figure out where we are and go for help," he said. "Hunter is safe until then."

"Except that Daniel Metwater is still out there," she said. "When he finds out you have the Smith brothers, and I've escaped, he'll be furious."

"He won't get past the hospital staff and the deputies who are guarding Hunter," Ethan said. "And we've alerted all the local law enforcement agencies to be on the lookout for him. He won't be able to go far."

"He has a lot of money and a lot of friends," she said. "He can do a lot more than you think he can."

"How did he get hold of you?" Ethan asked. "What happened?"

"He came to the house. He said he followed me from Ranger Headquarters the day before. I guess he had been watching, waiting to catch me alone. Anyway, he was furious. He hit me and I guess I passed out. When I woke up in the car, he started talking about drowning—about what it did to a body, and how he had to identify his brother based on a tattoo." She shuddered, remembering the horror of his words. "I was terrified I was going to die."

"Why was he angry with you?"

"He said I knew too much and could get him in trouble. I tried to tell him I was only interested in proving that his brother had murdered Cass, but he said David *hadn't* murdered her—that he hadn't done any of the bad things people thought he had. He said that was one thing David and Cass had in common. It didn't make sense, really."

"What do you know that could get him in trouble?" Ethan asked.

"I can't think of anything. All I have are those news articles I printed off the internet. Everything in them is public knowledge."

"If David Metwater isn't guilty of the crimes people think he committed, maybe it's because Daniel Metwater did them," Ethan said.

"But that can't be right," she said. "Daniel was always the good brother. He ran the family business. He bailed David out of jail. He sat on charitable boards. The articles in the scrapbook were full of stuff like that. He couldn't have faked *all* of that."

"He's managed to fake an identity as a peace-loving prophet who is only interested in spiritual matters," Ethan said.

"When I first came to live with him and his followers, I thought that was true," she said. "I never believed that he could predict the future, or that he had all the answers, the way Asteria and some of the others believe, but when he talked about how his brother's death had led him to seek answers in a simpler life, I thought he was telling the truth. And I saw how he had made a difference in people's lives. There are members of the Family who are former drug addicts or cons, and they turned their lives around because of Daniel Metwater. I thought if he did that much good, how could he be bad? I guess I was as naive as everyone else."

"You weren't naive," Ethan said. "He's an expert at deceiving others, which tells me it's a talent he's been honing for a long time. When he's back in custody, I think it will be worth digging deeper into his past activities."

"If you can find him," she said.

"We'll find him," Ethan said. "He's arrogant and thinks he's above the law—that will work in our favor." He lifted the tarp a little. "The rain has stopped. I'll see about starting that fire now."

He left and she felt bereft—colder both physically and emotionally. When they were back in the real world—when Hunter was safely with her again and it was time for her to move on to whatever the next phase of her life might be—how would she find the strength to say goodbye to this man who had come to mean so much to her?

Ethan had been kind to her—maybe he even had some feelings for her. But he had a full life already—he had an important job and friends and family—all the things she had never had. She didn't even know how she would fit into that kind of world.

ETHAN MANAGED TO find enough dry wood and tinder to get a good blaze going. He settled next to Michelle in front of it, and extended his hands to warm them. "That should help dry us off and thaw us out," he said.

"I'm impressed." She held her own hands out to the flames. "You really were a good Eagle Scout."

"Don't be too impressed." He pulled a lighter from his pocket. "I had this."

"Ethan Reynolds, don't tell me you're a secret smoker."

"Nope." He pocketed the lighter once more. "It's part of the emergency kit we all carry—first-aid kit, whistle, pocketknife, et cetera." He patted a pouch on his belt. "First time I've ever had to use it, though."

"You're still a good Eagle Scout," she said. "Isn't their motto 'be prepared'?"

"If I was that good, I'd have some emergency food stashed somewhere," he said. As if in agreement, his stomach growled.

"Food would be nice, but we won't starve before morning," she said.

"You're right." He patted her shoulder. "Why don't we lie down and try to get some rest?"

"I'm too keyed up to sleep," she said. "I've been worried about Hunter for so long—knowing he's safe I feel so much lighter—nothing else that has happened to me matters now that I know my baby is safe and I'm going to see him again."

"I'll admit I'm keyed up, too." He studied the inky sky—clouds still covered the stars. "As soon as it's daylight we need to get out of here, and we need to start searching for Metwater and bring him in."

"I don't want to think about Metwater anymore tonight," she said. "I don't even want to think about tomorrow." She slipped her arms around his waist and cuddled against him. "Now that I'm dry and getting warmer, I think we should take advantage of this time alone."

He caressed her shoulder, enjoying the feel of her soft curves against him. "Oh, yeah? What did you have in mind?"

"This." She pulled his face to his and kissed him, the crush of her warm mouth to his banishing the last chill from his body. He gathered her to him, lying back and pulling her down with him so that her soft breasts pressed against his chest, her body heavy against his arousal. She opened her mouth to deepen the kiss and he plunged his tongue into her, tasting warm sweetness. Forget food, this was what he needed right now— to taste and devour her, to quench the hunger that had been building in him ever since he spent that first night in her bed. He didn't believe he would ever get tired of making love to Michelle.

He caressed her bottom, then slid his hands up her back and around to cup her breasts. She arched against him and growled out a sound of pleasure. Fighting his own impatience, he pulled off her shirt, then made quick work of her bra. His lips closed around one taut nipple and her low moan pierced him, desire hot and urgent.

He shifted to focus on her other breast, but she slid down, out of his reach, and looked down into his eyes, firelight playing across the side of her face. "Officer, we need to get you out of this uniform," she said.

"I've heard some women find the uniform sexy," he teased.

"I prefer you naked." She started unbuttoning his shirt. "I want to feel skin against my skin, not some pointy badge."

His badge didn't have any points, but he got the message. And skin-to-skin contact sounded good to him, too.

It took a few moments for both of them to peel out of their still-damp clothing. He spread the clothes over the tarp to form a makeshift bed; then they lay down side by side, stroking and caressing, exchanging long, drugging kisses, letting the need build again. He threaded his fingers through the riot of curls around her face. "You have the most amazing hair," he said.

She laughed. "This mess? I thought men were into long blond tendrils or raven tresses or silky red hair. My hair is plain old brown, and there's no style to it—it just grows and kinks."

"I like it," he said. "It's a little wild—like you."

"Oh, you like wild, do you?"

"I do."

"I can show you wild." She moved over him, hands on either side of his head, straddling his torso. When she took him inside her, he let out a low groan, and when she began to move in a slow, sensual dance, he lost focus. She took his hand, and guided it down between them. He licked his thumb, then began to stroke, feeling her tighten around him. He felt very close to the edge, and tried to pull back, but she increased the tempo of her thrusts, driving them both up and over. She came with a loud cry, bucking hard, taking him deep inside her. His own release overwhelmed him, and he clung to her, riding the wave until he was utterly spent.

She pressed her forehead to his, and he felt more than saw her smile. "Wild enough for you?" she whispered.

His answer was a kiss, one he didn't break as she eased off him and moved to his side once more. He broke the contact and looked down into her eyes. "You're amazing," he whispered.

She closed her eyes. "Yeah. Amazing."

He wanted to tell her he loved her, but caution held

him back. He didn't want her to freak out or push him away. She hadn't had much love in her life, as far as he could tell. And too many people who were supposed to love her hadn't followed through on that love. Words weren't going to be enough for her.

She had her baby and a new life to get back to. He couldn't see her sticking around for a cop, of all people. He was the kind of man who liked to look after people—maybe too much, his mother might say.

She was a woman who valued her independence, who sometimes chafed under his overprotectiveness.

She fell asleep in his arms. He watched the firelight play across her face. She looked younger in repose, the tension around her eyes and jaw relaxed. He wanted to take away all the reasons for that tension, to show her that she didn't have to bear all her burdens alone. But after being on her own for so long, did she even have it in her to trust? She was like the feral cats his mother fed. She could care for them, but they would never come inside and live with her. They would never make her world theirs, or allow her to be more than a peripheral part of their lives.

MICHELLE WOKE TO bright sun in her eyes and a soft breeze across her bare skin. She blinked, then sat up, hastily pulling up the shirt she had apparently been using as a makeshift cover. In daylight, their camp looked even more pitiful than she had imagined it last night—a dirty blue tarp and some pieces of plywood beside a campfire of driftwood.

A rustling to her right set her heart to thudding and

she searched in vain for someplace to hide. What if Metwater had found them? What if he had already hurt Ethan and was coming for her?

Then Ethan stepped from the underbrush—barechested and barefoot, uncombed hair and a day's stubble transforming him into sexy backwoodsman. She hugged her knees to her chest and grinned at him. If it wasn't for Hunter and her growling stomach, she wouldn't have minded spending another day or two camped out with this hot cop. But she needed to keep playing it cool. She couldn't let him see how much he had come to mean to her. She didn't do needy.

"I don't suppose you found any coffee back in there?" she asked.

"Nope." He crouched beside the remains of last night's campfire. "But I think I've figured out where we are."

"Oh?" She pulled the shirt around and started to put it on, then realized it was his.

"I would say keep it—it looks better on you," he said. "But I might need it." He handed her her shirt and, aware of him watching, she began to dress.

"Where are we?" she asked as she hooked her bra.

"We're on an island in the lake, maybe half a mile from shore."

Her heart sank. "No way can I swim half a mile," she said.

"We still have the kayak," he said. "In daylight, with calm water, we shouldn't have any trouble getting to shore. From there we can walk to a store or a marina with a phone."

She shuddered at the memory of the terrifying last moments in that kayak, but nodded. She had done plenty of things in her life that had frightened or repelled her—she ought to be good at it by now.

"As soon as you dress we can leave," he said. "I'm hoping we end up near someplace with coffee. And food."

She stood and shoved her feet into her still-damp tennis shoes. "Just give me a minute to, um, freshen up in the woods," she said.

"Oh, sure. I'll finish dressing myself and get the boat ready."

She slipped into the underbrush, searching for a spot that was well out of sight. When she was finished, she ran fingers through her hair and smiled as she remembered what Ethan had said last night. All her life she had envied women with more manageable hair, but maybe hers wasn't so bad after all.

"Police! Keep your hands where we can see them!"

Fear replaced contentment as the man's voice, sharp and commanding, cut the peace of the morning. Scarcely daring to breathe, Michelle tiptoed to the edge of the woods and peered out.

Ethan, still shirtless and barefoot, hands in the air, faced two uniformed men with guns drawn. The men were very young, and she didn't recognize the uniforms. They also looked nervous, which made the weapons in their hands look that much more dangerous.

"He's got a gun," one of the men said, a blond. He nudged something with his foot, which she realized must have been Ethan's gun belt, which was lying on the tarp with the rest of his clothes.

"My ID is in my back pocket," Ethan said. "I can show you—"

"Don't move!" the blond ordered. He bent and scooped up the gun belt. "You need to come with us," he said. "And don't try to make trouble."

Chapter Seventeen

The two Forest Service employees were young and nervous, Ethan thought. A dangerous combination. Better to cooperate with them now—and enjoy their embarrassment later when they realized what a mistake they had made. He kept his hands up and his eyes focused on them, and prayed that Michelle would stay hidden.

"What do you think you're doing? For goodness' sake, he's a cop."

Of course Michelle wouldn't stay hidden, any more than she would have backed down if someone tried to intimidate her. Wasn't that one of the things he loved about her? But as the two men focused their attention on her, Ethan couldn't help wishing she was a little more subdued.

She stood at the edge of the clearing, hands on her hips, hair a wild nimbus around her face. "He's part of the Ranger Brigade and he saved my life, so you need to put those guns away," she said, reminding him of a mother scolding a pair of little boys with water pistols instead of real weapons.

The Forest Service badges looked back at Ethan. "Is she telling the truth?" the dark-haired one asked.

"Yes. If you'll let me get out my ID, I'll prove it," Ethan said.

"All right," the blond said. "But do it slowly. No sudden moves."

"Of course." He carefully reached back and took out his wallet and flipped it open to his badge and ID.

Both men leaned forward to scrutinize it, and a red flush worked its way up the blond's neck. He holstered his weapon. "Sorry," he said. "We didn't realize you were a fed."

"We got a message to be on the lookout for a dangerous escaped felon," the dark-haired young man said as he, too, put away his gun. "They said he might have killed a cop and be hiding out in the area. When we saw you out here by yourself—where no one is supposed to be—we thought you were him."

"He killed a cop?" Ethan asked. Was this Metwater they were talking about, or someone else? "What cop?"

The two exchanged looks. "An FBI agent, I think," the blond said. "And he may have murdered someone else. And he kidnapped a baby."

"We're talking a really bad dude," his partner said.

That sounded like Metwater, all right, Ethan thought. Though he hoped they were wrong about the cop part. The other FBI agent on the Ranger Brigade was the commander. He pushed aside the thought. He couldn't dwell on those worries. "I think we're looking for the same guy," he said. He picked up his shirt and put it on. "How did you guys get out here?"

"We have a boat." The blond motioned toward the water. "We're assigned to patrol this area. Mostly we ticket drunken boaters or folks who don't have life jackets. This is about the most exciting thing to happen since we've been working here."

"How long have you been working here?" Ethan asked as he slipped on his gun belt. Even though he had lost his gun in the fight with Metwater, the belt was part of his uniform.

The two exchanged glances and the blond went red again. "About two months," he mumbled.

Michelle joined them. "If you have a boat, you can get us out of here," she said.

"Uh, sure, we can take you." The blond looked around. "How did you get here anyway?"

"It's a long story." Ethan clapped him on the back. "And it involves that fugitive you're looking for. We'd be grateful if you could take us back to my vehicle."

"Sure." He turned to Michelle. "Ma'am, are you an officer, too?"

She laughed. "No. I'm an innocent bystander." Without a look back, she strolled past the three men, headed toward shore. Ethan grinned and followed.

Thirty minutes later the Forest Service Rangers—Clint and Joe—delivered them to Ethan's cruiser—which was cordoned off with crime scene tape and surrounded by Rangers. Marco Cruz looked up from taking measurements and grinned. "I'll bet you've got a heck of a story to tell," he said, coming over and clapping Ethan on the back.

Lance joined them. "We saw the blood and the signs of struggle and feared the worst," he said.

That explained the story the Forest Service Rangers had given him about a dead FBI guy, Ethan thought.

"Daniel Metwater was trying to drown me, and Ethan saved me," Michelle said. "We got away, but we ended up spending the night on an island in the lake. Then these two gentlemen found us this morning." She introduced the two officers, diplomatically omitting the fact that they had mistaken Ethan for a fugitive.

"It's a long story," Ethan said. "You can read my report later, but what I want to know now is have you found Metwater?"

"No," Marco said. "We've been watching the camp, but he hasn't shown up."

"His name and face and a description of the car are all over the area," Lance said. "We'll find him."

"We will," Ethan said. "He hasn't got the ego to lie low for long."

"I don't care about Metwater right now," Michelle said. "I need to see my son. Where is Hunter?"

"I'll take you to the hospital to see him," Ethan said.

"He's doing fine," Lance said, correctly interpreting her worried look. "The hospital was a safe place to keep him until the two of you could be reunited."

Since Ethan's cruiser was covered in fingerprint dust, he borrowed Marco's. As they headed toward Montrose, Michelle fidgeted, unable to sit still. "Tell me the truth," she said. "Is Hunter really all right? Those men didn't hurt him, did they? If they did—"

"As far as we can tell, they took good care of him,"

Ethan said. "And he's too young to remember anything. He'll be fine."

He parked in the visitors' lot at the hospital and led her in the front entrance and up to the pediatric floor. He was surprised to see his mom, in pink scrubs and white clogs, cuddling a baby to her shoulder. Even more surprising was her hair, which was cut fashionably short and streaked with blond.

"Hunter!" At the sound of Michelle's voice, the baby lifted his head and began to flail his arms. Ethan's mother turned, and when she saw Ethan and Michelle, a smile bloomed on her face.

"He definitely knows his mama," she said, walking toward them.

"Michelle, you remember my mom, Nancy," Ethan said.

But Michelle scarcely acknowledged either of them. She was pulling Hunter into her arms, covering his head with kisses and making little cooing noises. "Oh, my sweet baby," she murmured, closing her eyes and rocking Hunter against her.

Nancy touched Ethan's arm. "Let's give them a moment alone," she said.

He followed her out into the hall. "Mom, what did you do to your hair?" he asked, unable to stop staring at her.

She put one hand to her head. "Do you like it?" she asked. "I always wanted to try really short hair, but your father would have fussed so. He never wanted me to change anything."

"You look good," he said. "You look happy."

She looked wistful. "I still miss your father terribly, but I'm figuring out how to build a new life on my own. It won't be the same life, but I want it to be a good one."

"You deserve that, Mom."

"I understand you've been busy with other things," she said. "But have you found out anything about my car?"

"We've got a lead on the people responsible for the thefts," he said. "But it's unlikely you'll see your car again. These groups work very fast to get rid of the evidence."

"The officer in Montrose told me the same thing." She sighed. "I talked to my insurance agent and he tells me as soon as they have the police report, he can process the paperwork to cut me a check for the value of the car." She made a face. "Not as much as I paid for it, of course. I can almost hear your father, reminding me how much a new car depreciates."

"You can buy another car," Ethan said.

"Yes, but this time I'll find a nice used one. Maybe that won't be so attractive to thieves."

"Used cars get stolen, too," Ethan said. "Buy a new car if that's what you want."

"Whatever I decide, maybe you'd like to help me pick it out."

Ethan put his hand on her shoulder. "It's your car, Mom. You should pick it out."

She smiled, clearly pleased. "You don't have to worry about me, son." She turned and looked through the glass as Michelle cradled her son, who smiled up at her, waving his hands.

"Look how happy he is to see her," Nancy said. "I would have been beside myself with worry if something like that had happened to you when you were a baby."

"It's good to be part of a happy ending," Ethan said. "In my job things don't always work out that way."

He studied Michelle, thinking she had never looked more beautiful than she did now, the lines of tension having vanished from her face, a broad smile softening her face, making her look younger and more open. "For a real happy ending, you have to finish the job," his mom said.

He pulled his gaze away from the mother and baby. "What do you mean?"

Nancy nodded to Michelle. "Have you told her that you love her?"

He didn't ask how his mother knew his feelings. She had always been able to read him; maybe that was something all mothers did. "I don't want to scare her off," he said.

"And you think saying nothing is the way to encourage her to stick around?"

He shoved his hands in his pockets. "She's been through a lot, Mom. I don't want to rush her."

His mom shook her head. "You are so like your father."

"What do you mean?"

"Did you know he never proposed to me? I had to ask him."

"I never knew that." He didn't know much about his parents' courtship. He had never given it much thought.

"Don't pass up a chance for happiness," she said.

"Your problem is that you worry too much about other people—about me, about Michelle, even. Think of yourself for once. Tell her how you feel."

"Yeah, I should do that."

Nancy put on her best mom-lecture face. "If you can face down armed men who want to kill you, you ought to be able to speak honestly with the woman you love," she said.

"You'd think." But sometimes talking about his feelings—especially when so much was on the line—felt a lot riskier than facing a madman with a gun.

MICHELLE COULDN'T GET enough of holding Hunter, or breathing in his scent, or taking in his smile, feeling his little fingers wrap around hers, or seeing the love in his eyes when he looked at her. She felt whole again. Strong again.

Footsteps on the tile hospital floors made her turn to see Ethan walking toward her. "Thank you again," she said. "For everything."

He didn't return her smile—in fact, his expression was serious. "You know this isn't over yet," he said. "Not until we've found Daniel Metwater and put him behind bars."

"Will you put him behind bars when you find him?" she asked.

"We have plenty of evidence to hold him now—his attempt on your life and mine, his link to the kidnappers. I think we can even connect him to the auto thefts in the area, through the Smith brothers. And while we're building our case against him, we'll keep looking for your sister's locket and any other ties we can find between Daniel and David's crimes. He won't get out this time. But until we have him, he's still a danger to you and Hunter."

"I know." She looked down again at the child in her arms. "We'll have to be on our guard, but I think he's running now. I think—or at least I hope—he won't waste time coming after me again."

"You'll need protection until we find him," Ethan said.

She gave him a sideways look, unsure how to interpret the words. "You mentioned something about a safe house."

"I was thinking of something a little different." His expression wasn't flirtatious or teasing. In fact, it was almost grim.

"Is something wrong?" she asked.

"You know I wasn't just doing this for you, or because it was my job," he said.

"What do you mean?"

"I'm as selfish as the next guy—I did this for myself. To stay close to you."

She eyed him warily, still not sure what that somber expression meant. Was he going to arrest her or something? "What are you saying?"

He looked away, then back at her. "I'm saying that I love you. And I don't want you to leave. I want you stay here with me."

Her heart leaped, but she struggled to maintain her composure. She couldn't get carried away. "Are you asking me to move in with you?"

"I'm asking you to marry me. Though I'll take moving in with me, if you want to try that first."

She shook her head.

She almost felt sorry for him, he looked so bereft.

"Are you saying no?"

"I'm saying no, I don't want to start with moving in." She took a deep breath. "And I'm saying yes, I will marry you." He was the best thing that had ever happened to her—well, except for Hunter—and she wasn't going to let him get away.

Now came the smile she had been waiting for. "Really?"

"Did you think I would turn you down?" she asked.

"I didn't know what to think. You're so independent—and I like that, I do. But I'm a cop and I know how you feel about cops…"

She silenced him with a kiss on the cheek. "You're not just any cop. You're the man who believed in me when no one else did—the man who made me see I'm strong enough to do anything—I'm even strong enough to give up a little of my independence to be with the man who means the world to me."

"I always thought I was good at taking care of people," he said. "You've helped me get better at letting them take care of themselves." He pulled her to him and kissed her, long and hard.

She laid her head on his shoulder. "I love you, Ethan Reynolds," she said.

"I love you, Michelle Munson." He stroked the cheek of the baby between them. "And I'll love Hunter, too. I want to be there for him the way my dad was for me."

"You'll be a great dad. And I think you'll make a pretty good husband, too."

"I figure if I mess up, you can keep me in line," he said.

"Hush and kiss me."

"Yes, ma'am."

* * * * *

LOVING BABY

TYLER ANNE SNELL

This book is for Holli Anne. I've been waiting for a heroine that I thought you'd be proud of, and I think Suzy is it! She's an awesome mom, an amazing person and is stronger than even she knows. Basically a rock-star human, like you! Thank you for being my beautiful, rule-breaking moth and also the best Anne out there. Love you to the moon and back, Perkins/Knope!

Prologue

"Well, this isn't good."

Suzanne Simmons looked down at the body with a growing sense of dread. It wasn't strong enough to scatter her thoughts or turn her stomach cold, but it did warrant a worried glance at Detective Matt Walker, standing next to her. His face was hard, his eyes sharp as they scanned the dead man at their feet. He crouched down.

"No, this isn't good at all," he agreed. "Not if that's Gardner Todd."

They lapsed into thoughtful silence as each did their own private inspection of the man without touching him. He was in his midthirties, white and dressed in work coveralls. His boots were new but dirty, with maybe a few weeks' use. He had a tattoo peeking out at his wrist, a silver ring on his right index finger and three bullets in his belly.

But if it *was* Gardner Todd, then his death was the least of their worries.

"I guess that, for once, our department of front porch justice got it right," Matt said after a moment. "Our caller *did* hear gunshots and not a car backfiring."

The detective was referring to the older woman named June who had called in to the Riker County Sheriff's De-

partment, swearing up and down she'd heard a gunfight
at the abandoned warehouse two blocks over from her
house. Both buildings were on the outskirts of Carpenter, Alabama, and that put the issue square in the sheriff's department's jurisdiction.

Though Suzy wouldn't normally be the one to answer
the call, and neither would Matt, they'd been only a street
over when it had come in. She might be the chief deputy now, but her sense of obligation to her county hadn't
changed with her promotion. Her soul was forever that
of the young deputy she'd been the first day on the job.
She took pride in every aspect of her work, even when
it was something small.

"Thank goodness for cordless phones, sweet tea and
an abundance of free time," Suzy said. "If she hadn't
been snooping on the neighborhood from her porch, we
might not have ever found him." She did another cursory
look around the old saw manufacturing warehouse. The
power had been off for years. Shadows dodged rays of
light that filtered in from the hole past the rafters, and the
few windows not broken or boarded up were coated in
dust, pollen and mildew. Like the rest of the large, open
room they were in. Suzy's sinuses pricked something
awful. She'd have to take an allergy pill when they got
back to her Tahoe. "I don't think this place gets visitors
on a regular basis."

"That may be true, but I don't think he was dumped
here *after* he was killed," Matt said, rising. He pointed
to the trail of blood that had first grabbed her attention
when they started searching the building. "For whatever
reason, he was here, and so was his killer."

Suzy eyed the two doors at the end of the main room.

The offices, most likely. They'd already passed the break room and bathroom up front.

"Let's finish going through the rest of this place before we dig any deeper into him," she said, pulling her gun back up. "If that *is* Gardner, then if all hell hasn't already broken loose, it will soon. We need to get out in front of this as fast as we can."

Matt agreed, and together they cleared the last two rooms before coming up to the back door. The lot the warehouse was on stretched wide but was empty. No people, no cars, just dirt, sun and a woman named June two blocks over, probably already gabbing to the whole town about what she'd heard. Which meant that whoever had killed the man inside had already left and had probably taken his car, too.

"I don't like this," Matt said at her side. "There's only two kinds of people who would kill Gardner."

"The brave and the idiots," she supplied.

He nodded.

"Either choice doesn't bode well for us. If you can kill the infamous Alabama Boogeyman, taking out a cop or two trying to solve his murder is easy pickings."

Suzy sighed. The beginnings of a headache started to throb, pressure wrapping around her right eye. It was going to be a long afternoon and night, she knew. Which meant that allergy pill needed to come sooner rather than later.

"I'm going to go pop some sinus meds and call Billy directly," she said after a moment of deliberation. "Go ahead and take some pictures of the body with your phone. While everyone knows I'm a fan of our *wonderful* Crime Scene Unit, we all know they can have lead in their feet. I'd rather have something we can refer to while we wait on them to process everything."

"You got it, boss."

Matt went back into the warehouse while Suzy went around it. Her head might have been focused and calm, but her gut muttered a warning. One she didn't listen to as she moved along the small strip of dead grass between the building and the side parking lot. Something felt off, but she wasn't sure what that something was.

Until she saw him.

A man wearing a jacket, despite the heat, hurried around the corner of the warehouse.

Between breaths, Suzy barely had time to register two things. She didn't recognize him.

And he had a gun.

Suzy reacted on instinct, pulling her service weapon up and yelling all at once.

"Drop it right now!"

The man was just as fast. His gun rose up in tandem, like they had planned the routine. It was the only reason Suzy didn't shoot right away.

She wasn't sure who had the upper hand.

"Whoa there, buddy," she said, hurrying over. "Sheriff's Department."

The man—thirties, dark hair, and thin-framed glasses—hesitated. Again, just like her, he didn't put down his gun. However, unlike her, he wasn't able to justify why he had one aimed at her in the first place. She was law enforcement. Who was he?

"Put your gun down!" Suzy yelled, voice a mix between grit and calm. She didn't want to agitate the man if she could help it. She'd prefer to talk him down if possible. The fact that she wasn't wearing a bulletproof vest was also a fact she was all too aware of. If she'd had the time, she would have cursed herself for leaving Matt before backup arrived.

But she didn't have the time. All thoughts were focused on the detective only a building away from her.

The man pulled his trigger before Suzy's brain could send the instruction to her finger to do the same.

The *bang* filled the afternoon air like it was a Fourth of July firecracker.

Suzy felt the weight of the world slam into her chest.

Then she was staring up at the sky.

Blue and white, and a little gray.

It was going to storm later. She hoped Justin didn't miss the bus. His mimi wouldn't be able to pick him up. Their car was still in the shop.

Another firecracker went off. Suzy tried to move to find the sound, but her body wasn't listening.

"Officer down!"

A face swam into view. It didn't belong to Matt. It didn't belong to the man who'd shot her, either.

"You're going to be fine," he said. His voice was so smooth Suzy closed her eyes to savor it. "Hey, you stay with me, okay?"

But even though Suzy wanted to, she couldn't follow the command.

Her last thoughts before diving into the unknown were about her son, the rain and the stranger with a voice like warm velvet.

Chapter One

James Callahan thrust his hands deep into his pockets and braced against the cold. It was ninety-two degrees outside but only thirty-eight in the freezer. When he'd set up a time to meet a man named Sully the Butcher, James hadn't thought the place would be in a meat locker at the back of a restaurant downtown. It was a little too clichéd for his tastes. But he was nothing if not flexible.

"You wait here, old man. Or should I say, Padre. I'll go get 'em."

The young man—and that was being generous—was standing so close that the heavy scent of cheap aftershave invaded James's senses. Not in a good way. Whoever this kid was, James bet his dad would be coming home that night to a nearly empty bottle of the stuff. Assuming he had a dad who was around. Usually people who nicknamed themselves Queso and worked for a man called Butcher didn't have a normal home situation.

"I can see now why you have to make a reservation for this place," James quipped. He tilted his head to the hunk of meat hanging off a hook right behind them. "It's pretty crowded in here."

James busted out a wide grin at his own joke, but Queso wasn't amused. His exit was accompanied by an eye roll. The man guarding the door—with no nicknames that James knew of—kept his post without moving a muscle. Not that he needed to. Those muscles were thick and tattooed until there was more ink than bare skin. He didn't need a nickname. His purpose was to intimidate without saying a word.

James bet he was great at that. Sully might not be world famous, but he did a good job of keeping his name in the minds of the criminal underworld throughout the state. His network wasn't as big as that of the locals running the city of Kipsy a half hour away, but he didn't let that stop him from dipping his toes into the rest of the county's affairs. Still, regardless of Sully's lack of infamy, if anybody found themselves in his freezer with muscle guarding the door, they had every right to worry.

But while James wasn't a criminal, he wasn't exactly a nobody, either.

"Well, well, if it isn't the golden savior himself." On cue, a small-statured man walked in and spread his arms wide. James was surprised for several reasons. One, the man was wearing a pink-collared shirt, khaki shorts and golf shoes. Two, he looked closer to James's age of thirty-two than the old, weathered man he had been expecting. "Can't say I ever thought we'd meet like this, but who am I to question fate?"

He extended his hand, and James shook it.

"I have to admit, I thought you'd make me wait a lot longer in here," he said by way of greeting. "Make me sweat it, so to speak."

Sully laughed the thought off.

"I'm not trying to get information out of you, Mr. Callahan. In fact, I hear it's the other way around. And *that* is what interests me. As for the freezer?" He shrugged.

"You know how the gossip wheel turns in this place? That doesn't stop just because we're not your average residents. If I don't keep up appearances, then that might send the wrong message to some of my associates. They might start questioning me. And I don't like questions."

"But you agreed to meet me."

Sully nodded. His hair, golden, thick and curly, was just another piece that didn't seem to fit the man or his reputation. Then again, James knew that images didn't always go hand in hand with reality.

"I don't like questions, but I do like mysteries," Sully informed him. "And it seems you walked into a big one."

"Gardner Todd's death."

Sully nodded, and his humor dropped a few pegs.

"What happened to him is…troubling," Sully admitted.

"That's a nice way to put it." James pulled a picture out of his pocket. "As is the man who presumably shot him."

Sully took the picture and was polite enough to examine it like he'd never seen the image of the dead man before. James bet there wasn't a cop or criminal who hadn't already seen it. It wasn't every day someone got the jump on the Alabama Boogeyman.

"You don't think he was the one who shot Gardner?" That surprised the man. "I thought the sheriff's department linked a gun he owned to the one that took out Todd."

"They did, and I do think he shot him," James conceded. "But what I don't get is why." He tapped the picture with his index finger twice. "This man's name is Lester McGibbon—"

"An unfortunate name," Sully interrupted to add.

"He lived in Atlanta and was suspected of corporate espionage but later cleared," he continued. "The man drove a Prius, had a soft spot for rescue dogs and took his son on fishing trips almost every weekend during the summer. He was white-collar crime through and through. So why did he come all the way to southern Alabama to kill the infamous Gardner Todd?"

James could feel his adrenaline spiking with every new thought. Even if he'd asked himself these same questions during many sleepless nights.

"So *that's* why you went looking for me," Sully said, a grin pulling up his lips. If they had been anywhere other than inside a freezer, James would have mistaken the man for some rich tourist, getting ready for a trip down to the beach a few hours away, perpetually retired and two seconds away from pulling out a margarita and donning a visor. "Because ole Lester was white-collar crime."

"It seems while everyone around here is still getting their hands dirty with armed robberies and drug deals, you've upgraded."

Sully's grin widened. Surprise mingled with pride lit his features, and his stomach rumbled with a laugh.

"Seems like the Bates Hill Savior is more well connected than I thought," he said. "And here I thought you only spent that fortune of yours on good deeds and photo shoots, not collecting rumors."

"They're not rumors if they're true," James pointed out.

Sully conceded to that with a shrug.

"I suppose not." The humor once again began to fizzle out. "Though I'd love to meet the people who provided my name and contact information to you. But I suppose you'll keep that to yourself."

James nodded. "You suppose correctly."

For a moment, James thought Sully would make it a point to find out the sources James had used to track the criminal. Sully might have taken his people off the streets and put them into offices, but that didn't undercut his abilities. Especially when he was trying to get something he wanted. You didn't get the nickname Butcher for no reason. However, he returned the picture to James and went back to the original topic.

"After the media released Lester's name, everyone in my line of work researched him. Not to mention, after he shot that woman cop, the entire county full of law enforcement tore through who he used to be. What makes you think I can answer questions all of those people couldn't? And why, for that matter, do you even care about what happened to Gardner Todd?"

James lowered his voice. Not to speak more quietly, but to convey what he said next was fact.

"Because I'd owe you one, and having a favor from James Callahan is gold in your particular line of work. The rest is none of your business."

A pregnant silence followed. It was just for show. James knew the moment the word "favor" had left his mouth that Sully was hooked. He was, at heart, a businessman first and foremost. He traded in deals and favors.

"That's quite the offer," he said after a moment. "No strings attached?"

James held up two fingers. "More like conditions," he said. "No one gets hurt or killed for this information."

Sully snorted. "You apparently haven't heard of my

persuasive charm. Who needs brutality when you can just smile and get what you want?"

James fought the urge to roll his eyes and continued. "And you call this number when you get anything." He pulled a piece of paper from his pocket and handed it over. "That's a private number. Only I should answer it. Which means you and/or any of your associates shouldn't feel the need to stop by the house. Sound good?"

He could tell Sully wasn't a man who was used to adhering to conditions he didn't set, but again, he was staring at the golden goose.

"Whatever you say, Mr. Callahan." The conversation was finished. They both knew neither one had any more to say. It was just theater when Sully motioned to the door. "I'll see what I can find."

Together they walked through the kitchen—past the staff and workers who didn't bat an eye—and to the back door that led into the employee parking lot. Queso stood next to the door, wearing slacks and a buttoned-up shirt that hung awkwardly off his thin frame. He zipped to attention as Sully neared, and James was reminded of being in boot camp back in the day. Respect and a little fear. The driving need to prove oneself.

James knew that need well.

"Take Mr. Callahan back to his car," Sully greeted him, then narrowed his eyes at the young man. "And make sure you go the speed limit this time. We're in small-town Alabama. Not street racing through the city trying to win a big score. The cops here won't have a hard time getting to you if you're blowing through the streets."

A look of quick shame followed by embarrassment crossed Queso's face. Sully cracked a grin. "Then again,

I'm sure James here could sweet-talk his way out of it. Last I heard, he was on particularly good terms with law enforcement in these parts. Especially the sheriff's department."

This time James didn't fight the urge. He rolled his eyes.

"I'd stick to the speed limit if I were you."

Because even though he'd killed Lester McGibbon before he'd had the chance to send another bullet into Riker County's chief deputy, James had spent the last four months learning the hard truth about Suzanne Simmons.

She didn't like him.

Not one bit.

"No, sir." Suzy looked the sheriff dead in the eye and shook her head again. "There's no way I'm doing it."

Billy Reed chuckled. Just like he often did when he thought Suzy was being unreasonable. He'd made the same sound when he'd suggested she liked Jonathan Flynn in the seventh grade and even had the same look when he'd tried to set her up with Rick Carmichael right out of college. There were many more examples throughout their nearly lifelong friendship, but those two came to mind. Or rather, how she'd felt about those two specifically. It was a feeling she associated with the name Billy was trying to attach her to now. She may have loved the sheriff like a brother, but that didn't mean she didn't think he'd lost his mind from time to time.

"I'm not asking you to date him," Billy pointed out, most likely knowing where her thoughts had gone. "I'm asking you to represent the Riker County Sheriff's Department at the town-hall social tonight."

"The social being held at the James Callahan estate," she interjected.

Billy chanced a look of mild exasperation.

"You know, he's not a bad guy. He single-handedly brought that town out of poverty. Not to mention he decided to make it his home. With all that money he could have his own island somewhere, but he chose Bates Hill, Alabama. That's got to count for something." Billy's brow drew in. The look didn't last long. "Though what he did for you is enough to say he's okay in my book for life. I don't understand why you're still so against him."

Suzy crossed her arms over her chest. She felt defiant. Protective. And she was trying to hide the scar between her breasts, even though her shirt was already covering it.

"I don't trust him for the same reasons you like him," she said simply. "His life trajectory doesn't make sense. A trust-fund kid, party animal, gives the tabloids enough material for years before disappearing. Then *bam!* He shows up to a smaller-than-small town to put it back on the map ten years ago with no reason other than he just wanted to do something good?" She shook her head. "Sounds like a movie I wouldn't even rent."

"Just because we don't know his life story doesn't mean you should write him off." Billy's face softened. "And just because Bates Hill and its residents are under our jurisdiction doesn't mean we need to know all of their secrets."

"True," she conceded. "But then, why was he out there that day, Billy? Why was James Callahan, of all people, at an abandoned saw manufacturing warehouse that just so happened to house the body of a murdered Gardner Todd?"

Billy's eyebrows knit together. No matter what he said next, Suzy knew he wasn't buying what he was selling. At least, not all the way.

"He was looking at real estate for one of his businesses. We even verified it with his attorney who showed up afterward. You already know that, and still you don't believe him."

It wasn't a question. Still, she responded to it.

"I believe that money can buy a lot of things," she said. "Including the loyalty of everyone around here. For all we know, his attorney spun the exact tale he wanted him to."

"So you think, what? James hired Lester McGibbon to kill Gardner and then shoot you?"

Suzy could tell that Billy didn't like being blunt about her being shot. It had been four months—four long months—and she still didn't like it, either. That bullet hadn't just hit her; it had very nearly killed her. Even now, she was still technically on leave from the department, unable to do field work for another month.

"No, I don't think he hired Lester," she admitted. "But I do think he's connected to Gardner. Somehow. And he's hiding it."

"Then what better reason than to go tonight? You can represent us *and* satisfy your curiosity."

Suzy tilted her head to see if she had heard him right. "You're saying you'd be okay with me asking him some questions?"

Billy nodded. "If you think there's something there, beyond the answers he's already given us all, then who am I to stop you?" He crossed his arms over his chest, his expression suddenly stern. "Just whatever prodding you do, please keep it *reasonable*."

Suzy couldn't help but smirk. "When have I ever been unreasonable?"

The sheriff was smart. He didn't answer.

QUESO WENT FIVE over the speed limit. James decided not to comment. Though the urge to get beneath the teen's skin almost won out.

Teen. That was what James really figured the dark-haired boy was. A teen who worked for an up-and-coming criminal organization that was tapping into white-collar crimes.

James wanted to give him a speech, to question his motives and push the boy to create different life goals, but then he remembered himself at that age and couldn't bring himself to deliver any lectures. What advice could he really give the boy that would ring true? He doubted repeating the speech James had gotten from his father all those years ago would light the fire that had moved him.

It had only been chance that, after his father had stopped yelling, the younger James had run into the bar where Corbin Griffin had been spending his last free night before taking off to San Antonio for basic training. The then twenty-year-old had shown James a way to prove himself outside of fame and fortune.

His joining the Air Force had surprised everyone; finding purpose and peace during his time with them had surprised him. Nine years after leaving, James still felt that swell of pride and gratitude for the time spent at his Special Operations job. Even when things had gotten hairy.

No, Queso needed his own Corbin Griffin. James doubted he would listen to him. Still, he wasn't going to say nothing. After the car rolled to a stop in the parking lot James's truck was in, he drew back and met the teen's stare.

"I don't know if Sully will get your help on what I'm looking for or not, but either way, it could be dangerous," he warned. "I suggest you stay away from it, but I'm sure that might only make you want to do it even more. Either way, if things get too hairy, you can reach me here." James pulled a card from his wallet. It had a different number on it than the one he'd given to Sully. "Or if you just want a different option altogether." He shrugged. "A few of my companies have scholarship programs that could use hardworking entrepreneurs. If that falls into your wheelhouse."

Queso cut a grin. "Haven't been called an entrepreneur before," he said. "Doubt a fancy title like that would even stick to someone like me. Don't you think?" Sarcasm. It blanketed his tone and posture. An invisible defense mechanism that James himself had used many times before in his youth. "Why don't you run along there, Padre, and leave your troubles to the boss?"

James got out of the car, hands up in defense. He left the card on the seat. Queso eyed it but didn't say anything. Maybe that was a good sign.

James finally got what he was hoping for. As he watched the little Miata take off down the road, thoughts of Suzanne Simmons were replaced by Gardner Todd.

And his killer.

If he could find out who wanted him dead, then maybe he could figure out Gardner's secret.

What did you want to tell me, brother?

Chapter Two

Suzy stood on the fringe of the crowd, pondering life.

Not in general, of course—she didn't have the patience for that one, or the right amount of caffeine in her, either—but on her own life. More important, the path that had led her, along with the Riker County Sheriff's Department, through the thickest of thicks and the thinnest of thins, all the way to standing on a rug that probably cost more than her two-bedroom rental.

It was a solid piece of decoration, almost as big as the foyer, and most likely heavy as the dickens. Without even attempting to lift the thing, Suzy could feel its weight in her muscles. While she struggled with biting the bullet and buying a rug from Target, James Callahan had probably imported the thing from Sweden or somewhere equally expensive.

It made her want to grind her teeth. And make sure to keep her heels off it, if possible. Her mother had taught her to respect others' property. Even if she didn't respect the people who owned it.

Suzy sighed. She probably did need to cut the man who had saved her some slack. Whether he lived in a mansion or a shack shouldn't matter. He'd killed the man who had tried to kill her and then kept her from bleeding out in the dirt. He had also visited her in the hospital more than a few times. And when he couldn't come, he'd sent flowers. But no matter how nice the man was, it was hard to reciprocate when you knew he was lying.

"If you keep making that face, it might get stuck like that."

Suzy turned to a woman she'd been hoping to see when tasked with attending the social.

"Well, if it isn't Mrs. Reed, fashionably late, of course."

Billy's wife, Mara, beamed but didn't deny the accusation. Instead, she pointed to her protruding belly.

"I blame this kid of mine," she replied. "He's been tap-dancing on my bladder all day. You're lucky Leigh got us here when she did. We had to stop as soon as we got into town for a bathroom break."

Leigh Cullen was Mara's business partner and friend; together they ran an interior-design firm in Carpenter. Over the last year it had really taken off. They were currently designing an office-complex opening in the heart of Bates Hill. While Suzy knew Mara wasn't a fan of fancy parties and schmoozing, she knew it was hard to pass up a chance to meet James Callahan in his own home. He might have been a millionaire, but he rarely opened his house to the public.

Now Suzy couldn't help but wonder why.

A hush fell over the crowd before she could voice the question. The man of the hour appeared at the bottom of the stairs. Mistrust aside, Suzy felt her focus snap to attention.

James Callahan was a man you immediately thought about taking to bed. At least, Suzy did. He was tall, broad shouldered and admittedly good-looking. He wore his black hair short, cropped above the ears with some height at the top. It made him look authoritative and crisp. The consummate businessman. Yet the most attractive thing about him, for Suzy at least, was the charm behind every smile. *That* was his weapon. And that was what he wielded against the audience.

"First of all, I want to thank each and every one of you for coming out," he began, crystal-blue eyes scanning the people closest to him. Town council members, the local police and fire chiefs, and the mayor. The "it" people of Bates Hill. "I know it's been a stressful year, so I'm glad that I was able to offer up some levity by way of a party. You all work very hard to make sure this town stays afloat, and for that, I say thank you. And, as a token of my appreciation, instead of boring you with a speech, how about this—" He scooped a champagne flute off a waitress's tray at the base of the stairs and held it up. "Please make sure you take advantage of the food, drinks and live music on the patio! And have fun!"

He cast that charming smile out to the crowd as a whole. Its effect spread quickly. Soon even Mara was grinning.

"I think that man could read the alphabet and people would cheer," she whispered. Suzy snorted but didn't look away. James's gaze swept over her and then stopped. Heat rose from her belly, but she tried her best to keep it from reaching her cheeks.

"Why don't we go check out that food?" Suzy suggested, breaking the stare.

She might have had questions for the man, but now that she was here, she needed time to collect her thoughts.

It didn't help that James Callahan looked damn good in a suit.

THE PARTY WAS going better than he'd expected. It was nearing ten at night, and most of the attendees were still there, the party in full swing. They rotated in and out of the house, splitting their time between dancing, drinking and mingling. Most did, at least. James noticed the chief deputy kept the same glass and company for most of the party. Only briefly did she step out to talk to the police and fire chiefs before they left.

James was surprised at how much of his attention Suzanne kept without even trying. Even when carrying on his own conversations, he felt hyperaware of her presence. Like she was a glowing blip on his radar. A sound he always heard. A woman he couldn't ignore.

It was surprising at best, distracting at worst.

The way her brow furrowed when she was having a particularly serious talk and the small smile she wore when he bet she was trying to be polite were details that filtered in seconds after he found her again in the crowd. She seemed most comfortable with the sheriff's wife and her friend. When talking to them, her body language changed to become more relaxed, more animated. She'd tuck her long dark hair behind her ear or widen her brown eyes before laughing. He knew those eyes were the color of honey in the right light.

He'd looked down into them when holding her bleeding body.

James had wanted to approach her the moment he saw her in the crowd, but given the cold shoulder she'd shown him for the last four months, he decided to keep his distance. She didn't trust him, that much he could tell.

And she had every right.

Because Gardner Todd wasn't just some thug gunned down as justice for his past deeds.

He was James's brother.

"Mr. Callahan."

James turned to one of his friends who ran security for his events. Douglas was several inches shorter and as bald as a worn tire. James had once seen him body slam a man much bigger than either of them like it was a breeze.

"I told you not to call me that," James said after excusing himself from the group he had been in. "Makes me feel old."

Douglas snorted. "Just wait until I tell you who just called me and what it was about." James already felt the sigh coming out of his mouth before Douglas could explain.

"Let me guess—it starts with Chelsea and ends with pain-in-my-backside."

Douglas laughed. "You got it, boss."

James rolled his eyes but didn't feel any real annoyance. He flipped his smartwatch around to see the date.

"Considering her bio lab test was last week, I'm assuming this call has something to do with the grade she got on it?"

But Douglas kept tight-lipped. "She wants you to call her back after the party," he said. "And told me I'm not allowed to tell you one way or the other."

James couldn't help but laugh. "I should worry how easily my sister wraps you around her finger, but then again, I'm there, too." He clapped Douglas on the shoulder. "I'll go call her now. I didn't help her study for that lab every weekend for the last month for nothing. Keep this party going in my absence. If anyone asks where I went, just tell them I'm in the wine cellar getting toasted."

It was Douglas's turn to laugh as James left the main

room and went to the small set of stairs in the kitchen. He bounded up them two at a time and headed toward his office. He pulled out his cell phone and was calling before he even reached the doorway.

SUZY WATCHED AS James was pulled from his conversation by a member of the security team. Whatever the situation was, it didn't appear to be serious, yet after they were done the man of the hour left the party. Curiosity filled her so quickly that before she had time to process what she was doing, Suzy had excused herself from Mara's side and followed the millionaire.

Billy's request that she question James within reason repeated in the back of her mind as she waited a few seconds before going up the stairs behind him. She walked slowly to keep her heels from making a sound until she was standing in the upstairs hallway. If James caught her now, she figured she could come up with a valid excuse for following him. Yet she found her feet stalling on the landing.

What exactly was she hoping to find?

Did she really expect the man to buckle beneath her questions, giving up answers that she had been looking for?

Suzy felt a swirl of adrenaline in her gut. Something she'd often experienced out in the field. A feeling she'd been missing for the last four months. For one small moment, she reveled in how it made her heart beat faster, her senses more alert and her mind more clear.

If James really *was* involved with what had happened to Gardner Todd, then that meant he was someone to exercise caution around. Add in his fortune and connections and being on his own home turf?

She was putting herself in a dangerous situation.

She was being careless.

Like not wearing her vest four months ago.

Suzy turned toward the window and stopped before going back down the stairs. The scar between her breasts heated up. She fisted her hands, remembering the look on her son's face when she'd woken up in the hospital. He'd just turned ten and was trying his hardest to prove to her that he was old enough to keep it together. He'd been trying to be strong. For her. For himself. It wasn't until she promised him it was okay to cry that he'd broken down on her lap.

The adrenaline spiked in her belly. Her nails bit into the palms of her hands.

Suzy never wanted to put him in that situation again. Not if she could help it. Not when she could avoid it.

She'd figure out what James was hiding, but not like this. Not creeping around in the shadows of his house. Not by putting herself in compromising positions.

No, she'd figure it out another way.

A *safer* way.

Suzy nodded to herself and fully intended on going back downstairs to the party, but movement outside the window caught her eye. The side lawn wasn't lit up like the back patio, but there was enough glow from the hanging lights that she could just make out someone moving toward the house. Slowly and not at all steadily.

Limping.

She sucked in a breath as the man moved closer. The light from the kitchen window caught him.

That was when she saw the blood.

He was covered in it.

The swirl of adrenaline in her stomach upgraded to a storm.

Chapter Three

Suzy hurried down the stairs, not minding this time that her high heels hit each step and sounded off like thunder crashing in the night sky. The chatter from the party in the center of the house kept going, uninterrupted. That meant no partygoer or security guard had spotted the bleeding man.

The cop in her rattled off four instantaneous questions in her head as she stepped toward the side door.

Who was the man?

What had happened to him?

Why had it happened to him?

Why was he at James Callahan's town social?

No answers came as she flew out into the night and straight toward the unknown. The lights from the backyard cast a glow across the small patio and garden, but were still too weak to show her any new clues to help answer any questions. The blood was there, dark against his face and arms, but she couldn't be sure *where* it had come from. His struggle to walk made her assume it was at least partly his.

"Whoa there, buddy," she said, trying for soothing tones while staying cautious. She went at him with one arm out, like a deputy trying to direct traffic, while the other hung back so her hand was never too far from the holster hidden against her thigh. If she needed to get to her gun fast, she could. However, it would be interesting for any bystanders, considering she'd probably have to rip the dress to get to it. A small price to pay for being prepared, but still, she hoped she wouldn't have to ruin it. Not only because she thought it was beautiful, but also because it was on loan from Mara.

The man's head moved enough that, even in the poor light, Suzy knew he was looking at her. Now she was close enough to guess that he wasn't a party guest *or* security. Instead of a suit, he wore jeans and a graphic T with some band's logo on it in neon orange. In fact, the more she tried to find the source of his bleeding, the more Suzy wondered if he was a man at all. He seemed too young.

"Inside," he groaned out, voice surprisingly strong. "I need to get inside."

He lurched forward. Suzy's reaction time since the accident had slowed, but she still managed to dance away from touching the blood on his arm. She latched on to his wrist instead.

"What's going on?" she tried. "I'm with the sheriff's department. I can help."

The man reacted like she'd stung him. Suzy felt his arm muscles coil a split second before he pulled out of her grip. The sudden momentum, plus the fact that she was unaccustomed to wearing heels, threw her off balance enough that she was forced to let go or fall.

"Get away from me," he hissed. "Where's Mr. Callahan?"

He turned back to the house, eyes wild, but that didn't mean she was done with him. Suzy took one step closer, pivoted enough to bring her back leg forward and kicked out at the man. The sound of fabric splitting was followed by a grunt as her foot connected with his stomach. She wasn't trying to hurt him, but she *was* trying to control him.

He toppled over and hit the ground. Suzy didn't wait for him to get his bearings. She flipped off her shoe and pressed her foot against his shoulder to keep him down.

"I'm Chief Deputy Simmons," she announced. "You *will* tell me what's going on and you will do so in a calm manner."

The man's eyes widened and flicked toward the house before coming back to her.

"I need to talk to Mr. Callahan," he said. "Right now!"

He bucked up against her foot, but Suzy wasn't having it. She applied enough pressure to keep him down.

"What you need is medical attention," she pointed out. "You're covered in blood."

The man twisted beneath her weight. "No, I don't," he managed around his squirming. "What I need—is to—talk to—Mr. Callahan."

Suzy's curiosity overrode her caution. She leaned over, careful not to press against him too hard, and fixed the man with a stare he couldn't misinterpret as something he could ignore. Even in the darkness.

"Tell me why, or I'm calling in the cavalry right now."

This time he didn't fight back. That didn't mean he was calm, though—not by any means.

"They found him," he practically yelled. "And now they're going after him!"

Suzy tilted her head on reflex, but she never got to ask another question. Someone else beat her to it.

"Going after who? Me?"

Suzy's hand was at her holster in a flash. The cool

night air moved across her upper thigh, confirming that she had, indeed, already ripped the dress. She didn't let up off the man as she turned to the new voice. Though it wasn't new to her at all.

"Going after who?" James repeated. His expression was hard, but Suzy couldn't read what emotion made it so.

The man struggled against her foot again, but this time Suzy let him up. She kept her hand on the butt of her gun.

"I don't know," he started, with eyes only for James. "But—but Sully gave me this address to get to you." He fumbled a hand into his pocket. If he hadn't been wearing tight jeans, showing he wasn't carrying a gun, Suzy would have pounced. But now that James was here, her captive's earlier feistiness had seemingly vanished. When he pulled out a paper and handed it to James, his hand shook. "He said it's what you're looking for. New information. I don't know who they are or who they're going after. He didn't have time to tell me."

Suzy didn't have to know the situation to understand that the stakes had just risen. James looked over the paper. His eyebrows threaded together.

Maybe he didn't know the situation, either. Confusion blanketed his expression.

"What happened to you?" he asked. This time, she heard the concern before she saw it. It was familiar in nature. James knew the man. "And who did it?"

Suzy half expected the man to remain silent, as he had with her, but again, having James there seemed the key to unlocking answers. The man took a deep breath.

"You were right," he said. "It was too dangerous." He raised one hand up toward the little light they had. Blood. Some was dry. Some wasn't. "It isn't mine," he said. "The blood isn't mine."

Suzy glanced at James. He still looked as confused as she felt.

"Whose blood is it?" she had to ask.

The man's gaze stuck to his hand.

James crouched down so he was at eye level with the other man. "Queso, whose blood is it?" Suzy didn't have a chance to question the name. She was holding her breath for an answer. "Queso?"

James reached out and grabbed his shoulder. It did the trick in focusing him.

"It's Sully's," Queso finally answered, voice low. "I don't even know if he's still alive. He made me run when the shooting started. He told me that getting you that address was too important." He let out an exhalation. It deflated him. "Padre, he said you're already running out of time."

"Okay, I've heard enough."

Suzy placed her hands up in defeat. She wasn't about to let this show go on any more. The story was lost on her, everyone's motivations just as hazy. She'd made a promise to herself not to willingly walk into situations exactly like the one she'd just walked into. Having a powwow with a man who had just confessed the blood he was covered in was not his own? A man who had limped from the dark of night to James Callahan's estate instead of to the police?

It was too much.

"I'm calling this in."

"You can't," Queso said hurriedly. His haze had been replaced with sheer panic in seconds. It hit every syllable in his words. "If anyone knows I talked to the cops, I'm done for." He shook his head and turned to James. "And you'll be out of even more time. Please, Padre, don't let her call them in."

Suzy grabbed her discarded high heel and tried to cool her mounting anger before it came to a head.

"I *am* the law," she reminded him. "And no amount of money is going to erase that fact. Now, can you walk to the house or do we need to carry you?"

Queso flapped his mouth open and closed. James answered for him.

But not with what she wanted to hear.

"Maybe we should go inside and take a moment to think this through, Suzanne."

If there was one thing Suzy disliked more than a man trying to tell her how to do her job—or when *not* to do it—it was a man calling her Suzanne.

"Either call me Suzy or Chief Deputy Simmons," she snapped. "And there's nothing to talk through. Something is going on, you're in the middle of it and I'm going to get answers this time around. Honest ones."

She grabbed Queso's wrist and pulled up. James helped but kept talking.

"I need to go see what's at this address. *Now*, not later," he tried. "You heard him. I'm running out of time."

Suzy whirled around as the side door banged open. The man James had been talking to before he'd gone upstairs had a towel in his hand.

"Listen, *Suzy*, this is my head of security, Douglas. Let him watch Queso until we know what's here." He shook the paper with the address on it. "Then we can do whatever you feel we need to do. Please."

All three men looked up at her.

"You're out of your mind," she exclaimed. "A bloody guy limps to your party and gives you an address, and then you want to go off without anything else to go on? Even if I wasn't law enforcement, I would think that's crazy."

Then James did something that surprised her. He almost closed the space between them, his blue, blue eyes never leaving hers.

"I know you don't trust me," he said, voice low. "You don't believe that I just happened to be out there that day…and you're right."

Suzy felt her eyes widen.

"Then why were you?" she had to ask.

Would it be this simple to get her answer?

James angled his body slightly, as if he didn't want Douglas to hear what he had to say next. Suzy couldn't help herself. She leaned in a fraction.

"Because Gardner Todd, my brother, asked me to meet him there." Before Suzy could react, he continued. "He said he needed to tell me something important. I never learned what that was, never even had a clue, either. Until this." Suzy glanced at the paper in his hand. "Listen, I'm not like my brother, but I am like you. I want answers, too. So let's go get some before it really *is* too late."

There was so much to process that Suzy couldn't land on any one point or question. In part, that was because of the pure urgency behind his plea. It bled through his words and into her. So sincere. So *real*.

James wasn't the only one surprised when she nodded.

"Okay, I'll go with you," she agreed. "But I'm going to need answers on the way. And, Mr. Callahan, if you lie to me again, no one will be able to help you. Not your money, not your lawyer, not even the entire town of Bates Hill. Got it?"

He nodded. "Yes, ma'am."

Chapter Four

Suzy shook her head. She might have followed the millionaire to and into his truck, but she was still having a hard time believing what he'd said.

"Gardner Todd had no family," she said. "At least, nothing in his files ever said that at any point he had a brother. Let alone that you're him."

The truck hit a series of bumps that rocketed Suzy off the seat. James threw his hand out to steady her. His palm pressed against her rib cage. Through the thin material of the dress, she could feel the heat of his skin. It momentarily distracted her.

"Like you guessed, some people will do anything for the right price," he said, unaware that his contact had put a hiccup in her thoughts. "And my father was all about knowing what somebody's right price was. It was easy to keep Gardner out of the spotlight. Easier, too, when Gardner ran away at sixteen."

"But why?" Suzy interjected. James pulled his hand back, setting it on the steering wheel. The dark night kept flying by the windows. "Why would he erase Gardner like that?"

A small smile pulled at the corner of James's lips. In

the dark of the cab, Suzy couldn't tell if it was a happy one. Given the subject matter, she doubted it.

"Gardner wasn't a crazy kid, if that's what you're after. But he drove our dad crazy. And it went both ways. My dad wasn't the easiest man to get along with, and for whatever reason, Gardner got the short end of the stick with him. They never had one big fight, just a hundred little ones. It was like everything he did rubbed Dad the wrong way." He shrugged. "And there's only so much anger and disappointment and resentment you can shell out on a kid before they eventually either become the person you made them out to be or a completely different person, despite what you tried to make them."

"You're talking about Gardner Todd here," Suzy said, still in disbelief that he was related to the man next to her. "The Alabama Boogeyman. The fixer who gets hired by the highest bidder. Notorious across the state for his role as being basically the best criminal handyman."

James shrugged again. "I never said he was perfect."

The truck slowed enough to hook a right. Beneath the tires was nothing but dirt and rock. They were in backcountry and only getting farther into it.

"If he really was your brother, father issues aside, why run away and give up a fortune? Especially if he could have inherited it."

The smile—and whatever it meant—disappeared from James's lips.

"I never got to ask. I was thirteen when he left. He sent birthday cards, but the last time I talked to him in person was a few days after Dad passed."

"But you were going to meet him at the warehouse."

James stiffened, then nodded.

"In the last few years he'd call me occasionally to talk.

Nothing devious or anything. Just about how I was doing and checking up on our sister, Chelsea, mostly. Honestly, I think he regretted not having a relationship with her, but as you've pointed out, he was in with the worst kind of crowd. And he knew it. He never tried to come around while I raised her, and I never invited him to."

"Until four months ago," Suzy offered.

"He called and I knew something was off. He said there was something he had to talk to me about. In person. Something important." James tightened his grip on the steering wheel. His knuckles turned white. A muscle in his jaw twitched. "By the time I got there... well, you know."

Suzy fidgeted in her seat. "So you have *no* idea what he wanted to tell you?"

He shook his head. "I have no idea what he wanted or why he chose to meet there. Or who wanted him dead. I might not be in law enforcement, but that doesn't mean I haven't heard about his reputation. If someone wanted him dead, it was a bold move. One not many would make. Especially not Lester McGibbon. At least, not on his own."

Suzy and Matt had already agreed on that point. Nothing in Lester's history suggested he would go from white-collar crime to taking on Gardner. Someone either bold or stupid had ordered the hit and gotten the man to do it.

"You think what Gardner wanted to talk to you about was related to his death," she guessed.

James reduced the truck's speed and leaned forward to get a better look ahead.

"When the Alabama Boogeyman has a secret for you and then gets shot three times before he can tell?"

"It's hard not to connect the two," she admitted.

"Damn hard."

He motioned out the windshield, but Suzy was already pulling out her gun. The country road was funneling them toward a house in the distance. Not a farmhouse—it was too small, and there was nothing else around the property that suggested the owners dealt with animals or crops—but something more quaint. One lone exterior light hung over the front door. There were no cars around.

"You've never been to this house?" she asked, already knowing the answer. In profile, she could see the way his brows pinched together. Along with her, he was seeing the house for the first time.

"I've never been here," he confirmed. "I didn't even know there were houses this far out here."

Bates Hill might have been a small town, but its country land ran for a good chunk of miles. As far as Suzy could recall, she hadn't been out here, either. Which meant she needed to be on her A game.

As easy as it had been to not trust James during the last four months, she couldn't help but believe that *he* believed the tip he'd gotten was genuine.

Suzy took the safety off her weapon.

James didn't stop in front of the house. Instead, he drove a circle around it and parked facing the road they'd come from. No one stirred inside.

"Ready, Chief Deputy Simmons?" There was a hint of excitement in his voice. It matched the small dose of adrenaline building in her. The danger of the unknown. The promise of getting justice. All in a day's work.

"Yes, but at the first sign of trouble I'm calling in the cavalry. Got it?"

James snickered. "I wouldn't have thought otherwise."

They got out of the truck and fell into a surprisingly comfortable rhythm. James led the way to the door and knocked, and when no one answered, he stepped to the side. He tried the doorknob. It turned, but he didn't open the door. Instead, he gave Suzy a look that made pride for her job swell in her chest. She pushed her shoulders back, brought her gun up, and looked ahead and nodded. James opened the door wide and waited as Suzy pushed in first, gun ready.

"Riker County Sheriff's Department!" she yelled, quick on her feet.

No one yelled or jumped out, but Suzy didn't slow. She went through the living area as soon as James turned on the light. No sign of anyone. She moved to the one bedroom and the attached bathroom, flipping on the rest of the lights as she went.

"It's clear," she called after checking the closets. She holstered her gun and went back to the living room. "Anything you recognize?"

The room was small and open to the kitchen. A modest furniture set centered the room while a bookshelf took up half the wall near the front door. James stood in front of it, scanning the books and odds and ends it housed.

"I don't know," he answered after moving to the next shelf. "Nothing so far. No pictures or anything that I think would constitute a secret worth killing to protect." He reached over and pulled out a book. "Unless someone really didn't like *Romeo and Juliet.*"

Suzy walked to a chest against the wall and opened it. It contained a few handwoven blankets and a shoe box. Carefully she lifted the small box out.

"Do you think this is where he lived?" she had to ask, taking the lid off. "Gardner, I mean. Did he ever tell you where he stayed?" The box was filled with blank envelopes and a pen.

"That's just another question I never asked. Though I assumed he had a place north of Birmingham. Definitely not here."

"Maybe this place *is* the secret."

Suzy placed the box to the side and pulled the blankets out. She tossed them onto the couch.

"A secret about what?" James asked, his focus still on the bookcase. "That whoever stayed here liked isolation and Shakespeare?" Suzy could hear the frustration in his voice.

"Your source could have been pulling your leg," she pointed out.

He turned and their eyes met. Blue glass. Sharp and clear. "You saw Queso. Do *you* think he was lying?"

"I think he was scared and confused," she admitted. "He might have misinterpreted what he saw or was simply given the wrong information on purpose."

James didn't agree. He didn't even have to shake his head to get that point across. He squared his shoulders defensively. "My source wouldn't do that."

He didn't elaborate past that, and Suzy didn't push. He stalked past her into the bedroom.

James might have told her one of his secrets, but he certainly had more up his tailored sleeves. Maybe jumping into his truck without a second thought hadn't been her best move. Answers be damned.

They spent the next several minutes in silence, both working their rooms. Suzy checked the side tables, went back over the bookcase and started pulling out kitchen cabinets and drawers. Whoever lived in the house had either left in a hurry or hadn't been there in a while. Almost everything was cleaned out of the kitchen.

Almost being the operative word.

"James!"

"Suzy!"

Suzy jumped and turned as they spoke at the same time. James walked into the living room, holding a cloth in his hand.

"I would say 'jinx,' but I don't think it works like that," he said. The joke didn't hold any humor. James's expression was blank. "I found this in the dresser. It was hung up between the drawers."

He held the cloth up. Only it wasn't just a cloth.

It was a small onesie. One with a rubber ducky sewn in the middle.

Suzy's heart began to race. She stepped to the side to show what she'd found.

"It was at the back of the cabinet. I almost didn't see it."

James's eyes widened. He picked up the can. His expression gave nothing away. "'Formula,'" he read.

"*Baby* formula," she said, wanting to be crystal clear in what they were seeing.

"Baby formula," he repeated. She watched as he looked between the canister and the rubber-ducky onesie. They clearly didn't have answers, but she did have a few guesses.

"If this house isn't a secret, then maybe whoever was here is." She took the onesie from his hand. His gaze followed it. "And I'm assuming Gardner never mentioned a baby to you."

James shook his head. "No, he didn't."

"So, maybe he was hiding someone here? Someone with a baby? Or—"

"Or the baby is his," James interrupted. And his blank expression gained some emotion. Anger. Concern. Something else.

Something Suzy found she wanted to combat or soothe. She wasn't sure which. He *was* James Callahan, after all. A man she'd spent the last four months distrusting with a vengeance.

"I was going to say *or* this has nothing to do with Gardner, and whoever your source was wanted you here. Where there just so happened to be a baby at one point in time." She motioned to the rest of the drawers and cabinets, all open and mostly empty. "We still have no evidence that Gardner is even linked to this place. Other than, like you said, the owner seems to love isolation and Shakespeare. But I can't imagine he's the only person in the world to like both. That could be nothing more than a coincidence."

James opened his mouth, but whatever he was originally going to say died on his tongue. In a move that was so quick Suzy reached for her gun, James spun on his heel and hurried to the bookcase. He grabbed a book and opened it, determined. He shook his head.

"This may or may not have been his place, but Gardner definitely was here at one point." He held the book up, cover open. From her spot, Suzy could see handwriting against the first page. "He didn't like Shakespeare, but our mother did." He tapped the signature. "She always signed the inside of her books." He smiled. "I thought Dad gave them all away when she passed."

Suzy looked down at the onesie in her hand. The rubber ducky was wearing a blue ribbon around its neck.

A not-so-great feeling started to mix with the adrenaline in her stomach. Confusion was never fun, especially when it came with urgency.

"So, if Gardner stayed here with a baby—"

The window next to the front door exploded in a spray of glass. Suzy flung herself to the floor as another window burst out of its frame. She didn't have to be on her feet to know what was happening.

Whatever Gardner Todd's secret was, it looked like whoever was outside was also looking for it.

And they'd brought guns.

THE FIRST SHOT pushed him to the floor. The second had him wishing he'd brought his gun in from the truck. The third, fourth, fifth and—hell, he'd lost count—the rest of the bullets that were plugging into the house had James low and crawling to the kitchen, hoping he and the chief deputy weren't about to have a repeat of what happened at the warehouse.

Suzy was on the floor but, thankfully, not on her back this time. He gave her a once-over the best he could, given bullets were still flying. No blood or wounds that he could see. She lifted her head up enough to meet his eye as the cabinets above them splintered.

James didn't waste any more time. He closed the distance between them and covered her with his body. She didn't fight him. Which was good, because whoever was outside wasn't done.

Once again James lost count in the barrage of bullets that continued to come. There was definitely more than one gunman. In fact, he guessed they were being shot at from both sides of the house, the way it was crumpling around them.

If they managed to not get shot, the house falling apart just might do them in.

James moved his head so his lips were right next to Suzy's ear. "How much ammo do you have on you?"

"Not enough!" she yelled back. "Only the clip in my gun."

James said a few choice words born of frustration. He just hoped their enemy's show of force would empty their own reserves. Maybe they could get away with only one clip. It wasn't like they had much choice. From what he'd already seen of the house, it was empty of anything worth fighting with. If the house was Gardner's, and James realized he was already convinced it was, then at one point it had to have been well stocked with weapons. But now?

Now it was picked clean.

James was still trying to come up with a better plan than trying to take on what sounded like an army with only one clip when the gunfire finally stopped. The house continued to groan in the aftermath. Half of a cabinet door broke free and bounced off his back. There was no time to survey the damage.

"You okay?" James asked, voice low.

"I will be when we get out of here," she replied hurriedly. James liked the fire in her voice.

He moved into a half crouch, careful to keep out of the view of the windows. Suzy followed until they were at the back door. Whatever slugs their mystery gunners had been slinging had trashed it and the windows. The walls were mostly intact.

And probably the only reason they were still alive.

James moved to the other side of the door as Suzy took up a spot next to it. He had a moment of déjà vu.

He held up his finger to keep her quiet and peered out of one of the bullet holes.

Less than a second later, he was certain that one clip was not enough.

He reached out and took Suzy's wrist.

"We need to hide," he said urgently. *"Now."*

Chapter Five

The world around them was moving so fast, but James couldn't help feeling as if they were moving as slow as dirt. It didn't help that not one or two but at least six men were closing in on the house from the backyard alone. It also didn't help that the only hiding place he could think of was hard as the dickens to get to. At least, when that hiding place was the attic and you were hopped up on adrenaline and trying to get a beautiful woman in a slinky dress up into that attic.

With no ladder.

As soon as he pulled the string down and the door opened, James had Suzy by the waist and was shimmying her upward. Under different circumstances, he might have taken a beat to appreciate the way her body felt beneath his hands. Just like Suzy might have, under different circumstances, had some words to say when his hands cupped her backside with vigor, pushing her up until she could pull herself the rest of the way. As it was, they both kept their mouths clamped shut.

The moment Suzy cleared the opening, she spun around and held out her hand. James was already one step ahead of her. He jumped, thanked his lucky stars that he was a tall man and managed to grab the lip of the opening. Before he could start pulling himself up, a sound he'd been hoping not to hear until he was hidden exploded through the house.

Someone had kicked the front door off its hinges.

James pulled all the way up, once again was thankful that one thing he'd kept from his Air Force days was his workout routine. Suzy grabbed his back and then his belt. Then it was his backside she was cupping.

Another bang sounded as what was left of the back door was opened with force.

James grabbed on to the closest beam and pulled with all of his might. The moment his feet cleared the opening, Suzy reached through the space and grabbed for the string attached to the door. James twisted around and put his arms around her waist in time to keep her from falling out. After two swipes she got it, and together they closed it as quickly and quietly as they could.

With absolutely no time to spare.

No sooner was the door in place than a series of voices could be heard in the room beneath them. James and Suzy didn't dare move. He didn't even release his hold around her middle, and she didn't complain.

"Check the closet and bathroom," one man barked.

"If they're in here, we got them already," said another. His drawl was pure syrup. "Nobody can take that much lead."

"They can if you're crap with your aim," said another man. The voice was a higher pitch than the other two. Younger. "You should have let me do the shooting, and not Ryan and skunk for brains here."

"I was fifty-fifty on killing him or keeping him alive," the first man said. "Either outcome I can work with."

"No one's in here," the person with the Southern drawl called from the bathroom. "The house is empty."

"So, whose truck is that, and where are they?" It was the third man who asked, and something in the back of James's mind rattled around at his voice. It sounded familiar. If only he could *see* the three people beneath them.

"It could have been Sully's boy who got free earlier," the first said. "Came out here to warn Hank that we were coming and left on his bike. Might explain how they got away before we got here."

James couldn't help but tense up. He felt Suzy turn her head enough to look at him. A lot of good that did in the dark. While there might have been more than a few Hanks in Alabama, James knew of only one who would be tangled up with his brother. If Hank had been at the house, then there was no doubt Gardner had once been there, too.

"Well, what do we do now?" the drawler asked. "We got all the boys here and no one to question."

The sigh was so loud, James heard it as though the man was in the attic with them.

"Looks like we'll just have to hunt down Hank and make *him* tell us where he hid the boy before anyone else finds out Gardner Todd's son is out there missing."

If James tensed at the mention of Hank's name, he turned into a statue at this new information.

Gardner had a son?

He had a nephew?

Suddenly everything fell into place. The urgency to meet in person. The secret he'd been trying to tell James.

Gardner had a son.

A son who was in trouble now.

Rage, pure as pollen in the spring, filled James so quickly that he had half a mind to open the attic door and bring down a heap of pain on the men in the bedroom. Had they been the ones who had ordered Lester to kill his brother? Why were they after the boy? What were they planning on doing with him after they found him?

Every question pushed adrenaline into James's muscles.

In the darkness of the attic, all he saw was red.

And then that red cooled.

Suzy moved her hand onto the arm he had around her stomach. Her fingers delicately wrapped his forearm. Then, in the smallest of movements, she brushed her thumb across his skin.

The rage in him quieted, and sense returned to him.

Jumping out and taking on the unknown number of armed men would only get him killed, and her, too. And then his nephew would still be in danger.

James squeezed her side to let her know he'd gotten the message.

"Go get Zach and the boys, and tell them to go ahead and hit the road," the first man said. He must have been the one in charge at the moment. James committed his voice to memory. "Keep your phones on," he called as one of the men's footsteps went back into the living room.

"What do you want me to do?" the third man asked. Not the guy with the Southern accent. Again, James felt like he could almost place the man's voice. "I mean, do we even know where Hank is?"

"No, but Sully does."

"I thought he was gone. In the wind."

"Doesn't mean we can't get him back. The sorry SOB

has a lot of problems, but his worst one is how he feels about his people. We find that boy he took a bullet for, and I bet we could smoke him out."

"If Sully hasn't already bought a one-way ticket to the great fire pit in the ground."

The first man laughed. It sounded like nails against a chalkboard.

"He may be soft, but Sully isn't about to let a bullet do him in."

Car doors shut in the distance. An engine turned over.

"And what if he doesn't know where Hank is? Heck, what if Hank is already on his way out of the state with the boy?"

Zach, the boys and the man with the Southern twang must have been leaving. James tried to split his attention, to see if he could hear if one or two vehicles were driving off, but he very much wanted the same answers as the unknown third man did.

"You may not have been in for long enough to know about Hank, but I used to run with him a few years back. He's not a stationary man, and definitely not a fan of the state. He came back for a reason. He won't leave until he's done whatever he needed to, and my guess is it wasn't being the father to Gardner Todd's kid. Now, let's start with his old woman in—"

Music—the chorus of the song "It's Raining Men," to be precise, courtesy of James's sister and how hilarious she thought it was to try to embarrass him when she called—filled the attic around them. He and Suzy both reached for his coat pocket and his phone, lit up and blaring.

"What the—"

James wrapped his hand around the phone and pulled

Suzy up and farther into the darkness, just as a shot sounded up through the attic door.

"We need light!" she yelled. No point in trying to pretend no one was home when The Weather Girls were belting out one of their most famous hits.

James held up the phone, giving them some light. Another bullet embedded itself in the roof above them. As soon as Suzy could see, she was playing hopscotch across the ceiling beams. The last thing they needed was to fall into the bedroom.

"Whoever you are, you're screwed!" yelled one of the men. James didn't have the time to figure out which one it was. He canceled Chelsea's call and used the phone as a flashlight.

The attic ran the length of the house and was by no means spacious. They hunched and clung to roof beams as they hurried to get out from above where the men were.

Not that that would make much difference when they decided to walk into the living room and unload a few more rounds into the ceiling.

"How close is the truck to the house?" Suzy asked James. A ripping sound pulled his attention to her dress just in time to watch the tear that was already there split all the way up to her hip. Lord have mercy—if they weren't running for their lives, James would have had to really think on the lacy number she was wearing beneath it.

"How close is the—" he repeated.

Suzy cut him off. "The vent!"

James followed her line of sight to the attic vent at the end of the house. With a jolt of excitement, he understood.

"Close enough," he said.

Another two bullets shot up behind him, too close for comfort. Suzy must have sensed it. The moment she got to another beam, she turned toward him, brandishing her gun.

"Move!" she yelled.

James didn't have to be told twice. He hurried around her and kept going toward the vent while she did some shooting of her own. He counted four shots by the time he made it to the beam closest to the vent.

Two bullets answered from the men below. James turned, worried she'd been hit.

"Hurry!" she shouted at him.

Holding two roof beams to steady himself the best he could in the small space, James pulled back his leg and then kicked out at the attic vent with all he had. The planks of wood splintered beneath the force. Suzy sent another few rounds beneath them while he kicked out again. Before he could clear the last two planks, he could already see the truck beneath them.

"This is going to hurt," he called over his shoulder. He moved his phone to allow more light to help her get the rest of the way to him.

"Not as much as getting shot," she bit back. "Trust me."

He wasn't about to argue.

He broke the last board, until all that was left was a hole they'd have to squeeze through. But, like Suzy said, it was better than the alternative.

"As soon as you hit the truck bed, I'm gunning it. So make sure you buy us some time with those bullets," he said.

"Yes, sir." Suzy nodded, turned and unloaded her clip into the floor.

As soon as the last bullet left her barrel, James moved through the hole that used to be the attic vent, grabbed on to its sides, said a quick prayer and pushed off.

WHEN SUZY WAS FIFTEEN, she had dared Billy to jump off the Wendigo Bridge on their way home from school. It wasn't that high above the water, but tall enough that Billy wasn't having any of it. By the time she'd decided to stop ragging him about it, Tommy Wexler and his cute older brother had shown up. The way Suzy had seen it then, she'd had no choice at that point. She *had* to jump.

She still remembered how her stomach had turned to nothing but butterflies as she stood on the old railing and looked down at the water. Billy had still been spouting concern, but promised he'd try to fetch her if she started drowning. The Wexler boys weren't as concerned, but said a few things that made her believe they'd be impressed if she did, indeed, go through with it. So she'd taken that first step without hesitation.

What Suzy never told Tommy Wexler—or Billy, for that matter—was that she'd seen her friend Melanie do the same thing the previous summer on a dare. It was a scary drop, but as long as she tucked her legs in and held her nose, she'd be fine. But Melanie had told Suzy that the real secret was in knowing you'd be fine before you ever did it. Confidence was key, she'd said.

Now, no longer a teen trying to impress a boy, Suzy realized that the key had never been confidence. It had been youthful stupidity.

And, boy, did she feel stupid jumping off a house in

an attempt to hit the back of a truck with a nine-or ten-foot drop in between the two.

She felt a slight fizzle of confidence spring up when James hit his target and none of his bones snapped in half. At least, none that she heard.

James landed in the truck bed on his feet, and a second later he was out and over the side. The moment he flung open the driver's-side door, Suzy held her breath and followed.

If she hadn't abandoned her high heels in the attic, she was certain her ankles would have twisted something awful. As it was, when her feet connected with the metal, a jarring jolt of pain radiated up through her. However, nothing felt terribly wrong. Though she was sure she'd be feeling it the next morning.

That was, if they made it to the next morning.

It wasn't like two full-grown adults landing in the back of a pickup were exactly quiet. If the gunmen hadn't already left wherever they'd been seeking cover when she'd shot at them, they'd leave soon to find them.

On cue, a man yelled from inside of the house. "They're outside!"

Suzy was whirling around, trying to get James's status on driving them away, when the engine roared to life. She barely had time to drop into a crouch and grab the side of the truck bed before the tires were kicking up dirt and rock.

The window between the cab and the back slid open just as two men ran out into the night.

"Hang on there!" James yelled through the window. The truck accelerating threw Suzy even more off balance. She slid down. More ripping sounds let her know

Mara's dress was tearing again. It sure wasn't made for the field.

A familiar bang cut through the night. One of the men stood defiantly in the backyard with his gun out, but his face, as well as his aim, was becoming obscured by the distance and night. It was easy to hit a house. Not so much a moving target.

Which told Suzy these men might be familiar with guns, but they weren't pros.

"You okay?" James called. He didn't let up on the gas pedal as he took a left, putting them back on the road. Suzy was flung to the side.

"If they don't kill me, your driving might!"

Through the chaos that had turned into Suzy's evening, she heard James Callahan howl in laughter. Despite everything, it made her smile.

But it didn't last long. A pair of headlights raced onto the road behind them.

"They're following us!" she yelled.

"Might be time to get in here, then!"

Suzy eyed the window opening and did some quick math. She was a slim woman, thanks to the job and the need to stay in shape that came with it, but her part-Hispanic heritage had graced her with hips on the wide size, just like her mother. The pickup wasn't old, but it wasn't brand-spanking-new, either. Its window wasn't made for a grown woman to slide through and into the cab. Actually, it was a surprise the millionaire was driving this dinky truck rather than some sports car or hopped-up truck with a lift kit.

"I don't think I can fit," she said. "The window is too small."

James didn't turn his attention away from the windshield. The headlights were bouncing in front of them as the tires ran across the same holes that had prompted James to hold her down earlier.

"Simmons, you just jumped out of an attic vent and into a truck. You can manage this window!"

Suzy glanced over her shoulder at the approaching vehicle. It was too close. If she got stuck, then she'd be one easy target.

"There's no time!"

She pulled out her phone. She should have called the department when they were in the attic, but she hadn't wanted to give their hiding spot away.

"Here!"

Suzy turned in time to see James passing her a present.

It was a gun.

A *loaded* gun.

"You know the saying 'it's like shooting fish in a barrel'?" he asked.

"Yeah?"

James turned to give her a quick look. He was smirking.

And, boy, she couldn't stop the thought that it made him look delicious from crossing her mind.

"You're the fish in this scenario," he said. "So make sure you don't let them get near the barrel!"

Chapter Six

By the time the truck made it to the main road, Suzy had opened fire on their pursuers. She got in three shots before another was returned. It hit the top of the truck. An awful noise of metal against metal sounded above them.

"You okay?" he yelled, even though he knew she hadn't been hit.

"Just peachy!"

Two more shots came at them. Both missed. James already had his foot to the floor. At this rate, they'd be inside the town limits within minutes.

Would the men keep coming at them until their ammo ran out? Or would they stick with them until they could get the upper hand another way?

James glanced in his rearview mirror just in time to see the driver of the car thrust his arm out of his window. The passenger joined in, hand and gun sticking out of his window, too.

"Get down," James just managed to say seconds before both opened fire. One of the side windows was blown off as James ducked. The windshield followed quickly. A gust of night air pushed into the cab.

"Still with me?"

"They have more firepower! We need a better plan!"

Suzy yelled back. This time there was no joke in her reply.

James cleared the glass off himself and squinted as the air made his eyes water. Suzy was right. At the rate they were going, getting into the town limits wasn't going to do them a lick of good. Not unless they had backup waiting.

They needed a better plan.

Or, at least, a different one.

"Could you hit their tires?" James yelled, already weighing the pros and cons of what he was thinking of doing.

Pro? It could get the two men and their seemingly endless amounts of ammo off their tails. Long enough, at least, to call and rendezvous with Suzy's law-enforcement brethren.

Con? It didn't work, and they were either killed by bullets or in a car accident.

James decided not to share these thoughts with the female gunslinger in the back of his truck.

"Hold on," he warned, making up his mind. "And then get ready to jump up and shoot!"

"Roger that!"

James gave her a few seconds to get a good grip. Then, with another silent prayer that he wasn't about to kill them both, he stomped on the brakes.

For the second time that night, the world around them seemed to change speed. The truck shuddered as it skidded to a halt. The glass on James and the front seat sprayed forward against the dash. The weight of a body rattled around the truck bed. He even heard Suzy yell out in surprise or pain or both. All of these things were followed closely by the horrible screeching sound of even more tires. James looked in the side mirror in time to watch the car behind them veer around the truck by what had to be inches. They rode their own set of brakes down the oncoming traffic lane before coming to a violent stop. It was a miracle they hadn't fallen into the ditch or flipped.

Now there were less than a few yards between them.

"Suz—" James started to yell. He was interrupted by a blur of fabric moving as the woman stood tall in the truck bed. All he could see was a beautiful pair of legs.

Then he was listening to the sound of her gunshots over the truck roof above him.

Three shots was all it took to deflate the back two tires of the gunmen's car.

"Hold on," he warned again. This time, as soon as he heard her drop down, James was punching the gas pedal. Instead of going past the front of their car, giving them more shots, he cut the wheel and took them the other way. Suzy might not have been chief deputy of the county they were now pointed toward, but that didn't mean James was about to risk the pair of thugs getting a good shot at her as they rode past into Riker County.

At least, James hoped the new direction wouldn't open her up to any more of their target practice.

Either way, he bet their chances were better than flashing their backsides at two men more than willing to kill them.

"You have your cell phone on you?" he asked after a minute or so had passed. Suzy was sitting up, her hair moving in the night air like she was underwater. He didn't need to be her best friend like the sheriff was to know her focus was behind them. The car and gunmen weren't following them.

But that didn't mean their friends couldn't.

Wherever the Drawler and the rest of the original group had gone, James just hoped they didn't run into them on the way to safety.

"Yeah, but it's dead." She turned so that her head was almost in the window. "Let me see yours. Because we both know it definitely works."

James couldn't help but laugh at that.

Ten minutes later and Suzy was finally done with the phone. She'd called ahead to the Calwarts County Sheriff's Department so a deputy could meet them and bring them in while another few were dispatched out to find the two gunmen behind them. She also called in to her department and put them all on alert since they had no way of knowing where the other group of men had gone. She even called in the sheriff, as best as he could tell from the snatches of yelling he heard through the wind.

By the time she had ended the call, the county road was being blocked off in front of them by two blue-and-whites. James came to a stop in front of the first car as a pair of deputies raised their guns at them.

"This is all you, *dear*," James said over his shoulder. He cut the engine and raised his hands. Before Suzy could come back with her own quip, a man stepped out of the second car. He wasn't in uniform but James could see a sheriff's badge clearly on his belt.

"Suzanne Simmons?" he called.

"That's Chief Deputy Simmons to you," she yelled back without missing a beat.

It made the man smile.

"Lower your weapons," he ordered his men. "We're dealing with family now."

James didn't get a chance to question that before the

sheriff was walking through the barrier toward them. He nodded to James, who lowered his hands and popped open the door.

"You hurt back there, Simmons? We have an EMT on standby."

"I'm a little banged up but I think I'm good."

"What about you, son?"

"Nothing some Icy Hot can't handle," James answered. He got out of the truck but hung back to help Suzy out of the bed. Goodness knew she didn't need it, but that didn't stop him from wanting to offer.

"My dress wasn't so lucky," she said, raising her voice. "So unless you want to see my undergarments, Sheriff Wayland, I suggest you stop in your tracks."

Like a criminal had just drawn a gun, the sheriff reacted instantly. He turned on his heel and walked back to his men without another word. James didn't make such a retreat. Instead he took a few steps back until he was staring up at her.

"Don't worry—I've already seen that lacy number you're trying to hide there," he defended, going around to the tailgate. He opened it and then kept his gaze high. "I'm just here to help now."

Despite what they'd gone through in the last half hour or so, Suzanne Simmons looked like she was still ready for whatever was thrown their way. Her hair was wild, her body was tense, and her dress was ruined, but she in no way looked defeated. James stripped off his jacket and held it out to her.

"This is the best I can do right now," he said, trying to coax her forward.

It worked. She dropped down on the ground next to him and wrapped the jacket around her, hiding the majority of the damage. Watching her do something as innocent as trying to cover herself with his jacket, James couldn't help but remember everything she'd just done.

It prompted an honest reaction from him. One that came out before he could censor himself.

"I don't know if anyone tells you this often enough but, Chief Deputy Simmons, you are an extraordinary woman."

Suzy lifted her chin and fixed him with a honey-filled stare. Her lips, red and plump and just asking for his, lifted at the corner.

"Don't I know it."

What the woman didn't know was James was two seconds from taking her in his arms and covering that smirk with his own, but as quickly as he had the thought, he remembered what had led them to this point.

His expression must have shown the change in feelings.

"Did you tell them about Gardner on the phone?" he asked.

If law enforcement knew that Gardner was his brother *and* had a son out there? It could jeopardize the baby even more. As well as his sister, friends and even staff. Any and all could be used to get information out of him. Not that he had much to give.

Suzy shook her head. It surprised him.

"I have a feeling that just knowing you're Gardner's brother won't make this situation any less complicated," she admitted. "I want to do as much as we can to catch those men from tonight, but if there really is a baby out there… We need to be careful and smart."

"We?"

That surprised him.

"I still don't trust you," she said, voice even. "So, I'm not leaving your side until this is finished. Got it?"

It was his turn to nod.

"Yes, ma'am."

"Good. Now let's get out of here so we can figure out what's next."

He turned to follow her but not before lowering his voice.

"How fast can you get us in the clear with these guys?"

Suzy didn't break stride.

"What? Why?"

Even as he said it, James felt a surge of adrenaline go through him.

"Because I think I know where Hank went."

THE CALWARTS COUNTY Sheriff's Department was a quick trip in Sheriff Wayland's Tahoe. Suzy had known the man for years, mostly because her father had been his friend when she was younger. Since he'd passed Suzy had kept a more professional friendship with the older man, occasionally grabbing a drink between their jurisdictions with Billy and Matt in tow.

After she'd been shot, Wayland had called, sent flowers, but hadn't visited.

He tried to make up for that in the car but Suzy assured him she'd taken no offense. Their jobs could become overwhelming at times. Not to mention busy. Like now, trying to find a swatch of armed men, barreling through possibly both of their counties while they tried to find the baby of the Alabama Boogeyman. Even thinking it made her feel insane. She'd only gone to a party and now she was a county away with a ruined dress.

Once they made it to the Calwarts department, all attempts to apologize for his self-conceived wrongdoings
came to a halt. Sheriff Wayland took them into his office and buckled down on trying to get a better idea of
what they were up against.

"Honestly, I couldn't tell you," Suzy said with true
frustration. "I didn't get a clear picture of how many men
were there, if they even were all men."

"It had to have been at least six before most of them
left," James supplied. "Then we just had the two after
us. Guns and ammo didn't seem to be an issue for them,
either."

"And you have no idea why someone would give you
an anonymous tip to go out to that house?" Wayland
asked this to James directly. He shook his head.

"I wasn't aware it existed until I found the note with
the address on my windshield." Suzy didn't know if
she was impressed by the fact that James was weav-
ing around stating direct lies or if it should be another
point under the Reasons to Not Trust James Callahan
list. Either way, she knew she couldn't hold it against
him too much. Considering it had been her idea to leave
the teen called Queso, Gardner, Hank and Gardner's
son out of it.

Still, she wondered if that had been the right call.

"Because of my wealth I'm no stranger to the occasional prank or attempt at extortion," he continued.
"Which is why I asked Chief Deputy Simmons here to
accompany me since she was the only law enforcement
left at the town-hall social. Though if I had realized it
was more than just someone pulling my leg, I wouldn't
have gone. I had no idea it was going to turn out the way
it did." That last part was the unequivocal truth. On both

their parts. Had Suzy had any inkling of what they were walking into, she would have trod a lot more carefully. Or at least brought more ammo.

Sheriff Wayland rubbed his chin. He looked toward the door and then to a paper on his desk.

"What is it, Sheriff?" She showed him a grin. "And don't tell me nothing because I can see it's something."

If Wayland was amused that she knew him well enough to know he was chewing on some information he wasn't sure about telling, he kept his mouth shut. Right up until James stood.

"If you don't mind, I'd like to call my sister back and make sure everything is all right."

He wasn't asking for permission, just being polite. Though he showed a small smile to her before leaving. Suzy realized as soon as he shut the door that he'd only gone so Wayland would open up to her.

Someone he trusted.

"We've heard some talk on the street about a group attempting to weasel their way into the criminal underbelly here in the South," the sheriff led in. "Just hearsay, mind you. Sounded more like some people talking big but nothing else. But now with what happened? It would be different if it had been just the two men, but at least six with that kind of firepower?"

"Seems like overkill," Suzy supplied.

Wayland let out a long breath.

"Or a show of force."

Suzy mulled that over while Wayland checked his phone. The laugh lines at the corner of his eyes were deep. Just not being exercised tonight. Which, by estimation since her phone was dead, was technically day. She bet it was at least one in the morning.

A deep exhaustion was starting to settle the longer she sat in her chair. There were only so many jolts of adrenaline that could go through a person before draining them completely when they wore off.

"Unless there's more you need from me, I'd like to go home." She stood, not caring if he protested. "We can go give our statements and then I want to point my head toward my pillow."

Wayland looked up from his phone, seemingly lost in thought for a moment, but then he nodded. He didn't stand but motioned to the door.

"I'll keep you updated on anything we might find."

"I'll do the same," she lied. There was already a small list of details she wasn't sharing. Suzy rolled her shoulders back, trying to physically get away from the discomfort of deceit. But somewhere in her gut she felt it was the right thing to do. If they had any hope of getting to Gardner's kid before their unknown attackers could. Once law enforcement knew of James's connection to the Boogeyman it would cloud protocol. And that wasn't something they could chance with a baby out there.

Her thoughts turned to her own son.

No, she wouldn't chance their situation from going any more sideways than it already had.

"And, Suzy?"

Her hand hovered over the doorknob.

"Yeah?"

Wayland's expression was blank.

"I don't know James Callahan like you might, but I know enough to guess he's hiding something," he said, solemnly. "Be careful and try to stay out of his trouble, okay?"

Suzy nodded.

"Okay."

But she knew it was just another lie.

"WHAT HAPPENS NOW?"

It was such a simple question at such a complicated time that James didn't know how to respond for a moment. Instead, he slid his phone into his pocket and took the time to really look at Suzanne Simmons.

They were outside of the Calwarts sheriff's department, just within the glow of the outdoor lights. But it was bright enough to show him a woman who was tired and worn, but ready. The dress he'd admired from the moment he'd seen her at the party, however, had clearly seen much better days. Even with his suit jacket wrapped around her waist, one of the slits that had split farther upward was visible. Not only could he see the side of the lacy number he'd nearly died for in the attic, but the tan, smooth skin above it, too.

James focused his attention back on the woman's face. Her eyebrows were raised.

"Well?"

"Well, I think it might be time to get you out of those clothes."

Her eyebrows shot up even more. She pushed out her hip and crossed her arms over her chest. The stance did nothing to help his concentration.

"Excuse me?"

James held up his hands in defense. "We *both* need to get into some different clothes," he amended. "We look like the poster couple for a zombie film."

Suzy's eyes traced the cuts he knew he had on his face and neck from the windshield's glass. He'd cleaned them up the best he could with the first-aid kit. After a good shower, he hoped they wouldn't look so severe.

"So, your plan starts with new clothes," she said after a second.

"My plan starts with getting into that." He pointed over her shoulder to a burgundy Altima.

"Whose car is it?"

James started toward it, placing his hand carefully on the small of her back to steer her along with him. Even as he moved, he felt the soreness vibrating in his legs. The jump from the attic might have hurt him more than he'd originally thought.

"Deputy Decker's."

"Deputy Decker?"

On reflex, James took her elbow as they started down the few steps between the department and the sidewalk. Her skin was as soft as it looked. Warm, too. It felt right. *She* felt right. Even in the smallest of touches.

He cleared his throat and let go. She was a distraction.

"He works here. Nice man."

James pulled out the key fob and unlocked the doors. He went for the passenger's-side door. Suzy didn't seem like the kind of woman who would let a man she didn't trust open the door for her—and James had no illusions about her still not fully trusting him—but she didn't fight it. He had to keep his gaze up as she maneuvered herself inside. However, in his peripheral vision he could still see her long bare leg when her dress parted at the movement.

"And he's just letting us take his car?"

James leaned over the passenger seat. "Of course not. I bought it." He shut the door on her look of surprise.

Suzy kept her questions in until they were back on the main road that ran through the heart of Calwarts County.

Without looking at her, he could tell she was listing off each concern and going over them all mentally before she said anything. Not only had he found she was a woman of action, he could tell now she was also a woman of contemplation. A combo that had helped make her chief deputy at a younger age than most, he was sure.

"There might be an up-and-coming gang in the area trying to establish itself," she started. "Sheriff Wayland guesses those men we ran into were a part of that group. I have to ask—did Gardner have any connections to local gangs?"

"No," James was quick to answer. "He was a gun for hire only. A floater. He liked not having ties to hold him down. He once told me the only anchor he really had to the past was his phone calls with me." Although James had known that as fact, saying it out loud to someone else made the truth in it hurt. Regret, anger and a growing ache of loss came together all at once in his chest. "But I guess that changed. Or would have, if he hadn't been killed."

"His son," Suzy said.

James let out a deep breath. A wave of exhaustion that was in no way physical washed away the rising emotions in his chest.

Gardner was gone, and there was nothing James could do about that. With his brother's death, their shared past had frozen without hope of ever changing their future. Losing the possibility of a different relationship was like losing his brother all over again. Just like when he'd heard Gardner had run away from school.

And just like when he'd found him shot to death in the warehouse.

"It's been four months since he died," James finally

said. "If Hank has had the boy this entire time, then I agree with our trigger-happy shooter from the house. Hank's waiting to do something. And considering I haven't been contacted for any reason, I'm assuming Gardner never told him who he really was. Who his family was."

"And who is this Hank?"

James rolled up to an intersection and stopped. All of the stoplights were flashing red. No other cars were on the road. It was just the two of them. He wondered if, under different circumstances, the two of them would have ever been in a similar situation. Just a man and a woman, tired in a car, making their way home together.

A different kind of ache started in his chest.

He ignored it.

"Gardner, as you can guess, never really talked about his extracurricular activities with me. But sometimes he would mention an associate named Hank. On more than one occasion, he even referred to him as his friend. He never mentioned any other names, so I think it's safe to assume our trigger-happy friends are talking about the same guy."

"And you know where he is?"

James held up his finger. "I know where he likes to drink," he said. "And if you ask me, that's better than knowing where he lays his head." He pressed the gas pedal down. It felt better to do that when not under extreme duress. "Which is why we're taking a road trip tomorrow."

That got her attention. "Where? And why not now?"

"While you were giving your statement, I made a few calls. The bar is empty minus the owner, and he doesn't plan to talk until he's had some sleep." James felt his expression harden. If only for a moment. "And I want us to be smart about this. Sharp. We can't do that with the way we look and the way we feel."

Suzy's head tilted enough that he saw her hair shift over her shoulder.

"The way we feel?" Her voice was off. It prompted him to look at her. He didn't understand the change.

"Don't tell me Action Hero Simmons doesn't get tired," he said. "Because I'll be honest—I'm feeling it, and I wasn't the one being thrown around like a rag doll in the back of a pickup truck."

Suzy snorted. "Right." She cleared her throat and rolled her shoulders back. "I'd also like to reassess our situation."

"Our situation?" He glanced her way again. She didn't meet his gaze.

"I don't want to be caught in another ambush. In a dress. With only one gun."

He couldn't argue with that.

James looked at the clock. By the time they made it back to his house, he guessed it would be nearly three. What Suzy didn't know was that, even if they did sleep, he still had pieces on the figurative chessboard. Moving without him, but because of him. He'd made more than a few calls while she'd been talking to the Calwarts deputies and detective. The less he told her, the fewer reasons she had to lie when questioned. Something he was still surprised she'd done with her fellow law enforcement.

She'd kept Gardner out of it. She'd kept Queso out of it. Hell, she'd even kept the baby out of it.

James didn't know if it was because Suzy believed in him, or if it was maternal instincts coupled with experi-

ence in the field that kept her from going in guns blazing with a county of deputies behind her.

Either way, he was starting to see that, while he'd
thought he knew everything about her through her reputation, she had a lot more surprises up her sleeve.

"I think the best we can do now is to head home, get
some sleep and regroup later in the morning."

"And by home, do you mean mine or yours?"

The question made sense, but the way Suzy said it
brought out another feeling in James that should be reserved for the bedroom.

Lust.

That was what it was. Front and center. A feeling he
couldn't deny.

But one he needed to right now.

"I wasn't going to kidnap you," he managed to joke,
trying to switch gears. "But I thought it might be a good
idea for you to at least clean up at my place before I take
you to yours. Unless you think you can sneak around
Justin before he has to get up for school."

"Don't forget my mother." A soft sigh escaped her
lips. "After the accident—well, she decided it would be
best to be closer to us."

"She lives with you now?"

Another sigh. "She took over Justin's bedroom. The
poor kid has been bunking with me since I got back from
the hospital. Though my injury…" Out of the corner of
his eye, he saw her hand move to her chest. Where the
bullet had hit. He remembered it in too much detail for
his liking. "I don't think he realized the danger of my
job until the accident. If he saw me like this?" She shook
her head. "Let's just say I'll take you up on your offer."

"Good." He smiled. "Because I already had clothes

for you brought to the house." Suzy whipped her head around so quickly that her hair went airborne for a split second. "Don't worry—it's not like I had them shipped in from France. I called my head of security earlier and got him to run to Walmart. He needed to get some things for Queso anyways."

"You didn't need to do that," she said. "I'll pay you back."

James slowed and then stopped at another intersection. He turned toward her and immediately fell into her eyes. They were like two pools of honey.

"Help me find my nephew, and help me find the person who ordered that his father be killed. *That's* how you can pay me back."

The chief deputy didn't miss a beat.

"You saved my life, so it's only fair that I can now help save his."

THE CALLAHAN ESTATE was surprisingly quiet. Over three thousand square feet, not including the four acres of land around it, the two-story house stood in the dark like an old friend with a welcoming hand outstretched. Suzy was surprised at the comfort she felt as they pulled up to it. Or maybe the comfort had more to do with the reaction James had to it. The moment he cut the engine, it was like he was shedding a burden from his body. His shoulders relaxed and his frown lessened as he walked with her into the house and showed her to one of the second-floor bedrooms.

"This is Chelsea's room," he said, motioning to the massive space. It seemed to double as a bedroom and a small office, though the desk was bare and most of the clothes in the open closet were gone.

"I don't want to intrude," Suzy started, taking in the various framed pictures on the walls, plastic trophies on a shelf and a few odds and ends that denoted a teenage girl had once inhabited the space. "Don't you have another two or three guest rooms?"

James waved the concern off. "None with a bathroom attached that's already stocked. Plus, she's away at college. She really won't mind. Just so long as you don't read her diary." He grinned. "Which may or may not be hidden in a shoe box beneath her bed."

James winked. "She might be good at science, but hiding things from me? Not so much." Before Suzy could really appreciate how much he clearly loved his sister, James's playful mood evaporated. "Your new clothes should be on the counter in the bathroom. There's a charger that should work for your phone in the nightstand. When you're done, I'll be in my office a few doors down. I'll leave the door open."

Suzy barely had time to thank him before he left. Then she made a beeline for the nightstand.

Even though her mother already knew she probably wasn't going to be home until early morning, Suzy still felt a surge of panic at being reminded that her only lifeline to Justin was dead in her hands. Although, logically, she knew that her mother was more than capable of finding her without a phone—she had been married to a cop, after all, not to mention that Billy, Mara and the sheriff's department were on their family phone's speed dial in case of emergencies—finding the charger lying at the top of the drawer made her breathe a sigh of relief. She attached it to her phone and plugged it into an outlet.

Suzy rolled her shoulders back. She knew she'd been doing it all night. They were sore, just like the rest of her. She let out another long, low sigh and stalked off to the bathroom.

Like the rest of the Callahan house, the shower was impressive. Or maybe Suzy was just too excited to wash the night off herself. At any rate, the warm water was just the thing she'd been seeking. She didn't even bat an eyelash at the fact that James's head of security had taken it upon himself to buy her a bra-and-panty set, along with a plain T-shirt and pair of sweatpants. Nor did she wonder at the fact that every article of clothing fit perfectly. She made a mental note to see if this head of security would be interested in trying to find her the elusive perfect pair of jeans.

By the time she finished up in the bathroom, her phone was partially charged. She turned it on and was met with one new voice mail. It was from her mother. Suzy sat down on the edge of the bed and hit Play.

"You're lucky I got ahold of Billy and he explained your phone was dead but you're okay. I was about to hunt you down if you turned it off on purpose. Anyways, just wanted to make sure you're okay and being careful. Billy kept his darn mouth shut about what you're working on—even though you're not supposed to be working yet—so I'll trust you two. Just make sure when you *do* get your phone working to at least text me that you're okay…or else I'm sending out the hounds to find you. Love you, Suzy Q."

Suzy usually cringed at her mother's nickname for her, but after the night she'd had, she couldn't help but smile. While Cordelia Simmons moving into the house had been stressful at times, Suzy was grateful for it now. She lay down on the bed and sent a text to her mother, assuring her she was okay. She also sent a quick text to

Billy, thanking him for covering for her. Suzy had only been able to tell him the bare bones of what had happened earlier—goons with guns in Riker County—before she'd had to switch gears to what was right in front of her and get off the phone. He'd promised to head back first thing in the morning.

Then she'd have to tell him what had happened.

Which made her wonder what really *had* happened. And why?

What had she gotten herself into?

Suzy took a deep breath. She still had a few questions for James Callahan.

Yet, as she compiled the ones she intended to go ask right then, the most pressing had nothing to do with the case. Instead, she found that her thoughts had strolled over into a more personal area. One that had no bearing on Gardner Todd or potential new gangs trying to make a name for themselves.

Was there someone special the millionaire had called after they'd just barely escaped death? Someone other than his sister? Someone who was just as worried as Suzy's mother had been about her?

Someone whose relationship with the man went past friendly and straight into his bedroom, only a few doors down?

Suzy closed her eyes, not liking the thought.

But she was too tired to question why it really bothered her.

Chapter Seven

She felt warm.

Suzy opened her eyes slowly, trying to blink some sense into what she was seeing.

Sunlight?

"I was starting to think I might have to throw some water on you."

Suzy rolled onto her side, away from the window that was the source of her current irritation. She groaned at the movement. Pain shot through her. On reflex, she put her hand to her chest.

"What the—" she started, confused. It didn't help that James was standing next to her, looking down with a grin.

"I'm guessing you feel as great as I do," he said. "Probably worse. At least I didn't have to wear heels during most of our wild night."

The haze of sleep was clogging up her thought processes. While she was looking at James, she couldn't understand why she was horizontal and he wasn't. And why the room behind him didn't look familiar. Not to mention why she was so groggy.

Then it dawned on her.

"Oh, my God, I fell asleep!"

James's grin widened. "You sure did. Even snored a little. I thought you'd keep sleeping, too, but then you seemed to smell this." He shook a cup in his hand. The unmistakable smell of fresh coffee met her nose. It did nothing to stop the panic and heat that crawled up her neck.

"Why didn't you wake me up?" she demanded. In another move that reminded her that her body had been through the wringer, she swung her legs over the side of the bed and stood. "I have a kid! I can't just fall asleep in strange men's houses!" Suzy scrubbed a hand down her face. "Not to mention, my mom is going to kill me," she groaned. It earned a laugh from the man. Suzy shot him a look that she hoped burned.

James held his hand up to stop the next onslaught of anger she was about to let out. "Don't worry. Your mother was very understanding when I spoke to her."

"What?" Suzy managed to ask around her pounding heart. Who needed coffee when you woke up and immediately panicked? She already had more adrenaline running through her than when she'd been shot at. "You *talked* to her?"

He shrugged. "It was less me talking and more of her asking what kind of cake I like." He cracked a grin. "But I got the general point across before we started talking about the pound cake she made me while you were in recovery at the hospital."

Suzy felt her eyebrows hit her hairline.

"I told her that, after the party, I asked you to look into an issue I was having with a local company and, after some sifting through boxes of files and some light investigating, I offered you one of the guest rooms to rest in when the coffee stopped working. That's when we started talking about cakes."

Suzy's hip jutted out before she could stop it. She narrowed her eyes for a moment, then burst out laughing.

James looked alarmed. As he should have.

"You lied to my mother?" She shook her head and took the cup of coffee from him. The man might have been good at keeping his cool in danger-filled situations, but he had no idea the minefield he'd just stepped into. "And you thought being shot at was bad?"

James held up his hands in self-defense. "Hey, I figured it was either going to be me telling the fib or you. If you ask me, I took one for the team." His expression turned serious. "I've only met your mother a few times in the hospital. I don't know your relationship with her, but I know from the hospital that she seems to genuinely care about you. Which means if we told her the truth right now—"

"She would worry more than she already does," Suzy finished. "Plus, it could put her in danger. She's not the type of person to just stand by when her flock is threatened."

James gave a small smile. "So, I told the lie so you wouldn't have to. I could see how much it bothered you to lie to the deputies and sheriff last night." Like a sucker punch to the gut, Suzy felt the same guilt as before. She gave James one quick, appreciative nod. "Now, when you're ready, come downstairs. While you've been sleeping, I've been busy."

James walked to the door. Suzy set down her coffee.

"You know, it should bother you, too," she said, all trace of humor gone. "Lying, that is."

James paused in the doorway. The jokes and charm he

threw around like his own personal weapons remained in their sheaths now. His voice was cold, even.

"Sometimes lying is the only way we can protect good people." Ocean-blue eyes swallowed Suzy for a moment. The room and everything in it seemed to disappear. All that was left was the two of them—and pain. "My brother taught me that."

And then he was gone.

QUESO WAS EIGHTEEN, and had a sprained ankle and a real bone to pick with James. These were the only three facts he'd been able to get out of the boy since he'd been shown into the kitchen by Douglas, who, judging by the look on his face before he went outside, wasn't particularly happy at being saddled with watching the boy.

"You can't keep me here, old man!" Queso yelled. "I'm legally an adult! I have rights, you know!"

James finished topping off his third cup of coffee since he'd found Suzy asleep. He'd tried to sleep, as well, knowing rest was a necessity for staying sharp, but the moment his head hit his pillow he'd started thinking about Gardner. And Gardner's son. He hadn't been able to go to sleep after that.

"Yes, you have the right to be tortured and killed," James conceded. "But I think it's better for the moment that you are neither kidnapped nor dead." Queso's eyes widened enough that James knew his blunt approach had hit home. He also knew that the boy wasn't stupid. On the topic of options, he had few to none, and James didn't have the time to baby him. "Until we can figure out who this group is and why they're pulling the strings they are, you have a target on your back. One that, as I've told you, they really want to come after."

"You said that guy said that Sully wasn't dead. That he was out there somewhere," Queso tried. He put his hands on the kitchen island in the middle of the room in an attempt to really hammer his point home. "Let me go find him. He can keep me safe."

James reached into the cabinet and pulled out a mug. He kept his body turned so he could still see Queso's face as he poured coffee.

"Listen, I get it. I really do," James started. "From what I can tell, Sully saved your life, probably in more ways than one and probably before the shooting last night. I'm also going to go out on a limb and assume you don't have family to turn to, or maybe you do, and you'd rather not.

"But Sully is a smart man, despite his decision to stay on the less-than-savory side of the law. He sent you here, to me, when he could have hidden you elsewhere or even taken you with him. Not to mention, he has plenty of people who could have come to me, instead, with that address. That tells me two things." James topped off the cup and placed it on the island between them. "One, he wanted to try to keep you safe because he knows it's about to get crazy out there. Two, as of right now, he knew *this* place would be safe."

James pushed the cup of coffee closer to the boy and pointed to the cabinet behind him.

"The sugar is in there, and the creamer is in the fridge." He didn't give Queso the room to speak. Not that he looked like he knew what he wanted to say anyway. His expression was thoughtful. "You stay here, make yourself at home and let me figure out who's doing this. Okay? And then, when it's over with, I'll be happy to take you anywhere you want. Deal?"

It took him a moment, but eventually Queso took the mug. "You got until Monday," he said. "Then I'm out."

"Deal."

James took his coffee out to the patio. It was a beautiful day, all things considered. Upper eighties, low humidity and blue, blue skies. The weatherman claimed rain in the weekend forecast, but James had tunnel vision. Today was the important day.

Today he was going to find his nephew.

He took a long drink of his coffee and wondered if Suzy's willingness to bend her code by lying and withholding information to help him had anything to do with a need for revenge she wasn't telling him about. It didn't take a rocket scientist to make the jump that the people who were after Gardner's son were the same people who had hired Lester McGibbon to kill him…which, in turn, had gotten her shot. Shooting her might not have been premeditated, but her nearly dying by his hand made the blame game stretch to the same people James was after. It aligned their goals, if revenge was hers.

But was it James's goal?

Hadn't he spent months trying to find his brother's killer, even before he knew there was a baby out there?

Was *he* after revenge for his brother?

And for what had happened to Suzy?

As unwanted as they always were, images of her almost dying beneath his hands as he tried to stop the bleeding took a front-row seat in his mind.

He shouldn't have gotten her involved. The same group of men who had destroyed the small house were currently after Gardner's kid. Sure, James realized that Queso showing up at the house might have forced his hand to include Suzy in his personal investigation, but he hadn't resisted the idea as much as he could have.

The last four months had been emotionally exhausting, as he'd tried to find the right thread to pull to unravel the mystery that was his brother's life. He realized now that when Suzy had stood next to Queso, shoes in her hand and fire in her eyes, and demanded he explain everything, maybe he'd wanted to finally share everything with someone.

Or maybe just with her.

James took another drink and then sighed. The door behind him opened.

Like his thoughts had summoned her, Suzy stopped at his side.

"Whatever you've found out, you can update me in the car," she said in greeting. Pure authority rang through each syllable. Suzy might not have officially been on the job, but he bet her mind was always ready for work. "As much as I appreciate the fact that I won't be slinking home in a ruined dress and barefoot, I really want to get into my own clothes. Not to mention a holster that's more accessible."

"I don't know—watching you pull a Glock out from under your dress was quite the sight," James chimed in. "I bet it would have made the bad guys stop in their tracks."

Suzy surprised him. In one fluid motion she was in front of him, eyes narrowed and attention firmly on his face.

"I understand you use charm and humor as weapons, so much so that I'm sure people don't even realize you're playing them," she started. "But I want you to know right now, James Callahan, that I'm not some Bates Hill resident or millionaire groupie hanging around for a show. What I am is a single mother to a boy who is still afraid of the dark and needs help with learning the right way to use a bat so he doesn't keep hitting fouls. A boy who has a deadbeat dad who never was in the picture and an overbearing grandmother who was in it too much at times. A boy who I refuse to leave behind by being careless and treating the *real* danger like it's anything but.

"So, while I can appreciate the smirks and banter and a joke or two to lighten the mood, what I need from you before we go any further is simple." She spread her fingers out and placed her hand flat against his chest.

When she spoke again, James had eyes only for her. "I need you to be on your A game, Mr. Callahan. Plain and simple. You bring your best, and I promise you I'll bring mine."

This time there was no humor in his response. All James could feel was her hand against his chest. He wondered if she realized that four months ago he'd been doing the same to her, trying to spot her from bleeding out.

"I've always brought my best with you," he said. "I won't stop now."

Suzy searched his expression for something—he didn't know what—until she was apparently satisfied. She tapped his chest before pulling away, a smile lighting up her face.

"Good. Now let's get out of here and find your nephew."

James held up his finger to stop her from leaving.

"Speaking of being on our A game, how good are you at role-playing?"

Chapter Eight

Cordelia Simmons was short, slim and proud of everything she did. Which was never limited to and always included following her daughter around, room to room, until she got the answer she was seeking. A Southern helicopter mom, born and bred.

Among many things, how Suzy had managed to get pregnant when she was twenty-one had always been a mystery to the woman. Even when Suzy mockingly went through the logistics of how such things happened, the older Simmons put her hands on her hips and *tsk*ed at her daughter.

The moment Suzy got out of the car, wearing sweats and James's sister's flip-flops, she knew her mother would show up in spectacular fashion. Not only had Suzy returned after spending a night away from home, she'd brought company along with her. The businessman was all smiles as Suzy looked over her shoulder and told him to stay in the car.

"Do you think she'll let that happen?" he asked. With a nod, he motioned to the front of her house. Suzy didn't have to turn around to know that her mother was already on the front porch.

"If you want us to leave within the next few minutes,

then I suggest you put your phone to your ear and stay put in the car," she said hurriedly, her voice low. "As far as she's concerned, I just spent the night *with* you."

A devilish look crossed James's face. It was meant to be teasing, she knew, but Suzy couldn't help but feel her body react to it. She only hoped *her* expression didn't give her away.

James responded with a smirk before pulling out his phone. It would only hold off her mother for a few minutes, at best. Which meant Suzy was already on a deadline.

She took a quick breath, pivoted and barely made it to the first porch step before her mother was all she could see.

"Honey, are you okay? Why didn't you come home last night? Are you feeling good? You look like a mess! Where's Mara's dress? Where are your shoes? You don't wear flip-flops!"

Suzy chose not to answer anything until she was inside her bedroom. That didn't stop her mother. She rattled off a few more questions before Suzy knew she'd have to bite.

"Mom, I'm okay. Like James said on the phone with you earlier, I've just been helping him with some things that he needed someone familiar with law enforcement to deal with." It wasn't a flat-out lie. Suzy just hoped her mother didn't see that it was a truth filled with cracks. "You know how I get with some cases. A little too focused, and time slips away from me."

Suzy made it to her dresser and started to root around for undergarments *not* purchased by the head of Callahan's security. Her mother stood her ground right behind her.

"So, you sleep with James Callahan instead of coming home? And on a school night, no less!"

Suzy let out a half grunt, half sigh—a sound that only her mother could compel her to make—and rolled her eyes. She might grow older every day, but her mother could make her feel like a teen in a second flat.

"Mom, you know I didn't sleep *with* him."

The elder Simmons crossed her arms over her chest and lifted her chin. She shrugged. "Well, maybe that wouldn't be such a bad thing if you did."

"Mom!"

She shrugged again as Suzy huffed away into her bathroom. A second later and she wouldn't have been able to shut the door. Thankfully Suzy threw the lock between them. Still, her mother wasn't perturbed.

"I'm just saying, you've definitely done worse," she called through the door. "A handsome, suave man like James? I'm just saying, he has my vote."

"Did you just say *suave*?" Suzy hedged, stripping down. "Since when do you talk like that?"

"Like what? Educated?" her mom shot back. Suzy wouldn't have done it had her mother been in plain view, but since she wasn't, Suzy smiled.

"You know what, Suzanne? I take it back. James probably deserves someone better than your ungrateful, sassy self."

Suzy felt her smile grow. Right up until the day her father had passed, he'd always said the thing he loved most about Cordelia Simmons was how feisty she could become over the smallest things. It kept life interesting, he'd say. The same opinion held true for Suzy now. While her mother wasn't always the easiest to get along with, Suzy knew she'd much rather fight with her mother than be without her.

"You need to calm down," Suzy said, half finished dressing. After hearing the plan James had hatched, she'd chosen a shirt she wouldn't normally wear out and about. For the past three years it had stayed in the back of her closet with the question of *will this fit?* hanging over it every time she'd glanced in its direction. Now she sucked in and pulled it down over her head, hoping her love of bread and pasta hadn't betrayed her.

"You're just mad because you think there's something going on between me and James, and that I'm not telling you about it," Suzy continued, voice slightly muffled as the blouse went over her mouth. She slid it the rest of the way down slowly. It wasn't until the bottom hit the waistband of her jeans that she let out a sigh of relief. Though one look in the mirror and she realized her mother was going to have a field day.

Red, sleeveless and with a neckline that plunged down into a deep V, it was a blouse made for an evening out, topped off with the rest of the night spent in. While she had a few dresses that did their job of making her feel red-hot, Suzy couldn't deny that a good pair of tight jeans coupled with this date-night blouse put them to shame. And the leather jacket she'd snagged made her feel even more slick.

She admired herself for a few seconds before applying some quick makeup and attempting to make her hair presentable. She even pulled out some perfume she saved for special occasions. It wasn't until she had her hand on the doorknob that she hesitated, wondering if her concern for how she looked was more for what she and James were about to do, or if it was more for the man himself.

Suzy took a deep breath. Then walked out to face her mama.

"Well, good gracious, Suzy Q," she started, looking her daughter up and down. "You come in wearing sweats and you leave to go clubbing? I know I said you should date him, but maybe space those dates out a little more."

"I'm still helping him with an investigation," Suzy defended herself. "And before you get all crazy, know that some of it requires some information gathering at a bar in Kipsy." She motioned to her outfit. "I don't want to spook anyone by looking like I'm a cop."

The older woman's face pinched. She frowned.

"That doesn't sound safe," she said. Her gaze flitted down to the spot on Suzy's chest that had a near-perfect circular scar. The shirt just barely covered it, but like Suzy, her mother would always know exactly where it was.

"It's important and urgent," Suzy said, not denying the situation deserved caution. "But I promise you I'll stay on my toes, keep my eyes open and be back in time to bring you and Justin supper. Okay?"

Cordelia's frown stayed put, but she nodded. Suzy gave the woman a quick hug, collected the rest of her things and was out the door and running to the car when her mother decided to get in the last word.

"Mr. Callahan, you better bring my girl back in one piece, or so help me, you'll have to answer to me!"

James leaned across the front seats and called out through the open passenger door. "Yes, ma'am!"

It wasn't until the door was shut and they were pulling away that he said anything to her.

"You definitely don't look like a cop."

There was no humor or charm lurking behind each

word. No punch line he was waiting to hit. Instead, his attention was beyond the windshield, focus pulling his expression tight. Which was good. What they were about to do wasn't a joking matter.

THE BAR WASN'T OLD, but it carried a vintage aesthetic that started with the wooden sign that hung in the window and continued through the main room with its leather chairs and wooden bar stools, and even carried right into the men's bathroom, where James admired the mirrors, worn, but hanging in there.

While he scoped the restroom out, along with a door that he assumed led to an office, he couldn't help but get swept up in admiring the establishment on the outskirts of the city of Kipsy. It probably didn't help that it was named simply The Tavern. He'd toyed with the idea of starting up a bar while he'd been deployed. Every idea he'd come up with had been just as simple but elegant. He wasn't a heavy drinker, but he'd always appreciated a good, solid beverage.

Now, sitting in a corner of the main room, James wished he could have a good, solid beverage other than the beer between his hands. It was for show. Mostly. He ran his fingers down the glass of his bottle, wiping away the condensation that had collected. It was his first beer, and he was doing his best to make it last. The adage "it's five o'clock somewhere" didn't feel right at ten in the morning.

"Are you sure your friend isn't trying to pull one over on us?" Suzy wasn't looking at him. Instead, her gaze was bouncing between the one wall-mounted TV over the bar that had been turned on with an old football game playing on it and the front door. Her drink wasn't as full as his. Neither was her patience. Occasionally she would bite her bottom lip. It made it harder to keep his thoughts on point. "He could be setting us up."

James started to peel the corner of his label off. He shook his head.

"She," he corrected her. "And Hale might be a lot of things, but a liar she is not. She said her contact called in a favor to get us this early meeting, assuring her friend that we weren't looking for trouble, just information. I believe her. He has no idea who we're looking for or who I am."

Suzy's eyebrow rose, but she didn't meet his eyes. Cheering blared out of the TV as a team scored a touchdown. The bartender, Rudy, who'd had to let them in and start his shift early, and had done so without comment, watched the game with little interest. He didn't watch James or Suzy at all.

"So, not only do you have a lot of contacts, but your *contacts* have a lot of contacts," she stated.

"What can I say? Everyone knows someone."

"True," she conceded. He watched as her long, thin fingers wrapped around her bottle and she took one lengthy pull. Again, James wondered what it would be like to be out with Suzy without the cloak-and-dagger, danger and deceit, and hidden guns. It was true, he'd spent the time she was in the hospital trying to get to know her when he could, but that had only resulted in polite miscommunications and then straight-up avoidance. He'd then taken to internet searches and veiled inquiries of people he knew who had grown up with her or worked alongside her. He had been curious then, just as he was curious now, about who Suzanne Simmons was outside of her job. Outside of the Riker County Sheriff's Department.

"Hale Cooper is the sister of one of my buddies from my old Air Force unit," James explained, hoping to make her feel more at ease. "Between deployments, I would tag along to some of their family get-togethers. Sometimes Chelsea was included, too. After I left the Air Force to come back here, I kept in touch with everyone, including Hale. She still comes to Chelsea's birthday parties every year." He smiled. "Basically, she's a good friend and wouldn't steer me wrong."

Suzy turned to look at him now. Her eyebrow had come back down, but he could still see a question there. One he usually got when Hale was around. "We never dated and never wanted to," he added. "It's more of a sibling bond. I would assume like the one you seem to have with our fearless sheriff." A barely-there smile crossed her lips. He'd hit the nail on the head with that observation. Not that it had been hard.

"My dad used to say that family isn't blood. It's who you decide to love and who decides to love you back. You work for it. You're not just born into it." Suzy's smile became more pronounced. James was surprised she was opening up at all. He'd only shared about Hale to ease her mind. Or maybe to let her know that he wasn't interested in his friend. At least, not in the way he was with Suzy.

The thought entered his mind so quickly that he nearly missed what she said next.

"One of the last things he ever said to me was about Billy," she continued. "He told me to look out for him because he was a good kid and he didn't have any brothers or sisters." Her smile started to fade. "I didn't know he was sick then, and trying to give me as much advice as he could, while he could, but after he passed I made sure to take what he said seriously. Though it wasn't hard. Billy's always been there, and when he couldn't be, he made sure someone was."

She snorted. It made James smile on reflex. "I got pregnant when I was twenty-one. Not ideal, but it happened. When I told Justin's father, he called me a liar and then said several very bad things. Half the school heard, because in my mind telling him at a college football game was an awesome idea, and I remember getting so sad. But then *so* mad. He just kept saying horrible things to me. He wouldn't stop. I was two seconds from punching his lights out just to shut him up when Billy appeared out of nowhere and did it for me."

"Good man," James added, meaning it. He'd already done the math and knew Suzy had to have had Justin when she was around twenty, but beyond that he hadn't known what had happened for sure. Especially not with Justin's father.

"Yeah, I can't deny it was really nice to have him shut up, but—" She held up her index finger. "The real moment I knew Billy had become my family for life was just after that, when Justin's dad left town. I hadn't had the guts to tell my mom yet, and my sister was out of state, so there was no buffer.

"I was sitting on the front porch, trying to get the nerve up, when Billy shows up in his dad's Bronco. I remember being so scared about the future, about being a mom, and a single one, at that. And there he was, goofy as hell with a smile to match. He walked up and just said 'You two are going to be fine.' Just like that. No lie, just confidence. He believed it so much that it was enough at that moment to help me believe it, too." She shrugged. "He's been Uncle Billy ever since."

Suzy's affectionate demeanor shifted so suddenly that James tensed. There was ice in her words as she spoke.

"Which is why we need to figure everything out before he gets back into town," she said. "I don't want to lie to him. Not after everything he's done for me."

James wanted to assure Suzy that he'd do everything in his power to make sure it all worked out, but the moment he opened his mouth to do so, a man walked into the bar. He nodded to the bartender, who immediately stood up and left.

The man didn't look their way until Rudy was out of the room.

Then the man walked toward them with purpose.

Chapter Nine

The man, burly and tall, bald and bearded, pulled a chair over and sat down heavily. He wore a dark shirt and dark jeans, and had tattoos across the skin that showed. Suzy estimated his age around upper forties. She didn't recognize him, and by the look on James's face, neither did he. However, he got right to the point, which Suzy appreciated.

"So, you have a question for me. What is it?"

Suzy wanted to adjust her stance so she could more easily get to the gun hidden beneath her jacket. It was an urge she had to tamp down, however. The point of their cover story was to hide the fact that she was law enforcement for as long as they could. They didn't want to spook the man if he wasn't on the good side of the law. And if he had any affiliation with Hank or Gardner, it was safe to assume he wasn't.

James kept playing with the label from his beer. He seemed so relaxed. A cool cucumber.

"We're looking for a man named Hank," James said. "A mutual friend told me and my girl here that we could trust him."

The man didn't give anything away. His expression

remained the same one of slight annoyance that he'd shown them the moment he walked in.

"I'm sure there are a lot of Hanks in the world," he answered. "What makes you think I know where this one is?"

James motioned to the bar on the other side of the room. "Because that same friend told me this is where he likes to drink, and since you own the place, I'm betting you already know who I'm talking about."

"Even if I did know who this Hank was, you haven't given me a reason to tell you," the man countered. "What's your business with him?"

"My business is my own," James replied. Suzy was impressed at the level tone, as if he were calmly telling a child no instead of refusing to answer a man twice his size.

"Meeting with you was a favor given to an associate, but I'm telling you now you're *in* my business. You can't make demands and expect me to buckle to them."

He crossed his arms over his chest. Suzy saw a new set of tattoos on the back of his arm. A snake with stripes coiled near his elbow. Although unique and adventurous, the rest of his tattoos were the standard macho variety. No gang-related symbols jumped out at her. The bar owner was tough, but if he was on the seedier side of the law, he didn't broadcast it in body art like some of the men and women the sheriff's department had handled in the past.

"I'm not trying to be disrespectful," James said. "It's just a personal matter we'd like to keep quiet. So why don't you name your price, instead. Payment for your information."

James didn't make a show of taking out his checkbook, like they did in movies. It was the best move to make, in Suzy's opinion. He was exuding nothing but confidence in his nonchalance. No fear or worry.

The man, however, was unimpressed.

"Money isn't a motivation to me. I don't know you *or* your lady. And I don't think any mutual friend of ours is going to change that fact, especially if it has to do with one of the people who may or may not be a patron of my bar."

He rose in one quick movement. James didn't flinch. Suzy's fingers itched for her gun's trigger. If the man was holding a weapon, it was well hidden. He took a few steps away from them and held his hand out to the door. "You can tell me right now who you are, who your friend is and what you want with Hank if you find him. Even with a pretty lady on your arm, I'm not a man who takes payoffs."

The urgency that Suzy had been feeling all morning finally came to a head. There was a child out there who was being targeted for whatever reason, and James and Suzy were on a short list of those who wanted to keep him safe. She felt the slithering shame of having already lied to those in law enforcement who would also try to keep the boy safe, and she'd simply had enough. James opened his mouth, but she stood and spoke first.

"Gardner Todd wanted us to meet Hank," she said. "And to be really honest with you, we're pressed for time. So instead of acting big and bad, actually talking to us would be preferred. We need to know where Hank is. Now."

Suzy couldn't read his reaction. He now looked mildly bored instead of annoyed. Still, his tone fell flat.

"Gardner Todd is dead," he said simply. "And has

been for months. Whatever business you think you had with him died with him. It has no place here."

"Don't you want to know who we are?" Suzy prodded.

He shook his head. "No, I don't. The favor was to meet you and I've done that. Now see yourself out. The beers are on me."

"Listen here, buddy," Suzy started, finger going up to stop him from talking over her. But instead of hearing authority in her voice, all she could hear was her mother. "We need to—"

"Did you ask anyone else to come meet us?"

Suzy and the man turned to James. He was on his feet, staring past them. For a second she thought the question was for her. Then the man answered.

"No. I'm assuming you didn't, either?"

Suzy heard a car door shut before she pivoted to look out of the front window. James swore loudly. The SUV didn't have bullet holes in it, but it was identical to the vehicle that Suzy and James had been chased by the night before. Three men got out. They were dressed in jeans and T-shirts. If they had guns—which, if it *was* the same people, she assumed they did—they were most likely concealed in the backs of their waistbands.

"No. They're not with us. But if it's the same people we ran into last night, then I'm betting they're here for Hank, too," she answered. "And I guarantee they won't ask you to talk like we did." She didn't recognize any of the men, but then again, she hadn't been able to make out any faces the night before. But she couldn't be certain if the same was true for the men. She *had* been in plain view during the chase and the following shoot-out.

"Just in case you don't know them, I'll tell you those aren't good men," James warned. His hand slid around hers. He started to pull her toward the back hallway. "It might be best that we leave while we can."

Suzy thought about standing their ground, testing their cover of boyfriend and girlfriend and seeing what happened next, but then the men stopped in their tracks and looked back at their car. Inside, the bar fell silent. James's hand tightened slightly. It was warm and reassuring. The men looked like they were waiting for something. Suzy didn't like it.

Neither did her gut.

"I'm calling in backup," she said, making a decision. Waiting to see if something bad was going to happen wasn't a strategy they should be using anymore. Not after what had already happened. She felt James stiffen, but he didn't argue. She glanced up to see his focus was on the bar owner. His arms were still down at his sides. If he drew a weapon, she'd be faster.

"You're cops?" he asked, voice low.

"I am," Suzy retorted, dropping James's hand and going for her gun. The bar's front windows were heavily tinted. It was easy for them to see out, but those in the parking lot would have a harder time making heads or tails of the people inside. Still, she felt exposed. She didn't like it.

Out of the corner of her eye, she saw James straighten his back even more. The men in the parking lot were still looking at their car. Suzy pulled her phone out with her free hand.

"I'm not a cop," he announced. "I'm James Callahan, Gardner Todd's little brother." Suzy couldn't help but turn at that, surprised. James's jaw was set. Hard. His focus was on the man in the middle of the room. "And I'm pretty sure you're Hank." He pointed out of the window. "Which means they're here for my nephew, and I'm not going to let them get him. What about you?"

Suzy had several questions—how had James known the man was Hank? *Was* he really Hank? How had the men in the SUV found them? But it didn't matter. The bar owner only had one.

"What was Gardner's real name?"

James didn't miss a beat. "Trick question. Gardner *was* his real name. He was named after our grandfather on our mother's side. All he did was drop the Callahan after he ran away."

Suzy held her breath, waiting for a reaction from the man at James's answer. Finally she got one. Now she could read his expression with ease.

Relief.

"He told me he was going to talk to his brother about the kid, but he refused to give me a name. He was more uptight about privacy than I was."

"Where is he?" James pressed. "The boy."

The bang of another car door shutting prevented an answer. All three turned to watch as a fourth man stood next to the SUV.

This time it was Hank who swore.

"Who are they?" Suzy had to ask.

The men came together and began their walk across the parking lot toward the front door. Whoever the fourth man was, he had changed the group's demeanor. They weren't there for a leisurely drink or two. They weren't there to ask questions politely. They were there for answers.

And blood.

A sentiment Hank already seemed privy to.

"Follow me," he said quickly, swinging around and

rushing to the back hallway. Suzy hesitated. James didn't. He had her hand again, fingers gripping hers and the phone in her hand. She let herself be pulled along as she realized that Hank was projecting another heavy emotion.

Worry.

"I don't know the first three, but the last fella is Grayton McKenzie," Hank called over his shoulder. Instead of leading them to the back door, he swung a right and headed through a fairly large but cluttered room.

The kitchen.

The bartender looked up from the sandwich he was eating. One look at Hank and he was as rigid as a soldier before a commanding officer.

"Rudy, I need you to go to the house and check on Patricia. Bring your gun." Suzy opened her mouth, but Hank was faster. "He's got a permit for it and no criminal record. But I need you to go with him and go ahead and send deputies out there. An ambulance, too."

"What? Why?" James was just as lost as she was.

"There are only two people who knew how to find me. Grayton landing on my doorstep means he either found me through Gardner or through my wife. If it was Patricia, then you'll need to get to my place fast. My lady plays by the rules, but she's a fighter, too. If Grayton and his boys went asking questions, she didn't give them answers easy." Rage and worry battled for position across his face. So did sincerity. He looked at James. "That's where your nephew is."

James's grip tightened around her hand. As if a current of electricity was running between them, she felt a charge of excitement. Excitement and caution.

"You're not coming with us?" she asked, trying to ignore the surge of adrenaline beginning to move through her.

Hank shook his head. "Grayton isn't the type of man to stop unless he's gotten what he wants. I want to find out what that is."

"You're outmanned," Suzy pointed out. She nodded back behind them. On cue, the antique bell James had admired over the front door sounded. "If we stay, there's a better chance of—"

"You make sure my wife and that boy are okay," he interrupted. "I'll deal with Grayton."

The two men looked at each other. Finally, James nodded.

"Hello?" a man called from the front room. "Can we get some service in here or what?"

"Now go," Hank said to Rudy.

He was wide-eyed but accommodating. He went to a door on the opposite wall and opened it, revealing the back alley.

"Hold your damn horses," Hank called out, already moving back into the hallway. "I'm comin'!"

"They could kill him," Suzy whispered, but James didn't pause. He pulled her along with him all the way until they were in Rudy's truck. Even then, he didn't let go of her hand until they were racing away from the bar.

HANK'S HOUSE WAS in the country, just like Gardner's had been. However, it was less off the beaten path and seemed more lived-in at first glance—garden beds in the yard, patio furniture on the front porch and even a wreath on the door. James knew that judging people based on their appearances wasn't always reliable, but he couldn't help but be surprised that the man they'd left at the bar lived in such a quaint place. There was even a little gnome wearing a flowered dress next to the mailbox.

Then again, according to Hank, he didn't live alone.

"Patricia is a really nice woman. I hope nothing bad went down here," Rudy said, breaking his silence. He'd kept his mouth shut as Suzy had spent the ride in the back seat on the phone with the sheriff's department. He hadn't even muttered a word when she'd called local police to The Tavern, making sure the officers knew that Hank was friendly but also a person of interest. James wanted to ask if Rudy had known Gardner, but he knew it wasn't the time. Suzy and the bartender weren't the only ones with guns. He had his compact .45 caliber in the holster at the back of his pants and wasn't afraid to draw if he needed to.

"It doesn't look like anyone is here," James said.

Rudy stopped his truck a few feet from the closed garage door. There were no other vehicles in the long driveway or on either side of the house. There was a house in the distance, but it was one heck of a walk. James squinted but couldn't make out any vehicles that way, either. If any of Grayton's pals were around, they were hiding well enough.

"Rudy, have you ever been inside?" James asked after Suzy hung up with whoever was on the phone. Rudy put the truck in Park but didn't cut the engine. "Do you know the layout of the house? Any good spots where someone might try to jump out and get us from?"

The man sucked on his teeth, brow furrowed. "The living room is right when you walk in, and there's a small hallway to the left with a bedroom and a bathroom. I've never been to their bedroom upstairs," Rudy answered. "Only time I've ever been here was at a Christmas thing

Patricia threw last year. I got plastered, and they let me sleep it off in the room downstairs. The kitchen's in the back with a door that goes to a patio. I think there's a shed behind the garage, but I was too wasted to really check it out at the party."

Suzy slid forward in her seat. Her service weapon was already out. She might not have been cleared for field duty yet, but James knew from the determination shining bright and clear in her eyes that not even the sheriff could have stopped her.

"Is Patricia the type of woman to take us out with a shotgun if she thinks we're a threat?" she asked.

Rudy hesitated, then nodded. "She'll protect herself, and if there's a kid in there, she'll protect him, too."

"Does she know you well enough that she'll believe you when you tell her we're friendly?"

Rudy didn't hesitate this time when he nodded.

"Hank doesn't have a lot of people he trusts, but I'm one of them." His chest puffed out in pride.

"Okay, leave the truck running but come with us. Keep your gun in its holster until I tell you to bring it out. Or we start taking fire," Suzy ordered. She shared a look with James. It was worried. "The closest patrol to us is a few minutes out. An ambulance is just behind them. But if there's a chance there's a hurt woman and kid in there?"

James understood. And agreed.

"Right behind you, Chief Deputy."

Chapter Ten

"Hey, Patricia, if you got a shot on us, don't take it! Hank sent us to make sure you're okay!"

Rudy yelled the same line three times before they made it to the front door. So far, she hadn't responded. No one had. It wasn't until they were smack-dab in front of the door that the sense of something being terribly wrong crept in. It wasn't locked, but it had been. The dead bolt hung in its intended spot, but the wood around it was splintered.

The door had been kicked in.

James turned to Suzy. She made a succession of hand motions that made him feel like he was back in boot camp again. She wanted him to go right while she went left when they went inside.

No dice, he thought.

"We stay together," he mouthed.

The urgency of the situation didn't give Suzy room to argue.

"Stay here," she whispered to Rudy, instead. "Keep an eye out."

The bartender nodded, hand hovering over the spot where his gun must have been hidden in the back of his pants. He might have originally seemed as big and bad as his employer, but James could see how unsettled he was. Nervous and not ready. Which meant he probably didn't find himself in this situation often.

Suzy led the way into the house, gun sweeping the room seconds before James did the same. Together they pivoted, ducked and moved through the living room, hallway and two guest bedrooms like synchronized dancers. Their flow never wavered as they scanned each room in silence.

James balanced being alert with being observant. *Southern Living* magazines were spread around almost every room alongside football paraphernalia and a few issues of *Jeeps* magazine. Fresh flowers were in worn vases in both bedrooms, while the bathroom was pristine. Both beds were made, the rooms they were in smelling as pretty as the flora around them. Yet, despite the bottom floor being pristine, there was one detail that made the unease in James's stomach heavier. However, he kept it behind closed lips as he led Suzy up the stairs to the one part of the house Rudy had never seen.

The master bedroom was small but, like the house itself, quaint. It was furnished with white linens embroidered with flowers and leaves, and an oversize leather chair in the corner with a quilt across it. A large window let in enough sun to warm the space. Again, not what James had expected from Hank, not in the least. Not that anything he'd learned in the past two days had been less surprising.

The master bathroom was pretty much the same as the bathroom downstairs, and both closets in the bedroom were filled with women's and men's clothing. One had a small box in the corner of it. Suzy popped open the lid to confirm it contained nothing having to do with a secret baby.

Once they finished, Suzy lowered her gun.

"Someone broke the front door to get in, but there are no signs of a fight." She motioned around the room. "And unless we're missing something pretty big, I don't think any baby lives here, or any older kids, for that matter. Do you think Hank was playing us?"

James shook his head. "I think Patricia *was* here. I noticed that there are no bags in this entire house." Suzy's eyebrow rose. He elaborated. "In the closet downstairs, under the beds, the cabinets…no duffel bags or luggage. Not even Walmart bags in the kitchen. Someone who is *this* neat with their house, and this organized, could easily handle fleeing with a kid without leaving any traces behind. I'm guessing it was Patricia. There are easily thirty issues of *Southern Living* magazine throughout this house, and every single one is neat and orderly."

"Suggesting Patricia wouldn't get sloppy if she needed to stay discreet," Suzy said. "Like if she needed to leave in a hurry with a baby no one is supposed to know about."

James nodded. He walked to the window and looked out into the distance. The driveway started at the end of a long, thin road that branched off an even longer county road. Both were in clear view.

"She could have gotten lucky and seen a car or two on the county road, and gotten ready just in case," he ventured. "If she saw them turn, then she could have had two minutes, maybe, to do something."

"But do what? Grab a baby and a bag with all of his belongings and then…hide? Run?"

James snapped his fingers. "Rudy said there was a shed out back," he said, suddenly remembering.

Suzy pulled her gun back out, and together they hurried to the backyard. By the time they were pushing wide the shed's door, which was hanging open, but not broken like the front door, the faint sound of sirens began in the distance.

And James was cussing up a storm.

"Or maybe Hank *did* play us," he snarled, moving out into the grass. Like the house, the shed didn't hold a woman or baby or anything out of the ordinary. "Maybe he's working *with* that Grayton guy. And I just gave him my name." He turned and kicked the side of the shed hard. Frustration raged through him in sync with the painful throb that shot through his foot. He didn't care.

"But someone *did* break in the front door," Suzy pointed out. "And, even though we don't know much about Hank, he seemed genuine in his concern for his wife."

James felt the anger in his words before they even came out. "Gardner was good at a lot of things, but he was *great* at lying. Who's to say his friend isn't just as good?"

Suzy was in front of him in a flash. She put away her gun and furrowed her brow. Her proximity sent a jolt through him. It was alarming, but not in a bad way.

"Get it together," she ordered him. "I know there's a lot going on, but we need to keep our heads on straight. Second-guessing yourself and the gut feeling you must have had about trusting Hank is going to get us nowhere. And it's *my* gut feeling that we aren't following a bad lead." Her voice softened. "So, if you can't trust yourself, can you at least trust me?"

It seemed like such a simple question. Could he trust Suzanne Simmons?

James already knew the answer.

Yes, he could.

The real question was, could she trust him?

He opened his mouth to ask it when movement over her shoulder caught his attention. Rudy walked through the back door and pointed past the two of them.

"They're going to the wrong house!" he yelled.

James and Suzy turned in unison. The county road curved around Hank's house and went alongside the house he'd noticed in the distance. A field of grass and a few trees were all that stood between the backyard they were currently in and the side yard of the other house.

"Maybe Patricia *did* have time to get out of the house," Suzy said, excitement making her words come fast. "She just didn't have a car to leave in, so—"

"She fled on foot. If she was fast enough and they went into the house first, there's a chance they wouldn't have seen her," he said. "I bet she made a run for the neighbors'!"

APRIL DONAVAN HAD been tending to some sod her son had laid the day before when she'd been startled by her neighbor running toward her, a bag on her shoulder and a baby in her arms.

"I know Patricia," she said now, nearly out of breath from the excitement. It probably didn't help that Suzy and James were two of many people bustling around her yard. The deputy she'd called was talking to the deputies Suzy had called, while the EMTs were packing up to leave. "Her and Hank have lived there for about a year, and both are really kindly—which at first I wasn't so sure of considering how, well, how—" She motioned to her arms.

"How *decorated* Hank is," James supplied. April nodded quickly, clearly relieved she didn't have to talk about his tattoos.

"But they've been over to eat a few times and I've been there, too, and they're just really nice folks, you know?"

"And in all that time you never saw any sign of a baby," Suzy clarified.

"No! Not even once!" April flung her arms out toward Hank's house in the distance. She shook them, all dramatics. "The first time I saw that baby boy was when Patricia was running at me, hollering about needing the keys."

This was the second time they'd heard the story since they'd gotten Rudy to drive them across the field. The local PD and some of Riker County's deputies had been directed to look for Patricia and the baby in the surrounding areas, while law enforcement on the scene was waiting for the next senior person to give orders. Since *technically* Suzy wasn't on duty yet.

"I didn't even get a chance to answer her before she was running inside and grabbing my keys off the hook," April continued, voice going higher and higher. "Then she yelled at me to get inside, lock the doors and call all of you! What's going on? Whose baby was that? Where's Hank?"

"That's what we're going to try to find out," Suzy said, turning on the soothing tone she used on Justin when he was upset. She reached out and squeezed the older woman's arm to try to reassure her with contact. "You did the right thing in listening to her and calling us out here immediately." Suzy nodded to one of the deputies from the department. Her name was Maria, and she had a natural way of keeping people calm in not-so-calm situations. At seeing Suzy's nod, she smiled wide. "Why don't you let Deputy Medina talk to you about what happens now?"

The crease across April's forehead lessened as she caught Maria's eye. She nodded and moved away, already recounting how crazy the afternoon had been to the deputy before she'd even gotten near Maria.

Suzy let out a sigh. The heaviness that only frustration could bring felt like it was pushing her down, trying to wear her out before she could finish the case. She couldn't deny she'd missed the feeling a little. Four months in recovery without working to search out justice had started to make her feel antsy, restless. Now? Well, one look at James and she wished the sense of purpose that washed over her at being a part of an active case wasn't at his expense.

He hadn't left her side since Hank's house, and he hadn't said a word since April had finished telling the first round of her story. Suzy knew it wasn't him giving up or being afraid. He wasn't the kind of man to give up so easily. Yet it was as if he was his own island, standing in the middle of a storm. Resilient. Mysterious.

Alone.

And, just like that, Suzy was consumed with the need to join him on that island. To brave the storm and help him navigate it.

Before she could voice any part of the feeling, though, her cell phone vibrated. Another sigh escaped her.

"Simmons," she answered.

It was Matt. He didn't waste any time with formalities.

"Suzy, The Tavern is a bloodbath over here," he jumped in. "Two dead and one unconscious and being transported to the hospital. Didn't you say there were supposed to be two more people? We're only counting four total."

James must have read the alarm in her expression. His brow furrowed.

"Yes, the owner plus the four men." Suzy hesitated. "Unless Hank's one of the deceased or hurt." James's eyebrows dipped even lower. "He's bald with a lot of tattoos."

A pause. "No, no bald men here."

Suzy's stomach dropped. "What about a man with black hair, shaved close to the scalp? Hank called him Grayton McKenzie?"

This time there was no pause. *"Grayton McKenzie?"* The sound of movement filled her ear. Then Matt was whispering. "Suzy, I don't know what you're in the middle of, but I think it's time we all had a talk. Grayton McKenzie isn't just your run-of-the-mill bad guy. He plays dirty, and if he's linked to what happened to you and James Callahan, then things only stand to get dirtier."

Suzy's stomach had already reached the ground. Now it was digging a hole to jump into.

RUDY HAD NO idea where Hank might have run off to—not that they knew if he'd done his disappearing act voluntarily or not. And on the off chance he had, Rudy certainly wasn't saying. Suzy watched from the front porch as Matt did what he did best: get someone to talk. Yet, through all the questions and answers, she believed Rudy was telling the truth.

He had no idea where Hank was or how to get hold of him. The same went for Patricia.

And James's nephew.

The millionaire had detached from her side as they'd gone back to Hank's house to meet with Matt. Even if Suzy had kept things informal between herself and James, Matt stuck to the book and wouldn't show the crime-scene pictures from the bar until James stepped away. Which he did without fuss, much to her surprise. He didn't even try to turn on his charm, not that it would have worked on Riker County's lead detective.

"The best I can guess right now is this guy here was shot from the front *and* the back, so I'm guessing he was caught in cross fire." He pointed to one of the three men who had gotten out of the SUV before Grayton. He was face down on the floor, next to the bar. Matt switched the picture to the second victim. Another man from the SUV. This one's neck was at an angle that made Suzy's stomach twist. "As for this guy, his neck is broken. No other injuries. Which meant he either let it happen or it was an opening move. A surprising one, at that."

"Geez," Suzy said with a low whistle. "And to think we were worried Hank was outmanned."

"Yeah, no kidding." Matt changed the picture again. This one was of a man on a gurney. "He had a gunshot to the stomach and was rushed into surgery. We're running his face now. Hopefully we'll get a hit soon."

"And Grayton McKenzie?" She hated to ask the question she already knew the answer to, especially since the name alone evoked an undeniable tension in the detective.

Matt rubbed the back of his neck and filled his chest with a deep breath. When he let it out, there was less worry in it and more anger. "I'm about to go talk to Captain Jones, who's become more familiar with him and where he might go than I am, but honestly, he hasn't been *seen* in a few months. In fact, the only person that *I* knew who had the juice to get him out..." In his voice was guilt, anger and a longing to change the past. All three created a shadow across his expression. It was a look she'd seen on him in the hospital after she had woken up from surgery. She'd tried to explain several times that he didn't need to react that way when he looked at her. He'd done nothing wrong.

"Let me guess." Suzy lowered her voice, careful with talking about the dead. Especially now that she knew his brother. "Our one man was Gardner Todd."

"Yeah," Matt confirmed. "His life was a mystery, but his death?"

Suzy put her hands on her hips and sighed. "Even more questions."

"And some I need to go ahead and start working on." Much like she'd done with April, Matt reached out and patted her arm. Working at the sheriff's department was more than a job to them. It was friendships and family. When one of them hurt, they all hurt. He gave her two good pats and then excused himself. He disappeared into the house, writing pad already out. The beginnings of a stress headache started to build between Suzy's eyes. She wanted a lot of things at that moment. Answers. A hug from her son. Coffee.

"Suzy."

The voice came from behind her. She could be blindfolded, drunk, half-asleep or buried in a box and she'd recognize that voice. Velvet smooth.

"James," she returned. Soon he was standing in front of her. All worry. All handsome.

"We need to get back to my place." He said it with enough force that she believed that need. Her mind jumped gears. Suddenly she was thinking about her own needs. Ones that twisted sheets and made her knees weak.

"We need to go back to the bar and grab your car," she said instead. "And then I need to—"

"I just got off the phone with Sheriff Reed," he interrupted. "We need to go to my house because he's already there."

"Billy's at your house?" she asked, confused. She hadn't talked to him yet. "I didn't even know he was back in town. Why is he at your house?"

James was all stone.

"Because we need to talk."

Chapter Eleven

Billy Reed was standing on the back patio, surveying the acreage with his hands in his pockets, wearing his cowboy hat on his head and his sheriff's badge on his hip. Suzy approached him with nerves in her chest and shame in her belly.

The last time she'd talked to him, she'd withheld information—important information—about Gardner Todd's child and the connection they both had with James. If there was already a nasty group of men willing to kill to try to get the baby *without* knowing his uncle was a millionaire and one of the most influential men in their county, then filling in the blanks for the public only would put the boy in more danger. Still, Suzy had lied to a man she trusted completely, and there were no two ways about it. She'd lied to her best friend. Not to mention her boss.

But would she do it again?

Once Billy knew about who Gardner *really* was, then all eyes would go to James. His life would never be the same. Even his sister and nephew would become subject to the prying eyes of an entire county. Not to mention the men and women who might try to seek out some kind of revenge on him as payback for Gardner's criminal activities.

This wasn't just about her loyalty to Billy or her department. She had to make a choice, right then and there. Loyalty or…

Suzy hesitated in her steps.

Never did she ever think she'd be where she was, trying to decide between Billy and the department and a man she barely knew. Yet that was exactly what she was doing.

And it was eating her up.

Especially when she realized her heart was betraying itself and leaning away from her makeshift family toward one she wasn't even a part of. Toward a man she couldn't trust.

Billy glanced over his shoulder but didn't turn around. Suzy came to a stop at his side. Her stomach was in knots. He spoke before she could make up her mind.

"So, James is Gardner Todd's little brother, huh? Can't say I saw that one coming." Suzy's mouth fell open, surprised. Billy took a deep breath and let it out slowly. He didn't seem as confused as she was.

He didn't seem confused at all.

"But why do they want Gardner's son if they never found out the connection to James and the Callahan fortune?" He turned, brow lined with contemplation. "Where's the boy's mother?"

Suzy's shock was replaced by his line of questioning, specifically the last one.

"No one knows how the mother is, though…" Heat crawled up Suzy's neck. It held shame and anger. "I realize now that we never asked Hank that question. We were so focused on Gardner and finding the boy, and then the men showed up."

Billy shook his head. "And that's another thing—Grayton McKenzie making moves all of a sudden? Very *public* ones, at that?" He took his hat off and rested it against his chest. "I knew Gardner's murder would have repercussions beyond what law enforcement might see, but this? I sure picked a fine time to go out of town, didn't I?"

"Yet you're already caught up?" Suzy ventured. No one at the department knew the specifics, and she sure hadn't told anyone.

Billy's index finger started to tap a rhythm against the brim of his hat. It was a thinking gesture he'd made since he'd been elected as sheriff. He was beyond contemplative, and Suzy couldn't tell what he was feeling. Thankfully, she never had to wait long with him. He always told her. Which made her feel all the more guilty about her recent silence on everything that had been happening.

"James," he said simply. "He called me while you were talking to Matt at Hank's place. Said he needed to tell me something he had begged you to keep quiet about before either one of you knew how big this thing was. That he was Gardner's kin and the grand prize all of your new buddies have been shooting for is his nephew. Matt had already looped me in that Grayton was involved. I was also told there's someone named after cheese dip taking refuge here by James's invitation." He shrugged. "All in all, it makes sense not to let the cat out of the bag about the Callahans, so I thought it best we make a more strategic move and have a meeting here. Gotta say, I don't mind the view."

His eyes roamed over the trees and grass out in the

distance. Billy Reed was a country boy at heart. He could spend hours admiring something others might have taken in in a glance. He was the type of man who took the time to appreciate his surroundings, and Suzy couldn't help but feel pride that he seemed to like James's home.

It was a thought that surprised Suzy. But she didn't have time to question it.

"I'll tell you one thing for certain, though," he continued, a small smile pulling up the corner of his lips. "Riker County is never boring."

He wouldn't get an argument from her. "You got that right, Sheriff."

To prove his point, Billy's phone chirped out some music.

"Mara," he announced after looking at the ID. "I can already hear her worry without even answering the phone."

Suzy couldn't help but laugh. While Mara would always worry about her husband, it never detracted from her strength. It was another reason Suzy felt close to the woman. Mara had been through her own trials and tribulations, and fought her way back to standing. She even had the scars to prove it. Still, Suzy could sense the worry before he answered.

"Then right now probably wouldn't be the best time to tell her that the dress she loaned me… Well, let's just say I won't be getting my deposit back."

Billy shook his head, still smiling. "I'll save that conversation for you to have with her later."

Suzy patted him on the shoulder. "Good man."

He excused himself and, walking onto the grass, took the call from his wife. Suzy wanted to take advantage of the interruption, so she hurried back into the house, thoughts picking up speed in tandem with her pace. James had gone to his office and it was there she found him, standing behind the desk, brow furrowed.

"You called Billy," she rushed, forgoing any attempt at beating around the bush. "You voluntarily told him about everything. Why? Now your family is vulnerable."

His eyebrow rose and ice-blue eyes found hers.

"If anything, *hiding* my family's past has made us vulnerable. Something I will do my damnedest to make right." His fist balled next to an open box on the desktop. "Telling the sheriff was the right thing to do."

A surge of insecurity pushed past Suzy's lips before she could understand where it was coming from. "You didn't trust me."

James gave her a questioning look. "I didn't trust you with what?" he asked, head tilting slightly to the side.

Suzy's heart started to beat faster. Her stomach started to flutter. She didn't understand what her body was trying to tell her mind. So she spoke without thought.

"You didn't trust me to see this through, to catch Gardner's killer and save your nephew," she said in a rush. "You decided you needed Billy's help more than mine."

Her cheeks burned as soon as the words left her mouth. What was she talking about? Billy was her boss—her family—and here she was, hurt that James had gone over her head? It didn't make sense. Suzy opened her mouth to try to take it back, try to cover up the feeling of vulnerability that must have shown on her face, but nothing came out.

James's expression turned sharp. He came around the desk and stopped close enough that she could smell his cologne. Or maybe it was his soap, still lingering across his skin. Waiting to pull her in.

The heat in Suzy's cheeks traveled south. Her heartbeat was all-out galloping.

"Telling him was never about not trusting you," James said, keeping his voice low. "I decided to do it because I didn't want you to have to keep lying for me. For my family. I don't want anyone else hurt because of me or mine. Especially not you."

The racing, the fluttering, the storm of emotions. They all slowed.

"You told your secret so I wouldn't have to lie to Billy." She spelled it out, to make sure she understood. "But you don't know me."

James's frown smoothed out into a smirk. "I know enough."

The rush of emotions and thoughts inside of her abated.

Her picture from earlier, of James as an island in the middle of the sea, shifted. Instead, she realized he was the man in the eye of the storm.

And she'd just broken through the clouds.

In two long steps, Suzy closed the space between them and, with less thought than it took to walk to him, she pressed her lips to his.

James didn't reciprocate as she moved into the kiss.

She didn't need him to.

All she wanted to do in that moment was to show him how much she appreciated what he'd done. From saving her life to telling a truth that could hurt him so she wouldn't have to tell a lie, he'd been more than good to a woman who had given him nothing but grief and suspicion throughout the past four months.

Suzy might have felt more comfortable shooting out of the back of a truck than expressing her feelings, but right then, it was the best she could do.

She ended the kiss as abruptly as she'd initiated it.

The man was no longer smiling.

"Sorry," she said, taking a step back. "I just—"

James slid his hand across the skin of her neck beneath her ear and then fisted it in her hair. He used the contact to pull her back to him. His other hand fastened on her hip, and she could feel the warmth of his hand through the thin fabric of her shirt.

Where her kiss had been impulsive, his kiss was intense.

Hot and powerful. Crushing and consuming.

He deepened the kiss by parting her lips with his tongue. It was a shock she realized was pleasant. Her body reacted of its own accord and leaned up and against him, wanting more. Needing more. She gasped into him as he pressed against her. His body also wanted hers— another pleasant realization as she wound her arms around his neck. He wasn't the only one who wanted to be closer.

Yet, in the blink of an eye, James broke the kiss.

And untangled himself.

"I'm sorry," he said, voice full of grit. "I can't."

A different kind of heat roasted Suzy's skin. Embarrassment? Disappointment? She didn't have a chance to dissect the full body blush that he no doubt could see. Without another word, James Callahan left his own office.

Suzy leaned on the desk. No matter the reasons behind either one of their moves, she couldn't deny one thing.

It had been one hell of a kiss.

She inhaled long and deep and then let it out slow and steady. The open box on top of the desk caught her eye. Needing a distraction, she peered inside. Stacks of pictures created a mountain. They were old, definitely from a disposable camera. At first glance she could see they were scenes of several strangers doing what people normally did in pictures. Standing in front of a Christmas tree. At a park. Playing in the snow. Laughing by a pool.

However, the one that sat on top of them all seemed to be the most important.

It only showed two people, standing with their arms around each other and smiling for all they were worth.

A teen and preteen.

A big brother and his little brother.

Gardner and James Callahan. Before life decided to show them how temperamental it could really be.

"WE MIGHT HAVE a lot of questions, but that's good, because that means we also have a lot of pieces, too."

James, Suzy and Billy stood around the kitchen island with determination, purpose and mugs of coffee. Suzy had swept into the room just after Billy finished making a phone call and, after James quickly filled the sheriff in on some specifics he hadn't had time to give on the phone, she was rallying their spirits.

"And having a lot of pieces is better than having none," she finished.

It was a simple observation, but it did the trick. James felt himself stand straighter and puff out his chest. Yet maybe the boost had less to do with her narrative and more to do with what had just happened to them upstairs.

Kissing Chief Deputy Suzanne Simmons was something he'd thought about, sure, but he hadn't counted on the feelings that had attached themselves to the act. The urge, the want, the need. It was like he'd been put under a spell.

He'd wanted more, and then he'd remembered why that was a bad idea.

He would soon become a target, if he wasn't already. Not only of Grayton McKenzie, but the general public. While Gardner had been a silent part of the criminal underworld in Alabama, there were still plenty of up-standing people who had known his name. Keeping his association from them and law enforcement had had a cost.

One he didn't want Suzy to pay.

Now he needed to focus.

And not on how the woman across from him had tasted.

"Okay, so, let's start making those pieces fit," James said. His voice came out a little too low. He compensated by clearing his throat. Suzy's eyebrow rose enough to let him know she'd noticed, but the sheriff started without hesitation.

"Gardner leaves his son with his friend Hank, who may look big and bad but his record is clean save for a few drunken fights back in the eighties, and goes to meet you to tell you something. Presumably that he has a son and you have a nephew." James nodded. "Lester McGibbon, a man who had no reason to kill, shoots Gardner in the warehouse."

"And then Lester shoots me," Suzy said matter-of-factly. "And James shoots him and he's declared dead on scene. His identity is kept under wraps for a week while the department and local PD try to get a hold on what might happen when the news of Gardner's death hits the streets."

James motioned to Suzy and then himself. "We go to the hospital, and while you're in surgery, I call my family attorney for an alibi so no one will find out Gardner's my brother." James paused, needing to explain further. "He's a good man and I tried not to lie to him, but I didn't want to put Chelsea in any danger from the blowback of the news getting out. But I also didn't know about the baby then. I would have done it differently had I known. My attorney chalks my going without him to look at a property up to my being impulsive and doesn't question it further. Oh, and, by the way, I own the warehouse now, if that can help us at all."

Billy nodded. Suzy looked surprised but nodded, too.

"For the next four months, I use every connection I have to try to figure out why Lester did what he did, until I come to the conclusion that he was hired to do it or maybe forced," he continued. "That eventually leads me to the name of a man who deals in information, using less-than-legal methods."

"Sully the Butcher," Billy said. While they'd been on the phone earlier, the sheriff had confirmed he knew of Sully, though he'd never had a reason to deal with him personally *or* professionally. Sully tended to stay north of Riker County and almost always under the radar.

"He met with me yesterday morning and agreed to try to find out who had ordered the hit on Gardner, but *without* resorting to violence. I knew he could get to the seedier parts of the criminal outfit around here easier than I ever could. I figured it would be safer for everyone that way." James shifted his gaze away from Suzy. While he had believed then what he said, a part of him now wondered if he'd gone to law enforcement in the first place instead, if he'd be sitting with his nephew right now.

"And then one of Sully's protégés shows up at the party last night with an address for you from his boss," Suzy said, picking up where he left off. "Someone ambushes Sully and his men, wounding Sully in the process, and then we take the address and go to a house in the country. A house that you guess belonged to Gardner."

"Men show up, armed to the teeth, and are told to go find Hank and Gardner's son," Billy said, taking over. "James tracks down Hank at a bar he used to hear Gardner talk about, and you two have a chat with him. He identifies Grayton, tells you where the baby is, and we find out that his wife had fled with the boy. Two of Grayton's men are found dead at the bar, one is in surgery now, and both Grayton and Hank are missing."

They shared looks with one another all around.

That was it. The whole story. No more lies or omissions.

"So, those are our pieces," James said.

"And there are some questions we need to answer before we can see that puzzle," Suzy jumped in. She ticked off each one on her fingers. "Where did Patricia go? Did Hank and Grayton leave the bar together? How did Sully get Gardner's address?" She hesitated before putting up her fourth finger. "And if Hank *is* with Grayton and knows who we are, what does that mean for us if he shares that information?"

That question hung heavy in the air.

Then crashed into the ground as someone screamed outside.

Chapter Twelve

James was the fastest. He'd bolted out of the kitchen before Suzy had time to step clear of the island. Billy was next. The aches from the night before came back with force as she followed, but she pushed through them.

A woman had screamed.

Had Patricia learned about James already and come to deliver the baby? Had she been followed? Were Grayton and his men on the front lawn, guns up and high as they stood next to the garden beds?

The possibilities had her breathing ratcheted up higher than when she'd been shooting out of the back of a pickup truck.

Was the baby out there, too? Right in the middle of harm's way?

Suzy shut down all lines of *what if* the moment she ran through the front door.

There were no droves of men with guns pointed at them. Nor were there any babies caught defenseless between them. Instead, there was only Queso, standing with his hands straight up in the air, a cigarette hanging limp between his lips, James's and Billy's guns both pointed at him and a girl clutching her purse to her chest.

"Chelsea?" James asked, clearly surprised. He wasn't the only one.

"What in God's name is going on around here?" she shrieked. "Why do you have a gun?"

James holstered the object in question. Suzy followed suit. Billy stayed firm in his stance.

"Why did you scream?" James replied, matching her volume.

She pointed to Queso, who wasn't moving an inch. "I dropped my phone and bent down to get it, and then saw *this* guy just staring!"

James turned so fast on Queso that it was nearly comical.

"You were staring at my sister while she was bending over?" he asked, volume still high.

The poor boy tried to sound tough, but his words lost their edge around the butt of his cigarette.

"No way, Padre! I was going crazy inside, so I wanted to take a smoke break." He pointed at Chelsea, hands still in the air. "It ain't my fault she didn't hear me walk up. I wasn't checking her out, just trying to figure out who she was!"

James's anger wasn't appeased so easily. Suzy walked over to his side and touched his elbow lightly. Then she nodded to Billy. He lowered his gun.

"This is just another reason not to smoke," she said, reaching out and taking the cigarette from his mouth. He made a face like he was going to complain, but she gave him a look she often used on Justin when he needed to think before he spoke. Suzy went to the sidewalk and ground it out. "Come clean this up and get back inside," she said. "I've got some more questions for you." No one complained at the order, and although Queso looked like he wanted to, the boy dropped his arms and complied.

Not before casting a dirty look at Chelsea, though. She returned it in kind.

"What are you doing here?" James said, rounding back to her when Queso was inside. "Why aren't you at school?"

"You told me not to come home!"

James waved his arms around wildly. *"So you came home?"*

The girl nodded with fervor. "Of course I did! You've never told me not to come home, so I figured something was wrong!"

"That makes no sense, Chels," he shot back.

"Well, I was right, wasn't I?" She pointed to Billy and Suzy. "Unless you're always ready with backup to come out, guns blazing, and I've just missed it all these years."

James dragged a hand down his face.

"I'm going to go ahead and try to find out as much as I can about Patricia." Billy jumped in, looking at Suzy. "Tell me if your talk with Queso brings anything new up. I'll put Matt and the captain on the rest. Keep your phone on you and let me know." He reached out to shake James's hand, then tipped his hat to Chelsea. "Take care."

Billy paused at Suzy's side. "I'm going to arrange for a unit to keep an eye on the estate entrance," he said, voice low so the others couldn't hear. "Still, stay on alert."

"Yessir."

They watched as Billy got into his Bronco. It wasn't until his engine turned over that Chelsea's confusion soured into concern.

"What's happening, James? What's wrong?"

James let out a sigh. He glanced at Suzy. She knew

what he was feeling. While Chelsea was his little sister, she was also like his daughter, in a way. The age difference plus the fact that he'd raised her made him a man caught between brotherly affection and paternal love. He wanted to protect her, but now he had to figure out how to do that. It was something Suzy couldn't help him with. Especially since she had no clue if Chelsea knew who Gardner Todd even was.

Suzy's heart clenched for the man who had rejected her not fifteen minutes before.

It was an odd sensation. One she decided not to dwell on.

"Why don't we go inside first," she suggested. "It's a little too hot out here for my tastes." Suzy smiled and held out her hand. "My name's Suzy. We've never formally met."

Recognition flared instantly behind Chelsea's baby blues. Seeing the two Callahans standing next to each other, Suzy couldn't deny the resemblance between them. They had matching dark hair—although Chelsea's was more styled than James's was—and clear blue eyes, and they even shared the same chin. Suzy had seen a picture or two of their mother in the house and saw that the female Callahan had inherited the matriarch's petite stature. If there was any of their father in her, Suzy wouldn't know. She hadn't noticed any pictures of him in the house.

Chelsea was staring at her intently. "As in Chief Deputy Simmons?"

Suzy was surprised but nodded.

"In the flesh."

A small smile picked up the corner of Chelsea's lips. Her gaze flitted to her brother, then zipped back.

"I'm glad to see you out and about." Her gaze jumped down for a second to Suzy's chest. Then her smile widened. "James has told me a lot about you."

It was Suzy's turn to smile. "Hopefully all good things."

"Are you saying there are bad things about you I should know?" James chimed in. It was his way of trying to lighten the mood, she knew, but it still sent a thrill through her.

She shouldn't have kissed him. Not with everything going on. Not without knowing if the chemistry between them was something James Callahan could have with anyone he wanted.

Suzy knew that the kiss had been a mistake.

He knew that, too.

But knowing something was true and accepting it as such were two completely different things.

THREE HOURS PASSED and no one had learned a thing.

Well, except for Chelsea. She'd found out she was an aunt and that her nephew was still missing. Apart from that, everyone attempting to find him had come up with nothing but dead ends. But not for lack of trying.

James looked down at his cell phone. He'd made so many calls that it was hot to the touch.

The well of contacts he'd used the first time to ferret out information about Gardner had dried up with the disappearance of Sully. Not even Queso could find someone who knew if he was still alive, let alone where he was. James couldn't help but feel sorry for the boy. Sully might not have been the best role model, but it was clear to James now that he was all the boy had.

Once again James came back to his nephew. And worry and guilt were immediately replaced with anger.

Why had Gardner waited to tell him?

Why hadn't he set up a better contingency plan?

Why hadn't Gardner listened to him all those years ago?

"Knock, knock."

James lifted his head. Suzy stood in the doorway. She was frowning.

"I think it's time I went home."

Another simple statement that had a strong effect on him. But it wasn't unexpected. They'd been together for almost twenty-four hours.

"I'm sure you want to see Justin."

She nodded. "I do. But I won't stop working on this. I'll work from home."

James waved a hand, dismissing the thought.

"You've already done more than enough, plus there's more people on it now. The sheriff's department included."

Suzy nodded again. But she still wasn't smiling. "I know it's not my business, but how did Chelsea take the news?"

James looked over her shoulder to the closed bedroom door. Suzy took a step closer so he could lower his voice.

"She's a tough cookie, but I threw her a curveball," he admitted. "One of many." He sighed. "There's a thirteen-year age difference between us. Sixteen years between her and Gardner. She was only a few months old when he ran away. By the time she could understand what a brother even was, he'd been scrubbed out of the family by my father. I honestly don't even know if he would have ever told her Gardner existed if it wasn't for me and my mother. Even then, it was something you just didn't talk about with the old man in the room."

James rubbed the back of his neck. Talking about his family wasn't one of his favorite things to do. Especially about his father and the divide he'd created. "Either way, I didn't like her not knowing him, and so I told her about the Gardner I'd grown up with when she was old enough. Not the one who'd earned the title of Alabama Boogeyman. I was trying to protect her. Trying to protect him, too. The Gardner that was still good, the one I was proud to call my brother."

James fought the urge to ball his hands into fists. Suzy had asked a simple question and here he was, again, regaling her with the epic dysfunction that was what it meant to be a Callahan.

"By the time she was old enough to want anything more than just stories from me, my father died," he continued. "It wasn't until I left the Air Force and became her guardian that we had to have a more serious talk about him. I wanted to be honest with her, since it was just the two of us. I wanted her to know what it was like to be trusted and loved by a parent, even if I was her brother. I don't think she knows how to process the idea of a baby Gardner out there when she barely knew how to process *Gardner* being out in the world but not a part of our lives before he was killed." He couldn't help but smirk at how much he'd divulged. "I guess I could have just said that from the start."

"It's only fair, since I talked your ear off this morning," she replied without missing a beat. "Sometimes you just have to say what you're feeling."

"True."

A few seconds of silence stretched between them.

James thought about Suzy and the bed behind him. He wanted Suzy. There was no doubt about that now. But he also wanted to keep her safe.

She'd already nearly died because of his family's baggage.

So, instead of pulling her in for a kiss he hoped she'd never forget, he said good-night.

"Sleep well, Chief Deputy," he added before she turned away. "You've more than earned it."

She flashed a quick smile. It looked as tired as he felt. Wary, even. Then she was gone.

James looked back down at his phone.

It was still warm in his palm.

A WAITING GAME. That was all it was now. And she wasn't happy about it. Patience wasn't her strong suit.

Aggression was.

Someone rapped on the door. It took all the calm she had left not to shoot through it. Especially when it was Grayton who peeked his head around it.

"I was wondering when you'd slink back here," she greeted him with a snarl. "Next time maybe I should send someone younger. Or maybe I should just do it myself. Heavens knows good help *is* hard to find."

Grayton tucked his chin but held her gaze. It was the only form of pushback she'd gotten from him in the last year. The only resistance he attempted. The rest of her cronies didn't dare even that much.

"We underestimated him. Hank," he tried. At least his voice was submissive enough. She loosened her shoulders. "He killed Lee and Ryan. Rocko is in the hospital."

"I know," she said. "I always know, remember? Your merry band isn't the only group I have on the payroll."

She adjusted the pearls around her neck until the clasp was at the nape. She was overdressed in comparison now that Grayton was there. His suit was covered in blood. No bullet holes but more than a few slashes. He had certainly fought his way out of the bar, all right.

Not that she cared.

He'd had one job, and he hadn't delivered.

Maybe he picked up on that thought. His eyes shifted from her for a split second before slinking right back.

"Then I guess you know that his house is crawling with cops right now."

"I do." She leaned over and rested her elbows on the desktop. "Old news may be news, but it's not something I like to deal in. Impress me or, my God, Mr. McKenzie, at least try. I'd hate to have to change our arrangement."

Instead of letting her threat make him squirm, he tried to stand taller.

"I didn't want to come back empty-handed. So I didn't." He took a step forward and looked very much like a man pretending to relax because he was on more solid ground. However, he'd been around long enough to know that solid ground didn't exist in their business. At least, not hers.

You either did well or you didn't.

And she didn't have patience for those who didn't.

"After Hank took off, I figured he'd run home to see about his woman," he continued. "The cops were already there. Deputies from the county, too. I recognized one of the detectives from a few years back who helped take out that dimwit who tried to take over Bryan Copeland's old drug business. He was talking to a woman. I'm pretty sure it was the same one who shot at us at Gardner's place. She got into a car with another man. And guess where they went?" He grinned.

She raised her eyebrow, knowing there was a fifty-fifty chance he was going to disappoint her with his answer. "Where?"

"That fancy house out in Bates Hill. The mansion."

That got her attention. She felt her brow furrow.

"Do you mean James Callahan's estate?"

Grayton nodded with fervor.

"Well, that *is* interesting. What does the Bates Hill Savior have to do with Gardner?"

While she was pleasantly surprised with the information that Grayton had brought her, she didn't expect him to answer that. He kept silent as she stood and walked around the desk. Her heels tapped out a soothing rhythm against the hardwood.

Soothing to her, anyway. Grayton couldn't hide the muscle in his jaw that jumped. It made her feel even more powerful. She sidled up to him and flashed a smile she hoped chilled his blood.

"I guess I'll just have to go and ask him myself," she cooed into his ear. "After all, isn't the old clichéd adage something about if you want anything done you should just do it yourself?"

That clearly surprised him. She had a front-row view of his eyebrows bunching in together. She liked the reaction. Those who stuck to routines never flourished. It was about time she changed her tactics from a behind-the-scenes style to a more visible one, out in the field.

"Now, Grayton." She brought her hand up and cupped the side of his face, turning it so their eyes met. "While I'm away, why don't you go get yourself cleaned up?"

He gave one precise nod.

Unlike her other minions, Grayton knew when to keep his mouth shut. It was done more out of fear than strategy, but she appreciated unquestioning loyalty.

Hot and pure anger heated beneath her skin.

Loyalty.

She didn't take betrayal lightly.

Before he could flinch at the change in her expression, she grabbed both sides of his cheeks and squeezed until his lips puckered. It wasn't until her nails bit into his skin that she spoke.

"After that, you're going to figure out who that woman was and why she's interfering with *my* business. Got it?" She nodded his head for him. Droplets of blood oozed out onto her once-perfect manicure. She applied another wave of pressure until he couldn't stop from wincing. She smiled and loosened her grip. He didn't move a muscle as she stroked the half-moon marks across his skin.

"Good," she cooed again. "Good boy. Because I really *do* like you, Grayton. I'd hate to have to deal with replacing you, especially when we're so close. But don't think I won't, if needed. I'm not above eliminating those who disappoint me."

She wiped the tops of her nails on his shirt and patted his chest. While she kept her smile in place, she knew neither one of them believed it held any mercy.

"Just ask Gardner."

Chapter Thirteen

James might have had more than enough money to hire a personal chef, but he wasn't about to deny the world his famous breakfast for dinner.

He stood in front of the stove and slung eggs into a pan while keeping his eyes on the bacon. Chelsea manned her usual post next to the waffle iron. Looking at her, now nineteen years old, he couldn't help but see the preteen he'd taught how to use it.

"So, you never finished telling me," he started. "I know you aced your lab, but what grade did you get on your final history project?"

After hearing the news that Gardner's son was just out of their reach and they'd been all but ordered by the sheriff to stay put, Chelsea had been quiet. That wasn't unusual for her personality. She'd always been more of a contemplative kid. While some people barely thought about the words before they came out of their mouths, Chelsea often overthought hers. Sometimes, if you paid close enough attention, you could almost see her picking the words in her head, careful to use the right ones.

It had worried James, at first. Coming home to raise a sister who was only ten had been enough to send him diving into the pages of countless parenting books, but it had been Chelsea's quiet and reserved personality that caused him to stress. That was, until he realized that listening more than speaking wasn't a bad trait, just different from how he and his brother had behaved. And their father, when he was around, had been the louder parent. It hadn't mattered who was right if no one could hear the other points being made.

James had felt right at home with the drill sergeants in boot camp.

"It wasn't as good as my biology lab, but it wasn't as bad as I thought it would be." She poured batter over the waffle iron.

"Are we talking low A or high B? Or are we more into the Cs?"

Chelsea's contemplative nature also came with a dose of perfectionism. While she was willing to slack when it came to chores or summer jobs, her grades were important to her. Doing poorly on a test, in her mind, was the equivalent of doing great to most other people.

"High B, *but* I could have done better." She huffed and brought down the top of the iron. "I blame that stupid guy I got partnered up with. He was more interested in talking about himself than in helping me. I should have done the entire thing myself, but all I could hear was you in my head." She cleared her throat and adopted a baritone. "'Doing someone else's work usually only hurts them in the long run, Chels. Especially if someone is trying to take advantage of your work ethic.'"

James threw his head back and laughed. "That goes double for talkative, self-involved college boys."

"Oh, don't worry. I already told him all about my big brother who did two tours in Iraq. Which is why I think he never bothered me *outside* of the library."

"That's my girl."

James finished scrambling the eggs and turned his attention to the bacon. This was something he couldn't deny he missed. The house seemed so much bigger when Chelsea was gone.

His thoughts reverted to Suzy. It had felt nice having her around the last two days. Even when she'd been sleeping in the other room, James had felt an odd peace start to settle, just knowing she was there. Throughout his time in Bates Hill, he'd dated a few women he'd considered introducing to Chelsea. Yet he'd never noticed their absence the way he did with the chief deputy.

They'd been through a lot of near-death situations. With the baby missing, a potential new gang rising and a man who could disappear as easily as Gardner could, stakes were high. Anyone could get caught up in the moment. Maybe that was all their kiss had meant.

Maybe without danger and bullets, their interest in each other wouldn't exist.

James didn't like that thought. Nor the one that came next.

With or without Suzy, his future was going to change. Because of Gardner's son.

What was the point of having the money he did and spending years networking for connections when he couldn't use them to help find his own flesh and blood? Shouldn't *someone* be finding something by now? Statistics alone should have been on their side.

"Will it be like this when we find him?"

James paused, spatula in midair. Apparently Chelsea's thoughts had found their way onto the same wavelength.

"What do you mean?"

She took her time in responding, choosing her words

carefully again, no doubt. Slowly she opened the iron and forked out her waffle. Then she was ready.

"Gardner's son. Our nephew. Will you raise him by yourself, too, here in the house, like you did with me?"

James looked over at her. She kept her eyes on the new cup of batter she was pouring into the waffle iron. There was guilt in the question. He knew it, because he'd heard it before. No matter how hard he had tried, he couldn't seem to fully convince her that, sure, leaving the Air Force had been hard, but it was nothing compared to what abandoning her would have been like.

Just like if he abandoned his nephew.

"Of course I will," he answered honestly. "But I won't be alone." He hoped she heard the smile in his voice. "You're going to be on diaper duty as soon as you step through the front door when you come back from college. Plus, I've already decided that after teaching *you* how to drive, I'm done with that forever. I've been in combat zones less terrifying."

"Hey! That's not fair." Her normal voice returned. "I wasn't that bad!"

"You weren't that good, either," he mumbled.

She laughed. "I heard that."

The weight that had settled on her shoulders seemed to lift a little. James was glad for it. While, technically, she was an adult, he didn't want her to bear the particular burden that came with being mixed up in Gardner's criminal life. They'd agreed years ago that they'd protect her from it, and James would be damned if he didn't keep trying. She was still trying to find her place in the world; she didn't need to be caught in a web of constant worry, too.

They finished each of their cooking duties and settled

around the table in the eating nook. It wasn't until she spoke that he noticed she'd made an extra waffle. Which made her next topic of conversation no surprise to him.

"So, I know you said that he needed to keep a low profile and he helped get some information for you about Gardner, but—" she dropped her voice "—is his name really Queso? Don't get me wrong, I love a good dip, but that's a little intense. And kind of ridiculous."

James snorted and then sobered. He couldn't help but picture the scene the night before, when a blood-soaked boy had limped into the house yet was only worried about his boss. His friend. Despite his rough-and-tumble persona, Queso had been a better guest than most.

He wasn't about to make fun of the boy now, especially when they didn't know what he'd been through. The ridiculous nickname might be covering up a pain that neither one of them could understand.

James decided to set the tone for Chelsea so she knew exactly where he stood on the boy.

"That's what he's comfortable being called. And we'll respect that until he tells us otherwise." James was stern enough to leave an impression. Chelsea nodded and dropped her gaze to her food. She danced her fork across her waffle. He eyed the extra one off to the side and sighed through a smile.

"I guess it wouldn't hurt to ask him to come eat with us," he said, standing.

"You make it sound like you think we're too good for him," she noted with her own smile. But it zipped right off a second later. Her eyes widened. "Or maybe *he* thinks he's too good for us?"

James couldn't help but laugh. Always concerned, that was Chelsea Callahan's natural state.

He mussed her hair as he walked past, earning a swat or two from her. "Probably a little of both," he answered. "But I guess it wouldn't hurt to try to get him socialized. I'd hate for him to miss out on my famous breakfast for dinner."

Queso had been given the run of the house, true to James's word. Instead of staying in the living room, glued to the TV, he'd surprised James by hanging out in the small library at the corner of the first floor. When James had been house hunting, privacy had been the number one desire on his list. It was the main reason he'd bought such a big house when there were only two of them to live in it. However, the library had definitely been the second reason he'd signed the papers. Built-in bookshelves lined two of the walls, while a large window that looked out into the backyard took up the third. James had done some of his best business thinking in that room.

Queso sat on the couch by the window. His head was bent over an open book. Whatever it was, he was halfway through it. Another surprise.

"Want your mind to be blown by the best bacon and waffles you ever had?" James asked in greeting. The boy jumped and slammed his book shut. Then he went on the offensive.

"You shouldn't just sneak up on people like that, Padre. Wear a bell or something."

James shrugged. "It's not considered sneaking if it's your house. I think it's just called walking then."

Queso snorted. It lacked any real humor, though. "I don't think I can consider this a house," he sneered. "It's got more rooms than a motel."

James shrugged again. He knew he lived in what most

considered a mansion, and that he was lucky for it, but he'd tried to keep everything inside its walls simple and modest. He had money, yes, but he never flaunted it or took it for granted. All he ever wanted to do with it was help people.

Queso threw the book on the cushion next to him and scooped up his phone. No one had called him since he'd shown up the night before. It was clear that that was eating at him. James guessed the rising anger coming off him wasn't meant for him at all.

"And how can you joke around and just stuff your face when that kid is out there? Is it a rich thing to not care? Don't you want to find him?"

James had expected the question. It didn't lessen the sting.

"Running around like chickens with our heads cut off isn't going to help anyone. Not *the kid* and not Sully, either." Queso's jaw tightened. "It would be different if there weren't people out there looking, but for us, the best thing we can do right now is calm down, take a beat and be ready for anything. Sarcasm and a hunger strike aren't going to get either one of us what we want."

Queso didn't look swayed by James's points. His expression had frozen in a sneer.

"At the very least, come and thank Chelsea," James added, when Queso didn't appear to be getting up anytime soon. "She already made you a waffle."

"She made *me* a waffle?" he repeated.

The sneer was replaced by interest, interest James realized he didn't like. Before he could pepper in a small speech about what was appropriate in terms of interactions with his little sister, a sound he truly didn't expect echoed through the house.

The doorbell.

He was so caught off guard by it that he froze to listen as the series of chimes played out a song.

"I'm guessing by your face that you didn't invite anyone over for that famous bacon of yours?"

James didn't answer. He pulled his phone out from his pocket. No missed calls or texts. The landline hadn't rung, either. If anyone wanted to come over they were supposed to call. Not to mention, there was a deputy patrol at the entrance of the estate. They weren't supposed to let anyone past until authorized by the sheriff or him.

"Stay here," James ordered, not liking how his gut twisted.

Queso didn't listen. He trailed behind James through the back hallway that led across the bottom floor and into the living room. A set of double glass doors separated it from the grand entryway.

"Queso, you need to hang back," James said, pausing before he opened the doors. "I can't keep you safe if everyone knows you're here."

"Who do you think's at the door, Padre?" Queso asked with a smirk. "Bad guys don't ring the doorbell."

James rolled his eyes. "Just get out of sight for a second," he said in a rush. "And keep quiet."

The doorbell chimed again. Fortunately, Queso listened. When he was out of the living room, James swung the glass doors wide and walked into the entryway, body already tense. He didn't know what he expected when he opened the door, but it surely wasn't who he found himself staring at.

Tall, slim and wrapped in a white pantsuit, a woman James had never met before was smiling at him. Her lipstick was bloodred, complementing the dark auburn hair that fell to the tops of her shoulders, and she had a large, expensive-looking purse at her side. He placed her age at around his.

What he couldn't place was one single reason why she would be standing on his doorstep.

"Mr. Callahan," she greeted him. "I'm so sorry to intrude, but I was wondering if I could have a moment of your time?"

Chapter Fourteen

The popcorn had burned, but Justin hadn't complained. He'd eaten almost all of it during the movie. Now the bowl was empty in his lap, a book open on top of it. Suzy had already gone over all his homework due Monday, while her mother had excused herself to take a bubble bath.

If routine held, she'd be out by the time Justin was winding down for bed. The three of them would talk until it was time for lights-out, and then Suzy's mother would fix a glass of warm milk and question her daughter about work and potential suitors before recapping what had happened on the latest TV show or book she'd occupied herself with that day.

This was their normal. The way the Simmonses operated.

This was where Suzy was comfortable.

Or had been comfortable, at least.

Now?

Now she finally had someone to talk to her mother about when she brought up men. Not that she would. When it came to James Callahan, Suzy realized he was the embodiment of a wild card. And after he'd broken their kiss earlier, he'd all but shuffled her back into the deck.

Which was for the best.

She didn't need to be giving in to any impulses, especially ones involving the millionaire.

Suzy sighed. She left her phone on the arm of her chair and stood. She was between phone calls with Billy and Matt and anyone else she could think of who might be able to help track Hank, Patricia or Gardner's son. No luck. It was like everyone involved had vanished into thin air.

Her heart felt heavy for James.

Impulses aside, he was just a man scrambling to save his family, and that in itself pulled at her heartstrings.

One look at Justin with his hair tousled, dark cheeks lined with freckles and round, chocolate eyes focused on his book, and Suzy couldn't imagine how desperate she would feel if she couldn't find him.

Justin raised his head, feeling her "mom stare," as he called it.

"Mom. You're staring. Again."

That annoyed tone that kids seemed to pull out of thin air laced his words. Suzy also couldn't imagine Justin as a teen. She wondered how James had handled that phase with Chelsea.

There she was again. All thoughts seemed to lead back to the man now.

"I'm just wondering how you managed to do this." She bent over to grab a few stray kernels that had found their way under the coffee table. "You know this stuff is supposed to go into your mouth, right?" she teased. "Maybe I should get one of those horse feeders and strap it around your head."

"Then you have to get Mimi one," he said matter-of-factly. "She dropped those!"

Suzy laughed, picturing her mother being just as messy, and put her hand out for the bowl. He gave it up but followed her into the kitchen.

"Mimi was worried about you today," he said, still using what he clearly thought sounded like an adult tone. "She called Aunt Mara and talked for a while about it."

Suzy felt a flutter of guilt, but she didn't show it.

"And you know this because Mimi told you?" she ventured.

Justin looked sheepish. "I heard her."

"You heard her as in you were eavesdropping, or you heard her as in you picked up the other phone and listened that way?" It was a trap. One that he'd been snared in before. Either way, he knew the outcome was trouble. Still, he surprised her by answering.

"I picked up the phone in the living room to listen," he admitted. Then added in a rush, "But I thought it was you! And I didn't listen to a lot of it."

She crossed her arms over her chest and narrowed her eyes a fraction. Honesty was the best policy, but she'd trimmed the truth when it came to explaining why she hadn't come home the night before. Justin knew she was working and that she was with James—a man he'd met at the hospital and said he liked—but she'd told him that it was nothing for him to worry about.

He *was* only ten, after all.

"We've talked about this before," she reminded him. "You don't spy on people unless you're getting paid to do it as part of a profession. And even that sounds a little uncool."

He dropped his gaze, but Suzy knew it wasn't just his curiosity that had prompted him to do something he knew would get him into trouble. He'd been worried, too. And he still was.

Suzy relaxed her posture and opened the pantry. There was only one thing to help ease his mind. Or, at least, distract it. Standing on her tiptoes, she reached to the middle of the top shelf.

"Next time—" She jumped up, trying to grab the box, but missed. "Next time you are worried—" She jumped up again. This time her fingers wrapped around the edge of the box she was aiming for. She pulled it out. Justin's eyes were wide when she turned back to him, box fully in view. "—just talk to me or Mimi. You can even call Aunt Mara if you need to. Okay? No more of this sneaking around."

He nodded, but his eyes stayed on the box. Like he was in a trance.

"Can I have one?" He clearly couldn't hold himself back from asking.

This wasn't exactly part of their routine, but she figured it might take his mind off everything. At least for a little bit.

"As long as we can eat them before your grandma comes out," she said, dropping her voice to a whisper. Her grin was matched by her son's.

Suzy opened the box of sugar-filled, prewrapped honey buns—their little secret treat that Cordelia Simmons had forbidden—and threw one to Justin. No sooner had he caught it, though, than the sound of shuffling slippers filtered from the hallway that led to the bedrooms.

"Hide them," Justin whispered, panicked.

A giddy excitement filled Suzy's stomach. She didn't have time to throw the box back onto the top shelf of the pantry, so she threw it in the other direction. Justin laughed as it soared over his head and hit the top of the dining room table on the other side of the kitchen cabinet. There was no way her mother hadn't heard that, but it was worth a guaranteed nagging in Suzy's future to hear a carefree laugh from her baby boy.

"Act natural," Suzy said hurriedly, whirling around to stand next to him. She threw her arm around his shoulders and pulled him to her side, knowing they looked anything but natural. Justin barely had enough time to thrust his honey bun behind his back before a purple robe and matching slippers came into view. Suzy prepared an excuse about it being the weekend, and sometimes that meant sugary sweets, when any and all responses died on her tongue.

Justin's honey bun hit the floor. Suzy's grip on his shoulder tightened.

A man walked in behind her mother.

There was a gun in his hand.

"I'M SORRY BUT have we met?"

It was a formality, and the only one James was going to extend to the stranger. The last two days had been filled with surprises. This woman might be another one he didn't want to experience.

"We haven't, I'm afraid, but I thought it was about time we did."

She held out her hand. A pearl ring was on her index finger and matched her necklace and earrings. A gold Rolex hung on her wrist. Whoever she was, she didn't mind flaunting her wealth. James knew for a fact, thanks to his friend Hale, that the high heels she wore cost more than most people made in three paychecks combined. Fashion aside, how she'd gotten past the deputy guarding the entrance was one of several questions that sprang to mind.

"My name is Katrina," she introduced herself, giving his hand a firm shake. "I'm a friend of Hank's."

James didn't have time to hide his surprise.

"Hank," he repeated cautiously.

She nodded. Her smile hadn't faltered since he'd opened the door.

The red flag that had begun to rise at the time of her arrival shot up.

"Well, to be honest, *friend* isn't as accurate a description as I'd like. He's more of a business associate. One I'm having a hard time finding at the moment. I was hoping you could help me."

"I'm sorry, but I don't know a Hank," he lied, deciding to keep his cards close to his chest. "If it's someone who works at one of the businesses I invest in or help run, then you'll have to be more specific." He put on his best grin. "I'm good with numbers, computers and making breakfast, but I'm afraid I'm bad with names and faces."

Katrina's smile didn't even dim a fraction. She adjusted the bag on her shoulder. "Oh, how silly of me." She laughed. It was soft but not sincere. "I suppose you being at his house earlier today might have been misleading. Perhaps, instead, you were trying to find someone else?"

James held his ground. Every muscle in his face was working overtime to not give away what he was thinking.

"I don't know what you're talking about," he said, deciding he wanted to see her work for the answer she wanted, hopefully revealing her hand in the process. How did she know he'd been at Hank's? Had she been watching him? Why would she? Did she know for a fact he was lying? "Aside from a trip to the city to help close on a deal for work, I've been here all day," he lied again.

Her smile grew wider. Instead of it adding more charm, it started to degrade her beauty. He'd hit a nerve.

"Mr. Callahan. James, if I may. I'm here to help."

"I don't understand what with. Even if I did know your Hank, it seems like you're here because you need *my* help. Not the other way around." He shrugged. "Which I also don't know how to give."

The briefest of muscle twitches ran along her jaw.

Something was wrong.

Katrina was wrong. His feeling only heightened when she responded.

"I would say I'd offer you compensation for your insight, but I guess it's hard to tempt someone like yourself with something as trivial as money. So, why don't I do this—" She looked down at her watch. James waited, alarm rising in his gut. "If you tell me what you know about Hank and where he is, then I won't order my man in your house to gut your sister."

Katrina raised her head and met his gaze. Her smile was back. It was genuine.

James didn't have time to process what she'd said.

A scream tore through the house.

"Don't worry," Katrina added quickly. "That was just to prove to you that that man is really *in* the house. I call the shots. And before you go all hero on me, let me make something crystal clear."

She took a step closer, straddling the door frame. One foot in and one foot out of his family's home.

"The only way your sister's insides remain inside is if I tell him not to touch her. You silence me, you kill her."

James's body vibrated with so many emotions, he couldn't sort out even one.

Katrina leaned in, still smiling. "Now, Mr. Callahan, be a good boy and invite me inside. It's been a long day already. I don't have all night."

RAGE AND FEAR coursed through Suzy, nearly blinding her. Luckily it didn't take over completely. She was able to hold on to enough clarity to recognize the man.

"Hank?" The bar owner had changed clothes and was wearing a hat. It did little to cover the gash across his eyebrow or the bruising around his eye. "What the h—"

"Grayton McKenzie is on his way to grab you," he interrupted. "You need to leave. *Now.*"

"What? How do you know?"

Suzy loosened her grip on Justin. Her mother's eyes were as wide as saucers. If the gun had been aimed at her, Suzy bet they would have fallen out of her face.

"Criminal grapevine," he said in a rush. "I maybe have a five-minute start on him. If you want out, you gotta go." As she had in the bar that morning, Suzy believed Hank's sincerity. Still, when he reached into his pocket, she got a little antsy. He pulled out a piece of paper. "Here's Patricia's private number. She knows to expect your call. She has the boy, but will only give him to you or Callahan. If you don't get him by tomorrow morning, she's leaving town with him and never coming back. You got that?"

Suzy took the paper and nodded. "What about you? You're not coming with us?"

Hank shook his head.

"I'm done being ambushed by that scrawny son of a—" He paused, looked at Justin and chose new words.

"I'm tired of looking over my shoulder and seeing Grayton McKenzie. So I'm going to do something about that. Tonight. Now hurry!"

Hank moved past them to the front of the house to keep a lookout while Suzy grabbed her mother and son by the hand and ran for the bedroom closet. Opening her gun safe took less than ten seconds, but it felt like hours to her.

"Here, Mom, take this." She handed over her personal handgun.

"Suzy—" Her mother started to object.

"Don't you do that," Suzy interrupted. "You were married to a cop. You can use a gun if you need to."

Suzy didn't wait for a response but led them through the house, grabbing her cell phone from the chair and the keys from the wall hooks in the entryway, and then all three were converging on the car.

"You drive," Suzy ordered her mother, tossing her the keys. Despite being in a purple bathrobe, scared, confused and wielding a gun she didn't want to be holding, Cordelia Simmons knew when she needed to listen to her daughter. She threw open the driver's-side door while Suzy pulled the back door open and all but pushed Justin in. She handed her phone to him. "You *stay down* and call Billy. Tell him Grayton is coming to the house. Can you do that?"

Justin's eyes were wide, terrified, but he nodded. It broke Suzy's heart, but she didn't have the time to reassure him. While she hadn't said it out loud yet, she'd already made a decision she knew her mother wasn't going to like.

She leaned in and kissed his forehead, then turned to her mom. "Drive straight to the station. Keep a normal speed so as not to bring attention to yourself. Keep Billy on the phone. Don't stop for anyone." Suzy threw the paper Hank had given her into the front seat. "When you get there, make sure James Callahan gets that number."

"You can't stay," her mother said, voice cracking.

"He knows who I am and where I live. This might be our only chance to get him."

Their eyes met, and then her mother glanced at Justin. She didn't say it out loud, but both women understood that it wasn't just their lives that were endangered by Grayton. Justin's was, too.

"You be safe, baby girl."

Suzy nodded. "I plan on it," she said with a quick smile. "Love you both."

The moment she shut the door, the car reversed. Suzy didn't move until it was turning at the end of the street. It was like watching her heart drive away.

She shook her head. Now it was time to focus.

She ran back into the house.

"We're not going to kill him if we can help it," Suzy told Hank, voice firm. "We're going to trap him. That's not a request. That's an order."

Hank didn't argue. "Your house, your rules."

It caught Suzy off guard, but she gave him a nod. "Good."

Hank turned back to the window. His entire body tensed.

Suzy hurried to his side and looked out. On the street where her mother and child had been traveling less than a minute ago was a black SUV.

"Whatever we're about to do, we need to decide on a plan," he said. "Fast."

Chapter Fifteen

"Now, now, James, don't blow a gasket," Katrina started. "She's fine as long as we're fine."

James sat down heavily. Angry didn't cover it.

He was furious.

Katrina had pulled her gun from her name-brand purse just after Chelsea had screamed. She marched him back into the kitchen, where he was now at the table, their supper still fresh on their plates. A man with a matching gun and a myriad of rough descriptors that indicated he would hurt James's little sister if ordered to held one of Chelsea's arms. He'd pulled her from the table and had her a few feet away, near the side door that led outside. James didn't like how easily they could use it to escape with her in tow.

Chelsea's eyes were wide but dry.

"What do you want?" James growled.

Katrina's smile finally took a turn for the tainted. It was chilling.

But nothing compared to the fire of rage he was feeling.

"The same thing I wanted at the door," she said, sliding into the chair opposite him. She leaned over to take a piece of bacon. "I just want information on Hank. For instance, why you were at his place this morning talking to a detective." James gritted his teeth. Katrina held her hand and the bacon up. "Let me preface whatever it is you're about to say with the reminder that I'm the only thing standing in the way of him producing a lot of pain in your baby sister.

"I know, I'm a broken record, but if I'm happy, they're happy. And I'm happy when I'm not being lied to. And I'm *very* good at knowing when I'm being lied to." She took a bite of the bacon. "Speaking of, I now know you weren't lying about being good at cooking breakfast foods," she said around the bite. "So, was that the only truth you told me?"

She wasn't unstable. Of that much James was certain. Instead, she was precise. From her wardrobe to her hair, from the way she walked and carried herself to the way her eyes never left his, she was very much a woman who knew what she wanted. James had no doubt she would do whatever it took to get it, too.

One look at Chelsea, and he decided he'd stick to the truth, or some of it, at least. He wasn't about to gamble with her life. Which also meant not telling the very determined, seemingly devious woman across from him that they were the siblings of the infamous Gardner Todd.

"I was with a Riker County Sheriff's Department deputy when she got a call from a woman about some people breaking into her neighbor's house. I convinced her to let me tag along."

Katrina's perfectly shaped eyebrows rose. "And why would you want to do that?"

"I may be good at business, but that doesn't mean I'm always excited about it. When I heard the call and saw we were close, I thought it would be more fun than crunching numbers all morning." He shrugged. "When we got there no one else was around. More deputies and local PD showed up after, and I tried to get the story of who lived there from the detective on scene. All he said was that a man named Hank was missing."

"Then why did you lie to me on the doorstep?"

"I don't know you." He spelled it out. "I didn't want you thinking I was involved with someone I wasn't on the off chance it got me or my loved ones in trouble." He nodded to Chelsea and the man. "Case in point, the goon holding my baby sister at gunpoint while *you* hold a gun on *me*."

Katrina leaned back in the chair without sacrificing her upright posture.

"So, that's it? You rode with your deputy friend to a potential crime scene and then just casually talked to a detective while there?"

James nodded. It was the truth, more or less. Enough that he could confidently say yes, anyway.

Katrina studied his expression before turning to the men and Chelsea. "And what were you doing today, little one?" she asked.

Chelsea didn't hesitate. "I drove here from school."

Her voice was even. It didn't waver one bit. James couldn't help but be proud. He looked back at Katrina. She seemed thoughtful.

Which, in itself, was troubling.

James's muscles tightened as she pushed back her chair and stood.

"So I guess I barged in here for no reason, then," she said with a laugh. "How impolite! My apologies, Mr. Callahan."

She surprised James by putting the gun back in her

purse. Her lackey, however, didn't lower his from Chelsea's side. "For your hospitality, I'd like to do you a favor now."

She put her bag down on the table and reached into her pocket.

"I had a boy in grade school who was obsessed with me. Followed me around, constantly passed me notes and even once snuck into the girls' bathroom to try to talk to me. He was a mess, I tell you. Always trying to steal a kiss from me or trying to look up my skirt. He tried it all, really, until one day I yelled at him to leave me alone in front of all of his little friends."

She rolled her eyes. "Oh, how it hurt his little pride. To try to save face, and his ego, he turned his obsession into anger. Started calling me names, throwing food at me in the cafeteria and even placing some roadkill in my locker once. I thought, given time, he'd get bored, but he never did."

She sighed, as if recalling a mildly annoying memory. "So, one day, I confronted him again. I told him *very clearly* that if he didn't stop his pathetic attempts at trying to earn the other little boys' respect, I would make him stop. I'll never forget his laugh. He told me, and I quote, 'You're just some little girl. What are you gonna do?'"

Hand still in her pocket, she walked around the table and stopped at his side. She leaned back against the table, eyes never leaving his. "He didn't listen to my warning. Put a stink bomb in my *new* locker. Horrible smell. I swear, still to this day, I catch whiffs of it. Oh, just the worst." She shook her head. The humor that she'd been telling the story with started to disappear.

"So I did what I had promised him," she continued,

voice going arctic. "I swiped a kitchen knife from Home Ec, lured him into a supply closet and carved the words *little girl* into his skin."

She finally pulled her hand out of her pocket. It was holding a closed compact knife.

"He never forgot who I was, and you better believe my locker was never home to anything other than my books after that. I can't be all that mad at him, though," she continued with a shrug. "He taught me the lesson I'm about to teach you."

Her smile came back.

James didn't like it one bit.

Especially not when it was followed by her opening the knife. The blade was small but undoubtedly sharp. Definitely a blade that could—and would—do damage, depending on the determination of the person wielding it.

"And what lesson was that?" he asked, trying to show the woman that she didn't scare him. That she didn't have the upper hand.

Even though she did.

On both points.

She looked at the blade for a moment before answering. "Underestimating a woman like me is not only foolish, it's dangerous." She flipped the knife around in her hand so quickly that James knew, without a doubt, he was about to learn how sharp it really was. "You may be telling me some of the truth, but we both know you're holding back on me, James." She held the knife up to his cheek. Chelsea gasped. "And I know why." She ran the knife slowly down his skin, careful not to break it.

"Just like that boy in grade school, you believe that my wrath isn't worthy of your compliance." The knife stopped at his jawline. She moved it off his face altogether. "However, unlike that boy from grade school, you're a man. One who has served in the military, become a business tycoon and even become a savior in your own right. I'm smart enough to know that simply carving my name into you won't get me what I want."

She moved off the table and over to the man. With a single nod from her, he changed positions. He stepped away from Chelsea and adjusted the end of his gun so it was aimed toward James.

James's heart hammered in his chest. He stood slowly.

It didn't stop Katrina from moving to stand behind his sister. She grabbed the hem of Chelsea's T-shirt and pulled it up and off her body, throwing it to the bottom of the stairs.

James balled his fists, already knowing what was coming.

"But I think it's a safe bet that carving my name into *her* skin might get that pretty mouth of yours moving." Katrina pressed the knife to Chelsea's chest, stopping above her sports bra and right next to the chain of her necklace.

The same gold heart necklace Chelsea had worn almost every day since she was ten. The same one James had given her the day he'd officially become her guardian.

The same one he'd clasped around her neck while promising her that he'd always, *always* protect her.

"Stop."

Katrina pulled the knife up, hovering above Chelsea's skin. She raised her eyebrows again.

"Ready to tell me what you're trying to hide already?" She gave him a dramatic pout. "Are you sure you don't want me to at least *try* to convince you? I've nearly perfected my knife—"

"I went looking for Hank to try to get information on Gardner Todd," he interrupted. There was no point leaving his brother's name out of it. He might not know Katrina, but he did know that she wouldn't let that detail be ignored.

Her eyebrows went as high as they could. She was genuinely surprised.

"And why would a man like James Callahan be looking for information on a man like Gardner Todd? A dead man at that, I might add."

He didn't hesitate. Not even for a second.

"Because he was my brother," he said. He nodded toward Chelsea. "He was *our* brother."

No one spoke for what felt like a long time. James didn't move his gaze from Katrina's, afraid that looking away might create suspicion at what he'd just said.

The red-haired woman seemed to be frozen, eyebrows high and knife low. Her goon wasn't as guarded with his expressions. There weren't many criminals in the South—and James was positive that was exactly what Katrina and her goon were—who didn't know Gardner's name. The news that he had a brother and that brother was a Callahan…well, that surprise showed clearly across the goon's face.

So much so that he didn't seem to notice movement behind him on the stairs. Katrina and Chelsea didn't, either.

Though James already knew who it must be.

"Gardner had no living family," Katrina finally said. "I even had some of my best look into it. You're lying."

Katrina pressed the knife back to Chelsea's skin. His sister whimpered.

"Let her go and I'll prove it to you," James said hurriedly.

"How?" This time she didn't pull the knife back.

"Upstairs, in my office," he started. "I have boxes and boxes of family pictures. There are even some on top of my desk already. I pulled them out this morning before I went to Hank's. Go take a look for yourself." There was movement on the stairs again, but James only had eyes for Katrina and her knife.

"So, the *savior* of Bates Hill kept Gardner Todd a secret."

"I did," he admitted again. He took two steps forward. The man with the gun glanced at Katrina. She didn't address his concern. "You got what you want. Let her go. You know everything I do now."

"You can't just drop a bomb like that and not have a shock wave follow it," she was quick to say. "I can't believe that's all you know."

Up until that moment, Katrina had only become overtly serious when talking about the lesson she wanted to teach James. Everything else had been peppered with smiles and dark humor. Yet something shifted now. Her eyes narrowed. Her lips straightened.

She tightened the grip on the knife, but pulled it away from Chelsea.

"James, what other secrets do you know?" With one decisive step forward, she came within striking distance. "And if you're *really* Gardner's brother, how come you don't know about me? Or is your acting better than I thought?"

James wanted to know the answer to that, too. Who was Katrina? What was her connection to Gardner? To Hank?

That was when it clicked.

James felt so stupid not to have put it together until then. Still, he needed her to say it.

"Why do you need to find Hank?"

Katrina's eyes burned bright and angry. No humor. No charm. No performance for the sake of performance. She lowered her voice. It was as sharp as her blade. "Because Gardner gave him something of mine, and I fully intend to get it back."

James didn't move a muscle. She was so close he could smell her perfume.

"What did he take?"

James held his breath.

Katrina looked murderous.

"He took my son."

Chapter Sixteen

James wished a lot of things.

He wished he'd talked to his brother more. He wished he'd made more of an effort to get him out of his life of crime. He wished he could go out on the back patio and have a beer with his older brother and talk about something as normal as football.

He wished he knew why his brother had kept his son a secret, what he'd planned to do with him and how James had fit into that plan.

Standing opposite Katrina, seeing Chelsea over her shoulder without a shirt on, terrified, he knew exactly why Gardner had tried to keep his son away from the woman.

His brother might have been considered bad, but James had a feeling Katrina was nothing but evil.

"Your lack of surprise is telling, Mr. Callahan," Katrina bit out. "Where. Is. My. Son?"

She brought the knife up to his throat.

It was the wrong move.

"Now!" James yelled.

Chaos exploded in the kitchen.

James grabbed Katrina's wrist just as Queso jumped out from the stairwell, wielding a bat. He slammed it down across the goon's back. The man stumbled forward. His gun clattered to the ground near James's feet. Katrina brought her foot up and tried to kick James between the legs, but he was faster. He blocked the kick with his free hand and then pushed the woman as far from him as he could.

Katrina's man wasn't down for the count, however. He regained his footing and roared, turning to face Queso. The boy had repositioned himself between Chelsea and the raging bull.

James dived for the gun. He needed to stop the fighting. If Katrina and her guy got the upper hand again, James and Chelsea would pay for it with their lives.

Yet Katrina was fast, too. She came screaming at him with her knife brandished high. With another war cry, she brought the blade down. He kept quiet as the blade slid against the skin on his back; he was focused on one thing.

"Stop!" he yelled, gripping the gun and rolling to avoid Katrina's knife again. He jumped up and trained the gun on her. The henchman didn't care. He took a swing at Queso. Chelsea screamed as the boy took the hit across the face.

But he wasn't about to go down that easily.

Queso executed what James would later look back on as the perfect swing. The bat connected with the man's gut. It stopped him in his tracks. This time when he staggered, he fell. Hard.

He didn't move—but his boss did.

"Stop," James repeated, taking a more disciplined stance. She was crouched down, coiling like a snake ready to pounce. He needed to make sure she didn't. "I'm not above shooting you," he added. "Drop the knife."

Katrina's eyes narrowed. They flitted between James and the gun, Queso and the bat, and then back to the gun. She decided to relent. The knife clattered to the kitchen floor.

"Chelsea, you okay?" James asked. In his peripheral vision, he saw her nod.

"Y-yeah. I'm good now."

"Go upstairs and call the sheriff's department from my office. Lock the door behind you."

Her voice was small but steady. "Okay."

He waited until he heard retreating footsteps to look at Queso. Blood gushed down his chin from a busted lip. Still, he grinned. "I told you bad *guys* don't ring doorbells."

Katrina didn't speak as they waited for the authorities. She didn't even object as James bound her to one of the dining room chairs using bungee cords from the garage that he sent Queso after. Her friend said even less as the two of them hog-tied the man.

"One hell of a punch you took there," James said while inspecting the makeshift knots behind the man's arms and legs. "Even better swing you gave back with that bat." James lowered his voice so Katrina couldn't hear. "Thank you for helping us out."

The boy pushed his hands into his pockets. He shrugged, trying for nonchalance.

"Thanks for being a rich dude with two sets of stairs. I wouldn't have been able to get the drop on big guy here without them."

When things calmed down, he'd make sure Queso knew how much James appreciated what he'd done, risking his life to save them. Until then, the best he could do was clap the boy on the shoulder, smile and go back to the task at hand.

He walked past Katrina to his cell phone, which was face down on the table. He had sent Chelsea upstairs to use the landline to put distance between her and Katrina, but now it was time to make his own calls.

Though someone had already called him. A missed-call notification scrolled across the middle of the screen. James didn't recognize the number. The voice-mail icon was next to it. He moved away so Katrina couldn't hear and played the message.

It was the sheriff. "This is Billy. Something happened at Suzy's house. Call me. ASAP."

James's stomach went cold.

When he looked at Katrina, all she did was smile.

SUZY ROLLED BACK her shoulder. It hurt. The pain must have shown on her face.

"You sure you don't want to go to the hospital?" Billy asked, cowboy hat in his hand. The day had been so long that he hadn't had the chance to hang it up when it turned night. Now he looked like a tired Alabama cowboy, leaning against the front wall of the sheriff's department, bathed in the glow of the streetlight not too far from the front steps. Suzy wondered how she looked next to him.

The last hour had been nothing short of tiring.

After her mom drove off, Justin had followed through with the plan. He'd called Billy, and soon the sheriff and his deputies were speeding toward the house. Billy had gotten there in time to watch Suzy tackle Grayton's backup, a man twice her size. The move had been her way of saying thank-you to Hank for the heads-up about Grayton, considering the angry stranger was two seconds away from putting several bullets into the bar owner. After she'd gotten the man to the ground, she'd kept the upper hand while her colleagues and friends helped cuff him.

Hank, however, had never had anything but the upper hand with Grayton. While she may have been angry at him, Hank was riding several waves of fury.

"You tried to get to my Patricia," he'd roared, holding a bleeding Grayton by the scruff of his shirt. "How did you know where to find me? Who do you work for?"

Suzy wanted the same answers, but not at the expense of Hank killing the man. She'd quietly, yet firmly, talked the bar owner away from Grayton while the deputies did their thing.

"None of this makes sense," Hank had said, shaking his head and trying to calm down. He'd jumped Grayton as soon as the man had broken through the back door. There was blood across his face, but Suzy had no idea who it belonged to. "Why does he want the kid?"

An hour later, Suzy was still waiting for that answer and, more urgently, one Alabama millionaire.

She and Billy had just gotten to the department when Chelsea called in. Matt had been close and had reported that both Callahans and Queso were okay. He was handling the transfer of the woman and man, two people whose identities Suzy didn't yet know.

Two more puzzle pieces.

She just hoped that when James showed up, they could finally finish it.

"I know it's none of my business, but I have to say it," Billy said after a period of silence. His voice was all business. She stiffened, waiting for some kind of admonishment from her boss.

"I think your dad would have really liked James."

That caught Suzy off guard. But she just smiled.

It didn't matter how she felt about James or how he felt about her, because either way, she believed Billy was right. Her father would have absolutely liked the man.

"Thanks, Billy." She meant it.

He shrugged. "I just call it how I see it."

Suzy laughed but cut the rest of the conversation short. The sound of car doors shutting pulled Billy and Suzy along the sidewalk and into the side parking lot. Two deputy cruisers drove to the back. Matt's Tahoe broke away from the line and slid into his parking spot. Suzy's stomach tightened. While she knew that James was okay, seeing was believing.

Four doors opened. Matt and Queso stepped out of one side. Chelsea walked around the back soon after. Then came James. Jeans had never looked so good on a man.

Suzy held her ground as he found her gaze.

Matt was the first to talk. "We have a situation," he began. "One I think should stay private until we get a better handle on it."

"Let's go talk in the conference room," Billy offered. He glanced at Suzy. "I think it's time we got on the same page."

He led Matt back to the front of the building. Queso nodded to Suzy but kept at Chelsea's side as they followed. James lagged behind. He was frowning.

"Are you okay?" he asked. "Matt told me what happened."

Something was off in his tone. It sounded hard—cold, even. Detached.

Still she nodded. "Yeah, nothing some Icy Hot and Advil can't take care of. You?"

He didn't nod. "I'll be better when this is all done."

He followed the group without another word. Like she was a stranger. Suzy couldn't deny it hurt a little, even though she more than understood it. A lot had happened to the two of them in the last few days.

But that night?

That night was different.

Grayton had come to Suzy's home. If Hank hadn't been there, who knew what would have happened to Justin? To her mother. A town over, James hadn't had a warning. By the looks on all three of their faces, she knew something bad had happened before their intruders had been detained.

They marched through the lobby and the hall to the conference room. Billy stepped to the side, next to the door, and motioned for Matt, Queso and Chelsea to go in. Suzy reached out and caught James's hand before he could follow. She nodded to Billy, and the sheriff went inside the room without them.

"What?" James asked, frown still firmly in place. The contact of her hand evidently did nothing to improve his mood, but he didn't pull away, either.

"Hank showed up and warned me about Grayton being on his way. He gave me and my mother and Justin time to escape, but I didn't want him to get away again, so I decided to stay," she said. "But *before* I made that decision, he gave me a number to call Patricia." James's eyes widened but she hurried on. "Hank said if either you or I didn't call that number by the morning, he'd told Patricia to take the baby and leave town."

"We need to call it," James said before she could get

another word out. "I filled Matt in about what happened during the ride over. He can tell Billy what happened. We need to call Patricia and—"

Suzy smiled. It clearly deflated his urgency enough to stop his current train of thought.

"You already called?"

She nodded. "I did."

Wrapping her fingers fully around his hand, Suzy pulled him to the office opposite the sheriff's. The nameplate read Chief Deputy Simmons, and it always made her feel a rush of pride.

Suzy opened the door wide. Justin looked around from behind the computer screen and smiled. Opposite him, in an oversize chair that Suzy had brought in herself, was her mother. In her arms was a baby boy.

"Patricia told me where she was and said I should meet her and get him," she said. "So I did that, too."

Chapter Seventeen

James's entire expression changed. Like God himself had reached through the roof and grabbed the burden of guilt and worry straight from his shoulders.

"That's him," James said, sounding almost unsure. But his steps were less uncertain. Suzy's mother stood so he could get a better view. "That's *him*." He peered down at the baby, seeing his green eyes, mop of golden hair and chubby little legs.

"Yep, that's him," Suzy agreed.

James shook his head and laughed. He took the boy in his arms without hesitation.

"No," he said. "I mean his face. It's all Gardner." James let out another loud laugh and stroked the baby's hair. The boy looked alarmed but didn't cry. "And *this hair*! He's got a full head of it! Wow. Suzy, is this a beautiful kid or what?"

James looked at her with such blatant love across his face that she knew right then and there she wanted some for herself.

She wanted some of James.

"He certainly is."

James put his finger against the boy's palm. When he squeezed it, James smiled ear to ear.

"Hey, Justin, why don't we go grab something out of the vending machine in the break room?" Suzy's mom asked, smiling too. "I think your mama and Mr. Callahan need to talk a little bit."

Justin nodded and came around the desk. He stopped next to James, who adjusted the baby so he could see him better.

"I like him, too," Justin said, sure in his words. "I didn't like the crying as much."

All the adults laughed.

"There's a family doctor we all know who's agreed to come in tonight," Suzy said after the door shut behind her mom. "Just to give him a once-over to make sure he's okay." She walked to James's side and played with the boy's little toes. "Patricia confirmed your theory about what happened earlier. She saw two SUVs and only had enough time to run to the neighbors. She met up with Hank after he left the bar. She said with the day they've had, the boy hasn't been able to really sleep, so I imagine he's going to crash hard soon."

"The boy... Did she not know his name?"

Suzy shook her head. She trailed her fingers up to the boy's tummy. He was wearing a onesie with a shark across the middle. She tickled its fin.

"No. According to Hank, Gardner said there was a letter that he wanted to keep with his son at all times just in case something happened to him. It had all of his information, including a birth certificate. Though everything was kept hidden. Hank didn't even know about this adorable little boy until the day Gardner went to meet with you." She looked into the face of a child who would never know his real father and sobered. "Hank looked everywhere but couldn't find it. He said there might be one more place, but it might take a few days to get to."

"Where *is* Hank?"

"Since he's been helping us, not to mention keeping this little guy safe, he and Billy came to an understanding. We won't put him on any official documents as long as he stays somewhere we can reach him at any time. As of right now, he and Patricia have left Riker County." Suzy lowered her voice. "To be honest, I think he ruffled quite a few feathers trying to get information on Grayton and his gang of men."

James stiffened. "I don't think it was Grayton's gang." He sighed and looked down at his nephew. "I think Billy's right. It's time for us all to get on the same page."

GETTING EVERYONE ON the same page was a lot easier with everyone in the same room. Baby Gardner, as they'd decided to call him for the time being, went back into the care of Cordelia and Justin while the rest of their makeshift crew got down to brass tacks.

They went into the conference room with the fragments of the overall picture—from what had happened at Suzy's house with Grayton to everything that Katrina had said at the estate—and were able to form something that finally made sense.

"Katrina and Gardner have a child together, Gardner decides he doesn't want her around the kid, takes Baby Gardner and hides him away with Hank," Detective Walker summarized. "She gets wind somehow that Hank has him and sends Grayton and company to try to find him. In the process, she unwittingly pays a visit to Gardner's brother and sister."

"Where she shows us how insane she really is," Chelsea added. "And apparently how much she likes knives."

She sat with Queso at the end of the table. Meeting her nephew had shaken her out of her fear over what had happened earlier. Though, James was sure, she'd have nightmares about Katrina for some time. Hell, he probably would, too.

"What's going to happen to her now?" James asked. "Last I saw, she definitely wasn't talking."

"Grayton either," Suzy added.

The sheriff cracked a grin. "In my experience, men like Grayton McKenzie are only good at one thing. And that's self-preservation. I think if we apply just the right amount of pressure in just the right place, we can get him to roll over on Katrina. Who, at this point, I'm going to assume is the brains. From what you've told me of her, she doesn't seem to be the follower type."

James had to agree with that.

"Either way, let us worry about the two of them," he continued. "No offense, but all of you look mighty worn out. I think you could do with a good night's sleep. Even if it is technically morning."

The sheriff's gaze went straight to Suzy, who was in the process of opening her mouth. He held up his hand to stop her.

"I'm not about to debate with you on this, Suzy."

"And for once I wasn't about to debate it, either," she responded with a snort. "But my house…"

She let her sentence trail off. Billy swiveled to James.

"I'm sure Mr. Callahan here wouldn't mind helping," he said. "Last I checked, he had more than enough room."

James felt his eyebrows rise. Billy elaborated before Suzy could.

"Before our star quarterback here tackled Grayton, his buddies had a little too much fun with their ammo. Shot up the place really good." Billy paused. "Let me guess," he said. "She didn't tell you *that* part?"

James shook his head. "No, she left that out."

"It's not that bad," she tried. "Just need to call some repairmen out tomorrow to work their magic."

"Not that bad?" Billy repeated. "Suzy, your house looks like Swiss cheese."

Suzy sighed. When she looked back at him, emotions he couldn't read flashed across her face. Then one he knew finally settled. Embarrassment.

"If it's too much, I can book a hotel room, no problem," she said.

James was about to tell her he was more than okay with her staying—in fact, the idea excited him in a different way—when Queso finally spoke up.

"The dude lives in a mansion," he said. "I think he can squeeze in a few more people."

James couldn't help but laugh. "That I can, and I'm more than happy to."

Suzy didn't join in the mirth, but she nodded.

"So, does that mean Baby Gardner gets to come home with us, too?" This time, it was Chelsea who spoke.

The question turned James's mood dark. There was no way, after everything that had happened, that he was leaving his nephew behind.

Luckily he didn't have to say that out loud.

Billy nodded. "Due to the unique nature of this case, for now I'm going to put Baby Gardner into your custody, James," he said. "But first thing Monday morning we're going to have to start the process of legally getting this all sorted and squared away. I assume you're going to want to adopt him?"

It was a question that Chelsea had already asked and he'd already answered, but James realized then that he'd never told the rest of them his plans. Not even Suzy. What did she think of that? Was it too much to handle if something were to happen between them? Having to raise one sibling and then raise a nephew? And a baby to boot? Was that more than the single mom was willing to take on, going from a two-family situation to dating a man who brought two more people into the picture?

Did she even want to take on anything with James in the first place?

And what did he want?

No matter the answer, it wouldn't make a difference. James was proud of his sister and knew he'd be proud of his nephew, too. He'd do his best to provide a loving and stable home for both for as long as he lived.

His family might not have been conventional, but they were his.

"Yes," he answered, unable to hide the pride in his voice. "I do."

Billy smiled. "Then come Monday, we'll see how to go about doing that. Deal?"

James nodded. "That's a deal, Sheriff."

GETTING EVERYONE BACK to the Callahan estate was an adventure. One that included a caravan of Riker County Sheriff's Department vehicles with Suzy's car in the rear. If it was overwhelming for James, he didn't show it. In fact, Suzy got the impression that he liked it.

Even when Baby Gardner started crying as soon as the group got into the entryway of his house.

"This is chaos," Queso said, giving the baby the stink eye.

"But it's the best kind," James responded, holding the car seat in one hand and the diaper bag Patricia had been using in the other.

"Is good chaos even a thing?" Queso asked back, raising his voice over Baby Gardner's cries.

James laughed. Chelsea rolled her eyes.

"If you can take on a man twice your size, I think you can handle being around a crying baby," she said.

Queso scrunched up his nose. "As long as I don't have to change it."

No sooner did the words leave his mouth than the smell of a soiled diaper filled the room.

"Ew, *gross*," Justin said from her side. Suzy mussed his hair.

"Hey, you used to do much worse than that," she teased. Her mother nodded.

"Amen to that," the older woman said.

"Looks like I'm about to change my first baby," James said with a laugh. He motioned to the stairs. "Chelsea, could you show Suzy, Ms. Cordelia and Justin to the guest suite?" He looked at Suzy. "There should be some new clothes and things for you three in there. If you need anything else, let me know."

Suzy's eyebrow rose. "Does that mean Douglas is around?"

James laughed. She liked how much he was doing that, now that they'd found his nephew.

"Yes, he did some shopping for me while we were at the department," he answered. Then he looked to Chelsea, though he spoke to the group as a whole. "There's already been several sweeps over the house to make sure everything is safe. The guards are back and here to stay for a while, just to ease our minds." Then James looked directly at Queso. "The door that was broken into was repaired, and the alarm will be set momentarily. If you have the urge to leave the house to smoke, the entire estate will know it."

"The lesson being, don't smoke," Chelsea muttered.

Queso rolled his eyes this time. "Chief deputy here already crunched my last one," he whined.

Suzy smiled. "And I'd do it again."

"Amen to that," her mother repeated.

It earned a laugh from Chelsea before she started a tour for the only two people who hadn't been in the house yet. Suzy hung back. She wanted to talk to James. But about what, she didn't know. Maybe about the baby. Maybe about Katrina.

Maybe about them.

"Queso, I need to talk to you before you go up," James said, stopping the boy midstep. His expression hardened. He didn't look Suzy's way.

Their one on one would have to wait.

Chapter Eighteen

Douglas had done it again.

He'd managed to pick out sleeping clothes with ease for the new estate guests. Suzy's mother was finally out of her robe and into a matching pajama set that was also purple, while Justin was sporting a Spider-Man shirt and shorts. Suzy was back to sweats and a T-shirt. This time, there was even slippers.

The same slippers she stepped into after an hour of being unable to sleep.

The bed made no complaint as she eased out of it, careful not to jostle her son or mother. While there was another bed they could have used, all three had wound up together. Neither her mom nor Justin wanted to admit it, but they were shaken by what had happened. After Suzy had gotten to the department with Baby Gardner, both had clung to her, trying not to cry.

Suzy traced her sleeping boy's face, peaceful now.

She could admit that the last two days—the last four months, really—had definitely shaken her.

Moonlight streamed through the part in the curtains, helping Suzy navigate the unfamiliar room to the door. She held her breath as it clicked open. A small light in the hallway showed a quiet second floor. Queso's and

Chelsea's doors were shut. James's office door was not. A faint light pooled on the hardwood.

Like a moth to a flame, Suzy was drawn to it.

And like he'd been expecting her, James was already smiling.

"Glad to see I'm not the only one who can't sleep," he greeted her, voice low. He stood next to his desk, the box of pictures in his hand.

"I think we're definitely in the minority on that front."

A baby monitor with a camera attached sat on the side table next to the couch that was opposite the desk. Definitely a new addition since yesterday—they were closing in on four in the morning. Suzy moved around to the front of the monitor and took in the view. The image of a sleeping baby made her heart warm. Being a single mother had been hard, especially when Justin had been that size, but Suzy couldn't help but miss it sometimes. The baby phase didn't stick around, even if their mother's love for them did.

"I just got him down," James said at her shoulder. "I came in here so I wouldn't wake him back up since I couldn't pass out as fast as he did. He's had one heck of a day."

"One thing I think every parent envies is their kids' ability to fall asleep at the drop of a hat." She sighed. She wasn't frustrated or angry. It was just an observation. One of many she realized she wanted to share with the man.

Suzy turned and was surprised at how close he was. A warmth of a different nature started to spread within her. Especially when she realized that the last time they'd been in the room they'd been in a lip-lock.

Twice.

"So, let me guess," Suzy started, putting some mental distance between his body and hers. "Douglas did more than shop for clothes while we were at the sheriff's department?"

James chuckled. "Big-time," he confirmed. "If he wasn't a friend, I think he would have up and quit. Thankfully, he took pity on me. He even bought a crib. Which I coaxed Queso into helping me put together." He smirked. "The kid's pretty good with his hands. Fast, too. Whines a little too much, but I think he's frustrated."

His smile dropped. A sigh pushed out and followed him as he moved around to the back of his desk. He pushed the chair aside, opened the top drawer and waved her over.

"I didn't say anything earlier because the whole Katrina thing really threw me, and then we saw Baby Gardner—which by the way, I really hope Hank pulls through with his birth certificate so we can stop calling him that—and it went out of my mind but…"

Suzy came to his side and accepted a card he pulled out. It was smaller than a normal business card and completely black. She ran her finger over the top of it. There was an indentation.

"It's in the shape of a butcher's knife," James explained.

"One of Sully's calling cards?" she guessed.

He shook his head. "That's Sully's card, period." He leaned against the desk facing the office's one window. Through the gap in the curtains, Suzy could see the dark trees in the distance. It was comforting in a way. Foreboding in another. "I spent a lot of time and money trying to find someone, *anyone*, who could get me information on Gardner. After months of rumors and hearsay, one name stuck out. The Butcher. It wasn't until I got the name Sully that I was able to set up a meeting. I'm assuming that, because of my status in the public eye, he met with me without his normal cloak-and-dagger routine. Which is good, because it's what he's known for." James tapped the card. "For instance, one of his unique practices is this. It's his ID, essentially. One that encompasses who he is. One he'd never let go."

"Where did you get it?"

James managed to look sheepish. "Out of Katrina's purse."

Suzy opened her mouth to point out this was the type of information to share in an official capacity and not behind closed doors in their pajamas. But James held up his hand to stop the thought before it could spring out.

"I know, I know. I shouldn't have taken it, but once I did I got sidetracked with everything else and forgot about it." He gave her a small smile. "I was going to tell you in the morning. Well, *later* in the morning."

Suzy ran her fingers over the engraved knife again.

"You think Katrina killed Sully." It wasn't a question.

James's frown was back. It deepened. Suzy put the card in the drawer and shut it. She was sure she knew him well enough to pick up on his unspoken thoughts.

"You can't be everyone's father," she reminded him.

"No, I can't," he agreed. "But I can be a friend."

It was such a pure sentiment that Suzy couldn't help but reach out. She cupped his face and with a genuine smile told him the truth.

"You're a good man, James Callahan," she said. "Don't let anyone ever tell you any differently."

It was one of the observations she had wanted to share with him. She had done it because she believed it needed to be said, not because she'd hoped for anything in return. So when he caught her hand as she pulled it away, Suzy didn't know how to react. Not right away.

Instead, she gave him a questioning look.

He returned the look. However, there seemed to be no question in his.

Slowly, as if he was trying not to spook her, he pulled her hand up to his mouth and turned so her palm was open toward him. Even more slowly, he brushed his lips against the skin of her palm. It took the breath right out of her.

Confusion melted away, replaced by something hotter.

His eyes found hers as he wrapped his other hand around her hip. Suzy felt her eyes widen. James's crystal blues held her gaze. He stood, and just as slowly as he'd done with her palm, he pulled her body to his. He kept her stare, as if waiting for her to deny him. Or simply waiting for her to stop him.

She would do neither.

His body was warm against hers, even through their clothes. Suzy's breathing had gone shallow. She searched his expression for proof that he was as affected by her as she was by him.

She found it in a kiss.

A warm and soft beginning turned to something hard and needy. And this time James didn't seem to have any plans to end it. One of his hands slid into her hair, while the other continued to rest on her hip. Keeping her close. Keeping her against him. Not that Suzy intended to pull away.

She maneuvered under his shirt, desperate to feel his skin against hers. He broke the kiss long enough to show he wanted the same thing. Soon both of their shirts were at their feet, and Suzy was staring down at a chest that shouldn't be real.

In fact, she laughed.

James didn't waste time and covered her mouth with his. It was a softer kiss. "Shh, woman," he whispered, pulling back a little but still keeping close. "If you wake the baby then I'm sending you in there. Why are you laughing, anyway?"

Suzy placed her palm against his stomach and grinned. "Not only are you a charming millionaire but you have abs of steel, too. It just doesn't seem fair for the rest of us simple folks."

James's smile disappeared. So did Suzy's. Had she offended him?

Before she could ask the dark-haired, sexy-as-hell millionaire, he did something else to surprise her. In one fluid movement, he picked her up and carried her to the love seat, only stopping long enough to lock the door.

Suzy tensed, waiting for the drop, but James was gentle. He eased her against the cushions, the cool of the leather sending a chill over her exposed skin. It wasn't until he was on top of her that she really got a show.

Starting at her neck, James trailed his lips down to her collarbone. She curled up against him when he got to her breasts. He thumbed her nipple until it puckered. His mouth and tongue took over next, eliciting raw pleasure in her. It was all she could do not to moan as he treated the other one to the same play.

When he was satisfied he'd been fair to the second nipple, he moved down to her waistband, where his kisses turned hard. Everything in Suzy was on fire, and somehow still managing to get hotter. James hooked the inside of her pants and, for the first time in her life, she praised God that she wasn't wearing her tight jeans. He slid them down and off in a second flat.

Then he did Suzy's work for her, which was good. She was already having a hard time not attacking the man. She didn't just want to be with him. She needed it. She needed him.

He threw his pants on the floor next to hers and lowered himself on top of her slowly, pressing against her and showing Suzy exactly how excited he was by her. Suzy couldn't help the small moan that escaped.

James seemed to enjoy it, but before he could show her how much, he looked into her eyes and smiled.

"Suzanne Simmons, you are anything but simple."

JAMES WOKE UP when he hit the floor. Pain spread through his side and across the cut he'd bandaged at the department. For a second he didn't understand why either hurt and, even more confusing, why he was on the floor. Then the details started to filter in.

First the floor—a burgundy rug on hardwood—then the couch he was staring ahead at—dark leather, a bit worn—and the last clue that reminded him where he was—the blanket that was half on the couch and half covering him up.

He was in his office.

Naked.

And he'd fallen off of the couch because it was definitely smaller than the bed he was used to.

The door was shut, but the room was bright. Sunlight was leaking around the curtains, meaning there was a good chance the rest of the house was awake. It was a thought that sent him scrambling. He jumped up, tripped over the blanket caught between his legs and barely missed falling flat against the floor. Again.

It wasn't until he found his footing that he even thought to look for Suzy.

The last time he'd seen her she'd been on the couch with him, wrapped in his arms and also very naked.

Now?

Now all he could find was his clothes.

He hurriedly put them on, trying to get his bearings—where was Suzy? What time was it? Did anyone know he was asleep in the office and naked to boot?—when he spotted his phone on the desktop.

He cursed beneath his breath. It was nearly eleven.

"Why didn't you wake me, Suzy?" he mumbled to himself while unlocking his phone. He had a new text message but nothing else.

It so happened the lone message was from the chief deputy herself.

You needed the rest. Don't worry, I'll take care of Baby G.

James let out a breath and smiled. He realized that trusting Suzy had always come easy.

The next few minutes were spent rushing through a shower that he had to admit felt great. Maybe, like she'd said, he really *had* needed some rest. He couldn't remember the last time he'd slept so soundly. Finally having Gardner's son had been a big part of that, he was sure. Just as James was sure having Suzy with him had helped, too.

When she'd told him he was a good man, it was like a piece of him that had always been missing fell into place.

And making love to her?

That was another feeling he wanted to experience again. Preferably many more times.

By the time he was dressed, he could have almost laughed at how excited he was to see her again. Like he was a schoolboy nursing the mother of all crushes.

He even skipped the last two steps on the stairs before sliding into the kitchen with more pep than he'd had in years.

Nothing was going to ruin his good mood, he decided.

So he was nowhere near prepared for the sight that greeted him.

Douglas was laid out on the top of the kitchen island. Blood pooled around him, dripping off the counter and onto the floor. James's own blood turned to ice.

Grayton McKenzie stood from his chair at the table, a gun already aimed at James.

The man smiled.

"You have only two options. You come with me, or they die," the man said. He shrugged. "It's as simple as that."

Chapter Nineteen

Suzy was going to be sick. Her head throbbed; her body throbbed; everything in the room throbbed. Light was pain. Sound was pain. *Breathing* was pain. If it wasn't guaranteed to hurt, she would have yelled out.

Not that she thought it would do any good.

The raw pain at her wrists, along with the full-body ache brought on by gravity, spelled out a situation that turned her stomach even more.

She was hanging up by her wrists, shackled to chains that were connected to metal beams in the ceiling. A ceiling that wasn't a normal ceiling. Suzy fought to find her footing against the concrete floor. The moment she was able to stand up, the pain in her arms and hands lessened considerably.

But that was the only good news for her.

Not only had she been jumped in James's house, she'd been brought back to the one place she'd never thought she'd visit again.

"It's a bit dramatic, I know."

Suzy whipped her head around so fast she whimpered at the pain. Katrina walked into view. There was blood across her white pantsuit. She motioned to the room around them. "But bringing you back to where this all started? Well, I thought it was worth being a *tad* dramatic."

Suzy couldn't help but look at the spot in the corner of the large room.

It was where she'd found Gardner, murdered, four months ago.

"Where's the boy?" Suzy asked, fighting through the fear beginning to spread within her.

Katrina raised an eyebrow.

"Which one?" she asked, feigning confusion. "My boy, your boy or *that* poor excuse of a boy?" Her dark eyes slid behind Suzy. She turned, igniting more pain, and saw someone else hanging in the warehouse.

Queso's body was completely slack. His face was covered in blood and bruises.

"Don't worry—he's alive," Katrina assured her when Suzy turned back to face her. "I'm smart enough to know that if I killed either one of you, James would feel personally responsible for your deaths. When I negotiate with him, I need him to be relatively calm. Which I don't think he'd be if I had let Grayton continue to beat on that one there." She took a few steps closer. The *click* of her heels echoed around them. "Plus, since *your* boy wasn't at the estate, I had to improvise. I knew you'd cooperate if I had someone to hold over you."

"Then why did you knock me unconscious?" Suzy ground out.

Katrina smirked. "Because I know you now, Suzanne Simmons. You would have looked for an opening and taken it to try to stop me. You might have even succeeded since I'm low on men at the moment." She laughed. "Though I have to admit that it did feel good.

Maybe it's better that your son didn't see you go down so easily."

Suzy's muscles tensed. She didn't want to give anything away about Justin. Especially if Katrina was thinking of trying to get him as some kind of leverage. Less than a half hour before Grayton and Katrina had shown up, Chelsea had taken Justin and Suzy's mother to the mall in Kipsy. She had a list of things to get the baby, and Suzy suggested they make a day of it. Justin had perked right up. So had her mother. They needed the distraction, the fun. It had only been Suzy, the baby and Queso in the kitchen when Katrina and her men had come in, guns blazing.

"As for *my* son, well, that's none of your business," Katrina continued. "Gardner should never have taken him in the first place." Her words turned bitter. She crossed her arms over her chest. Suzy had so many questions for her. How had she gotten out of the sheriff's department, for starters? Yet she became transfixed by the woman. If happiness was contagious, hatred was consuming.

"The damn fool thought he could pull one over on me," Katrina continued. "Thought he could slip quietly out into the night with *my* flesh and blood and I not know?" She laughed. It was more of a cackle. One that was born of frustration and anger, long built up, if Suzy had to guess.

"Killing him was too easy a punishment, if you ask me."

A surge of anger went through Suzy. While she hadn't specifically talked to James about who had hired Lester to kill him, once Katrina had shown herself, it seemed obvious. It was one of the questions Matt had been hoping to ask before they'd left the department for the estate.

Now Suzy at least had confirmation of that theory.

"But that man was nothing if not quick on his feet when needed. Well connected, too," Katrina added. "I guess if he *hadn't* had a few tricks up his sleeve, he wouldn't have been the infamous Alabama Boogeyman. Not that that did him any good in the end."

"What do you want with James?" Suzy asked. While she wanted to know everything that had led Gardner to the warehouse months ago, Suzy had to be more concerned with the future. Especially since the present involved her and Queso chained while a no-doubt vicious woman ranted and raved, flipping between pure anger that Suzy could almost feel and malicious pride at what she'd done. There was no telling how she would react to James, considering he'd already bested her once.

She didn't seem the type of person who took kindly to losing.

The smirk she adopted could mean a number of things. She took a step closer and lowered her voice. "For all his hype and glory, Gardner believed in moderation. That included money. Money he never seemed to warm up to telling me the location of, or even how much he had. Instead of spending any more of *my* money and time looking for it, I'm going to go to another, more viable source."

"James," Suzy offered.

Katrina nodded. "The golden-boy savior himself." She snorted. "Heck, if I had known the connection, I would have had Gardner killed a lot sooner and tried my hand at little brother, instead."

The anger in Suzy ratcheted up another level. An

almost overwhelming sense of protectiveness toward James washed over her. It pushed out a question she'd wondered about since the night before.

"If you wanted to kill Gardner so badly, then why have a kid with him?"

Katrina scoffed. "It's hard to be a woman in my line of work, with my goals and ambitions, especially around here," she said. "When I first came to Riker, these rednecks with their simple ideas and lack of go-get-'em had the gall to look down on *me*. They didn't take me seriously. So I had to make them. It worked, mostly, but there were still some players out there I wanted to see quake at the very thought of me. So I decided I'd do some out-of-the-box thinking."

"You became partners with Gardner," Suzy guessed.

The woman nodded. "The idiot was lonely," she said, voice lacking any ounce of empathy. It made Suzy grit her teeth. "Convincing him that I loved him was too easy at first. Then I think he started to see the cracks. The poor guy had gone so soft that I knew if I got pregnant with his child, he'd stay by my side. A partnership that was good for business. Savvy, if I do say so myself."

Suzy was disgusted. "You tried to trap him," she bit out.

"It was nothing personal, just business."

Suzy couldn't think of a more personal thing than having a child with someone. Yet Katrina was acting like she'd never even entertained the idea that their kid was anything but a ploy to attach herself to Gardner.

"But Gardner saw through you," Suzy said. "He saw you for what you were and tried to leave."

Katrina's smirk started to slip. "He betrayed me,"

she hissed. "By stealing *my own child*, he made me look weak."

"That's the only reason you even want your son, isn't it?" Suzy realized the truth. "To prove to a bunch of criminals that you have your house in order. You don't even care about him, do you?"

Suzy was incensed. It seemed to feed Katrina.

"Aw, let me guess. You think all women should be mothers, and the fact that I could care less offends your maternal soul."

Suzy leaned as close to the woman as the chains would allow. A modicum of pleasure passed through her when she noticed the slight look of surprise on Katrina's face. It made the pain of moving worth it.

"*You* shouldn't be a mother," Suzy seethed. "And, in my book, you aren't."

Katrina glanced up at the chains. They rattled at Suzy's movement.

"Well, Suzy, tell me how you feel, why don't you," Katrina said with mock hurt. Suzy wasn't going to let the weight of the topic go. All she could think about was that baby boy growing up and knowing no love from the woman who had birthed him. If he were to stay with Katrina, he might not even have a chance at any type of love that was healthy and normal. The thought pushed Suzy close to her breaking point.

"Take me out of these chains and I'll show you instead," she threatened. "Or are you afraid you might break one of those manicured nails?"

As a woman who worked in law enforcement, Suzy had been underestimated by her fair share of people because she was a female. But she knew that a woman wasn't any less talented at her job just because she had pretty nails or liked wearing makeup.

Suzy also knew how to read someone. Knowing where their buttons were and when to push them was a part of the job she was constantly learning.

However, with Katrina, she'd just hit the jackpot.

The woman's lips narrowed; her nostrils flared. Dark eyes turned to slits.

Suzy couldn't help herself. "Looks like I hit a nerve," she said.

Katrina wasn't amused.

In record time she pulled something out of her pocket. Suzy didn't even have time to flinch away as Katrina drove the knife into her stomach.

But she had time to scream afterward.

"I think it's important to note the difference between our morals, Suzy," Katrina said at her ear. Suzy's vision blurred. "You might fight fair, but I *always* fight dirty."

IT WAS A bad case of déjà vu.

James stood at the back of the warehouse his brother had died in. He'd been back countless times since, trying to find some answers, but now everything felt different. That was because everything *was* different.

He'd lost a part of his family here. He wasn't going to let that happen again.

"No funny business, or Ryan here will break your knees," Grayton said, stretching tall and wide as soon as his shoes hit the dirt. The man named Ryan had been James's back-seat companion for the ride over. He had more weight and muscle than Grayton and James combined—not someone you'd bet against in a fight. James had spent the car ride trying to decide if the knife in the man's boot was the only weapon he had on him, or if he'd managed to hide a gun beneath his T-shirt. "Now, let's get this over with."

James let Grayton lead the way. So far, he'd decided to go along with the man's orders, let him think James wasn't going to resist. If he had been a smarter man, Grayton would have realized by now that James really only had one option.

Gather as much information as he could.

Then hit them all where it hurt.

It was a plan that was immediately put to the test. Two steps in and James was already seeing red.

Anger *and* blood.

Ryan grabbed James's shoulder and stopped him from running forward as Grayton swung his gun to face him. "Suzy!"

In the middle of the room, Suzy hung by her wrists. A knife was protruding from her stomach. Blood soaked through her shirt beneath it.

Katrina stood in front of her, smiling.

"And, just think, if you hadn't been such a heavy sleeper, then none of this would have happened," she said in greeting.

James was livid.

It didn't help matters when he saw Queso slumped against the wall in a similar fashion. If Chelsea, Justin and Cordelia were in the warehouse, at least they weren't hanging in this room.

"What did you do?" James roared, directing his rage toward Katrina. She gestured him and her men forward. Ryan's strength and Grayton's guns were the only things standing in the way of James unleashing his fury.

Katrina waved her hand in the air, dismissing his concern. "Don't worry, James," she said. "The chief deputy isn't dead. She's just unconscious." Her eyes trailed down to the knife. "Though I'm sure that can't be good. I suppose we should get down to business sooner rather than later."

Katrina snapped her fingers. From one of the warehouse's offices stepped another man, one James didn't recognize. Unlike Ryan, he was slight. Also unlike Ryan, he had a gun at his hip.

And Baby Gardner in his arms.

Chapter Twenty

"Let me make things simple," Katrina said, walking over to the two. She placed her finger on top of the boy's head. He started to fuss. "This is mine, and no matter what you do here today, he will stay mine. When I leave this ghastly building he will leave with me, and you will never see him again." She shrugged. "These are facts, not points of negotiation. However, here is what *is* up to you to decide."

She waved the man away just as Baby Gardner started to cry. James wanted to go to him, but knew the baby would probably be safer in the closed office than out there with them. Katrina moved until she was in front of James. Her smile never dropped.

"You can wire your fortune, using the computer in the lobby, to my untraceable account in the Caymans or I let Little Miss Authority here bleed out, dying near the same spot my dear Gardner did. Then I'll move on to the boy." She motioned to Queso. "And then I'll hunt Suzy's kid and gut him before it's your sister's turn." James's blood was boiling. "*Those* are your choices, Mr. Callahan."

"It's hardly a choice," he growled. His entire body was nearly vibrating with anger.

"That's the spirit. Grayton, make sure he does what he needs to," she ordered, waving her lackey to the front of the building. It was the only place that had power. Since James had bought the building, he had slowly started to work on converting it into something. He didn't know what yet, but in a weird way, working on the idea had made him feel closer to Gardner. Though now James wondered if he'd ever come back to the warehouse if they all managed to get out.

"Ryan, take our young friend in there with them," Katrina continued. "If Mr. Callahan gives either one of you any lip, start breaking the kid's bones. I don't care which ones."

James could barely keep it together as they walked out of the room, leaving Suzy behind. While he had no doubt that the vicious woman would do as she promised if he didn't cooperate, James also believed that it wouldn't matter if he did transfer the money without complaint. Katrina would kill the three of them and then disappear forever with his nephew. Which was why James was trying to shed his anger and focus as Queso was dragged into the room by his chains. He needed to make a move if they were all going to get out of the warehouse alive.

And not just any move. A smart one.

"Before you get any ideas, know that we made this really simple." Grayton pointed to the lone table. A laptop was on it, plugged in and open. A cell phone sat next to it. "You're going to put that on speaker while you call whoever is in charge of your finances to give you the account information. Then this is over."

Grayton waited for James to get in front of the screen. He kept the table between them, his gun at the ready.

"Without my phone I don't know his number," James said. It was the truth. "I'll need to look it up."

Grayton weighed that request for a moment then motioned to Ryan. "Watch him."

Ryan obliged and took up a spot at James's shoulder. He was glad the brute had stepped away from Queso. The boy was starting to stir.

"Don't worry about him," Grayton said. "Worry about the lady with the knife in her gut in the next room."

That got James going.

He pulled up a search window and went about contacting his adviser, while being hyperaware of Queso's progress. A plan was starting to form. Maybe not the smartest one, but it was a plan, all the same.

And it required Queso's help.

"So I have to admit, after hearing a little background on you, I'm surprised you're taking orders so easily," James started. He kept up the appearance of searching around. "Grayton McKenzie, the errand boy for Gardner Todd's ex. Interesting that you traded your reputation for *that*. And who are we kidding? You're going to be her babysitter now, too. You've gone from being the top guy to cleaning diapers full of it."

Ryan surprised James by snorting behind him. Grayton was trying to play it cool, but anger flashed across his face at the sound. He stood up straighter and stared daggers at his brother in arms. It gave James the opening he needed. He looked over at Queso.

His eyes were open. And he was looking right at James.

"Shut up," Grayton said.

James took his hands off the laptop's keyboard and held them up in defense. "I'm just saying," he responded, hoping Queso was coherent enough to follow what he was about to try to convey. "If there's one thing I know about babies, it's that they can be a *distraction*."

The world around them seemed to slow. James felt a

surge of adrenaline fill his veins. Every muscle tightened within him. All he needed was Queso to take the hint.

He didn't have to wait long. The boy's voice came out loud and clear.

"Padre's right about that."

It distracted Grayton, giving James an opening.

And he wasn't about to waste it.

Grabbing the underside of the table, James flipped it up. Before anything could settle, he bulldozed forward, using it as a battering ram. Together they connected with Grayton.

The man didn't have time to form his own attack. Instead, he was knocked off his feet and hit the ground hard. James kept the table on top of him, stomping down once before pivoting around. Every ounce of training and his workouts kicked into gear as James looked into the eyes of the charging bull that was Ryan. He was a big guy. A direct hit was going to hurt.

James decided he'd just not get hit.

Instead of readying a punch, he used the man's forward trajectory against him. James stepped to the side just enough that he could grab the front of Ryan's shirt before the man's beefy hands could land a blow. He took Ryan's momentum and employed it to his advantage. He swept the man's left foot out from under him while pulling down hard.

James pivoted once more, following the arc until Ryan's face connected with the underside of the table. He groaned and tried to roll onto his back to get up, but James was faster. He kicked downward against the man's cheek.

It wasn't enough pressure to kill him, but enough to make his body go limp. A breath eased out of him as he slipped into unconsciousness.

"Padre, gun," Queso called.

James whipped around the table just as Grayton moved his arm forward. He was trying to grab the gun that he must have dropped while the table was being pushed into his body.

"I don't think so," James huffed, adrenaline still running high. He scooped the gun up before Grayton could even touch it. If half of his body hadn't been trapped beneath the table, which was now beneath Ryan, there was a good chance he would have been able to get at least one shot off before James could adapt.

James crouched down, level with the man's eyes, and aimed the barrel of the gun at Grayton. When he spoke, he made sure his words were crystal clear.

"I'm going to give you something your boss wouldn't," he said. Grayton's eyes widened. "Mercy."

Relief flashed across the man's face. Still, James wasn't a chump. He used the own man's gun to knock him out.

Then James and Queso were the only conscious ones in the room.

He didn't want to let the streak of good luck die. Moving as fast as he could, James fished in Ryan's pockets until he had a key for Queso's chains and a cell phone.

"Where are Chelsea, Justin and Cordelia?" he asked as he went through the process of unlocking the clasps. There was blood on them where they had dug into Queso's skin.

"Shopping in Kipsy. It was just me and Suzy when crazy chick showed up."

James let out a small breath he'd been holding, relieved.

"Well, there's a piece of good news," he muttered.

The second the last clasp came undone, he handed Queso the cell phone.

"Call in backup and EMTs," he said. "Tell them an officer has been stabbed in the stomach and needs immediate care."

Queso rocked to his side, obviously trying to get up. "You need help now," he tried, wincing. He looked like someone had used him as a punching bag. "She had another guy with her at the house."

James shook his head, checked his gun and then pointed to the phone.

"Suzy needs you to make that call. *Now.*"

He didn't wait to see what the boy would say. Gun out, ready to pull the trigger when needed, James went back out into the main warehouse.

Neither Katrina nor her last lackey met him there. Surely they'd heard the ruckus. James kept looking left and right, walking softly. No one jumped out or shot at him. That was good…but it also gave him a bad feeling.

Had Katrina already jumped ship? And with his nephew in tow?

James stopped at Suzy's side, eyes going straight to the knife.

This time it was he who had been distracted.

"Move and I shoot." Shame and anger set James's shoulders straight. "Drop the gun, slowly, or we shoot you both." Katrina's voice was calm. Steady. She meant what she said.

James didn't need to keep looking at Suzy—the beautiful woman he'd been lucky enough to fall asleep holding that morning—to know the risk wasn't worth her life.

His life, maybe, but not hers.

He did as he was told.

"Kick it away from you and turn around slowly," the lackey ordered.

Again, James followed the direction.

Katrina wasn't smiling anymore. "Do you know how a man like Lester got the drop on the infamous Gardner Todd?" she asked. Her voice was ice. "Gardner became sloppy. He didn't see a threat that was right in front of him. He was cocky. Just like you." She nodded to the office. The door was open. He'd been so transfixed by Suzy that he hadn't even heard them walk out.

"Some would call walking into the unknown courageous," he offered. "And one thing Gardner never lacked was courage."

"Courage has no place in this world," she snapped. "All it does is get people like you into a grave faster while pissing the rest of us off." Her stance changed. It hardened. She'd just come to a decision and was resolute about it. "I'm over it. And, just like Gardner, I'm over you."

A gunshot exploded through the warehouse. Followed by another. Then one more.

Baby Gardner started to cry.

James looked on, wide-eyed, as Katrina fell to the ground with a cry. Her lackey dropped next.

A fourth person moved farther inside the room.

It was Sully.

He looked rough, slouched and holding his side with one hand and his gun in the other, but he was still standing.

James couldn't claim the same.

Sully cursed something wicked and called out to him. But it was too late.

James clutched the bullet wound in his stomach and stumbled to the ground. The last thing he saw before the world got dark was the face of a beautiful woman.

Chapter Twenty-One

Suzy smelled the cake before she ever saw her mother.

Cordelia peeked around the door mere seconds before walking in uninvited, cake tin in hand.

"I brought cake," she whispered, holding the tin up as if Suzy hadn't seen it. "He said pound cake was his favorite. So here I am!"

Suzy put her finger to her lips, and the older woman's eyes widened. They both glanced at the hospital bed in the space between them. James was asleep. He had been since that morning. The night before, he'd woken up for the first time since surgery. But then Suzy had been asleep, riding her own wave of pain medications. The same thing had happened that morning. It felt like they were star-crossed lovers, just waiting for word when the other one was conscious.

Finally Suzy had given up and decided to park herself on the couch in his room. If Katrina's knife hadn't managed to miss her major organs, Suzy knew it would be a different story. Yet the tides had turned and she was the one in the hospital room who was in the better condition. Though the nurses were keeping an eye out on her. If she moved around too much she would be banished back to her own room.

She wanted to thank James for what he'd done.

She also just wanted to know he was okay.

The doctors might have already given him two thumbs up after his surgery, but she needed more proof. And she desperately wanted to see the man smile.

"Where's Chelsea?" her mother asked, putting the cake tin on the table that already held a myriad of flowers. All were from residents of Bates Hill. Once word had gotten out that their beloved millionaire was in the hospital, the floral population in the private wing had grown exponentially. "Did I miss her on the way up here?"

The older woman went to Suzy's legs, picked them up carefully and then sat beneath them. She readjusted the blanket so it was over both of them. Very much a woman who meant to stay for the long haul.

It warmed Suzy's heart.

"They finally cleared Queso to leave, so Chelsea took him back to the estate," she answered. "I suggested she look after him for a few hours, and I said I'd call her if James decided to stop auditioning for Sleeping Beauty."

The older woman smiled. She looked over at James. "Maybe he just needs to be kissed by his one true love," she suggested.

While Suzy might have warned her mother off the week before, flustered by the suggestion and even opposed to it, now she found herself smiling.

"I heard his friend is doing better now," her mother said, apparently deciding not to push the topic of kissing James Callahan. Though Suzy knew that would probably only last until both were discharged from the hospital.

"Douglas? Yeah, thank goodness Queso sent first responders to the estate, too, when he made the call for backup. The doctor said Douglas might not have made it another hour, otherwise."

The older woman nodded and then patted Suzy's leg. "It's been one heck of a year," she pointed out. "One too many hospital trips for my liking."

Suzy tried to reach out to touch her mother's hand, but the stitches across her knife wound pulled. She lowered herself back down. Her mother frowned. "One too many scars on my baby girl."

"Mom, didn't you hear? Guys dig scars. Or, wait, is that just chicks?"

It took a moment, but her mother laughed. "Oh, Suzy Q, I do think you're the best thing I've done in my life." Her expression softened. "I'm sure wherever your daddy is right now, he's so proud of you."

The warmth in Suzy's heart grew in size. While they often drove each other crazy, at the end of the day, their love was strong.

Being reminded of that did Suzy some good. She surprised her mother by being completely honest, no humor attached. "Billy told me that Daddy would have liked James. I believe him, too. Even if he hadn't taken a bullet for me, I think he's one of the best people I've ever met or will meet."

Her mother's smile was back in force. "I agree." There was a glint in the older woman's eye, a look that told Suzy her mother had, indeed, picked up on the fact that Suzy and James had gotten close. In more ways than one. "He's got a big heart. But…"

Suzy felt her eyebrows rise. While she'd been more than ready to criticize James the week before, now she'd gotten to know him. Gotten to know his family. Understood that he would always do his best to help people, especially those closest to him. He was a compassionate man, and that, above all else, had made her fall in love with him.

Which was definitely something she hoped to explore with him when he was out of recovery.

So, what strike could her mother have against him? "But?" she repeated.

Her mother let out a long, low sigh. "But when you two need a babysitter, please look somewhere else, because, honey, I already did my time with you and Justin, and goodness knows I need all the help I can get when it comes to beauty sleep."

Suzy wanted to laugh but knew the movement would upset her stitches and be more than painful. Instead she smiled. Her mother, tough as nails, had a habit of becoming cranky if her eight hours weren't met.

"Mom, Mara has been babysitting the last two days. Not you," Suzy reminded her. "You and Justin weren't even in the same house with them!"

Her mother shrugged. "I'm just letting you know that, while I don't mind helping out every now and then, you two are young enough to take on the task of trying to get that baby boy on a normal sleep schedule."

Suzy rolled her eyes and glanced at James.

He was looking right back, smiling.

The worry that had clenched itself around her heart like a vise finally loosened.

"Is it just the pain meds or do I smell cake?" he asked.

And just like that, Suzy felt like she could fully breathe again.

TWO WEEKS LATER, James was sitting on his back patio, enjoying the weather and holding his nephew, when Hank approached him. Hank didn't wait for an invitation and took a seat in what James was hoping would be Suzy's chair when she arrived for lunch. He had two envelopes in his hand.

"I hear you took out Grayton McKenzie with a table," he said in greeting. "I have to say I'm sorry I missed that. I guess your brother wasn't the only one who could think on his feet."

James smiled. He considered it a compliment. "I hear you took out two men with your bare hands at Suzy's house, not to mention the men you fought off at The Tavern," he pointed out. "Maybe we're all a little like Gardner at the end of the day."

Hank chuckled. The baby in James's arms wiggled but didn't wake. Hank looked down at the boy. The sleeping baby seemed to sober him.

"While I'd really get a kick out of you describing handing Grayton his backside in detail, I got my lady in the car and some business to finish before we leave." He took the first envelope and set it down on the patio table at James's side. "This is for you from me. Well, from your brother, really. It's the deed to the bar. It's yours now."

James couldn't hide his surprise. "The Tavern? I can't take your bar."

Hank grinned. "Never was really mine," he said. "When I first met Gardner I was pretty down on my luck. I had problems on problems, and nowhere and no one to turn to but the bottle. I find myself at an old bar, wasted and alone, when this guy takes a seat on the stool next to me and just starts talking. At first I didn't know what he was yammering on about. He opened with a joke about the weather, but he kept going, and then I started yammering, too. The next thing I knew, I was a regular and Gardner was a friend.

"Then, soon after that, he offered me a job. Said I had good character and he needed someone like that to take over the bar and run things." He shrugged. "I thought the man was crazy for just giving it to me, but I took the job with pride. Gardner floated around after that, but when he was in town he'd come in. Eventually he started opening up a bit, talking about how he wished his brother could see the place. Said you two used to talk about owning a bar when you were younger."

James smiled. Gardner had named the bar The Tavern because they had picked it out when they were boys.

Hank didn't miss the smile. "Anyways, since I can never repay Gardner for what he did, I thought I'd at least do something he never could." He motioned to the envelope again. "I think he thought one day he'd finally show the place to you, so it only seems fitting."

James kept his smile but shook his head. "I appreciate it, I really do, but I can't take your bar. I'll just come in and drink at it, instead."

This time Hank was the one who shook his head.

"Because of it and Gardner, me and my lady are good on money. Plus, we're feeling restless. Might hop on up to North Carolina to see some of her kin, or just jump a plane to Hawaii for a few weeks." He shrugged. "I don't need the bar anymore. And, really, I think I was always just holding on to it for you. All I ask is that you keep Rudy on. He's a good guy. Deal?"

James didn't have to think long. "Deal," he agreed.

"Good." Hank put the second envelope on the table. Unlike the other one, it had the letter *J* handwritten on its front. It was also much thicker. James sat straighter. "I can't speak for Gardner on most things, but what I can say is this. He loved that kid in your arms, and he loved you and your sister something fierce. In that envelope is proof of both. But that's something you should read on your own. I won't spoil it."

Hank stood. He held his hand out. James shook it.

"And now it's time for me to go. You take care of yourself and that little boy."

James stood, moving the sleeping child to his other arm. The baby stirred, but again didn't wake.

"You too, Hank. I can't thank you enough for everything you did."

The man smirked. "Buy me a drink whenever I'm back in town and we'll be square," he said.

James laughed. "I guess now I know just the place."

Hank didn't linger. He walked around the side of the house and was gone. A few seconds later the back door opened.

"Hey, Padre, was that Hank?"

James turned to see Queso walking over. Like James and Suzy, he'd had to be hospitalized after the warehouse. Or, more accurately, after what had happened at the estate. According to Suzy, Queso had done everything in his power to try to protect her and the baby. Just as he'd tried to help Chelsea and James when Katrina had first broken in. James was still trying to find a way to repay him for both. He figured giving the young man a place to stay for a while was the least he could do. And, he had to admit, he was happy that the boy had agreed.

Sully had come in and helped save the day, shooting both Katrina and her henchman before either could finish the job on him or kill Suzy. When Sully had gone to get the information that James had asked for on Gardner after they'd met in the freezer, Sully had been ambushed by Katrina. She'd nearly killed him. He, however, had decided to only wound her and not end her life when the opportunity arose.

"I want her to sit in a prison cell, letting everyone know that Sully the Butcher doesn't stand for anything she did," he'd told James in the hospital. At the time, James had made his own decision not to mention that a lot of the anger Sully was feeling had to do with the beating Katrina's men had given Queso. Sully might pretend to be tough, but there was undoubtedly a soft spot there for the boy.

Which made his insistence that Queso leave his organization surprising. Or maybe not.

"I don't think that kid ever believed in what we do," he'd said. "I think he just needed to belong somewhere."

Now that somewhere included being with James, Chelsea, Baby Gardner, Justin, Cordelia and Suzy. Since they'd been released from the hospital, they'd all seen a lot of one another.

"It sure was," James answered, scooping up the envelope with The Tavern's deed in it. "Too bad you're not twenty-one yet. Because apparently, Queso, we now own a bar."

The boy looked confused but didn't have time to ask for an explanation. Baby Gardner started to fuss.

"Chelsea sent me out here to get him," he said. "It's time for his food."

James passed the baby over with a laugh and then looked at the second envelope on the table.

"You two head in," he said. "I need to read something first."

Queso didn't question him. However, he did pause in the doorway. "Oh, and, Padre? You can call me by my real name. It's Jensen."

Then the boy was in the kitchen, the door shut behind him. James couldn't help but smile wide.

"Deal," he said to himself, sitting back down. He opened the envelope, trying to ready himself for what he was about to find.

It was a fool's errand.

Gardner had managed to fill the envelope with three things. The first was an official birth certificate. His son had been born in Birmingham, and his name was Adam. James took a minute to let that sink in. An unexpected weight lifted as he finally knew the name his brother had given his only son.

The second thing was a letter to Adam with a note to read it when he was eighteen. James made the decision not to open it himself.

The third thing was the one that consumed James. It was a letter to him, typed in small font over the front and back and dated a week before Gardner died. It was long and heartfelt, and for the first time James had a clearer picture of his brother's last ten years. Gardner told stories about his life, along with hopes he had for the future, and fears and regrets he had from the past. He apologized for who he had become, but said he was proud of who James had turned into. And then he told James what he had already guessed. Once Gardner became a father, he'd planned to leave his criminal life to do right by his kid.

This was hard to process all at once for James. He knew he'd spend years going over the letter, reading it when he missed his big brother, but there was one line that James would never forget.

Just remember, kid, life is chaos, but that never has to be a bad thing.

As he put the letter back in the envelope, the sound of laughter came through the back door. James watched as a conga line of people marched out with food on their plates. Chelsea had Adam and both were giggling at something while Jensen balanced their plates. Justin and Cordelia were right behind them, having their own conversation, which meant the woman he'd seen every day since the hospital was not far behind.

Two seconds later he was staring at that beautiful face, grin and all. She dropped her plate off at the patio table and walked over with purpose. That purpose included a kiss against his lips and a laugh. She eyed the envelopes and then his face, picking up on the emotions he'd just flown through at receiving each, he had no doubt. James liked to believe he was hard to read but was finding there was one woman who had no problem doing exactly that.

She dropped into the chair next to him and leaned over, expression turning serious.

"You know, I realized today that you haven't had an empty house in weeks. Just say the word and me and mine could stay clear for a few days if you need a break. Or longer. It's up to you."

Even though she was offering, James could see the hesitation behind it. She didn't like the idea of them spending time apart.

Neither did he.

He felt a smile as genuine as they came pull up the corners of his lips.

"Oh, no you don't, Suzanne Simmons. You're not getting off that easy." He motioned to his stomach. "I took a bullet for you, so, by my calculation, I think you owe me at the very least several years of companionship." Suzy started to mimic his smile. He reached out and took her hand. "Plus, I'm pretty sure I'm the one that got you into trouble with the sheriff's wife over a dress I helped ruin?"

Suzy tossed her head back and laughed. James didn't

know what he would do in a world where he couldn't hear that sound every day.

"I guess you do owe me, then," she decided. "And it was such a nice dress. Definitely worth a few years of trying to make it up to me. Though maybe you can start trying… Say, tonight after everyone goes to bed?"

There was a mischievousness in her eyes that excited James to no end. He pulled her to him and gave her another kiss.

"Ew, gross," Justin called from behind them.

"I second that," Jensen added.

"I think it's adorable," Chelsea tacked on.

"I second that," Cordelia said.

Suzy broke the kiss and sighed. She was still smiling.

"This is what we're signing up for, you know? One big, messy family. It'll be chaos."

James didn't miss a beat.

"But the best kind."

* * * * *

LET'S TALK
Romance

For exclusive extracts, competitions
and special offers, find us online:

f facebook.com/millsandboon

◎ @millsandboonuk

𝕏 @millsandboon

Or get in touch on 0844 844 1351*

For all the latest titles coming soon, visit
millsandboon.co.uk/nextmonth